THE SEVENTH WINTER

OTHER BOOKS BY HAL BORLAND:

The Dog Who Came to Stay
The Amulet
High, Wide and Lonesome
This Hill, This Valley
The Enduring Pattern
An American Year
Rocky Mountain Tipi Tales

POETRY:

America Is Americans

JUVENILE:

Valor
Wapiti Pete

THE
SEVENTH
WINTER

by Hal Borland

———◆———

J. B. LIPPINCOTT COMPANY
Philadelphia & New York
1960

To Barbara:
". . . which can say more
Than this rich praise,
—that you alone are you?"

1

The storm came down out of the mountains, quiet as fog, and Jeff Ross didn't like it. It was only the middle of November and a blizzard now, even a heavy snowstorm, could mean trouble at the ranch. That was his first thought, of his cattle. But close after it came the thought that a storm would trap him here in this big house on the hill. With Loretta and the girls, and Tommy.

He stood at the west window of his office, a corner room on the first floor of the house, and he looked down across the roofs in the valley and beyond to the first range of foothills. At nine o'clock this morning, two hours ago, there had been only a mist in the mountains, and now the peaks were beginning to whiten. A thick haze was creeping down the canyons and spreading eastward. Bill Sanders had reminded him yesterday, hoping Jeff would let him go back to the ranch, that this was a seventh winter. The last long, hard winter had been in 1864, and this was 1871.

"Superstition!" Jeff said to himself now, and he crossed to the other window and looked southeast, out toward the plains. Beyond the horizon, on Bijou Creek, he had a ranch and four cow-camps, and close to ten thousand head of cattle. Everything he owned, except this house. More than he owned, for he had notes out on those cattle.

He stood there, staring at the overcast plains: Thomas Jefferson Ross, a dark-haired, smooth-shaven man in his late thirties, one of the few businessmen in Denver who didn't wear a beard. Until the past year he had been almost wiry, but now he was putting on weight. Getting chunky, as Loretta said; Loretta always managed to find the kindly word. Jeff knew he was getting a paunch, the way a man does when he stops eating cow-camp fare and begins eating napkin meals three times a day, when he quits the saddle for a chair at a desk.

"I wish Bill was out there," he muttered, and he turned back to the big roll-top desk and picked up the papers again. They had the figures on last winter's operations, and those figures added up to the fact that it cost him a dollar and twenty-one cents a head to carry his cattle last year. He hoped to get that down to a dollar ten. John Iliff, he understood, had his per-head down very close to a dollar. But Iliff's herd was almost twice as big as Jeff's, and the per-head cost went down as the herd size went up. To a point, of course. Interest could eat you up. So could winter losses.

He spent another hour over the figures. But he was just making motions, and he knew it. He was worrying about the storm, and he was thinking about the past, the days before the war. When he only dreamed of being a big cattleman. Everything was simpler then, in Texas, at least. And up here there wasn't anything but buffalo and Indians, and a few trappers willing to bet their scalps that they could take a few bales of beaver skins before the Indians caught up with them. He, Jeff Ross, was one of the first cowmen to come up here, see the possibilities in this grass; and now everything was changed. For him, at least.

Down there, before the war, a cowman was a king with God knew how many cattle out in the brush. Cattle grew like mesquite. And were worth just about as much as mesquite, sometimes worth only what their hides and tallow would bring. Now and then a cowman wanted a little cash and gathered a herd and sent them to market. But he counted his wealth in cattle and sons, not in dollars.

And now, up here, a cowman was like a banker, a damned nickel-watching banker figuring interest. And cattle weren't brush-poppers. You bred them up, with blooded bulls. Jeff had been one of the first to do that. Put meat on their carcasses, bred some of the meanness out of them. And you worried about snow and winter, as he was worrying right now.

Before the war, he thought. Before the war I was a brush-popper myself, a cattle drover who knew the long trails and the far places. Now I'm an old Shorthorn bull in a pen. I built the pen, but it's

8

a pen just the same. And a storm's coming and I'm acting like a goddamned banker, niggling over figures!

He pushed the papers aside and went to the door. He called Jenny from the kitchen and told her to bring his noon meal to him here in the office. Then he went back to the west window and watched the storm. The peaks were hidden and the curtain of snow was down out of the canyons. A gusty wind was rising, rattling the bare branches of the cottonwoods in the yard and skittering the crisp leaves.

Jenny brought his food on a tray and put it on the desk. A cup of thick soup, a thick slice of pot roast in dark gravy, two boiled potatoes, two slices of bread, a piece of apple pie, a cup of coffee. And a linen napkin.

As he spread the napkin in his lap Jeff thought of the noon meal at the ranch. A plate of beans boiled with salt pork, a chunk of sour-dough bread, a cup or two of ranch coffee. His belly almost growled at the thought, but his heart didn't leap at the sight of the food in front of him. He picked at it, ate the meat and the bread and half the pie. He sipped at the coffee. It had no bite, no flavor. Jenny had no idea of how to make coffee.

He pushed the tray aside and went to the other window and looked toward the ranch once more. Snow had begun to fall here on the hill, big cottony flakes. And he knew he had to get out of the house. This house full of Loretta and Tommy and the girls and all those other things a man can't fight.

He put on a hat and a dark ulster and went down the hallway and out the back door. The outside air was just cold enough to make him catch his breath as he went along the brick walk toward the stable. The puffy white flakes were beginning to give way to grainy pellets and the walk was crunchy underfoot.

When he opened the door to the big red-brick stable the smell was like the past itself. Smell of prairie hay, of chopped corn and oats, of horses, of manure with its faint ammonia odor. It bothered him to be so aware of those smells. They were a part of his youth. Was he getting old?

He turned left, to the carriage room with its odors of axle grease and harness oil and varnish and leather upholstery. Alongside was the saddle room, the saddles on their pegs, each with its folded, sweat-smelling blanket over it. Jeff could feel the cantle at his butt, the firm fork between his thighs, and unconsciously he stood a little straighter. And resented that, too. A man shouldn't have to remember the way he hunches his shoulders against the pelt of sleet and the way he sits tall and high in the saddle in the sun. He should know those things without remembering.

Then he heard Bill Sanders' uneven footsteps, the thud of his crutch, in the alleyway. Jeff turned toward the box stalls. Bill, carrying a pail, heard him coming and waited. Bill was tall and lean and graying and he had a crooked left arm, an elbow broken at Elkhorn Tavern and never set right. He also had a bad leg, but that was temporary, a bone-break he got at the ranch five weeks ago when a cut-bank gave way and pitched his horse into the creek.

Bill said, "She's a-coming for sure." There was a soft trace of Texas in his voice.

"I don't like it," Jeff said.

"But not tonight. She'll just pester along, building up, and tomorrow we'll really get it."

"Tonight."

"Late tonight, maybe."

"Your arm tells you, I suppose."

"Yep." Bill grinned and led the way down the line of stalls. He had chopped grain in the pail.

"Which horse are you graining at this time of day?"

"Lady. She's been off her feed. Gave her a warm mash this morning, but she didn't go for it. Don't blame her. I don't go for mush either." Lady was Loretta's personal buggy horse, too dainty, too pampered, for Jeff's taste.

"How are the blacks?"

"Fat and sassy. They need work." Bill opened the door to Lady's stall and put a few handfuls of chop in her feed box. Lady, a dainty-legged bay with white feet, sniffed the chopped grain, nosed at Bill, and began to eat. Bill put a few more handfuls in the box and rubbed her neck fondly.

They went back down the alleyway to Bill's quarters, a big, square room in the corner of the stable, originally the coachman's room. It had a bare floor, a built-in bunk, a plain wooden table, two kitchen chairs and a small coal stove. Jeff had urged Bill to stay in the big house, but Bill was stubborn. As soon as he could manage crutches he moved out here. "The house is too rich for my blood.

And I smell of horses." He did come to the house for his meals, but he always ate in the kitchen.

There was a coffeepot on the stove. Without asking, Bill set out two tin cups and poured them two-thirds full. He handed one to Jeff, who sipped it and sat staring out the window. It was good coffee, ranch coffee. He wished Bill was at the ranch. But not with that game leg, not on a crutch. Sam Royce would have to run things out there till after Christmas. Then Bill could go back and take over. Sam was a good hand, but he thought that cattle should take care of themselves.

Jeff said, "Remember our first winter on the Bijou?"

Bill nodded. "Big snow the end of November, then open plumb up till New Year's."

"But we got hell all through January. Snow and ice."

"December was good. So was February."

"March was mean. By late March we were jerking cows out of every little slew."

"We got 'em out, didn't we? Less than two per cent loss as I recall."

"Just lucky."

"A little luck and a lot of hard work and a man makes out. You've made out all right."

Jeff was staring out the window again. "If this was to be an early winter, Sam might have trouble."

"Why don't you let me go out, Jeff?"

"Because the doctor said no! He said you shouldn't get in the saddle for at least another month. That's why. Damn it, you don't even use your crutches half the time! Or you peg around on just one."

"I've seen men still with splints on them riding, day after day. So have you."

Jeff dismissed it with a gesture. "All Sam needs is a little pushing. And you wouldn't sit in the house and push. Are the blacks sharp-shod?"

"I shod them fresh last week."

"The light wagon greased?"

"Yep, and I can put the curtains on in five minutes."

Jeff considered for another moment, decided. "Leave the curtains off. A man needs air."

Bill gulped the last of his coffee, set the cup aside and got to his feet and winced with pain. "How soon are we leaving?"

"You're not going. I'm going alone."

"Jeff, just let me—"

Jeff handed him his crutches. "Use them, you damned fool. Both of them. Or you'll be here till next summer."

Bill tucked the hated crutches into his armpits, leaned on them. "How soon do you want to leave?"

"Half an hour." Jeff set his tin cup on the table and went back to the house to tell Loretta.

Loretta and the girls were in the second-floor sitting room. Loretta was three years younger than Jeff, a handsome woman with an auburn cast, pink skin, blue eyes, just a trace buxom. A damned pretty woman, Jeff sometimes said. She had square, capable hands still marked by hard work. But it was her eyes that one noticed, deep blue eyes that had a faintly haunted, troubled look. She wore a light blue dress and she was sitting on the dark blue sofa with the girls on the floor at her feet.

Jane was almost twelve, dark as her father, tall and gangling. Jane's eyes were large and dark, and they had in them a brooding, defensive look. Lissie was eight, blond as her mother, still in the chubby stage, no longer a baby, not yet really growing up. The girls were playing jackstraws, Lissie with whoops and giggles, Jane with a patient air of condescension. Tommy was between them in age. Tommy was upstairs, on the third floor, with the new nursemaid.

Loretta, too, had been watching the storm and thinking of the ranch, especially of their first winter there, which was one of the happiest times of her life. But as she watched the storm she knew that Jeff would be restless. And worried.

He worried too much, especially since they moved to Denver. She sometimes wondered if they should have left the ranch. But Jeff needed this house, wanted it. He needed success and every-thing that went with it. There were other reasons, of course, for moving to Denver. The girls needed proper schooling, and there was always the hope that Denver doctors could do something for Tommy. As it turned out, they couldn't; but the hope was there.

She was thankful for the ranch, thankful in a way even for to-day's storm. A woman's life can be filled with little things and she can find importance that way. But a man, Jeff's kind of man, needs something beyond home and family. Jeff, she thought, had always been going, doing.

It is a woman's lot to wait, she said to herself. Jeff needs me, in some ways. But not always, not all the time. He never has needed me all the time. I understand that. I know his need for man-freedom. I understand him, and I love him, and I respect him, especially his pride. Take away a man's pride and what is left?

So, understanding him, knowing his worries and his restlessness, Loretta was not surprised when she heard him come up the stairs. She read his purpose even in his footsteps.

Lissie heard him first when he came to the door. She shouted, "Papa!" and ran to him. Jane got to her feet, smoothed her dark dress and stood at Loretta's knee, watching, waiting. Jane always made Jeff feel uneasy.

Jeff patted Lissie's head, not thinking of her at all, and he glanced at Jane, whose eyes were almost challenging. He turned to Loretta. "I'm going out to the ranch."

Loretta nodded. "Yes?"

"I won't be here for supper. I'm leaving right away."

"I'll tell Jenny." Then she asked, "There's nothing wrong out there? They didn't send for you?"

"No. But if this storm builds up—" He shrugged.

"I know."

Jane was staring at him, hurt in her eyes. Loretta watched her, apprehensive. Lissie begged him to watch her lift a special straw. Jeff watched and said, "You're very clever, Lissie."

"Now you try, Papa!" Lissie begged.

"No, Lissie. I haven't time." He turned back to Loretta. "I'll try to be back by the end of the week."

Jane glanced at her mother, then back at him, and her lips tightened angrily. Jeff turned away, went down the hallway to his bedroom.

Fifteen minutes later he was back, in heavy breeches, boots, woolen shirt, his ranch clothes. He was carrying the heavy coat he wore in the saddle. He paused in the doorway. The girls were back at their game. Lissie looked up and blew a kiss to him. Jane didn't even glance up, but she said good-bye tonelessly.

Loretta went with Jeff to the head of the stairs. He paused there and looked up the stairway toward the third floor, toward Tommy's room and the nursemaid's quarters.

"How is he today?" he asked.

"He's all right." For the first time Loretta's voice was faintly defensive.

"And the new girl?"

"She's very good with him."

"You'd better keep her." Jeff glanced up the stairs again. Loretta hoped he wouldn't go up, hoped he wouldn't and wished he would. But she knew it would be painful to them both if he did go. There was nothing he could do for Tommy. Or for her.

Jeff decided not to go up. "Well," he said, "I'll be on my way." He kissed her on the cheek and went downstairs. He looked back from the foot of the stairs, waved once, and went toward the back of the house. Loretta waited till she heard him close the back door; then she climbed the stairs to the third floor.

Tommy's room was on the south end of the house, where it had the winter sun. Bessie Magruder, the new nursemaid, sat in a rocking chair knitting, her chair across the room from the big cradle beside the window. Jeff and Bill Sanders had made the cradle that first winter at the ranch, made it first as a spindle bed, then added rockers. It was only four feet long, but it was ample for the sleeping child beneath the patchwork cover.

Loretta went into the room and Bessie looked up, then got to her feet with a meaningful glance at the child in the cradle, a glance that said he was sleeping. Bessie was an angular woman in her early thirties, sandy-haired and long-faced. She was an old maid; it was written all over her. An English girl who had come to America ten years before to find a husband, had worked briefly as a housemaid in Philadelphia, had gone to Pittsburgh and learned practical nursing, had moved down the Ohio eventually to St. Louis, disdainful of the laborers who would have made her wife. And come to Denver a year ago as nursemaid for a family of small children. The family's coachman had made what Bessie considered improper familiarities, and she had packed and moved out. Loretta had heard of her a few weeks ago, had met and talked with her, and had hired her.

Bessie cried over Tommy the first time she saw him, and all her thwarted motherhood had gone out to him. Her dreams of "a proper marriage" had leached away, and now she wanted, more than anything else, to have a home, a haven, a child to care for. She found them all in the Ross household. Here she had a home virtually to herself, the whole third floor of the big brick house. A home, a child who needed her, a mistress who asked only Bessie's love for her invalid son. And a man who seldom invaded her domain, a man who was her ideal of a household head. Jeff was "in business," and he wasn't interested in Bessie, never interfered with or even suggested what she should do. So she lived here, had her own quarters, made her own schedule, lived Tommy's life, and was content. Bessie was born to serve, knew nothing but service, wanted nothing more than to be needed. She had found her place in life, at last.

She got to her feet, laid down her knitting, and whispered, "He's resting, Missus. I fed him and changed him, and now he's getting his rest."

Loretta moved quietly to the cradle, looked down at the child. His face was a strange combination of cherubic features and wizened expression, premature age overlying stunted childhood. He had beautiful features, clear skin, a baby mouth, long, dark lashes. Physically he was a baby and always would be, a baby no more than three years old. His arms, in the flannel gown outside the coverlet, were thin as reeds, and his baby hands were tightly clenched. Beneath the covers, Loretta knew, was the baby body with the bird-thin legs, the twisted feet that would never walk. He was a cruel caricature of a normal child, and in his face, even as he slept, was a painfully distorted look of thwarted age and maturity.

He was sleeping quietly. Loretta watched him and thought: My baby. My son. The only son I shall ever have. I love him. I shall always love him. And wonder why he is not whole.

She turned to Bessie, saw the sweet, benign look on Bessie's face. Bessie, too, loved Tommy. And Loretta thought: Thank you, God, for Bessie.

She and Bessie went back to the doorway. "Is there anything you need?" Loretta asked.

Bessie shook her head. "No, ma'am. Nothing at all. We've got things in hand and he's doing very well."

"You know, Bessie, if there's anything you need, anything you want, you just have to tell me."

"Oh, yes, Missus." Bessie hesitated, then said, "Miss Jane was up this morning."

"Jane?" Loretta knew nothing of any visit from Jane.

Bessie nodded. "While I was rubbing his legs, easing the pain I know he has in them. It's that makes him cry, you know, the pain in his legs. I was rubbing his legs, and Miss Jane came up."

"Did she want anything special?"

"Just to see him, Missus. That's what she said. Her exact words was, 'I come to see my brother.' She said it kind of defiant like, as though I'd not let her see him. It struck me strange, though I suppose it's natural enough. Some folks hides a sick child like him, afraid somebody'll see them, I suppose."

Loretta said, "It's all right, Bessie, any time Jane wants to come up. Or Lissie either."

"Miss Lissie hasn't been up."

Loretta glanced again at Tommy, sleeping peacefully, and she said, "Thank you, Bessie," and went back downstairs. Back to the hallway and the window there that looked out on the street. It was still snowing, but she scarcely saw the snow except as a shifting curtain. She was thinking, for no special reason, of that strange, half-mad old trapper, Jake Starling.

He came to the ranch the second winter they were there, a bearded man in dirty buckskins. He looked and acted half Indian and he talked in a rambling way of the old days. He said he used to trap beaver on the Bijou and that he had lived with the Cheyennes and this was a favorite camping ground of theirs.

Old Jake came into the house and he saw the crib with Tommy in it. He went over and stood and looked at Tommy for several minutes. He muttered strange words and he made gestures, up and down and in the four directions, and he lifted his head and blew his breath as though he was blowing smoke toward the sky. Then he turned to Jeff and Loretta and said, "This is an Old One, this baby. A wise one."

"Why do you say that?" Loretta asked.

"He is," the old trapper said. "He has wise things to say."

"He doesn't talk," Jeff said.

Old Jake smiled, a pitying smile. "Of course he talks. You don't understand." He glanced at Tommy again. Tommy, aware of the strange voice, wrinkled his face into a frown and made his usual unintelligible sounds, his way of demanding attention. The old man listened, then slowly shook his head. He turned back to Jeff and Loretta.

16

"Hear? Annnh! I remember one like this among the Crows. Nobody could understand what he said till a war party came back with a Nez Perce prisoner, a squaw. She listened, and she understood. She told the Crows what the child was saying, and it was wise.

"This Nez Perce squaw was the only one who could understand, so she cared for the child and told the Crows what he was saying. He knew when it was going to storm, and he knew when the buffalo would come. Many things this child knew. For a year that child and the squaw who could understand ran that whole band of Crows."

Jake hesitated, slowly shook his head.

"Then what happened?" Loretta asked.

"Then this Nez Perce squaw told the Crows the child had said they must make a raid on the Blackfeet. They did, and only seven of the war party returned. The Blackfeet killed all the others. So the Crows killed this Nez Perce squaw."

"Killed her! But why?"

"She lied. She lied about what the child had said, so that she might have revenge on the Crows. So they killed her. And soon after that the child died."

"But why—"

Jake dismissed the matter with a shrug, would say no more about it. He looked at Tommy again and shook his head and walked away. Jeff gave him a quarter of beef and told him he could trap on the Bijou, but old Jake said he was too old to trap. He said he was looking for the Cheyennes, who would take care of him.

When he had gone, Jeff said Jake Starling was a crazy old man. Maybe he was. But the Cheyennes never gave them any trouble at the ranch, though they occasionally came past when they were hunting buffalo in the fall. Once a small band of them came to the ranch to beg for food and Loretta asked them about the old trapper. They said he was dead. They seemed to respect his memory, and Loretta was sure they left the ranch alone because of what Jake Starling had told them about Tommy. Once she said that to Jeff, and Jeff smiled. "We haven't had much buffalo trouble, either. Suppose the old man told the buffalo, too?"

But it did seem more reasonable than the thought that Tommy might have wise things to say. Tommy was just a maimed child, not a strange, mystic being. But she was glad, both glad and proud, that they didn't keep him locked away, hidden like some horrible secret.

She watched the snow a little longer, then went back to Jane and Lissie in the sitting room.

Bill Sanders had the blacks hitched and waiting, the buffalo robe ready to tuck over him and the oil lantern to put at his feet. Jeff took the reins and got into the seat, then turned and said, "Better toss my saddle in the back. Never know what a storm's going to do."

Bill put the saddle in the wagon, covered it with its blanket and tucked a yellow slicker over them. "If you have to ride," he said, "better use Topsy. She fights the saddle, but she's got more bottom than Nig. If you can stay on her the first five minutes."

"You've ridden her, haven't you?

"Yes."

"Then I can." Jeff pulled his hat down, tucked the robe over his lap and slackened the reins. The blacks swung into the alley, dancing, eager to go, and Bill closed the big carriage-room doors.

Jeff held the team down for the first few blocks, till he was on the street leading east, toward the flats. Then he let them out for a little while, to warm them and settle them down. He filled his lungs with the thin, chill air and welcomed the bite of snow in his face. There was less than an inch of snow on the ground and he was traveling with the storm, which was moving east. With good luck he would be at the ranch in eight or nine hours.

He settled into the seat, felt the warmth begin to build up in him after the first chill. He began to feel alive, to feel his body take hold and generate its own warmth as it never did when he stayed indoors. Coop a man up in a warm house or an office and he lost his energy, became a prisoner of a stove or a fireplace. But then, Jeff thought, men become prisoners of a lot of things that don't have bars at the windows or locks on the doors. Men devise all kinds of prisons for themselves.

His ears began to tingle. He took a thin woolen scarf from his pocket, put it over his head under his hat, drew it down over his ears and tucked the ends inside his coat. It was the scarf Jane gave him two years ago this coming Christmas. When he'd opened the package and seen what was in it he'd thought it was just a scarf Loretta had helped Jane pick out at a store. He had thanked Jane, but she seemed disappointed. Later, in privacy, Loretta had told him that Jane made it, picked out the material and spent hours fringing and hemstitching it. "See that stitching? It took her days. Her fingers are still sore."

Jeff had tried to make his thanks more effusive, but it was too late. Jane looked at him with that cool, vaguely suspicious air that said, without a word, that her mother had told him what to say. Jeff had tried to make up for her hurt by wearing the scarf often. He should have worn it in plain sight today, when he said good-bye. That, too, was a thought that came too late.

Then he remembered that Jane was born on the eighteenth of November. She would be twelve years old day after tomorrow. He had forgotten. Loretta should have reminded him.

And he remembered that Loretta had reminded him, last week, and he had asked her to buy a gift for Jane from him. He never knew what to get for the girl. What he chose was either too old or too young, expensive jewelry or childish toys. So he told Loretta to buy something and he gave her twenty dollars.

"This," Loretta said, "is far too much."

Jeff said, "I can afford it."

"That's not the point. Maybe you can afford to spend it, but you can't afford to spoil her."

And Jeff, trying to be light about it, had laughed and said, "Girls *should* be spoiled!"

Loretta didn't laugh. She gave ten dollars back to him.

So that was why Jane was so sullen. Because he wouldn't be home for her birthday, didn't even mention it. But he knew that wasn't the whole of it. He didn't know what the whole of it was, but he was pretty sure it involved Tommy. He didn't know why, but he had the feeling that a good many painful things involved Tommy. Well, they would all have to get that one into place, as he had.

For some reason, Bill Sanders' words came back to him: "A little luck and a lot of hard work, and a man makes out."

I've made out, Jeff thought. And with very little luck. I didn't wait for luck. I played the cards as they fell. Life isn't draw poker. It's stud, and you play what you are dealt.

19

He glanced around for landmarks, saw that he had come almost five miles, was halfway to Schuyler Station. He knew every rod of the trail to the ranch, but he was glad to have the railroad tracks to guide by in weather like this. The Kansas Pacific tracks were still new, completed to Denver less than eighteen months ago, and you couldn't depend on the trains in the winter. Ice, blizzard, even drifting buffalo, might hold up a train for several days. There were three stations between Denver and the Bijou—Schuyler, Box Elder and Kiowa, none of them more than a water tank and a crude shelter; but those stations were like knots on a string that led where he wanted to go.

The snow was still falling about as it was when he left Denver and the wind held in the northeast. Bill was probably right. It would pester along until tonight, then settle down to business. The wind would whip up toward dusk and make it mean. Jeff didn't care what it did. It was going to be a storm, something tanigible to fight. He had been fighting intangibles too long. Fighting bad dreams, as he did when he was a little boy. Only these dreams were real. His mother wasn't going to come wake him up and say, "Jeff, it's just a dream. Everything's all right, Jeff-boy!"

He couldn't have been more than six when that happened, because they still lived in Warren County, Kentucky. His father was part-time farmer, part-time drover, and like all drovers he had restless feet. He would be at home long enough to plow and plant in the spring, then be off with a herd of market cattle, to New Madrid, to Memphis, to Louisville. He would be home again in the fall to harvest half a crop from his untended fields, then he would be off again, perhaps this time all the way to New Orleans.

Then Jeff was six and his sisters were eight and ten, and his father sold the farm and announced, "We're moving." He packed the family's belongings in two wagons, put Jeff on a pony to herd the loose stock, and headed west. He went all the way to Lamar County in north Texas, and he settled on new land along Bullard Creek.

For two years the Rosses lived a settled life on the Bullard Creek farm. Then Jeff was big enough to harness a mule and hold the handles of a cultivator, and his father took off again as a drover. Jeff grew up tough and wiry, and determined to escape the cornfield.

His mother fostered Jeff's discontent. "I want you to be a law-yer," she said, and she taught him to read and write and started him toward an education with what few books she had and could borrow. She did her best by him, gave him a start.

Then Jeff was sixteen and he told his father he was all through with plowing corn. His father said, "I guess you're ready to be a cavvy boy." A cavvy boy herded the spare horses in a trail crew and did the dirtiest, dustiest jobs.

Jeff shook his head. "I'm ready to learn to be a lawyer."

His father snorted. "No son of mine is going to make a living by his wits!"

"As near as I can see," Jeff said, "that's about what you do."

His father threatened to trounce him. Jeff said, "Try it." He was as big as his father, and almost as tough.

His father said, "All right, go be a lawyer. Get out!"

Jeff walked all the way to Dallas, the new town on the Trinity River. A lawyer there told him that if he would go to the new academy for a year he could come into the office and read law. Jeff got a job as stable boy at the hotel for meals and a place to sleep, swept floors and chopped wood at the academy to pay his tuition. Then he began reading Blackstone in the lawyer's office.

Meanwhile, with no one to plow the corn, his father sold the Bullard Creek farm to a newcomer from Kentucky and he, too, went to Dallas, which was becoming a trade center with a thriv-ing cattle business. But there was no healing of the estrangement. Jeff's father prospered as a drover, but Jeff struggled along at the law office and the hotel, chore boy at both places with little time to read law.

Another year and Jeff went to his father's office. His father looked up from his desk, as at a stranger, and demanded, "What do you want?"

"I'm looking for a job, as a drover."

"I thought you were going to be a goddamned troublemaking law man."

"I've changed my mind."

"And now you come crawling to me for a job."

"When I crawl, it'll be a cold day in hell."

"I can use a cavvy boy." It was an insult, meant as one.

Jeff turned and walked out. He went to his father's chief competitor and signed on as a trail hand taking a herd to New Orleans.

Jeff had grown up with talk about cattle, trail herds, drover's business. He learned fast. Within a year he could guess a steer's weight within twenty pounds, at a glance. He could ride around a herd and estimate their number within five per cent. He could make a shrewd guess at how many of the herd were wild-eyed brush-poppers and how many were tame enough to trail well. And he had begun to learn about the trails and the markets.

On that first trip Jeff came to know the open country and the wide sky. He knew sweat and dust and bone-weary fatigue; but he also knew the glory of sunrise, the smell of dawn, the shimmer of starlight. He rode drag and cursed the dust. He rode flank and swing and heard music in the creak of saddle and the jingle of spur and bit-chain. He rode point and was the tallest man in the saddle.

And he told himself that the time would come when he would have his own cattle, his own grass and water and herds on a hundred hills. When he would be a cattleman, a rancher.

By the time he was twenty he was a trail foreman and had been to Vicksburg, to Memphis, to Cape Girardeau, to New Orleans. He knew the trails and he knew the commission men. He knew the best hotels as well as the dives and the gamblers and the easy women. He knew how to handle a crew and a herd. He had been through sleet and blizzard, hail, rain and lightning. He had dickered and bullied and fought with Indians and white outlaws. Jeff Ross was a man, and proud of his manhood.

It was then, the summer Jeff was twenty years old, that his father sent for him. Jeff sent back word that his father knew where to find him.

He had known for months that his father was heading for trouble. He had kept up with the situation and waited, knowing that trail work was a young man's job and that his father was getting toward fifty. A trail boss of thirty-five was an old man, and his father had lost his best trail boss last spring, had to take his last herd of the season to Memphis himself. He lost twenty per cent of the herd on the way.

So Jeff sent back word that his father knew where to find him, and he waited. Two days later his father came to Jeff's hotel room, walked in unannounced and said, "I sent for you. Why didn't you come?"

22

He was weathered as an old saddle and stiff in the knees, but he was still rawhide-tough and he could bellow like a range bull.

"Any man that wants to see me can come find me," Jeff said. "Have a seat."

The old man glared at him and remained standing. His bushy brows half hid his angry eyes and his long mustache drooped over the wattles that were beginning to show under his cheeks. "You've got a big opinion of yourself, haven't you?" he said.

"Why not?" Jeff demanded. "I'm not asking anything of anybody. What do you want?"

His father was not exactly uneasy, but Jeff knew he would have been happier in his own office. If you're going to attack, it's always better to choose your own ground. But this time Jeff had chosen the ground. His father cleared his throat, and he said, "You've done pretty well for yourself." It was a growl, but it was a concession. "What are you going to do next?"

"Set up in business for myself."

"What kind of business?"

"As a drover," Jeff said. "In another five years, at most, I'll run you out of business."

One tip of his father's mustache tweaked. Jeff knew the sign. He was both amused and annoyed. "Why didn't you come see me," his father asked, "and tell me that face to face?"

"I figured you'd find out soon enough."

His father reached in his pocket, brought out his knife, opened the blade and sat down. He began to pare his nails. Jeff waited. At last the old man looked up and said, "So you think you can run me out of business?" He was smiling openly now.

"That won't be hard, the fix you're in," Jeff said.

His father went on paring his nails. Finally he looked up again. "Jeff," he said, "I always figured there was two ways to get what I wanted. One was to lick the other fellow. The other way was to join him."

Jeff didn't answer. He knew the offer had come hard, and he knew it was an offer. But he wasn't going to make anything easy for his father now.

His father waited, shifted in his chair. At last he demanded, "Well?" It was a bellow.

Jeff smiled at him. "I'd figured on going it alone. I don't need any help. Besides, you're too old to handle a trail herd." The insult was studied, and he let it sink in. Then he said, "You should have learned that, by now."

His father shouted, "Goddamn it, Jeff!" and he snapped the blade shut and put the knife back in his pocket. "I'm not asking to join you! Who do you think I am?"

Jeff was still smiling. "Why didn't you say what you mean?"

His father was on his feet now, pacing the room. At last he wheeled back and faced Jeff. "All right, I'll say what I mean. I've done my trailing. I need someone to take the herds. I'll handle the business here, but I need a trail boss. Someone I can trust. Someone as by-God tough as I am!"

"As you used to be," Jeff said.

"All right, as I used to be!"

"Back when you told me to get out," Jeff reminded him. Then he said, "The last time we talked, you offered me a job as a cavvy boy. Remember?"

"I wanted to see if you had any guts," the old man snapped. "If you were fit to be called my son."

Jeff shook his head. "I'm not trail-bossing for anyone from now on. You or anyone else." He started to turn away.

His father caught him by the arm. Jeff stiffened, and his father relaxed his grip. "Goddamn it, Jeff, I'm not asking you to crawl, but I won't beg, either. I've offered you a partnership. Take it or leave it!"

"Full partner?" Jeff asked. "In charge of the trail and the markets at the other end?"

"Yes!"

"I'll take it," Jeff said. "Get a herd ready. I'm going to take them through to St. Louis."

"St. Louis? You're crazy!"

"Crazy to get five dollars a head more than they're paying in New Orleans?"

"It's too long a drive. No! No, not to St. Louis!"

Jeff shrugged. "You don't want a partner. You want another cavvy boy." He turned and walked away.

"Jeff!" his father bellowed.

Jeff turned his head. "Good day, Mr. Ross."

His father strode over to him. "Stop this damn nonsense, Jeff!

I made my offer. What more do you want?"

"I want to handle the trail and the market at the other end."

His father eyed him for a moment, then thrust out his hand. "We'll go down and drink to Ross & Son."

But Jeff refused the hand. "To Ross & Ross," he said.

His father glared, then smiled, and he said, "I guess you are my son, Jeff." And they shook hands and went downstairs together.

So they became partners. And Jeff took the first Ross & Ross cattle to St. Louis.

Jeff liked St. Louis the first time he saw it. Until then, New Orleans had seemed the height of elegance and civilization; but St. Louis was a busy American business city as well as an old Spanish-French town. New Orleans was pleasant, but St. Louis was exciting, and not only because of its business, its money. There was an aliveness, a vigor about the whole city. Even the women in St. Louis were exciting, and those of New Orleans weren't, to Jeff. And when he thought of women, Jeff meant the respectable ones, the ladies.

So Jeff turned to St. Louis. The Planter's Hotel became a kind of second home to him, a place where he was known and deferred to. It was in St. Louis, through John Laughlin, the cattle dealer and commission man, that he met Amy Caldwell.

Jeff roused himself from the memories, looked around again for landmarks. He was approaching Box Elder, the second station, twenty-two miles from Denver. Almost halfway to the ranch. Box Elder was on the bank of a dry, sandy gully in which there was flowing water only after the spring thaw or an occasional summer cloudburst. Nine miles beyond Box Elder was Kiowa Creek, another dry bed, and twelve miles beyond Kiowa was the Bijou, the first stream of flowing water.

Dusk was closing in, a gray dusk that settled around him in a shifting white world. The blacks were trotting on the flats, easing to a walk on the long slopes, then trotting again. The snow was about three inches deep. It had beaten itself into the horses' coats till they looked ghostly in the twilight.

Jeff shifted in his seat and knew that his legs were numb. He had sat too long. His fingers were icy. He looped the reins around the whip in its socket and thrust his hands inside his coat to warm them. The wind was coming now in sharp gusts, the cold deepening. He readjusted the scarf, drew a fold of it up over his mouth and nose. When the blacks slowed to a walk at the next rise he drew them to a stop, pushed back the buffalo robe and stepped down to the ground. He had to get the cramps out, get his blood to moving.

He spoke to the horses and they started up the slope. Jeff's knees buckled at the first step and he would have fallen had he not grabbed the iron rail on the wagon seat. He held to the rail and forced his legs to walk, and slowly life began to creep back into them.

He walked all the way up the long slope and his legs felt fully alive again. It was stupid of him to have sat so long. In weather like this, a man should be out and walking up every hill.

The blacks began to trot down the far side of the rise. The reins slipped from Jeff's numb fingers. He stumbled, almost fell, then ran and caught the tailgate of the wagon. And drew himself up, lay across the slicker-covered saddle, catching his breath, until the horses slowed to a walk again. Then he shouted them to a stop, recovered the reins, knotted them and slipped the loop over one arm. He walked up the next slope, and the next.

He came to the dry bed of the Kiowa. The wagon crossing was a quarter of a mile downstream. Jeff didn't want to risk bogging team or wagon in the loose sand so he turned downstream to the crossing, then angled back to the track. In good weather, or in daylight, he would have taken the short cut, angled across from the Kiowa Crossing directly to the ranch. But this was no time to get lost and spend an hour or two finding the trail again. He would follow the railroad to the Bijou, then go down the valley to the ranch. Another three hours.

He plodded on, his breath coming easily now. Maybe he wasn't as tough as he was when he first saw the Bijou, but he hadn't gone altogether soft.

Then he thought back. As a matter of fact, he wasn't tough when he first saw the Bijou. He was a sick man. Still getting over the malaria. And still getting over Amy. If it hadn't been for the war he might have got over Amy Caldwell sooner.

"I'm all over Amy now," he told himself. But even as he said it he began thinking about her, remembering.

2

Amy was the youngest daughter of Andrew Caldwell, a man whom nobody, not even his wife, ever called Andy. Andrew was a farmer, a dour, moody Scots-Irishman who stood six feet three in his socks and had shoulders like one of his own oxen. He arrived in southern Illinois in the late 1830s with a pregnant wife, three small daughters, a rifle, an axe, a plow, and the determination to build a home and a competence. He built a house, a barn, the necessary sheds, and he plowed a field and planted it. Before his first crop came to harvest his wife was brought to bed with her fourth confinement. Andrew planned on a son. A farmer's wife may welcome daughters to primp and pamper and help with the washing, but a farmer needs sons.

To make sure of his son's safe delivery, Andrew went fifteen miles and brought back the nearest midwife, an earthy crone who peddled herbs and was called Snagtooth Liz. She took charge, bullied Andrew, wheedled the girls, and eased Mary Caldwell's delivery.

Andrew, who had spent the day at the barn to escape the cries and moans of Mary's birthing, was summoned. Old Liz came from the bedroom with the newborn babe in her arms.

"So," Andrew said, "you've got my first son."

Old Liz grinned at him. "I've got your baby."

"My son," Andrew insisted.

"And if it's not a son?" Old Liz demanded.

Andrew stared at her, anger rising in him. "I've already got three girls, you old witch!"

27

"So that's the thanks I get!" Old Liz shouted at him. "That's the thanks you give your poor wife, on her bed of pain!"

Andrew reached for the baby. Old Liz drew back, laughing at him.

"Give me the baby!" Andrew ordered. "I'll see for myself."

The old midwife began to laugh and backed away, out of his reach. "You should have told me," she said.

"Told you what?"

Old Liz cackled. "If I'd only known, I could have left it dangling instead of tucking it in, and you'd have had your son! But it's too late now." She flipped back the blanket and revealed the baby's undeniable femininity, almost triumphant.

Andrew stared for a moment, flushed, and snapped, "You foul-mouthed old slut! Be damned to you!" And he strode out the door and back to his barn.

So Amy Caldwell was born, Andrew's fourth daughter. And from that day forth Andrew slept alone, and Mary slept alone, and Andrew put all his vigor, all his dogged energy, into the land. For another fifteen years. Then the Illinois Central built its line from Decatur to Cairo and laid out a townsite and named it Centralia, just four miles from Andrew's farm.

By then Andrew was forty-five, his two oldest daughters were married, and Andrew's dreams of affluence had begun to fade. When a young farmer from Ohio came along and offered to buy the farm, Andrew sold it to him. He sold the farm and moved to Centralia to become a storekeeper. A man without sons can deal over the counter just as long as he can add two and two and come out with four. Or so Andrew Caldwell believed.

Amy at fifteen was a young woman, and every young man in Centralia was aware of it. She could have married within a month after they moved to town. Her oldest sister had married at fifteen and now, at twenty-one, she had four children. But the more Amy saw of marriage, including that of her own mother, the less she thought of it. Marriage was babies and washing and cooking and cleaning. Marriage was a man to care for, to pick up after, to humor, to say yes to when you didn't mean yes at all. Marriage was drudgery and submission, and Amy wanted none of it. Not with her mind, she didn't, though there were yearnings and excitements in her body that sometimes gave her mind quite a tussle.

28

Even so, the urgings and the hungers of her young body might have got the upper hand had Andrew not had his leg under a barrel of molasses just two months after he opened the store. He was trying to start a bung and put in a spigot, and his foot slipped, his bung starter missed, and he knocked the rack loose. The barrel came down on his leg, and there he was, a storekeeper with his leg broken in two places. The doctor splinted it and put him to bed, and Andrew ranted and fumed. And young Amy took the key to the store and went down and opened the doors and became a store-keeper. She escaped early marriage by selling bed ticking and calico, by trading sugar for eggs and coffee for butter.

It was three weeks before Andrew could hobble around on crutches, and by then Amy had straightened out his account books, rearranged the stock, washed the windows, swept the floor, and begun to show a profit. Amy had a head for figures and she had an instinct for business. Besides, she had found something that could use her mind, something that could make her more than a submissive woman.

Andrew got up on crutches and came hobbling down to the store. He looked around with a scowl and said to Amy, "Go on home. You've been here long enough."

Amy had no notion of going home. If she went home now she would never come back, and she knew it. She said, "I'll go home just as soon as you don't need me any longer."

Andrew snorted. He needed someone to help, and he knew it. And Amy had only skirted defiance; she hadn't openly defied him. "You shouldn't have come here in the first place," he said.

Amy said, "I've taken in ten dollars today."

"Don't lie to me!" Andrew snapped. The whole of the last week he had been in the store he took in only eighteen dollars.

Amy opened the cash drawer and showed him the money. She took out the ledger and flipped it open on the counter. First to Andrew's disordered entries, then to her own neat, orderly accounts. Andrew glanced at it and growled, "Anyone can set down such sums." But his belligerence lessened a little.

A farmer was at the door, a shifty man from south of town. Amy put the ledger away and closed the cash drawer. The farmer came to the counter and said to Andrew, "Hear you been laid up. I need sugar and coffee and I got a tub of butter. Will you trade?"

29

Amy spoke up. "Bring in your butter."

The farmer looked from one to another of them. Andrew said, "I'm in business to trade. Bring in the butter."

The farmer brought in a firkin of butter. Andrew picked up a dab on his forefinger, tasted it, and told Amy to weigh up ten pounds of sugar. Amy said, "In a minute," and came around the counter with a butter paddle in her hand. She dug two deep pats from the tub. The farmer caught her arm, looked at Andrew and said, "I won't be suspicioned by anyone!"

"That's a plenty," Andrew said to Amy. "Weigh up the sugar."

Amy went back behind the counter and began scooping corn meal from a barrel into the scale. The farmer exclaimed, "Sugar, not meal! I got plenty of meal!"

Amy emptied another scoopful of meal into the scale. "I'm giving you as much meal with your sugar as you're giving me lard with your butter," she said.

Andrew snapped, "Amy!" the farmer sputtered indignantly.

Amy picked up the paddle again, dug deep in the tub once more. This time she brought up a pat half yellow, half white. The whole lower half of the firkin contained lard.

Andrew stared at it. The farmer swore at Amy. Andrew shouted, "Get out, you thief! Get out of my store!" And the farmer picked up his tub and scuttled back to his wagon and drove away.

Andrew rubbed his chin and cleared his throat. He eased himself on his crutches and growled, "Put the meal back in the barrel, Amy." His voice was gruff and he was giving orders. But Amy knew it was only a token command. She emptied the meal back into the barrel, and she knew she was in the store as long as she wanted to stay.

So Amy was on her way to becoming a business woman. Andrew never admitted it, but within another year she was virtually running the store, making all the decisions that mattered. But she still made the gesture of deferring to Andrew, remained only his clerk and reserved for him the status of storekeeper. She still swept the floor and tended counter, but she kept the accounts and she knew to a penny how the business was doing. And she told Andrew what to buy from the occasional drummer, decided the price of what they had to sell or trade.

Centralia grew and business prospered. Within two years Amy

persuaded Andrew to move to bigger quarters in a better location. She hired clerks and broadened the business, which had started as little more than barter with farmers. Amy made the store an emporium where Centralia's women came to buy dress goods and corsets and buttons and shoes, and to which they sent their men for the groceries and the housewares. And the time came when Amy went to St. Louis with her father and bought the merchandise for such trade.

Amy was approaching twenty by then, and she'd never been seriously courted. Centralia's young men were in awe of her and the older men were all married. But at last George Bradley mustered courage and asked her to go out with him.

George was a teller in the bank and, at twenty-four, Centralia's woman-shy bachelor. An only child, George had been tied to his widowed mother's apron string all his life, and his mother was a prim and domineering woman. She wanted George to be a banker, a bachelor and a bulwark in her old age. Almost from the cradle she had lectured him on filial duty and the perils of sex. Then she died at the age of forty-three. Of her own meanness, some said, but more likely of a burst apppendix. And there was George, twenty-four, motherless, lonely, and more ignorant of the facts of life than any farm boy of ten.

George decided to court Amy Caldwell and Amy, more curious than eager, encouraged him. Without knowing, Amy was still fifteen years old in such matters, for she had grown right past the customary courting age with no experience at all. If either of them had been just a trace less naïve, Amy might have been a mother and a banker's wife at the age of twenty-one. But George knew neither the sweet nothings and gay inuendos of the city nor the crude directness of the backwoods, and Amy had only instinct and yearning curiosity to guide her. George's kisses were tentative and his caresses fumbling, and Amy's responses were impatient and exasperated.

But George persisted and Amy endured and eventually, by sheer instinct, they approached the rudiments of intimacy. Whereupon George became panicky. "Amy!" he exclaimed. "What are we doing? If we sin, and they find out at the bank—" The consequences were too awful for George to put into words.

Amy, in an agony between astonishment and frustration, thrust

31

him away. "I thought you were a man!"

George, on the verge of tears, said, "Amy! Now you have to marry me, Amy!"

"Never!" Amy cried. Then, having to drive the hurt of her own frustration deep into him, she said, "I am already so sinful, George, that you probably will go straight to hell, just knowing me!"

George cried, "Oh, what would mother say?" and retreated in horror. That was the end of the courtship.

For almost a year after that Amy didn't look at another man except across the counter at the store, and her ideas of marriage took shape in her mind without interference from her emotions. She would marry eventually, since it was woman's destiny to marry. But when she did it would be an older man, not a George Bradley, a man of experience and a man of means. A man who would humor her, pamper her, lavish her. Who he would be, she had no idea.

Then Matthew Hilliard came into the store one afternoon and spent twenty minutes talking to her. Matt Hilliard was forty-five years old, a widower with two grown and married children. He was reputed to be the wealthiest man in Centralia. He was a director of the bank, owned several business buildings, lived in the finest house in town with servants and a coachman. Gossip had it that he was courting a wealthy widow in St. Louis and was waiting only a decent year after his wife's death to marry her.

He gave Amy a large grocery order, but he was in no hurry about it. He talked with her as he ordered, obviously a man with a purpose. But Matt Hilliard was not an impulsive man. He talked and he smiled and he took his time, watching Amy, appraising her. And at last he said good day and tipped his hat and said his man would call for the order.

He came in again two days later, to buy a new robe for his carriage, and again he talked with Amy at length. And Amy knew then that Matthew Hilliard was going to offer her more than pleasantries and a friendly smile.

A week later he asked her to go for a ride with him in the country. "I am thinking of buying a farm and I'd like your opinion of it."

Amy smiled and said, "I am no farmer, Mr. Hilliard."

"True, true. But you have a business head on you. Besides, it is a pleasant afternoon for a ride."

Amy said that this was a busy day and she couldn't take the

afternoon off. "Some other time, perhaps."

Matthew Hilliard said, "I shall stop and pick you up Sunday afternoon."

So on Sunday he took her for a drive into the country. He talked about himself and his plans, and he deferred to her with pleasant, restrained gallantry. He stopped at the farm he had mentioned, drove about the fields, looked at the house and barns. And when they got back in the high-wheeled buggy he asked Amy's opinion. The owner, Amy told him, was asking too high a price.

"What, then," he asked with a smile, "it it worth?"

She mentioned a figure.

"You are shrewd, Amy," he said, "but too conservative. He will sell for a hundred dollars less than he asks, and in five years it will be worth twice that. That's the difference between land and groceries. In the store it's a matter of immediate profit. With me, it's a matter of investment and ultimate profit. Besides, I have other plans for that farm while I wait for its value to rise."

"What plans?"

"I need such a place to keep the cattle and mules I buy and sell from time to time." He smiled. "You see, I plan ahead."

As they talked, Amy began to get the measure of the man. Matt Hilliard did plan ahead. He weighed the odds and the prospects, then acted. He was a man you could count on. He fitted her plans.

The courtship was neither hasty nor insistent. Matt Hilliard was too sure of himself for that. But it was a courtship that left no doubt of its purpose. And, after her experience with George Bradley, Amy wanted no fumbling or precipitate assault on her emotions.

Matt Hilliard courted her for six months, and when he proposed to her he did it with a fine combination of sentiment and practicality. "Amy," he said, "I trust that what I am about to say to you will come as no great surprise. You must know that I have given it the most serious thought and that I am not speaking in any impulsive way. It is much too important a matter, for both of us." He paused a moment, then said, "Amy, I hope that you will consent to be my wife."

Amy had thought that when this moment arrived she would know exactly what to say. Now, however, she searched for words.

Matt sensed her confusion. He said, "Don't try to give me your answer now, my dear. Weigh your answer well. I know that I am older than you, but I hope that will prove to be a virtue. I am a mature man who has proved himself. I am no stripling still in search of his place in life. On the other hand, you, Amy, are no child. You are old enough to know your mind. And you, too, have proven yourself. I know your worth and I greatly admire your character. I hope you know how well I can care for you and how completely I shall cherish you. I believe that I can make you the happiest woman in Centralia."

A month later Amy went to St. Louis to visit John Laughlin, her mother's brother, and to buy a trousseau. She met Jeff Ross at the Laughlin house.

Jeff was in St. Louis with a trail herd, and the day after he arrived John Laughlin said, "Jeff, Mrs. Laughlin and I would like to have you at the house for dinner tonight. We have two pretty girls out there, my daughter Anabelle and her cousin who is here on a visit from Centralia. Will you come?"

Jeff went.

The Laughlin house was one of St. Louis' lesser mansions, lavish but not really ostentatious. Jeff was no stranger to such places. Dallas could equal them, right down to the silver, the china, the mahogany, the crystal and the linen. Jeff had been born in a log cabin; but so, for that matter, had John Laughlin. Only shiftless farmers lived in log cabins all their lives.

Jeff went and he met Anabelle and Amy. Anabelle was an only child, eighteen, pretty, shy and spoiled. Amy told him later that Jeff had been invited as an eligible young man for Anabelle. But when he met the two of them Jeff looked right past Anabelle to Amy, and if the Laughlins didn't know what was happening they must have been blind.

Amy was tall for a girl, and she was slender. Her hair was the color of a strawberry roan horse, not red and not brown but a little of both, wavy and full of lights. Her eyes were a kind of blue-gray, an odd color that looked almost green. Her voice was a note or two deeper than that of any other woman Jeff had known, but it was as feminine as a petticoat. Everything about Amy was feminine that night, so feminine that Jeff felt masculine as a stud-horse.

He wanted Amy Caldwell, and he knew it from the minute their eyes met.

Mrs. Laughlin had seated Jeff beside Anabelle at the dinner table. Some other young man, whose name Jeff didn't catch and never took the trouble to learn, was seated beside Amy across the table from him. But Anabelle and her mother and father and the anonymous young man might as well have dined in the kitchen for all that it mattered to Jeff and Amy. Yes, Amy felt it too. For them, there were only two people at the table. Jeff undoubtedly made the proper responses when the conversation demanded, though he had no memory of it later. He and Amy didn't exchange half a dozen remarks. But it wasn't words that mattered, then. Later they couldn't talk enough.

No doubt there was a roast and everything that went with it. There must have been a rare wine, knowing John Laughlin. There was whiskey later, for the men. Jeff remembered the whiskey because it had no effect, none. Jeff was not a drinker, seldom took whiskey; but that evening it might as well have been coffee or water.

And when he left, the evening over, he said good night to Amy almost as casually as he did to Anabelle Laughlin. Anabelle's eyes were bright, probably with held-back tears, but she laughed and nodded and turned and hurried away. Amy said, "Good night, Mr. Ross," in that low-pitched voice and without the trace of a smile. Jeff, forgetting everyone else, said, "I must see you." Amy said, "Yes," as simply as that. And John Laughlin went out with Jeff to where the Laughlin carriage and coachman waited to take Jeff back to his hotel. John, knowing that another stratagem to get a man for Anabelle had failed but knowing too that a man's world is business, not matrimony, said, "A pleasant evening, Jeff. Very pleasant indeed. We enjoyed having you with us. I'll see you at the yards tomorrow. Nine o'clock?"

Jeff said that would be splendid, vaguely remembering that they still had to make final settlement for the cattle.

For a week Jeff saw Amy every day. She came to luncheon with him in the public dining room at the Planter's. She went for drives with him in a hired trap. She had dinner with him and they went to the theater, saw a troop of players up from New Orleans.

And Jeff asked her to marry him.

He had hired a buggy and matched bays and they had gone for a ride out west of the city, into a wooded valley where June lay like a spring song. Wild roses climbed the rail fences and robins and redbirds were full of song. Jeff let the horses ease to a walk and he turned to Amy and said, "I want you to marry me, Amy."

Amy showed no surprise. She looked away and said, "Please, Jeff, don't spoil it."

"That," Jeff said, "is why I am going to marry you. So we will never lose it."

She smiled at him, then, and she took his hand between hers. "Jeff," she asked, "why aren't you already married? Surely Texas has plenty of pretty girls who would be glad to be Mrs. Thomas Jefferson Ross."

"Because," Jeff said, smiling, "I never met you until now."

"I am serious," she said. "Why?"

He reined the horses off the road into a small grove of walnut trees where the afternoon shade dappled the grass. "I've told you why," he said. "That's the sum of it. And now I'll ask you the same question. Why did you wait?"

Amy looked away and he saw the touch of a sad smile on her lips. Then she sighed and opened a small silk reticule in her lap and drew out a little blue velvet box. She closed the purse and held the box cupped in her hand for a moment. Then she looked at him and said, "I am going to be married, Jeff. This fall."

"You are what?" He couldn't believe her words.

She opened the box. It held a ring, a large solitaire diamond set in a yellow gold ring. Jeff stared at it for a moment, then said, "That doesn't mean anything. You are going to marry me."

"I have promised him." She closed the box and put it away. Then she said, "I'm sorry."

"Sorry? For what?"

"That I deceived you."

"If that ring means anything to you," he said, "you would have worn it from the start."

"Would it have mattered, if I had?"

He didn't answer.

"Would it have changed things?" she persisted.

Still he didn't answer.

"I don't think so, Jeff. And after that first night—well, I just couldn't wear it. I couldn't hurt you."

"You had to wait till now!"

"We've had this week, Jeff. There's that to remember."

"You are not going to marry him!"

"Oh, but I am." Her voice was calm, quiet. "He is the kind of man I should marry, the kind I planned to marry. He will give me the things I want."

"I can—" And Jeff bit back the words. Damned if he would plead or crawl.

"Yes?" she asked.

He picked up the reins, backed the team around and turned toward the road again. Then he checked the horses, put an arm around her, drew her to him and kissed her. A fierce, possessive kiss. She pushed against him for a moment, then returned his kiss, and for a long moment they held the embrace. At last she drew away.

Jeff said, "Well?"

"We'd better go back." For the first time her voice was tense.

He sat waiting, watching her. She flushed and wouldn't meet his eyes. At last she repeated it. "We'd better go back. Take me to town." She was trembling. She clasped her hands in her lap, clasped them so tight that her knuckles were white.

Jeff spoke to the horses and they went back to the city.

Not a word was said between them until they were within two blocks of the Laughlin house. Then Amy said, "Jeff, I shall never forget you."

Jeff, by then, could laugh. He laughed and said, "Of course you will. But I do hope you find it difficult."

"Don't be cruel," she said. "Please!"

"Cruel? I want nothing but your happiness." He was smiling at her.

She put her hand on his arm. "I don't expect happiness, Jeff. All I want is contentment."

The current between them was still so vital, so alive and tingling, that he wanted to thrust her hand away. It was like pain stabbing at him.

"If that's all you want," he said, "I hope you find contentment. That, I understand, is rather cheaply bought."

Then he was turning in at the Laughlins'. He drew up to the

marble carriage block, got out, went around and helped her down. As they went up the steps of the veranda she said, "You might say something kindly, Jeff, for me to remember."

"I have said," he told her, "that I hope you find what you want. Contentment."

"Is that kind?" Now she, too, being safe on the Laughlin veranda, could laugh.

"Then," Jeff said, "I will add that it has been a pleasant week. I thank you."

"And still you can't be kind." Her voice was little more than a whisper.

They were at the doorway. She faced him, a smile on her lips, hurt and something between defiance and pleading in her eyes. "I wish you would write to me," she said.

"I'm not much of a hand at letters," he said. "Especially when there's nothing to say. You are going back to Centralia?"

"Tomorrow. And you?"

"I'll be gone tomorrow too."

"You've been generous, Jeff."

"Thank you."

"That's all you have to say?"

"We've said enough, Amy. Both of us. Good-bye."

She hesitated just an instant, then turned and hurried indoors.

Jeff drove back to the hotel, left the team with the doorman, told the man at the desk he was checking out at once. Less than an hour later he was out at the stockyards, getting his own saddle horses from the stable. Before dusk he had ridden fifteen miles, was well out of St. Louis on his way to Springfield, heading for Indian Territory, for home. He rode all that night, stopping only to change mounts, to get as far from St. Louis as he could before the light of another day.

A month later, in Dallas, he received a letter from Centralia. There was only one sentence: "When can you meet me in St. Louis? Amy."

Jeff waited two weeks. Then he wrote an equally brief note back: "The tenth of October. Jeff."

Jeff put the memories aside now, in the darkness and the storm's swirling snow, and looked for landmarks. He sensed rather than saw that he was approaching Bijou Creek.

He came to the last ridge above the stream and turned north, down the ridge where the wind had blown the hilltops bare. He was glad to see the bareness, feel the open grass beneath his feet. If this wind kept up, continued to sweep the ridges this way, the storm wouldn't cause too much trouble for the cattle.

The blacks, headed into the wind, didn't like it. They fought the reins. Jeff held them into the storm for half a mile before they sensed where they were going and stopped fighting him.

Another hour and a half and he would be at the ranch house, a fire searing his back and a cup of scalding coffee in his hand.

He ducked his head and plodded on, and the memories were with him again.

She wrote and asked if he would meet her in St. Louis. It was as clear as that. Obviously she wasn't married. So he wrote that he would be there in October and she wrote, "I'll be there too." And Jeff wrote, "Bring your wedding dress."

So he went to St. Louis. Before he left Dallas he rented a house, he was so sure that he would bring back a bride.

He arrived in St. Louis and saw John Laughlin. John made no mention of Amy. But, Jeff told himself, John wasn't interested in woman matters. He went to the Planter's Hotel and checked in. There was no message for him there.

Jeff began to wonder, and his wonder became annoyance. She had made a fool of him once. Was she up to it again? The least she could have done was send a message, say she was delayed or she wasn't coming, after all. He wondered, and he tried to tell himself it didn't matter. He was here on business.

But he knew that it did matter.

He ate alone that night, and he told himself that he should have known. Amy had changed her mind again. Very well, if she was that way he wanted none of her. He decided to close up his business as quickly as possible and get out. Go home and forget her. That's what he should have done in the first place. He shouldn't even have answered that first letter from her. But a man does foolish things.

He was busy the next day till late afternoon. When he returned to the hotel the clerk handed him a message. It was from Amy.

It said only that she was in town, at a nearby hotel. Jeff changed clothes and went over there, still annoyed. She might have sent word that she was going to be delayed.

He went to her hotel and sent a message to her room. She came downstairs and he greeted her with a handshake and led her to a divan in a quiet corner of the lobby. She seemed almost smug, and yet there was something like fear in her eyes.

"Well," he said, "I hope you had a pleasant trip."

"Pleasant enough," she said. "Were you worried?"

"Why should I worry?"

"When I didn't get here yesterday."

"I wondered if you'd lied to me again."

She flushed, then laughed. "But you didn't worry?"

He didn't answer the question. He said, "You should be hungry. Shall we have dinner at the Planter's?"

"Of course."

"I saw John Laughlin. He didn't know you were coming?"

"I didn't come to visit the Laughlins."

He reached for her left hand. There was no ring. "Are you hiding it in your purse again?" he asked.

"A ring didn't seem to matter before."

"To you it did. And I expected to see a wedding ring this time."

"Oh, Jeff! Let's not start right out quarreling. You asked me to come. Here I am."

He didn't dispute her. "I'll call a hack," he said.

They went to the Planter's and Jeff asked for the table where they had eaten before. He ordered a light wine, New Orleans oysters, prime roast of beef. As they ate, the barriers began to ease away, the strangeness and the remembered hurts. They always did that to each other, brought out the hurts, then came to the laughter and the aching need. And they seemed always to come back somehow to the hurts again.

They ate, and they went for a walk in a park beside the river. They walked and they fell silent, and Jeff felt the tensions building up in her. At last he said, "What's wrong, Amy? You've turned remote as a stranger."

"I shouldn't have come," she said.

"But you came."

"It didn't matter to you whether I came or not!"

"Should it matter?"

"Of course it should!"

"Then I do have a claim on you?"

"You always said you did."

They walked in silence, and at last he said, "We'll be married tomorrow."

She didn't answer.

"Next week we'll start home. To Dallas. You brought that wedding dress, didn't you?"

"No."

"Why not?"

And she flung at him, "Jeff, you tangle me in words! I don't know *what* to say! Why must we talk, talk, talk? Why can't we just *live*! That's enough, isn't it?"

"That depends on what you mean by live."

"Talk, talk, talk!"

"If you didn't come expecting to marry me, why did you come?"

"You wanted me to!"

"Did I ask you to come?"

"Jeff, you know that I have been yours ever since that first evening we met, and—and— Oh, now you have robbed me of my last refuge, my pride!"

He took her in his arms and kissed her, and there was no reluctance in her. She clung to him, held his lips, his arms.

At last he said, "We'll be married tomorrow."

"No." She drew away from him.

"Why not?"

"I—I didn't bring the wedding dress."

"We'll buy one."

"No."

"So you're still afraid. What are you afraid of?"

She caught his hands. "Jeff, I'm getting cold. Let's go somewhere and talk."

"Where?"

"Your room."

They went back to the hotel, up to Jeff's room. It was a big corner room, one of the hotel's best. Its furniture was upholstered in red and gold plush, long, heavy drapes at the windows,

41

a big four-poster bed, a long couch, a big walnut dresser, several chairs, a rug patterned with red roses a foot across.

Jeff turned up the gas chandelier and Amy wandered restlessly about the room.

"Well," Jeff said, "how do you like it?"

"Like what?"

"The room. This is where we'll be tomorrow night."

"No, Jeff. Not tomorrow. I'm going home tomorrow."

"You're what?"

She crossed the room and stood at the window, staring out at the street, her back to him.

He waited, and at last she turned to face him, and she said, "Jeff, I am not going to marry you. Ever."

Jeff said, "I never did care for cowards."

She said, "Maybe you're right, Jeff. Maybe I am afraid. But not of you." She came a few steps toward him. "I told you once what I wanted of life, and of marriage. I still want that, and I intend to have it. I'm afraid not to."

Jeff said nothing. He stood staring at her.

"Jeff," she said, "you've been in love with me since that very first night, haven't you? And probably I'll always be in love with you. That's something to remember, isn't it?"

"You came here to tell me that?"

"I came, Jeff, to have something to remember."

"You're making it something to forget."

"Do you think you can ever forget me?"

"I heal quick, Amy. I'll forget."

She looked at him with anger and bafflement in her eyes. Then she said quietly, "Jeff Ross, I hate you."

And he took her in his arms.

Later, she was sitting in front of the mirror over the dresser, buttoning her blouse, watching herself in the mirror, watching Jeff standing there behind her.

Jeff said, "That's a pretty enough wedding dress you've got on. Unless you want another, we'll make it do tomorrow."

She smiled at him in the mirror, then opened her purse and got out a powder puff. "Jeff," she said, "you told me once that you never saw a river you couldn't cross, an Indian you couldn't bluff, or a horse you couldn't ride."

"That's not quite the way I said it, but—"

"That's close enough." She turned and looked up at him, and her eyes were dead serious. "Some day," she said, "you will. Just as you found a woman who wouldn't marry you. . . . Please take me back to my hotel, Jeff."

"Amy, you can't—"

She stood up. "Please, Jeff." She was as cool, as dispassionate, as though they had just eaten dinner in the public dining room.

He picked up his coat, put it on, picked up his hat. She took his arm, smiled up at him and said, "We said all that needed saying, Jeff." And they went out the doorway and along the hall and down the stairs, Amy with her head high and her eyes calm and assured.

They walked the few blocks to her hotel. The streets were almost deserted, for it was nearly midnight. In the lobby of her hotel Jeff said, "I'll call for you at nine o'clock in the morning." She smiled and shook her head and he stepped to the desk.

He handed her the key to her room.

She said, "Good-bye, Jeff."

"Good night, Amy."

"I said good-bye." And she turned and ran up the stairs.

Jeff watched her go, and the bafflement turned to anger in him. Anger both at Amy and at himself. Then he went back to the Planter's and into the bar. He ordered a double whiskey, drank it and another, then ordered a bottle. He sat there alone and drank, too angry to stop, and at last someone helped him to his room.

He didn't waken till ten o'clock the next morning. He hurried to dress, and he went to Amy's hotel. The clerk said that Miss Caldwell had checked out early that morning.

Jeff finished his business, caught the train to Memphis, bought a saddle horse and went on home to Dallas, touchy as a range bull with a sore back. Six weeks later he married Loretta.

Two weeks before his marriage, a letter came from Centralia. As usual, it was only one sentence: "Remember me kindly." It was signed, "Amy C. Hilliard."

Jeff didn't answer it.

The cold was bitter, now, and Jeff was walking every step of the way. The wind cut like a wire-edged knife. His cheeks were raw from the slash of the snow and the scarf across his face was stiff with ice from his own breath.

He wrapped up the memories of Amy and put them away, like a pack of old love letters. He was through with Amy.

He peered toward the valley of the creek to his right, made out its dim features through the snow and the darkness, just enough to know where he was. The ranch was only about a mile ahead. He was almost home. Strange how the ranch was home to him, always would be. The house in Denver wasn't home. It was just a house, a big, showy house where Loretta and the children lived.

He was stiff and tired as a dog, but he had an inner warmth of satisfaction that eased the weariness of the flesh. He had faced the storm and done what he set out to do. He wasn't too soft to make it out to the ranch in the teeth of a blizzard. He had fought the storm, and he had won, was in sight of victory right now.

Then he was on the last ridge, the bluff just west of the ranch house. The buildings were down there, just ahead, in the bend of the stream, sheltered on the north by the big grove of pines. The house, the long, low barns, the pole corrals and open sheds, the haystacks in the stack yard. Jeff Ross's Pothook Ranch, named for the brand that started out as a lazy J, the letter "J" on its side, but re-named the Pothook by Bill Sanders.

The blacks angled down the steep slope toward the shallow ford and Jeff drew them to a stop at the water's edge. He climbed into the wagon and crossed the black current dry-shod, and he drove up to the door of the peeled-log house and shouted till he raised an answering shout inside. Then he drove to the barnyard and began unhitching the team. His stiff fingers were fumbling with the neckyoke when Sam Royce and Harvey Bird came hurrying from the house, Sam swinging an oil lantern. It was almost midnight. The storm was still rising.

3

In the big house in Denver, Loretta couldn't sleep. The storm was a bad one, but she wasn't actually worried about Jeff. Jeff always got where he was going. He would get through to the ranch, one way or another, she knew that. She wasn't worried about anything, really. She had learned that worry never solves a problem; it only makes a problem seem more difficult. For that matter, the only problem she had that wouldn't eventually solve itself, somehow, was Tommy. And maybe the problem of Tommy was solved, for the present, with Bessie.

It was difficult, though, to know what to do. The girls needed her, and Jeff needed her, in some ways. Yet all of them were, in most ways, largely self-sufficient. Tommy was the only one who was really helpless, completely dependent.

Strange, Loretta thought, lying there in the big, dark bedroom, how the needs change. They could all go on without her, one way or another, except Tommy. And yet, to be clear-headed and practical, Tommy was the least important of them all, though he had dominated their lives for ten years. Jeff, she thought, was the only one of them who seemed able to rise above it. But Jeff was a man.

Then she thought: Tommy is the only one who needs, actually needs, love. I love him. Do I love him too much, simply because he is so helpless? Because he is a helpless part of me? Does a mother always love the most needful one, even cherish the need? Is that what being a mother means? Jeff leans on my love, needs to know it is there; but Jeff needs to get away from it, too. As he needed to go today. A man can't be prisoned by love. A woman can. Is. I need Jeff. He is a part of me. Not as Tommy is and always will be, but as breathing is a part of me. The breath I take does not need me. I need it to go on living. I need Jeff here in bed with me. Not always, but from time to time. I need the knowledge of him as well as the love his body knows for mine, the fact of his being even when he is unaware of me and my needs. I need him now.

She got out of bed, put on a robe and slippers and went across the hall to his bedroom. He used it as a bedroom only occasionally, but he kept his clothes in its big closet, used it mostly as a dressing room. It had a faint odor of him, of his clothes, of his body. Jeff was an immaculate man, always had been, but there was the faint, masculine smell of him in this room; and when she opened the closet door it was even stronger. Not as strong as the horse smell that was always about him at the ranch, but even with a touch of that, too, since Jeff always had been, always would be, a horseman.

She stood there at the closet for a long minute, then turned away, content, somehow assured.

She went back into the hallway, still restless. The house was dark and had that strange, empty feeling of night. The snow still beat on the windowpanes, coming now with the swish of strong gusts, and the wind moaned.

She went downstairs, her eyes now fully adjusted to the darkness. Even without dim sight, she could have moved confidently about the house, for she knew where every chair, every table, was. She went to Jeff's office, opened the door, had the scent of him again, felt his presence. She crossed the room, stood at the south window and looked out, toward the plains, as Jeff had stood that morning. Off there somewhere in the darkness and the storm Jeff was nearing the ranch. She could almost feel the cut of the wind, the bite of the snow.

And at last she went back to the hallway, to return to her bed. Then she smelled the coffee, and somehow in the darkness and the storm it brought back the memories.

She went to the kitchen, which had a faint, rosy glow from the drafts in the kitchen range, where Jenny had banked the fire for the night but had forgotten to close the drafts completely. It was comfortably warm, and in the glow she saw the coffeepot at the back of the stove, simmering. She got a cup from the cupboard, poured half a cupful and sat down at the kitchen table. She tasted it, and the bitterness brought the memories flooding.

She was twenty years old. Twenty, and her mother nagged, "Loretta Graham, what *is* the matter with you? You've had a dozen chances and turned them all down. You're an old maid right now. Don't you *care?*"

Of course she cared. But her mother had a right to scold. Widowed when Loretta was ten, she was left with no resources except her nimble fingers and her skill with scissors and needle. Naturally, she wanted her daughter to marry. Naturally she scolded.

Loretta could have married at sixteen. Not much of a marriage, perhaps, though the boy turned out all right. He owned a feed store now. But even at sixteen Loretta knew that Jeff Ross was the man she wanted. And Jeff didn't know that Loretta existed. Not really. Jeff was a drover, a hard-riding man who went to far places, saw distant cities, and came back with money to waste. Except that Jeff Ross wasted little money in Dallas.

Jeff was the man she wanted, and she hoped every time she saw him that he would look at her and say, "Why, Loretta Graham, you are beautiful! I never knew it until now. Loretta, I love you!" Silly, of course, but she wished exactly that. And he never did. But she hoped and dreamed, and for three years she refused every boy who tried to court her. Refused them for reasons she couldn't reveal to anyone. Loretta Graham became an old maid, just as her mother said, an old maid who had passed up her chances and settled down as a seamstress with her mother.

Her chances passed. And the time came when Jeff Ross met the girl in St. Louis whom he was going to marry. Word gets around, gossip. Loretta heard it, and she refused to believe it. No! He couldn't! But Louise, Jeff's older sister who had married a Banta, was one of Loretta's mother's customers, and one day when she was at the house ordering a new dress she said in passing that Jeff had gone to St. Louis to bring back a bride. Loretta heard and had to believe, and her heart cringed and began to cry.

Those were difficult weeks, with her mother asking over and

over, "Are you sick, Loretta? You're pale as a ghost and you hardly say a word. What *is* the matter?" And how could Loretta tell anyone, most of all her mother, that she was dying inside?

Loretta said, "There's nothing the matter with me. I have a headache, that's all. Just a headache." And her mother said she was either bilious or in love, and since she couldn't be in love she'd better take a physic.

September passed. Loretta hardly left the house, because she knew Jeff Ross was soon due back and she didn't want to meet him on the street and blurt out, "Why, Jeff Ross, I've always been in love with you and now you've gone and married someone else!"

Then the day came when Louise Banta came for a fitting and said, "Well, Jeff is home."

Mrs. Graham, her mouth full of pins, said, "I didn't know he'd been away."

Louise laughed, and Loretta held her breath. "He went," Louise said, "and he came back mad as a bear with a sore paw."

"Mad?" Mrs. Graham asked. "What about? . . . I think we'd better take a dart right here, Louise."

"About some girl," Louise said. "That girl in St. Louis. Jeff doesn't talk, but he'd rented a house to live in, and now he's come back alone and he's living at the boardinghouse again."

"Well, that's too bad," Mrs. Graham said. "Now I'll pin up the hem."

Loretta thought she was going to faint. She got up and went to the kitchen for a glass of water, and she stayed there till Louise had left the house.

Two days later Loretta was going downtown to match a spool of thread, and she saw him. He was coming up the walk toward her, there on the street, and his face was like a thundercloud. Loretta wanted to turn and run, wanted to dart across to the other side of the street, wanted to drop right through the board walk. Then he was right there in front of her, not seeing her at all, and she was so nervous she dropped her purse. She hadn't meant to. Not Loretta! It slipped from her hand and she tried to catch it, and instead she knocked it right in front of him. He almost stepped on it.

He stopped and stared at her. Then he reached down and picked up the purse and handed it to her. He frowned and he said, "You are Loretta Graham, aren't you?"

She said, "Yes!" And her throat couldn't utter another word.

Jeff looked her up and down, head to toe, as though he had never seen her before in all his life. Then he said, "How are you, Loretta?"

She said, "I'm fine," and she wished she could get past him and run.

Then Jeff grinned at her, maybe sensing her nervousness. He grinned and he said, "It's a fine day, isn't it? A fine day."

She said, "It looks like it might rain, and we need rain."

Jeff looked up at the sky, then back at her. He said, "So it does," and he started on. Then he turned and came back. "Loretta," he said, "if it doesn't rain it'll be a nice day for a buggy ride. I'll come over to the house for you at three o'clock."

And Loretta said, "I'll be busy at three o'clock. It would be better if you came over right after supper." She didn't know why she put him off, but she did.

She went on down to the store and matched the thread and went home, and it wasn't until she had been home almost an hour that it struck her. Jeff Ross had asked her to go out with him. Jeff Ross!

He came for her at seven o'clock, in a buggy with the top down. They drove out into the country, and Jeff talked and Loretta listened. She never did remember what he talked about, but that didn't matter. They had driven about three miles when the clouds thickened and lightning flashed. The thunder boomed, and it began to rain so quickly they both were soaked before Jeff could put the top up. It wasn't funny at all, but they laughed about it as though it were the biggest joke in the world. Jeff drove back to town, and Loretta said he just had to come in and get warm and dry, and she had to get out of her wet dress.

The kitchen was the warmest room in the house, with the supper fire still smouldering. Jeff said some hot coffee would be just the thing to fix them up, and he poured half a cup from the pot still simmering on the back of the stove. He tasted it and made a face and asked, "Did you make this stuff, Loretta?" She admitted she had, and he laughed and said, "I'll have to teach you to make *good* coffee!"

Loretta said for him to go ahead and make a pot the way he

49

liked it and she would change her dress. She went to her room and when she came back he had built up the fire and the coffee pot was boiling. She got out cups and he poured it, and they sat down at the kitchen table. She tasted it and exclaimed, "What is this, anyway!"

"Coffee!" Jeff said with a laugh. "Coffee the way it should be. Black as midnight, hot as hell, strong as the devil. You test it by tossing a silver dollar in the pot. If it sinks, the coffee's too weak."

It was the first time Loretta had tasted real ranch coffee. She drank a whole cupful, and she didn't sleep a wink till long after midnight. It probably wasn't the coffee, though. Jeff kissed her when he said good night, and he wanted to see her again the next evening. She knew she shouldn't have let him kiss her, not the very first time she went out with him, and she shouldn't have promised to see him again so soon. But she did, both. She knew, that very first evening, that she hadn't waited all this time for nothing. At least she wanted so desperately to know that she felt she did know.

Sitting here now, in the big brick house in Denver, with the storm outside and Jeff out in the storm, she felt warm and glowing with the remembrance. She sipped the coffee, which was strong but not as strong as ranch coffee. Jenny had never learned to make it right, never would.

She sipped the coffee and remembered Jeff's courtship, which scandalized her mother. For three weeks Jeff saw her almost every evening, and her mother said, "Loretta, I don't care if you *are* twenty years old, there'll be talk!"

Loretta said, "What do I care?"

Her mother said, "Well, if you don't, I do! You're acting like a hussy, Loretta Graham!"

"Mother," Loretta said, "I don't care what you say, or what anyone says. Maybe I am a hussy. But I love him."

"Loretta!"

"I do!"

"You hardly know him!"

"I've known him all my life! I've known him forever!"

"Don't you care what people think?"

"No!"

"You're no daughter of mine. Oh, Loretta, the things you do to me! The way you talk to your own mother!"

Jeff courted her only three weeks. Then he asked her to marry him. She said yes. She had no pride about it. She said yes, and he said, "Name the date. There's no need to wait long, is there?"

"None that I can see, Jeff," she said. "But I want it on a Sunday. It seems more a marriage, somehow, on a Sunday. I'd like it to be two weeks from next Sunday. Is that too soon?"

"That's fine," Jeff said.

And now Loretta's mother was horrified. A wedding in two weeks? After practically no courtship? "Oh, Loretta! How could you do such a thing?"

"We've set the date," Loretta said firmly.

"Two weeks to make a wedding dress!" Then: "Loretta, tell me the truth. Do you *have* to marry him? Are you—are you going to have a baby?" Her voice was a horrified whisper.

"No!"

"Tell me the truth!"

"No!"

"Everyone will say you are, and you know it."

"I don't care what they say!"

And Jeff faced the same thing. He told Loretta. Both his sisters came to him, horrified, and asked the same question. Jeff told them to mind their own business.

Talk? There always is talk, about someone. Dallas had its share of weddings that led with surprising celerity from the altar to the baptismal font. It even had its occasional birth without benefit of marriage. Loretta let such talk go right over her head. She and Jeff were married just as they had planned, in the church, the second Sunday in November, with only the Rosses and Loretta's mother present.

Loretta was happy at the altar, happy and frightened and wondering at the grim stiffness of Jeff beside her. Jeff had a thin smile on his lips as he looked out at the family, defiant. Then she saw that the defiance was not really at his family, for he wasn't looking at them. He was looking beyond, into the unknowable distance.

They were married, and they went to the hotel, and Loretta

knew deferred love, deep, plunging body love that engulfed her and left her weak and spent. She slept and was renewed and wakened, and marveled at Jeff, there in the bed beside her. She touched his lips, his cheeks, his hair, and he stirred and whispered, "Amy."

She drew away from him, stricken. She fought the tears, knew that the lump in her chest was a stone, for it could no longer be her heart. The tears came, and she fought the sobs, telling herself that Jeff was asleep, he was dreaming. And she whispered over and over, "Jeff, Jeff, if I haven't got you, I haven't anything."

And at last Jeff opened his eyes and lay staring at the ceiling, and that grim, defiant look he wore all through the ceremony was on his face. Then he sensed her crying, and he turned to her and said, "Loretta."

She couldn't answer. She couldn't say a word.

He said, "I don't know what I said or did, but I'm sorry, whatever it was."

She couldn't tell him what he had said. Not then or ever. But she could say, "Jeff, I've always loved you. Always."

And he said, "And now you're my wife." He drew her to him, held her close, made her his again. And it was enough, for then, enough. She was Jeff's, and every fiber of her being knew it. Some day, she told herself, I'll be his even in his dreams.

Three days at the hotel, seeing no one. Then they went to the house Jeff had rented. And a week later Jeff got on his big bay horse and went about his business. Loretta began making a home for her man.

Loretta sipped at the coffee again. It was cold; it lacked the bitter hotness, the strength of the devil. She set it aside and went to the window and looked out at the turbulent darkness of the storm. Then she closed the drafts on the stove and went upstairs and back to bed.

There are the things to remember, and there are the things to forget. Remember the kisses, forget the good-byes. Remember the loving, forget the pain. And yet, one cannot always command the memory.

The years, those early years, were strange and difficult, shot

52

through with ecstasy, yet marked by loneliness and wondering. No marriage is completed at the altar. Marriage is what comes after the public declaration.

Jeff was always going or coming, it seemed, busy, restless, needful of action. He would come home weary but jubilant, grateful for ease, for comfort, for Loretta, full of talk of far places. But always a man of moods. And a stranger, in many ways, a beloved stranger. Home for a little while, then off again, into his man-world. So there was the ecstasy and the loneliness, the living and the waiting. And the living was worth the waiting, even during her first pregnancy.

The child was to be a boy. Jeff insisted on that. A son, his first son. That was typical of Jeff. He demanded what he wanted of life, and he wanted a son. She laughed at him, said, "It may be a girl, you know. We will have daughters as well as sons."

"Girls like you," he said, "boys like me. But we start with a boy."

The first child, however, was a girl. She was born in November, the fall of '59. A relatively easy birth, the doctor said, for a first child, and Loretta had a sense of fulfillment. But she knew Jeff would be disappointed. When he came into the room she looked up at him and said, "I'm sorry, Jeff. I wanted a boy as much as you did. But she is a beautiful baby, isn't she?"

Jeff looked at her and at the baby, and he said, "Yes, Loretta, she's beautiful, I guess. But she doesn't look like you. She's got dark hair. She'll never be as pretty as you are."

"Her hair may change." Loretta glowed inside. Jeff so seldom said sweet, endearing things.

"You're all right?" he asked.

"Tired, just very, very tired."

He leaned over and kissed her. He looked again at the baby. Then he looked again at Loretta and he said, "The next one will be a boy."

Was it then, when Jane was born, that the change came? No. It was later, the next spring. That was a good winter, a happy winter, though Jeff spoke often of the troubles that were brewing in Washington. But the next spring he took a trail herd to St. Louis, and he came back like an old range bull on the prod.

It wasn't only because of the certainty of war, though he said the fat was in the fire and trouble was sure to come. It was something else, and after a time Loretta knew it was Amy Caldwell, that woman in St. Louis. The woman he had planned to marry, and didn't. Loretta had thought that Amy was all through and done with, but she wasn't.

How do you fight a thing like that? How do you meet the eyes of a man who looks at you and looks away and all but says, "You are the woman I married, but I wanted someone else"? A man who speaks her name in his dreams.

Fight it? You don't. You can't, really. Not a woman six hundred miles away, a woman you have never seen. You know that he came back to you. To you, the woman he did marry. You know that he is the man you love. So you wait, and you hope.

Loretta waited, and hoped, and Jeff's angers eased away. He was almost himself again by summer. He might have taken another herd to St. Louis that fall, but he didn't. He took a herd to New Orleans, and he came home more worried than ever over the war that was coming. He talked bitterly of the election of that lawyer from Illinois as President, and he was disturbed by the opposition to old Sam Houston, back in the governor's mansion in Austin. But he no longer had Amy Caldwell's face in his eyes when he looked at Loretta. Loretta wasn't in his eyes either, but that hurt less than the other.

He talked of the ranch, the ranch he wanted and hadn't been able to get. It seemed almost an obsession. He had talked of it ever since they were married, but as something in the future, something he was working toward. Now he talked as though he had planned to have it by now, had been thwarted somehow. And she had the feeling that she had thwarted him. She hadn't, knowingly; she had always been willing to do whatever he wanted. But now he talked as though everything were against him, and he had to fight, fight, fight. Even fight her. He was touchy. He was short-tempered.

But he threw himself into business, local business, all that fall and winter. Trying to make money, trying to get ahead. Then Texas voted secession, and there was the attack at Fort Sumter. And the next thing she knew Earl Van Dorn was recruiting a brigade of Texas cavalry. And Jeff was like a man in a cage, restless as a trapped wolf.

Loretta herself brought the matter to a head. "Jeff," she said one evening, "you want to get away, don't you?"

He looked at her, startled. "Get away where?"

"Away from here. You want to join Van Dorn."

He didn't answer.

"And you think you shouldn't leave me."

He stared out the window, then turned to her. "I don't know what to do. I planned to have the ranch by now."

"Maybe it's a good thing we aren't on a ranch. I can take care of myself here in town."

He shook his head, then stared at her. She wondered if he guessed that she was pregnant again. She hadn't told him, partly because he was so remote, so touchy, and she wasn't going to tell him now.

"You want me to go?" he asked.

"If you weren't married you would go, wouldn't you?"

"Yes."

"Then I want you to go, yes."

"I guess you won't miss me, then."

"I'll miss you terribly, Jeff. But I still want you to go."

He said no more about it, but he began putting his affairs in order. He had the house paid for. He put it in her name. He paid up his debts, gave her most of the cash he had, sold all but one buggy horse for her and his own two favorite saddle horses. Then he enlisted.

When it came time to say good-bye she almost told him about the coming baby, almost promised that this one would be a boy. But she checked herself. Motherhood was woman's business, and she was sending him away with a laugh and a kiss, free.

It was almost seven months before he had a furlough long enough to get home. When he found her nearing the end of her pregnancy he demanded, "Why didn't you tell me?"

"Because you might not have gone, and it was important to you to go. Having you here wouldn't have shortened my time one hour, Jeff." Then she said, "How long can you stay? I hope you're here when our first son is born."

"Five days." He smiled. "So it's going to be a boy this time?" He was pleased, but not as pleased as she had hoped. He was remote, the familiar stranger, pleased to be home but vaguely uneasy. Pleased with Loretta, but uneasy even with her.

It bothered her, baffled her, until she realized that this was the same strangeness she knew so well from his returns from the long trail trips. But now it was multiplied. War was more than a long trip up the trail and back. War enforced its own allegiance, created its own breed of men for a time. Men different from other men, men who were alien to home and peace.

Jeff was at home for five days, but she knew that the visit was only a lull in the bigger theme, not really a return. War was the reality. Home, wife, even the child about to be born, were unreality, a kind of remembered once that existed somewhere on the rim of life but were not actually a part of it.

Five days, and Jeff the stranger, the courteous man who in many ways was more considerate, perhaps even more in love, than ever before, said good-bye again and rode back to war, back to his present reality.

The baby was born the sixth day after Jeff went back to his command. It was a long, difficult birth and the doctor said later that he was fortunate to save either of them, Loretta or the baby. But Loretta was triumphant. The baby was a boy. She named him for Jeff and she wrote a long letter as soon as she was able, telling Jeff all about his first son.

She was in bed for a month after Tommy was born, and her mother had to move in and take care of her for almost three months before Loretta regained her strength. But she was sustained by the thought of Jeff's pride in her, the thought that now he had everything he wanted. The war would soon be over—it couldn't last forever—and he would come home and have a wife who loved him, a son to be proud of; and he would start his ranch. Everything he wanted, surely.

But as the months passed she knew that something was wrong with the baby. He was a slow baby, distressingly slow. He didn't sit up. His eyes didn't seem to work right. His arms were stiff, and his feet seemed twisted.

She asked Dr. Carter what was wrong. Dr. Carter pursed his lips and tweaked his nose and said, "Sometimes a baby like this takes a while to get going." He said, "Mothers worry too much. If you had six you wouldn't have time to worry." Finally he said, "Have patience, Loretta."

But she knew, as a mother knows.

Jeff came home again, and she watched, fearful, when he saw the baby. But Jeff said nothing except, "He's a good-looking boy, Loretta." She didn't know until long after that Jeff, too, went to Dr. Carter, and that Dr. Carter gave him no more satisfaction than he had given Loretta.

Jeff was home again for only five days, and again he was the visitor, the familiar stranger, gentle with her and seemingly with a proper pride in the children. But still the stranger, the guest from another world. Then he went back to the war.

The war years. The loneliness, the waiting, the never-knowing. As the months passed and the hopes for an early end to the war faded, she worried. Others from Dallas died in battle or of disease. Letters from Jeff were brief and far apart. He was at the battle of Elkhorn Tavern, at Vicksburg, at Corinth. Defeats, all of them. Yet Jeff went through the war without a saber cut or a bullet wound. Three horses were shot from under him, she learned later, yet he ended the war as a casualty from malaria and dysentery. He was mustered out and sent home to stay in January of '65. Bill Sanders brought him home, assigned to him on detached duty, for Jeff was too sick to travel alone.

He came home to stay, and by then there was no doubt about Tommy, who was going on three and was still as helpless as a baby of six months. Jane was past five. And Loretta was in her third pregnancy.

His first night at home they sat at the lamplit table after they had finished supper and Loretta said, "It's good to have you home, Jeff. You don't know how good it is!"

"Why?" he asked. "Why do you say it's good?" He wasn't much more than a skeleton, and he was so weak he could hardly stand.

Loretta, heavy with child, in her eighth month, said, "If it's good to my way of thinking, why should you question?"

"I don't know what you're talking about. You wanted me to go. Now you say it's good to have me come back."

"I knew you had to go, Jeff. Now you have come back, and I'm trying to tell you I'm glad you are here. I need you, Jeff."

"Because you're going to have another baby?"

"No!" He didn't mean to be cruel; she knew that. But it hurt. "No!"

57

"You haven't needed me for three years and a half."

"I've needed you desperately, Jeff."

"You made out."

"That's not enough!"

He didn't answer.

"Jeff, you didn't marry me just because I needed you then, did you? You needed me, too, didn't you?"

Still he didn't answer.

"Have we changed so much?"

"Everything has changed."

"We are older, Jeff. Shouldn't we be wiser?"

Jeff sighed. "I'll get to work as soon as I can."

"That isn't what I meant! You know that isn't what I meant!"

And he flared, "A man can't just sit!"

"I've learned to."

"Well, I won't!"

She got up to clear the table. Jeff sat there, his head in his hands. She had the dishes almost done before he got unsteadily to his feet and went to the bedroom.

He hadn't said one word about Tommy. Not then nor ever after did he have critical or bitter words about Tommy. The baby was a blow to his pride, a deep and baffling disappointment. She saw that in Jeff's face, read it in his mind. But there was no recrimination, ever.

Lissie was born three weeks after Jeff returned home, another healthy, sound baby, a fair-haired girl. When Jeff saw her he said, "At least, she looks like you. She'll be pretty too, when she grows up." And Loretta named her Melissa, after Jeff's mother.

Jeff's dysentery eased but the malaria still racked him. He began getting outdoors and with Bill's help he began riding again. Less than a month after Lissie was born he said, "I'm going to get back to work."

"To work? Doing what?"

"I'm going to gather a trail herd."

"Jeff! You can't! You're still sick!"

"Not that sick."

"You can't take a trail herd anywhere, can you? The war's still on!"

"The war," he said, "is almost over. They would recall Bill

if it wasn't. It can't last more than another month or two."

"But—but—"

"But what?" He growled. He was a sick man, sick in heart as well as body, and she knew it.

"Nothing," she said.

That night he had a malarial attack, first the chills, then the fever, then the sweats. She wanted to call Dr. Carter, but Jeff refused. "I've got quinine," he said.

She was up most of the night with him. After the sweat he slept, exhausted. The next day he was almost too weak to stand on his feet; but he sent for Bill, saddled his horse and set out to gather a trail herd.

Loretta went to Dr. Carter, asked him what she should do. He said, "I don't know whether there's anything you can do, or that I can either. All I could do for the malaria is give him quinine, and you say he has that. But it's more than malaria with him."

"You think he's worried?"

"We're all worried, Loretta. But Jeff Ross never was a buggy horse. He don't even like the feel of a saddle on him. Have you two been quarreling? About the boy, maybe?"

"No! No, Dr. Carter, we aren't the quarreling kind."

He sighed. "Maybe what he needs is a trail drive. Sun, air, activity. He'll have the shakes and the sweats. He's still a sick man. But he'd fret himself to death, cooped up here. You know that, don't you?" And he concluded, "If you want to keep your husband, Loretta, let him go. That's the best advice I can give you."

She went to Jeff's father. The war years had aged him, taken much of the fire out of him. But he snorted, "Jeff's a damn fool, thinking he can get through to St. Louis with a herd!"

It was the first she knew that Jeff intended going all the way to St. Louis. She thought immediately of Amy Caldwell, and her heart sank.

"I told him I'd have none of it," the old man said. "But that didn't stop him. Did you let him have any money?"

"I haven't any to let him have."

"He's a crazy man, crazy as a bedbug. Let him go. Good riddance."

She made an opportunity to talk to Bill Sanders. Bill had liked Loretta from the start. "Jeff's not crazy," Bill said. "He's taking cattle on commission, not spending a cent. He's getting a trail crew together the same way, no pay till they get to market. Jeff knows what he's doing, Miss Loretta."

"But he's still sick!"

"Jeff's not a man to die in bed. You know that. Nor to die poor, if there's a way to make a dollar."

"Tell me, Bill, is he going just to get away from me?"

"He's never said that, never hinted a thing like that."

And she knew that Bill was speaking truth.

She said, "Take care of him, Bill. Take care of him, for me."

A week later Jeff had his herd gathered, his crew ready to go. He rode in from out on the flats where he held the herd, to see her before he left. He came in and looked around the house, the stranger again, the familiar stranger. He looked around the house, looked at Lissie in her cradle, at Tommy in his, at Jane playing with her rag doll. Then he said to Loretta, "Well, I'll be on my way. Good-bye, Loretta."

"How long will you be gone?"

"I don't know. It all depends."

"Depends on what, Jeff?"

He didn't answer. He kissed her and went out to his horse and swung slowly into the saddle and rode away.

She stood there at the door and watched him out of sight. Then she went to the bedroom and cried, the bitterest tears she had ever known. She prayed, "Dear God, I never lifted a finger to stop his going, now or ever. I know he is sick. I know he may never come back. But dear God, if he is to die, let him die with the memory of my kiss, not hers."

The bitter wish, the hope that he might never live to reach St. Louis.

Perhaps, she thought now, I need the hurt to know the happiness, the bitterness to know the sweet.

4

After his hours in the storm, the ranch house felt warm as an oven to Jeff, though there was a thick scum of ice in the water pail on the bench beside the door. He took off his coat and stood for a moment savoring the smells—coffee, cooked beans, pine pitch, wood smoke, and the mingled odors of human presence. Then he squatted in front of the fire to warm his hands, and the weariness weighed on him. The cold began to tingle out his finger tips and toes.

Sam put fresh wood on the fire and Jeff poured a cup of coffee from the black pot and spooned a plateful of beans from the kettle simmering at one end of the fireplace. The fresh wood flamed and lighted the room, winter quarters of a ranch crew and masculine as fly-front pants. There were the homemade pine table and benches, the bunks built against the wall, the bare floor. A rick of firewood was heaped to the ceiling all across the far end of the room. In one corner were the big bags of supplies, coffee, sugar, flour, beans. Beside the door were two shovels and an axe. On pegs above them were rifles and a shotgun. At one end of the fireplace hung long strings of red chile peppers. On the hearth were smoke-black pots and the Dutch oven.

Loretta, Jeff thought, would be dismayed at the thoroughness with which practical males had taken over. When she was here the whole place had the civilizing comfort and decoration of a woman's hand. But she hadn't been here for a year and a half.

He sipped the coffee and ate the beans and let the fire's warmth seep into him. Harvey Bird went back to bed, soon was snoring. Sam Royce sat on a bench, his bootless feet to the fire, and asked about things in Denver, about Bill Sanders' leg, finally asked if Jeff had seen any drifting cattle on the way in.

Jeff smiled wryly. "I was doing good to see my own horses. There could have been two thousand head of cattle down in the timber and I wouldn't have known it."

"They won't drift much," Sam said hopefully. "If they do, they'll come back when it lets up. Or we'll pick them up on spring roundup." Sam yawned. "Pete's down at Cottonwood." Pete Wallace, the third member of the winter crew and the youngest, was riding the camp circuit, checking on the cattle.

Sam yawned again, stood up and pulled off his pants. He went back to his bunk. Jeff watched him, frowning, wanted to snap out at Sam but holding his tongue. Sam wasn't slack, really. He just didn't approve of weather like this, never would. Come spring and Sam could understand both the weather and the cattle. He would be downright sentimental over a motherless calf. He would work eighteen hours a day tailing bogged steers out of the mud. He would go hungry and sleepless on roundup, if need be. But a steer caught in a blizzard—well, Sam was Sam about such matters. That's why Jeff had to come out here today. After all, they were Jeff's cattle, and Jeff knew what a blizzard could do to them.

Then he thought: There's nothing to do tonight. Just wait and rest and be ready to go into action when the storm lets up.

He suddenly felt bone-weary. He finished his coffee and banked the fire. He stripped to his shirt and long drawers and went to the bunk in the corner nearest the fireplace, his personal bunk and never used by anyone else. The blankets were icy but comfortably rough. The rawhide cording under the cornshuck tick creaked and gave under his weight and he settled into the familiar hollows for hip and shoulder.

Sam called to him, "Guess this is better than sleeping in a snowdrift under a pine tree."

"Much better," Jeff said.

Two minutes later Sam was snoring. But, weary though he was, Jeff lay awake, watching the glow from the fireplace and listening to the roar of the wind and the sleety swish of the snow at the windows. Listening, and remembering how he came to the Bijou in the first place.

He went to the war to get away. He knew that now, could admit it. But there was no escape, really. A man has to live with himself. And when his war was over he came home sick and broke. Back to the same things he had tried, and failed, to escape. In a way, he was typical of Texas itself, defeated, ruined financially, and still caught in a union it chose in the first place, then tried to get out of.

He came back, and he hadn't been home one day before he knew he had to get away. Not only from home and Loretta, but from everything. The old childish dream of running away, probably. But he could excuse it. He had to get back to work. If he lived— and he didn't care much whether he did or not—he didn't intend to live on scraps or charity.

As soon as he could get about he went to see his father. The old man shook his head. "Face it Jeff, the old days are gone. We're broke, every damned one of us, and we'll be broke for the next thirty years."

"I won't!"

"I hope not, Jeff. But there's no way out. We're a defeated province, Jeff, overrun with the curse of our own cattle. Get yourself a little patch and grow beans and potatoes for your own table."

"I'm not down to that."

"You will be. Just thank God you haven't got a ranch on your hands. There's not even a market for hides and tallow, any more."

"I'm going to find a market for beef."

The old man smiled and shook his head, and Jeff knew he would have to go it alone. And he did. Barely able to sit in the saddle between bouts of malaria, he and Bill Sanders began to gather a trail herd and assemble a trail crew.

Bill had been detailed to bring him home, and Jeff had kept him there, on one pretext after another. Nobody seemed to care very much, and that circumstance itself convinced Jeff that the war was practically over. Anyway, Bill became his trail foreman and they assembled a herd. The ranchmen offered him his choice of their cattle, even gave him horses for his trail crew. All he offered was to take the cattle to the best market he could find and to take one-third of what they brought as his commission.

Bill was a native Texan. His father had been one of Stephen Austin's colonists in '21 and had been with Fannin's doomed

63

little band at Goliad in '36. So Bill was left fatherless at eleven. His mother remarried, but Bill went his own way, became cavvy boy, then cowhand. Jeff met Bill in the cavalry when Bill was assigned to his troop. He was Jeff's kind of man, one who could take orders and see that they were carried out, come hell or high water.

Jeff made Bill his sergeant and twice offered him a commission. Bill would have none of it. "Jeff, if it wasn't that you seem to need me, I'd resign as sergeant and go back to trooper." Bill saved Jeff's life at least once. And when Jeff was mustered out and invalided home he requested that Sergeant Sanders be detailed to accompany him. So there he was when the war ended; there he was when Jeff started north with that trail herd in the spring of '65.

They headed north in the middle of April. They went up the Kiamichi Valley into Choctaw country. Jeff had had friendly relations with the Choctaws before the war, but times had changed. Truculent young bucks were now in command and the more tractable older leaders were sulking in their lodges. The Choctaws cornered Jeff's outfit and demanded impossible toll for passage across their land.

Jeff had his men pull the herd together and hold them while he dickered and bargained for three days. Finally he told the young leaders that unless they reached a reasonable compromise he would turn the whole herd back to Texas and the Choctaws wouldn't get so much as one steer. And at last they agreed on a hundred head, Jeff's choice, as toll. Jeff told Bill to have the men cut out the culls and footsore cattle for the Indians, and they went on.

North of the Choctaws were the Cherokees, also eager to levy toll. Jeff had had more trouble with the Cherokees in the past than with the Choctaws, and he had no hope that they had changed for the better. So he pointed the herd east, toward Fort Smith, thinking he might find a market there for at least a part of the herd, hoping the garrison was low on meat.

The fort was low on meat, but the commissary officer still remembered the licking he took from a detachment of Texas cavalry three years before. When Jeff rode in and talked to him he found that the man wouldn't take a Texas steer as a gift.

Jeff rode back to the herd and swung around Fort Smith and turned north, up through the Ozarks. But every mile of the way he met increasing hostility. Texas cattle carried ticks and infested the local cattle with fever to which Texas cattle had become immune. Later, Jeff admitted that his trail herd was a menace to every roadside farmer with a span of oxen or half a dozen milk cows; but at the time the opposition seemed only one more degree of punishment for a sin already expiated. The South had lost the war. Must the North forever continue to beat the carcass of that dead, lost cause?

He bribed and bullied his way northward, an unwelcome outlander in a hostile area, still hoping to reach Missouri. But his dream of getting to St. Louis began to fade. As he approached the state line he heard that Missouri farmers were rallying to turn back his herd. They sent word that they would shoot every Texas steer that crossed the state line. They added that sometimes they had trouble telling a Texas steer from a Texan.

Jeff knew it was senseless to try to get much farther. He swung the dwindled herd westward into the corner of Kansas, to Baxter Springs. There he found a buyer willing to take his cattle at twenty dollars a head. St. Louis would have paid thirty, but he would never have reached St. Louis alive. Maybe he could have got through alone, but the cattle couldn't.

He had just under six hundred head. He sold them, paid off his men, and had about fifteen hundred dollars left as his share. He sent it all home to Loretta.

When Jeff left Dallas he was so sick that he couldn't sit in the saddle more than half a day at a time; but he was damned if he was going to die in a trap. Neither in a trap of his own making, with Loretta, nor one of Amy's making, in the memories that deviled him. If he died, he was going to die a free man. If he lived, he would go on through and have it out with Amy, once and for all. If he died on the trail, that was the way it was meant to be. Bill would take the herd on through.

But after two weeks on the trail things began to change. The malaria was still in him, the sweats and chills, the aches and the desperate times when he wanted to die. But between his bad times there was the boundless sky, the endless folds of the earth, the flaming dawn, searing midday, comforting night. There was lash of rain, bite of dust, flooded streams to cross, stampedes to check. There was the old enchantment—there was no other word for it—

that he had known on his early trips as a drover. He had almost forgotten it, except in an occasional night dream.

Then he had the run-in with the Choctaws, got some of the choler out of his blood. And the wrangle with the commissary officer at Fort Smith. And the constant encounters with the Ozark farmers who wanted to bar his way. Wrangles and arguments and tense encounters. Man-problems.

Gradually he came to know that he had almost forgotten this world of man-problems, this world where a man handled his own life or soon had no life to handle. In the war your life was at the mercy of a vast machine that rolled on and on to an inevitable end. He went to the war because it seemed the only thing to do, and he lost himself in the machine; he went to escape himself, the problems he had created, the woman-problems. To get away from the barriers he had built, the cages that seemed too frustrating for a man to master. He got away from them, into that vast inevitability of war, and he survived; and came back to those same cages. Back to himself again.

And now he was out where a man could live again, and breathe. Where a man could see once more the dream of grass and water and his own cattle on a thousand hills. He knew again that he was alive, that his years were neither tagged nor numbered.

Who can ever draw a line between birth and death and say that it is a man's life? A life surely is more than a span of years. It is a man, flesh, blood and bone, passion and emotion, choices offered, decisions taken. It is love and hate and exultation and regret. If it is anything, it is choice and circumstance, and it is failure and triumph, known, tasted, gulped down or spewed out. It partakes of God and the devil and all their works, the sweetness of honey, the bitterness of gall.

Without putting it into words, Jeff Ross knew that life was more than the going and the coming. It was the doing and the being. It was the knowing.

Now he knew that he had come on this trail drive because he had to know life again before he died. And, whether life had any meaning or not, he tasted the sweetness again. Caring came back. Even as an animal, he didn't want to die.

Here he knew again that once he had dreamed dreams. Here, where a man could be himself, not his memories and regrets. And he knew that he didn't want to go to St. Louis any more than he wanted to go back to Dallas. He didn't want to hear Loretta's voice when he talked to Amy any more than he wanted to see Amy's face when he looked at Loretta. He didn't know what he wanted, but he wanted neither of those things. He wanted himself, whoever he was. And he hadn't known himself for a long time.

He took the trail herd to Baxter Springs and sold them, and he said to Bill Sanders, "Do you want to go back home, or do you want to go with me?"

"Where are you going?" Bill asked.

"I don't know. West, I think."

"I'll go along."

So they chose four horses from the saddle herd and they sold the rest of them. They laid in fresh supplies, packed their gear and rode away. West.

They went up the Neosho for two days, then crossed to the Verdigris, went on west. Across Fall River and Walnut River, and on to the Arkansas. They went up the Arkansas to the Great Bend and they crossed the divide and came to the Smoky Hill River and went up that stream, leaving farms and towns behind.

The year before, all the plains had been seething with Indians, plundering and killing in retaliation for Chivington's massacre of Cheyennes and Arapahoes at Sand Creek. But Jeff and Bill rode through a land of comparative peace. They had only one tense encounter with Indians, well down on the Smoky Hill. It was a Pawnee hunting party, and they were surly and insulting. But they apparently didn't think that two men and four horses were worth the trouble their killing would stir up. They were after meat, not plunder. They went their way, and Jeff and Bill continued westward.

It was a strange land to Jeff, and the strangeness increased as they left the headwaters of the Smoky Hill and pressed on across the rolling flatland. It was an almost waterless land, yet the grass was lush, the hills covered with a tight-curled mat of buffalo grass, the swales belly-deep with bluestem and wheat grass. Sandy runs followed an occasional valley, proving that water did flow in a spring thaw or after a summer cloudburst, but there were virtually no live streams. Yet the travelers never thirsted for long. Even on the high flats there were buffalo wallows that caught the intermittent rain like big wash basins. It was brackish water, often alkaline, but it slaked thirst. And if you dug in the sand in one of the gullies, sometimes you would find cool, sweet water only a foot or so beneath the surface.

You could look for miles and not see a tree or a bush as high as a man. Then you would drop into a hollow and find a line of willow brush and a few cottonwoods along a bone-dry gully. Not enough to shelter cattle from a summer sun or a winter blizzard, but a break in the eternal monotony of grass.

"Did you ever see so much grass in your life?" Bill asked, awed.

"No. Nor so little water."

"A lot of room, though."

"Room for a million head of cattle."

It was the first time Jeff had mentioned cattle since they left Baxter Springs. He hadn't consciously thought of them. Not in this barren, hostile, forgotten land.

But, thinking of it now, he knew it wasn't barren. Not with all this grass. It wasn't forgotten, either. Nobody had ever known it to forget, except the Indians. And damn few of them. And it wasn't really hostile. It didn't even know that man existed. A man could live and die here and nobody but the buzzards and the coyotes would know or care.

But he liked this land, for some strange reason. Perhaps because he felt better than he had in months. He had the chills and fevers the whole way of the trail drive, sometimes was almost too weak to stay in the saddle. But the attacks had diminished as he put Baxter Springs behind him. He hadn't had a chill in almost a month. Life was worth living. Maybe that was the reason he liked these waterless flatlands. A sick man hates any land.

And yet, it baffled and angered him with its extremes. The sun could be like a searing torch and the huge white clouds could be like taunting sails on the horizon of a vast blue sea. Sometimes those clouds piled up and lightning flashed and thunder shook the very hills. The storms were as vast as the flats themselves. Once a slashing rainstorm sent horse-high torrents foaming down the gullies, racing walls of water that ran themselves out in a few hours. Once a hailstorm roared like a hurricane and covered a strip two miles wide with hail three inches deep, hailstones so big they killed half-grown antelope.

It was a violent land. Jeff thought again of cattle, and he thought that winter blizzards here would whoop across the flats with a force that would blow a steer all the way to the Gulf. And yet, that violence was only a part of the land's strength.

Cattle. The thought persisted. Find water here and this land would be the biggest ranch God ever made, bigger than man ever dreamed. Water. And some kind of shelter, from those winter storms.

A man would have to be big and tough, to make out here. And the land itself dwarfed you. Dwarfed a man even while it challenged him. A man would have to make his own importance here.

"One thing," Bill said, "a man can see. There's no brush, and there's no mountains."

"And no shelter. You'd have to cross cattle with coyotes, so they could dig holes to hide in."

Day after day they kept on westward, the hills seeming never to change, never to have an end.

Bill said, "Know where you're going yet, Jeff?"

"I'm going till I find a river."

And then, one afternoon, they saw a thin, bluish line on the western horizon. The next day the line showed a few jagged peaks. Another day and the mountains were clear to the eye. And Jeff knew there was an end to those high, waterless plains.

"There should be sweet water in those mountains," Jeff said. "And shade."

Bill said, "If they're anything like the Ozarks, you can have them."

Jeff said, "I'm going to go and see."

They kept on. Late the next afternoon they topped a rise and saw, only a few miles ahead but still a long way from the mountains, a valley and a line of green that had to be trees. The green line reached a dozen miles north and south before the hills cut it off at either end. Jeff looked at Bill, and Bill said, "It's a mirage."

But the horses knew better. They hurried without being urged. Jeff and Bill rode the last few miles down through the breaks, the rough slopes and gullied hills, into the valley of the Bijou.

There were pines and there were cottonwoods and aspens. Just before they reached the timber a flock of prairie chickens rose in front of the horses and went rocketing off to the north. As they approached the first stand of pines an elk snorted in the brush and slipped quietly away. There was a flash of white as a big mule deer lunged through the aspens. And Jeff was sure he saw a turkey hen and her flock of poults scurry away in the tangle.

There was a stream. Not a river, but a broad creek with a full flow of clear, icy water. And there were shade and shelter, aspens that whispered, pines that sighed, and cottonwoods that rattled their big, stiff leaves. Summer shade, winter shelter.

They camped beside the stream, and they had venison instead of rancid salt meat, sweet water instead of the brackish dippings from a mud puddle. And Jeff said, "We'll stay and look around."

The next day they rode down the valley to the fork of the stream, saw that it drained a huge upland and was timbered all the way. Good pine for buildings and corrals. The stream flowed north. Jeff guessed, rightly, that it emptied into the South Platte. The Denver Trail followed the Platte. Off to the south a few days' ride was the Arkansas, and the old Santa Fe Trail. Between the two rivers and their trails was a vastness of grass.

They rode back to their camp, and Jeff said, "A man could build a cabin there and be sheltered by that stand of pines."

"And put his corrals over there, and his barn," Bill said.

"We'll look upstream tomorrow."

There was timber upstream, too, and a good flow of water. And those same hills of grass, hills of buffalo grass, swales of bluestem for hay.

Then they rode on in to Denver.

Denver, which was still half a day's ride east of the mountains, was a mixture of the new and the primitive. Some of its crude log huts, built by the first settlers seven years before, still stood on the banks of Cherry Creek. Yet it had brick hotels almost the equal of those in St. Louis. It had a race track patronized by men in stovepipe hats and tail coats and women in silks, and it had the cheapest of saloons, gambling dives and bawdy houses. It had banks and busy stores, and Indians and ragged miners shuffled the streets and searched the garbage heaps for food.

Jeff and Bill spent a week in Denver. They heard rumor, gossip and outlandish truth. The Union Pacific, driving westward to link the two seaboards, had chosen a survey route sixty miles to the north. Because of this, some said, Denver would be deserted in another five years. The Kansas Pacific, building west from Kansas City, promised to reach Denver within another year or two, and others said the railroad would make Denver boom and thrive beyond any dream. The mines back in the mountains, some said, were already worked out. Others said the store of precious metals had scarcely been scratched, that they still held a store of wealth bigger than the world had ever known.

Jeff listened, and shrugged off such talk. What happened to Denver, one way or another, didn't matter to him. More important was the talk he heard at the livery stables. Tales of freighters, unable to buy hay, who turned out their foot-sore oxen to die on the flats and who, come spring, found those oxen fat and sound, wintered on buffalo grass. Tales of beef herds down on the Arkansas and out on the Platte, thriving the year around. And when he made the rounds of the markets he found that grass-fed beef was selling for as much as forty dollars a head in Denver.

He went to the leading bank and asked to talk to the president. After much argument, he was sent to see a vice-president, a man in a black suit and with an undertaker's air. He stared at Jeff as though Jeff were a mule driver just in from the mines. Jeff wore his trail clothes, the only clothes he had with him, but the striped pants and the brush jacket were clean and the boots were blacked. And Jeff was shaved and barbered. Back home that would have been enough for any banker.

But this man glared at him and demanded his name and business. Facing the worst and beating him to the accusation, Jeff said, "I'm a Texan, a cattle drover, and I can deliver beef cattle to Denver by the thousand. Will you lend me money if I need it?"

"What security have you?" the banker asked coldly.

"I'm not asking for a loan," Jeff said. "I am asking if money can be borrowed, say next winter, if I decide to bring in a trail herd."

"Money can't be borrowed without security," the man said.

"It would be secured by the cattle," Jeff said. "And by my own word."

"I don't know you. Who do you know in Denver?"

"Not a soul."

"Who have you dealt with here?"

"No one. I have dealt in St. Louis, in Memphis, in New Orleans.

Before the war. A few weeks back I took a trail herd to Baxter Springs, in Kansas."

"I haven't any money to loan on Texas cattle," the man said.

"There's Texas cattle down on the Arkansas," Jeff said. "Likely some on the Platte, too."

The man said nothing.

"If you had money," Jeff said, "what would be your interest?"

The banker considered, then gave Jeff a thin, triumphant smile. "Five per cent. A month."

Jeff nodded. "I understand. You don't like Texans, and you don't like me. Is that it?"

The banker shrugged. "I don't even know you."

Jeff got to his feet. "You will know me," he said. "The time will come when you'll beg me to borrow money." And he walked out.

He went back to the hotel and he said to Bill Sanders, "Come on, we're going home." He had made up his mind.

"To bring in a herd?"

"To bring in cows. We're going to cover those hills, out there along that creek, with Ross & Sanders cattle."

"Ross cattle."

"What do you mean? We're partners, Bill."

Bill shook his head.

"Why not?"

"You're not a partner kind of man, Jeff. But I'd like to be your foreman."

Well, Jeff thought, I came up here, and I covered these hills with cattle. It was a nothingness until I came and began making my mark here.

Memories of the trail trip, the trip up here with that first herd, began to come at him. He pushed the memories away. A rough trip. A long, rough trip.

He shifted in his bunk and the rawhide creaked. He was finally getting warm, the last of the storm's icy chill easing out of him.

A rough trip. But he came and began making his mark, a mark that will endure for a few years. And after that? After that it's somebody else's problem. If a man can't do his own name credit and honor, why should he expect someone else to do it for him?

Every man must make his own mark, not delegate the job to his son. Begetting is no great achievement. Jackrabbits beget. Coyotes beget.

I came up here, he thought, and here I am. And Loretta's there in the big house in Denver. It's been a long, rough trip. A lot of forks in the trail, since I started out, a lot of choices made. And maybe a man shouldn't think back and wonder about the choices. But you had to know, didn't you? Or did you ever know? And did it matter, in the long run?

Not tonight, it didn't matter. He was here, where he belonged. Playing the cards the way they fell. As Bill said, "A lot of work and a little luck, and a man makes out."

The beat of the storm lulled him at last. The weariness of the day and the trip crept over him. He slept.

5

Jeff wakened the next morning to a day that never brightened much beyond the thin light of a normal dawn. The wind held strong out of the north and the air was thick with fine snow, blizzard snow that drifted deep in every hollow and sheltered place.

Sam Royce was cooking breakfast when Jeff wakened. "It's a chore day," Sam said, "nothing else. Couldn't get a mile from the house and be sure of getting back."

They ate, and Harvey Bird, who had wallowed to the barn and done the morning chores, reported a six-foot drift behind the house and a drift higher than that across the horse corral. After breakfast Jeff went out to see for himself.

The wind almost took him off his feet, but he made his way to the barn. There was no way to tell how much snow had fallen or how much was still coming down, for the drifts were still shifting under the drive of the wind. Probably as much snow was being lifted from the ground as was falling from the sky. One good thing, though. That wind was still clearing the ridges and the hilltops. Once the storm ended, there would be open grass for the cattle.

He went into the barn, saw that the blacks were fed and in good shape. Six rough-coated Texas ponies, saddle horses, were also in the barn. They watched Jeff with rolling eyes and loud snorts. The presence of a man meant one of two things to them, feed or work. They had already been fed. Seeing Jeff, they hauled back on their halter ropes and hunched their backs against the expected saddles, laid back their ears and swung their heads, ready to fight the bridle. Outside, in the horse corral, the rest of the pony herd sensed Jeff's presence and began to squeal, kick and charge through the drifts, full of frost and fight. Jeff went out to watch them and he said, "You'll get some of that vinegar worked out of you just as soon as this lets up." He paused to look at the stack yard and to see that the feed racks were full for the outside ponies, then went back to the house.

Harvey Bird was putting new latigo straps on a spare saddle. Harvey was in his middle twenties, dark as an Indian. He probably had Indian blood. He had come north with a herd Jeff bought from Charley Goodnight last year, Jeff had liked him and he had stayed on. Harvey must have been born in the saddle. He was an instinctive cowhand, one of the best Jeff had ever known. He could do anything and he had that rare knack of anticipating orders, working with you at every turn. But you could ride with him all day and he wouldn't speak a dozen words. He was as quiet as Sam Royce was voluble.

Sam was making stew. Sam liked to cook in the winter, but he wouldn't lift a pot all summer long. Sam was one of the original crew that came north with Jeff, but he went back to Texas and didn't come back till two years later, when Jeff brought in a trail herd of yearlings. That time he stayed.

Jeff sometimes thought Sam stayed up here just to complain about the winters. From April till December he was one of the spryest men within a thousand miles, seemed to think he was still a stripling in his teens. But from December till April he was ninety-nine years old, barely able to get around. All summer long he carried a mouth organ in his shirt pocket and played jigs and reels and stomp-dance tunes. Come the first snow and he put the mouth organ on the shelf over his bunk and wouldn't touch it till the grass was green again. Once Jeff asked him to play a tune on a winter night and Sam said, "When you hear the birds begin to sing again, then old Sam will make music. Not till then, Jeff, not till then."

Actually, Sam was only a year or two older than Jeff. But now, with winter upon him, he hobbled about as though he were worse off then Bill Sanders. But when Bill was hurt, Jeff had no choice but to put Sam in charge. Pete Wallace was just a boy and Harvey Bird wasn't cut out to give orders. Sam might argue when you told him what had to be done, he might think up a dozen reasons for not doing it, especially in winter, but eventually he would try to see that your orders were carried out. And Sam could get along with anyone. That was important in any winter camp. In any normal winter there wouldn't have been any gamble in leaving Sam in charge till Bill could get back. But this wasn't a normal winter.

Sam looked up as Jeff came in and took off his heavy coat. "I suppose," Sam said, "you're going down to Cottonwood today. Visit with Pete for a while."

"Tomorrow," Jeff said. "Tomorrow we'll all get out and go down to Cottonwood."

Sam sighed and reached for another chile to break into his stew pot. "Tomorrow," he said, "there'll be five feet of snow." He paused to rub his back. "I shouldn't ever have left Texas."

"Want to go back?" Jeff asked.

"Want to go back? Jeff, if Bill was here to take over I'd start drifting right now, today. I'd drift all the way down to that warm, sunny, sweet-smelling Gulf."

Jeff smiled. "As long as you're here, Sam, we're going to work those cattle. Tomorrow, if it lets up a little, we start busting them out of the yards."

Sam looked pained. "Why, Jeff? You know they can't drift. They'll wait, and it'll loosen up in a few days if *we* just wait." He put the lid on the stew kettle and set it on the coals.

Wait, Jeff thought. Wait for the thaw. Damn it, you didn't wait for anything, except summer and winter. And, sometimes, next year. Or you waited out a storm, as now. Otherwise, you made your own terms. Or tried to.

Was that the difference, one man from another? He sometimes wondered. Was it something inside, something born in you, that made some men wait and other men go and do? You knew what you wanted and you went out and took it, or you just had a yearning for something and waited for it to come to you. Was that it? Or wasn't it that simple? He used to think it was, ten or fifteen years ago. Now he wasn't so sure.

He said, "We aren't waiting. We're going to get those cattle up on the ridges, find some grass for them. Hear that, Sam?"

"I hear. Lordy, how my old knees ache! Don't know that I could even reach the stirrups today." He sighed. "Well, I suppose you want to beat the tar out of me at black-jack. All right, the cards are over there on my shelf. I ain't won a game in two months."

The day dragged past. They played cards and ate, and Sam found new aches to complain about. And Jeff listened to the storm. Then it was dusk again. They did the evening chores.

The wind was easing off, now, coming in gusts rather than a steady blow. The air was still filled with biting snow, but Jeff guessed that most of it was blow-snow. And when they had finished the chores and started back to the house Jeff saw a handful of stars twinkling icily through the blown snow. The sky was beginning to clear.

By bedtime the whole sky was clear. The storm had blown itself out. Now the cold would clamp down.

The second morning dawned dazzling. The late sun rose with brilliant sundogs and by the time they had eaten breakfast a twinkling cloud of steam hung over the barn and all along the stream was a glittering mist of frost crystals.

"We'll go downstream," Jeff said, "and try to get as far as Cottonwood. I want to see how many cattle are yarded in the timber. We've got to get them out."

Sam rubbed his back and groaned. "This snow can't stay, Jeff. They'll be out in a few days."

"Damn it, Sam," Jeff snapped, rising to Sam's bait, "this isn't Texas!"

"Cattle," Sam said, pulling on his coat, "are cattle."

"And if cattle don't eat for two or three days they begin to lose flesh. Carry them into January in good shape and they can take the rest of the winter. If they begin to lose ground now they'll die like flies in February."

But Sam was already on his way to the barn, hobbling through the drifts like a maimed old man.

They saddled horses and rode off the frosty-morning cussedness. Sam grunted and groaned till he hit the saddle, then rode like a youngster. They started downstream, Jeff and Sam on the west side, Harvey Bird on the east.

The ridges had been blown almost bare. They made a maze of tan streaks criss-crossing the dazzling background of snow-covered plains. In the valley, among the trees and underbrush, drifts were

77

piled five and six feet deep. The stream was ink-black, edged with a lace of ice that covered only the deep, quiet pools. In many places the water flowed through canyons, drift canyons whose tops were ice-smooth but whose lips, even over the water, were curled and swirled like a baby's hair. The whole world was new, fresh-made, untracked. And the sun was already beginning to warm the air. By midday there would be melting.

They were half a mile north of the house when Jeff saw the first cattle, a herd of fifty or sixty head in a grove of pines at a bend in the creek. They had tramped down half an acre of snow, made themselves a yard. They saw the horsemen and turned to watch, their breath making steam clouds. Now and then one of them bawled and the echoes rattled back from the hills.

Jeff reined his horse toward a gully, picked his way among the drifts. He found a hollow leading down from the ridge, forced his horse to wallow into it. The snow came to Jeff's knees, he in the saddle, and the horse tried to turn back. Jeff quirted and spurred and the horse lunged, wallowed and slid down the slope and into a four-foot drift. Jeff let him blow for a minute, then quirted him on through the drift and into the yard of cattle.

The steers surged away, wild-eyed and snorting. Jeff rode around them, tried to drive them toward the opening he had made. They started to mill. He quirted those nearest him, forced them toward the opening, hurried four of them into his horse's tracks and drove them toward the hilltop. They scrambled up the slope and stood there on the ridge, puffing and resentful. Then they nosed the grass and began to graze. But they lifted a head between bites and looked balefully at the horsemen.

"No thanks from them," Sam said. "They weren't hungry."

"If it melts today and freezes tonight," Jeff said, "they'd be damned hungry by tomorrow night."

They rode on, and now they found a bunch of cattle in every timber patch. Harvey Bird was working the cattle on his side of the stream. Jeff and Sam took turns on this side.

By noon they had driven close to twenty-five hundred head up onto the ridges or opened the way for them to get there. The cattle would go back to the timber for shelter, but once they had broken trail out they could reach the grass, even if the deep drifts crusted over. And by noon the melt had set in, softening the top of every drift.

They kept on, toward Cottonwood Camp, and about two o'clock they saw a horseman off to the west. It was Pete Wallace, on a lop-eared roan, the ugliest horse on the place.

Sam was down in the timber, breaking out a bunch of steers, when Pete joined Jeff. The ugly roan picked his way through a drifted hollow and jogged up onto the ridge where Jeff was waiting, and Pete said, "Howdy, Mr. Ross," just as though he had expected to meet him there. Pete was a round-faced, tow-headed boy of nineteen. He looked like a farmer, rode like a farmer, but he was as reliable as sunup.

"Thought you were at Cottonwood," Jeff said.

"I was about halfway there from Comanche when the storm hit," Pete said, "and I figured I'd better go back. I had had a fresh deer hung at Comanche, and there wasn't nothing but beans at Cottonwood." He grinned.

Jeff had four line camps, Cottonwood, fifteen miles downstream from the home ranch, Comanche over on Comanche Creek just above its junction with the Kiowa, East Camp out on the flats to the east, and South Camp up the Bijou beyond the railroad. During the winter months the hands took turns riding the camp circuit, checking on the cattle.

"How are the cattle over on Comanche?" Jeff asked.

"Yarded up, mostly," Pete said. "I broke trail into all the yards I could find. Didn't waste time trying to drive them out. Figured they'd follow my trail out when they got hungry."

That was Pete Wallace, simple, direct with his own solutions.

"Good boy," Jeff said. "Is there plenty of coffee at Cottonwood?"

"Plenty."

Jeff saw that Pete's horse was in good shape, hadn't been worked too hard. Pete was one rider who took care of his horse. Jeff ordered him to go across the creek and help Harvey Bird, then said, "We'll all meet at Cottonwood and warm up."

Cottonwood was only two miles ahead. The camp consisted of a cabin about ten feet square with an open shed at the back for the horses. It had a fireplace, a bunk and a big tin-covered box for food. Only a bear could have done much damage, and the log walls and roof would discourage most bears. Any human traveler, except Indians, was welcome to stop and rest and eat, obliged only to replenish the supply of firewood before he moved on. But there were few travelers. The food stowed there in the fall, flour, salt, sugar, side meat and coffee, usually lasted all winter, pieced out with venison.

Pete and Harvey reached the camp first. They had a fire going and the coffee cooking when Jeff and Sam arrived. The fire had already begun to warm the small room. You could no longer see your breath. Pete, who was to spend the night there and go on to East Camp the next day, had grained his horse and laid out his gear.

Harvey got out the tin cups and poured coffee and while they drank it they compared notes. They had freed close to five thousand head of cattle along the Bijou. Pete estimated that he had seen about fifteen hundred head on Comanche and Kiowa. That left close to thirty-five hundred head somewhere else on the range, on down the Bijou, over on Kiowa, or in the breaks to the east. Pete would have a look in the breaks tomorrow on his way to East Camp.

"That means they aren't drifting much," Sam said. "They were scattered just about the same way two weeks ago when I rode the circuit."

"Bar H cattle are drifting," Pete said. "I saw about fifty head of Bar H stuff over on Kiowa. That's Hilliard cattle, ain't it?"

Sam nodded.

Jeff frowned and started to say something, then reconsidered.

Sam said, "They must have drifted all the way from the Platte. Kind of early for them to drift down here." Then he shrugged. "That's the Bar H crowd's worry."

Jeff got to his feet, began putting on his coat. "Let's get going," he said.

Sam groaned, rubbed his big, rough hands in the warmth of the fireplace. Then he, too, shouldered into his coat and he and Harvey Bird and Jeff went out into the early dusk. They tightened the saddle cinches and started for the home ranch. It would be a long ride, for they would have to take a roundabout way, zigzagging the bare ridges. And the horses were tired.

The sun had just set behind a dark cloud bank, splashing the cloud with fiery red that spread a rosy glow across the rolling white hills. Jeff didn't like the look of that cloud but he was reassured by the color. Red sky at night means clearing. Clearing, however, meant deepening cold. The snow was already beginning to crust. In a few more hours the day's melt would top all the drifts with ice that would cut like a knife. That's what Jeff had been afraid would happen. That's why he had insisted on breaking the cattle out of the drifts today.

Well, they'd got them out. Jeff had been right, on all counts. If the cattle had been left in the yards, waiting for a thaw, they would have been iced in, starving. Now they could get to grass, and they could get back to the timber for shelter. And they wouldn't drift.

He thought of the drifting cattle Pete had seen, the Bar H cattle. Hilliard cattle.

He thought of Amy. Amy Caldwell, who married Matt Hilliard.

Amy married Matt Hilliard, and sent that message to Jeff announcing it just two weeks before he married Loretta. She married Matt Hilliard, and less than a year later they moved to St. Louis where Hilliard went into business as a commission man, a livestock broker.

Then, in the spring of '60, Jeff took another herd to St. Louis. Not to see Amy. That was all over with. To get the premium price that St. Louis was paying for cattle. But the second day he was there he walked into the Planter's at midday, picked up his key at the desk and turned toward the stairs, and someone called his name: "Jeff! Jeff Ross!"

He knew the voice, even before he turned to look. Amy.

She was just getting up from a chair. She had been waiting for him in the lobby. She stood there, smiling, and he went over to her. She looked almost the same as when he last saw her, but when their eyes met he saw questioning and appraisal in her.

"Why, Amy," he said, "what are you doing here?"

She laughed. "Why so surprised? You knew, didn't you, that I live in St. Louis. I came to have luncheon with you. Or are you too busy?"

He hesitated, wondering at her purpose. Then he said, "As a matter of fact, I'm not busy. Please do." Her whole appearance was that of the young wife of a prosperous city man, and he noticed that she wore a broad wedding band as well as the engagement ring.

She took his arm and he led the way to the dining room. A waiter seated them and took their orders, and when he had left them Amy looked across the table and said, "Well! How are you, Jeff? You look tired and thin."

"I'm just in," he said. "A man doesn't get much rest on a trail drive."

"Uncle John said you were here with a herd."

He watched her, still looking for some clue to her purpose. "You look well," he said. "Marriage seems to agree with you."

"I have what I wanted." There was the first hint of defensiveness in her, the first chink in the armor of her self-assurance.

"Lucky, aren't you?"

She smiled. "I wouldn't call it luck. I planned it. And you, too, are married? Happily, I suppose?"

"Yes."

"How fortunate we are. Aren't we?"

Their food came. As they ate he saw the assurance return to her eyes, even her gestures. But he kept wondering why she had come.

At last she said, "So we are both married. Happily. And we have things to remember."

So that was it. He looked at her and said, "I haven't a very long memory, Amy."

Her eyes were intense. "I have, Jeff. We were wonderfully foolish, weren't we?"

"What," he asked, "are you having for dessert?" He looked around for the waiter.

She laughed at him. "Foolish. And yet, perhaps far wiser than we knew. One must have memories."

The waiter saw his signal, came to the table. "Two coffees," Jeff said. "No dessert."

When the waiter had left them, Jeff turned to Amy. "You haven't changed a bit, have you?"

"Do you really think so, Jeff?"

"Yes. You still think you can eat your cake and have it too."

"Oh, Jeff!" she exclaimed. "But you always did have that cruel streak in you." She watched him for a moment, then said, "Why don't you want to be friends, Jeff?" She reached out and touched his hand, lying on the table.

Jeff looked at her hand, capable, cared-for. She had servants, obviously, and her clothes were expensive. She was wearing matched beads and earrings, warm green gems lighter than emeralds, probably tourmaline. They enhanced the greenish lights in her eyes. He was sure they were expensive; otherwise she wouldn't have worn them to this meeting.

He drew his hand away and she asked again, "Why not?"

He said, "You have friends, I'm sure. I'm just a cattle drover that you once knew. Let it stand that way."

"That's the way you want it?"

"That's the way it is."

She smiled. "You still haven't found the river you couldn't cross?"

"No."

"I've never known anyone like you, Jeff," she said quietly. Then she asked, "How long will you be here?"

"I leave tomorrow."

"You're going back to Dallas?"

"Yes."

"I had hoped you might come to dinner."

"I am busy."

"I'm sure Matt would like to talk with you. About beef. And about Texas, and the war that is coming."

"I'm no politician. I'm just a drover."

"Matt has beef contracts with the Army. It might be well to know him, Jeff."

"So has John Laughlin. I've dealt with John a long time, and I've always found him an honest man."

"You are hard and tough, aren't you, Jeff? But you aren't happy. Will you ever be?"

"If you were happy, Amy, you wouldn't have come here today," he told her.

"Oh, but I am happy!"

"Then why did you come?"

"I wanted to see you." The pretense was gone now, the parrying done. She said, "Oh, Jeff, one can't just forget, wipe the memory clean. I had to know you couldn't either."

83

He sat for a moment meeting her eyes. Then he knew that he must end it. He looked at his watch.

She said, "Yes, I must go too."

They left the table, returned to the lobby. He said, "I'll call a hack for you."

"No need," she said, and even in the stiffness of her back, the firm tilt of her chin, he saw something close to defeat. She said, "My carriage is waiting just down the street."

"I'll walk with you."

"No." Then she asked, "When will you be here again?"

"I don't know when."

"And if war comes?"

"I am a Texan."

"Yes." She held out her hand. He took it, and he said, "Goodbye, Amy."

She hesitated an instant, then asked, "Have you any children, Jeff?"

"Yes." The question puzzled him.

"I have a son. A son two years old."

He met her eyes, and he knew the question was in his face. The question she wanted him to ask.

She smiled, and she said, "Good-bye, Jeff," and turned to the door.

Then she was gone.

He went to the door a moment later, saw the coachman step down from a carriage waiting halfway down the block and help her in, then return to the seat and drive away.

That was the last time he saw her. After that, the war. Matt Hilliard, he understood, made a fortune in Army beef contracts during the war. And after the war he supplied beef for the railroad construction crews, established his headquarters in Cheyenne, eventually put a herd of cattle down on the Platte and set up a ranch just above the mouth of the Bijou.

Jeff never met Matt Hilliard, had no wish to. Matt died last spring. The Denver newspaper printed an obituary and said that the bulk of his estate went to his widow and their son, Matthew Hilliard, Jr., a boy almost thirteen years old.

They had been riding almost an hour and the cloud bank had scarcely moved. The stars had come out, stars with almost as much glitter as they would have in January. The night was full of a dim, reflected light, a deceptive dusk that make you think you could see things a mile away and yet obscured the trees in the valley just to the left. Now and then, when they were close by, Jeff could make out a bunch of steers, still grazing; but most of the cattle had gone back into the timber. The only sounds were the soft crunch of the horses' hoofs in the thin snow and the creak of saddle leather and the clink of bit chains. And, now and then, the high-pitched, wavering howl of a coyote.

Jeff was tired. His calves ached and his ribs were sore.

Bone-weary and gut-hungry, Jeff put away the memories and the wondering and was one with the night. And the night was a part of forever.

The cloud bank meant nothing. It had eased over the horizon and was gone by the time they reached the ranch house. But the late moon had a halo, a close rim of reflected glow, indicating high overcast.

By the next morning the sky was full of high-flying scud. Goose feathers, as Sam said.

To work out the muscle soreness, Jeff rode upstream that day with Harvey Bird to see how many cattle there were and how they were faring. The temperature hovered at the freezing mark and last night's crust was so firm that when Jeff tried to break trail to the first bunch of steers his horse had to rear and strike the snow with its forefeet to break through.

They found only about five hundred head between the home ranch and the railroad. By then it was past noon and the sky had turned leaden, so they went back. Before they had gone a mile it began to snow, light, feathery flakes that drifted down as gently as fuzz from the cottonwoods in June.

Jeff had hoped that it would blow over or that it would come as rain. November rain could be mean, but it would clear the ground. Icy rain would be hard on the cattle, but not as hard as more snow. They had good winter coats. But when the snow started Jeff knew that there would be no change to rain. He asked Harvey Bird, "How much of this stuff are we going to get?"

85

Harvey glanced at the sky and said, "Tell you tomorrow."

It was as good an answer as anyone could give. The way the sky looked, it could snow all day and all night. But not another blizzard. Just a snowfall, a quiet, lazy snowfall that would lie on the hilltops as well as in the valleys. Snow that would bury the grass.

There were two inches of new snow by the time they reached the home ranch, light snow, so fluffy that it puffed from beneath the horses' hoofs like dust. As they rode into the barnyard Jeff noticed that there was as much snow on the tops of the corral posts as there was on the ground.

It snowed all afternoon and all night. By the next morning it was eight inches deep, on top of the old crust. Eight inches of new snow stood on the corral posts, too. It had come without a breath of wind, and Jeff knew there were eight inches of it on every hilltop, every ridge that had been blown clear by the earlier storm.

The snow stopped while they were eating breakfast, and by midmorning the sun came out. That deceptively friendly sun. It was going to melt again, on the top, just as it had before. Melt that would turn to ice. Jeff and Sam rode downstream, halfway to Cottonwood, that day, and they found a good many of the cattle out of the timber, on the hills looking for grass. By early afternoon, when Jeff and Sam turned back to the ranch, the sun was making bare patches where the cattle had wandered along the ridges. Jeff was hopeful. But even before they reached the ranch the temperature began to drop. A wind came up with the dusk, a raw, cold wind, and that night it froze a half-inch crust on the new snow.

Now they were in trouble. Even Sam knew that; but he insisted that the cattle could last it out. "It'll loosen up in a few days," Sam said. "My God, Jeff, it's still November!"

"It could last a week," Jeff said. "We've got to get them up onto the hills again and break up that crust so the sun can go to work. Put boots on the horses. Let's get going."

They made rawhide boots to protect the horses' legs from the icy crust. Then they saddled and set out, downstream.

It was slow going. The horses were wary of the crusted snow, and even with the boots they were soon cut and bleeding around the hoofs. But the cattle had to be driven out of the timber. The riders quirted and spurred, crowded the bawling steers up the old trails and onto high ground. The cattle's gashed legs left trails of blood, but they also left the crusted snow so broken up that the sun could get to work on it. Although it didn't seem to be much above freezing, by the time they turned back toward the home ranch Jeff saw that the melt had uncovered a good deal of grass in the tracks. Almost half the cattle were still on the hills, picking at the grass, at sundown. They were hungry.

They went home on limping horses, the rawhide boots cut to tatters. The men ate and fell into bed, almost as tired as the horses. And an hour after they turned in Pete Wallace arrived, on foot. Pete's horse had given out that afternoon, midway between East Camp and the home ranch, its legs so badly cut by the crust that it couldn't travel another mile. Pete had left the horse in a grove of cottonwoods, hung his saddle in a tree, cut his saddle blanket into strips, wrapped his feet and legs in them, and come on in, afoot. Pete's own legs were gashed and raw, the blanket strips cut to pieces by the ice. The going had become so painful after the first three miles, he said, that he waited for darkness and enough cold to harden the crust. "I could walk eight or ten steps before I broke through," he said, wincing from the bite of the turpentine with which he dosed his legs. Pete finished turpentining his wounds, ate three plates of stew, and crawled into his bunk.

The next day they took spare horses and all four of them worked downstream, changing mounts often. They worked all the way to Cottonwood and, despite the raw wind, the sun opened big patches of grass where they had broken the crust. Jeff wasn't sure they were winning this fight with the weather, but he knew they weren't losing. Not yet.

That night Jeff announced that they would begin working the outlying camps the next day. "We'll double up on it. Sam, you and Harvey go to Comanche. Pete and I will go out to East Camp. We'll work those areas, and if everything goes right we'll meet at Cottonwood."

Sam frowned and rubbed his knees. "That's sure doing it the hard way, Jeff. This weather should loosen up tomorrow or the next day. This stuff should melt loose by the end of the week."

Jeff was too tired and too worried to think that Sam was being funny. "Goddamn it, Sam, stop growling about your aches and pains!" he snapped. "Sure it could melt. Sure it could loosen up. But it could also freeze up tight as a drum. Then we'd be up to our chins in trouble. You know it as well as I do!"

"I still say—"

"You don't approve of winter! I know, Sam. I know. I've heard it all before. Who does? We've got about five thousand head out on grass again, but there's that many more still in the timber somewhere. Or in the breaks. And by now they're getting damned hungry." He glared at Sam. "What do you want to do, drift for Texas in the morning, or go over to Comanche with Harvey?"

"Jeff," Sam said, "I was just joshing. You know what I'm going to do. But good God almighty Jehosephat, I *don't* like this kind of a winter!"

The next morning was raw and cold. Travel was difficult. Jeff and Pete had to take turns breaking trail because their horses couldn't take more than a mile of it at a time. Even the spare horses, which started out running and bucking, full of frost and foolishness, soon settled down, content to trail the man in the lead.

It wasn't going to be a day of melt. The sun was in sight, but it was masked by overcast that robbed it of its warmth. Mid-morning seemed almost as cold as it had been at dawn. Jeff wondered when this weather was going to break.

Pete was in the lead as they came to a broad draw with a clump of cottonwoods in the bottom. He turned and shouted something to Jeff, who was trailing the spare horses, something Jeff couldn't make out. Then he heard a horse nicker among the cottonwoods. They came closer and he saw the old lop-eared roan, the horse Pete had to leave when he walked in. He had tromped out a small yard among the trees and had nibbled off all the twigs within reach and even gnawed the bark from some of the trunks. A horse can survive quite a while on such browse, if he has to. The roan seemed to be in pretty good shape, but he was glad to see them, just the same.

Pete recovered his saddle, put it on one of the spares. The old roan joined the train and they went on. But by noon they had come only about ten miles from the home ranch. And they had seen only forty head of cattle.

Afternoon and the overcast thinned. The sun began to soften the crust a little. Four miles from East Camp they came to the

88

Little Breaks, an area of scarred hills and shallow gullies. There they found the first real bunch of cattle.

Jeff was in the lead. He worked down a gully where the drifts stood as high as his head. The wind really whooped it up out here on the treeless flats. Sometimes the drifts piled up fifteen feet deep. Jeff worked his way up the gully, and there at the foot of a twenty-foot cutbank close to a hundred steers were trapped between the sheer wall and a drift higher than their backs. The cattle were packed tight in the small yard.

Jeff found the lowest drift and yelled back to Pete, "Crowd the horses! Drive them right past me!"

Pete quirted the loose horses, sent them lunging past Jeff. Their momentum carried them through the drift, lunging and plunging, clear into the cattle yard. Jeff followed. The cattle milled and bawled, and Jeff shouted and quirted them. The leaders found the opening the horses had made and began lining out. As they stumbled up onto the flats, Pete turned them and headed them east.

From there to East Camp it was easier going. They kept the cattle ahead of them, forcing them to break trail for the tired horses. Along the way they picked up close to two hundred more steers from little pockets among the hills.

It was dusk when they reached the camp. They milled the cattle, forced them to tromp out a corral in the drifts, and they left them there with all but two of the horses. The horses would paw for grass and the cattle would eat after the horses. They would stay there for the night.

Pete put the other two horses in the shed and grained them while Jeff got a fire going in the cabin. He got out the supplies, cut salt meat, made coffee and pancakes. And Jeff thought wryly that he was getting a bellyful of the camp fare that he had been wanting, there in Denver.

While they were eating, Pete said, "Tell me, Mr. Ross, how does a man get to be a cattleman? I mean, where does he start?"

Jeff smiled. "He starts with grass and water. He gets himself grass and water and cattle, and he's in business. After that it's just a matter of staying in business."

"That's the way you started?"

"That's the way any cattleman starts. I came up here after the war and found this place and brought in my first herd."

"I guess that's the hardest part, getting started."

"No, I wouldn't quite say that. The hardest part is to keep going."

Pete didn't understand that, of course. How could he? You learn that, if you ever learn, only as the years begin to roll over you. What barriers are there, when you are young? You decide where you want to go, what you want to do. It looks easy, after that, because life is big and welcoming, yours for the taking. When you are young.

Pete stared at the fire, then turned to Jeff with glowing eyes. "Did you feel the way I did when I saw this country for the first time, Mr. Ross?"

"I don't know, Pete. How did you feel?"

"Like I was looking at something nobody had ever seen before." He said it softly, as though it were a precious secret, something almost holy. "I didn't feel any bigger than an ant. And at the same time I felt so tall I could touch the sky, if I really tried." He frowned, aware of his own words and self-conscious. "You know what I mean?"

"Yes, I know what you mean."

Youth, Jeff thought. Dreaming dreams and needing someone to say it's all right for you to dream. Then he thought of himself when young. Not the first time he saw this country, but on his first trail trip, down across east Texas. Maybe, he thought, it isn't so much the place you see as the eyes you see it with. I was just about Pete's age.

"I wanted to holler," Pete was saying. "And at the same time, I didn't want to make a sound. I just looked at the hills and the sky, and I saw a hawk sailing up there and I said to myself that if I wanted to I could spread my arms and fly like that. Only I didn't want to fly. It was enough just to be there, with all those hills and all that sky. I looked at the hills and I thought God made all those hills and that grass just for me." He looked at Jeff, self-conscious again. "I guess maybe He did, didn't He? Just for folks like you and me."

"That could be." That wasn't the way Jeff thought of it, but it would do. He thought that God made the grass for cattle, and he, Jeff Ross, was going to own the cattle. Maybe it came out to the same thing.

"I was thinking about that today," Pete said, "when we picked up old Roanie. The other night, when he played out on me, I had that same feeling. There I was, all alone and having a kind of a hard time, but it was still the world God made for me. I knew everything was all right, because it was my world."

"You never thought you might not make it on in?"

Pete was surprised at the question. "Oh, I knew I'd make it. I knew I'd get to the ranch. I just got to thinking that God made that world and He gave me my chance to be a part of it, and it was up to me from there on. God didn't owe me anything. Nobody did. I had to make it on in, because there were all these things I had to do. Like having my own ranch, some day."

Jeff poured another cup of coffee, sipped it and stared at the fire. He wished his own life was as uncomplicated as that. Why was it that a man got himself so tangled up?

Pete watched him a moment, then took the last pancake and began eating it. He had already said more than he intended, revealed so much of himself that he felt almost naked. But Jeff didn't notice.

Jeff thought: My life was that simple, once. I felt that way. I didn't know that youth has so many dreams they can't all come true. That's what hurts, once you start remembering. Somewhere along the way you found that you had to pick and choose. You had to make the choice, follow one or two dreams and forget the others. You learned that you couldn't really fly like a hawk, and you told yourself it didn't matter, because you didn't want to fly. You just wanted to walk, or ride a horse. So you picked a dream or two and tried to follow them. And, if you were lucky, you forgot the other dreams. And if your horse played out on you, you walked in. You got there. God didn't owe you anything. Nobody did.

I don't know when my horse played out, he thought, but I've been walking for quite a while.

Jeff felt very tired. He wanted to sleep, rest, forget. He glanced at Pete, staring at the fire with youth on his face and in his eyes. Pete, who would love and marry and pick one among his dreams to follow. And, if he was lucky, forget the other dreams.

Jeff got to his feet and went outdoors to relieve himself and to look at the stars. The overcast was almost all gone. The stars seemed very close. But he knew he couldn't touch them, even from the highest hill. All he would get if he tried was a handful of darkness.

He went back inside, took off his boots and his pants and got into his blankets. To sleep. To rest. To be ready for tomorrow.

The next day they drove forty or fifty steers ahead of them from one cutbank to the next. They found fifty steers trapped here, a hundred there, two hundred in the next gully. By taking fresh steers from each bunch they broke trail without laming the horses. And they opened a whole network of trails across the flats where the sun could go to work. The haze hung on, but the storm was passing, the siege ending. The cold began to ease and the melting continued after sunset.

By the third day the melt had really taken hold. The crust began to soften and all the trails they had opened showed big bare spots of open grass. By the third night they had freed more than fifteen hundred head, had them out in the open and grazing again.

The fourth day they went on to Cottonwood Camp. All the hills were beginning to show open patches and there was slush in every draw. If the weather held, and it seemed likely to, the range would be open again within another week.

Sam and Harvey were at Cottonwood when Jeff and Pete arrived. They had found about two thousand head of cattle on Comanche and Kiowa. All told, they had accounted for close to ninety-five hundred head. Jeff was satisfied, but he told Sam to send someone down to South Camp and have a look, see if they couldn't turn up the remaining five hundred head.

They went back to the ranch house. It was still thawing.

Jeff decided that if the weather held through the night he would go back to Denver the next day. He would leave the blacks and the wagon here and go back in the saddle. It would be slow going with the wagon, even if he could get through.

The thaw continued all night and the morning dawned clear. Jeff saddled a horse, put a spare on a lead rope, and headed for Denver. He had been gone ten days.

6

When he brought the milk to the kitchen that morning, Bill Sanders told Loretta that he expected Jeff home that day.

"Do you really think so?" Loretta asked.

Bill said yes. He and Loretta had discussed the weather and the ranch every morning since Jeff left. Bill would say that today they were breaking the cattle out of the yards in the timber, that now they would have to reopen the trails, that this day they would be out at the line camps. Bill knew the problems, knew how Jeff would handle them.

So now Bill said, "By now they've got all the cattle out. They've been to the line camps and the grass is opening on the ridges. It'll melt a good deal today and there's clear weather ahead for a while. So I figure Jeff'll head for home. Keep the coffee hot."

It was the Wednesday before Thanksgiving. Loretta told Jenny to get the goose ready for tomorrow and to bake a spice cake. Thanksgiving never had meant much to them until they moved to Denver. It still didn't mean much to Jeff, not nearly as much as it did to Denver's New Englanders. But Loretta observed it, and she knew that Jeff liked roast goose and spice cake any time. If Bill was wrong, if Jeff didn't come today, they would have Thanksgiving dinner anyway. The girls always enjoyed it.

After the midday meal Loretta and the girls went to the sitting room for the rest hour, relaxation before the afternoon nap. Sometimes the girls played a quiet game, sometimes Loretta read to them, though reading had become more difficult since Jane had decided that the child stories that delighted Lissie were far too young to interest her. This day Loretta had sewing to do and she suggested that they play a game. But they weren't interested in games. Jane went to a window and stared moodily out at the melting snow. Lissie said, "Tell us a story, Mother."

"What about, dear?" Loretta asked.

"About a storm!"

Jane, still at the window, said, "She's told us about all the storms that ever were."

"No, she hasn't," Lissie insisted. "Besides, storms are exciting." She thought for a moment, then said, "Then tell us about a trip."

"Which trip?" Loretta asked with a smile. She was lengthening a dress for Lissie, who seemed to be growing an inch a month.

"Any trip! Trips are exciting too!"

Jane said, "There wasn't but one trip. The trip from Texas to the ranch."

"Oh, darling," Loretta said, "there were many trips. Your father made lots and lots of trips."

"You didn't." Jane was still at the window. "Papa always went alone. He always goes alone."

"I didn't go on the trail trips with him," Loretta said. "Women never go on trips with a trail herd." She wondered why Jane seemed to relish saying the hurtful thing. Did the child know, by some uncanny instinct, that she could hurt her mother with such statements? "But your father always told me about them when he came home." Then she said to Lissie, "We were all on the trip from Dallas up here."

"Even me?" Lissie asked.

"Even you. You don't remember because you were just a baby."

"You," Jane said, "cried all the way."

"I didn't!" Lissie exclaimed. "Did I, Mother?"

"No, dear. You were a very good baby. Jane is teasing. You were only a year old when we started, but you were a good little traveler. You seldom cried."

"Was it a long, exciting trip?" Lissie asked.

"It took more than six months, more than half a year."

Jane had come over from the window to the sofa. "A man got killed," she said. "The Indians shot him and he bled horribly. Lots and lots of blood."

"Jane, stop it!" Loretta said.

"He did," Jane insisted. "And another man got shot. He bled too, and Father burned him with a hot iron because he got shot. You cried, Lissie. You cried and cried."

"Jane," Loretta said firmly, "you cried too, when those things happened. Your father didn't burn the man. He cauterized the wound, to clean it and help it heal. You were both very good girls the whole trip." She smiled. "Now sit down and be quiet and I will tell you some stories about the trip."

Jane reluctantly sat at the other end of the couch and Lissie sat on a cushion on the floor. Lissie was excitedly expectant, but Jane already had a superior air of boredom. Loretta turned to Jane. "And no interruptions."

Loretta told them first about the day they left Dallas, the excitement of leaving and all the strange sights and sounds of the first day on the trail. Then she told them about the day when they had to stop, weeks later, and repair a wagon and she and the girls picked wildflowers. They were two of the most beautiful days she could remember, and the happiest.

When she had finished the wildflower story Lissie said, "Mother, when will the sand lilies and the larkspurs be here again? I want to go and pick a bouquet!"

"Not until next spring, Lissie," Loretta said. "It's just the beginning of winter, now."

"I can't wait!" Lissie exclaimed.

Loretta laughed. "I'm afraid you'll have to, dear. Most of us spend our lives waiting, for something."

"I won't," Jane said quietly.

"You won't what, Jane?"

"I won't spend my life waiting. For anything!"

"I hope you don't have to, Jane. But most people do. Now you've had your stories. Run along and take your naps."

Both girls kissed her and Lissie said her thanks. They went to their rooms. Loretta picked up the dress again, measured the hem, pinned it and began sewing. And the whole trip, that six months trip from Dallas to the Bijou, began unwinding in her memory, a varicolored thread with knots of remembrance.

They started in April, early April, the weather still uncertain. The first few days were sunny and springlike, but the fourth day it snowed. Not much snow, and the snow turned to rain about noon, chill rain, and the air raw and cold. Loretta was miserable.

They were going up Denton Creek and after the noon-stop the wagons, as usual, went on ahead of the cattle to the night camp ground. There the drivers unhitched the mules, turned them loose to graze and saddled horses and went back to help with the cattle. Only the cook and his helper stayed with the wagons, and they had to cut firewood, start the cookfire, begin getting supper under the tarpaulin stretched as a shelter beside the cookwagon. Loretta sat in her wagon, not knowing what to do. Lissie was fretful. She was cold and hadn't yet got used to being cooped up in the wagon. Tommy was crying, as he always did when the wagon stopped. Tommy liked the motion of the wagon.

Jane sat huddled beside her mother, a comforter around them, for almost an hour. Then the riders arrived with the cattle and put them on a nearby hill to graze. The men built a rope corral and drove the horse herd inside and chose fresh mounts.

Jeff came up, on a tired horse, and rode about giving orders. He saddled a fresh horse that was skittish and didn't like Jeff's long, flapping slicker. Jeff was tired and short-tempered. He gave the horse its head, let it buck, and there was a vicious round of pitching, Jeff's slicker flapping and his quirt slashing. Loretta covered her face, afraid to watch, fearful that the horse would fall in the mud and break Jeff's leg, or even his back. But Jeff won, as he always did, and the horse didn't fall. Jeff rode past Loretta's wagon, his face glowing with triumph, and didn't even see her.

Then Bill Sanders rode past, and he did see her. He stopped and asked, "Cold, Loretta? You look half frozen."

Her teeth were chattering so much she could hardly speak, but she said, "I'm all right." Jeff had told her before they started that he would make the wagon as comfortable as he could and that she needn't do any cooking, but that she would have to look after herself and the children. The men would be busy with the cattle. So she told Bill, "I'm all right," and Bill rode away, and she wished she hadn't come.

Ten minutes later Bill came back with two riders. They brought two tarps and put up an awning for her. They dragged in a load of firewood and built a fire. Loretta thanked them and they went back to the cattle. She pulled a wooden bench from the wagon, helped Jane down and brought Lissie, and she brought Tommy from his bed and held him in her arms until the warmth of the fire had quieted him. Tommy went to sleep and she put him back in his bed, bundled in quilts against the raw cold, and went back and sat with Lissie, a comforter around them, their chill misery somewhat abated. Jane stood at the fire looking like an orphan in one of Jeff's old brush jackets.

The riders got the cattle settled for the night. The cook's helper brought plates of food for Loretta and the girls, fried steak and gravy and sour-dough bread and fried potatoes, greasy fare but hot and satisfying. Then the cook began beating on a dishpan with an iron spoon and shouting, "Come and get it!"

The riders came in, wet and silent, and ate standing under the cook's awning. They came in twos, ate quickly and left. Jeff was the last to come. By then the night herders were making their rounds. Loretta could hear them when there was a lull in the beat of the rain on the tarp overhead, the men calling or singing to the cattle, restless in the darkness and the storm.

Jane was over at the cook's fire, watching, when Jeff rode in, unsaddled his horse, filled his plate and tin cup. He came over to Loretta's shelter and sat down on the bench beside her. He was so tired he just sat, for several minutes, before he even took a gulp of coffee. Then he said, "Nice little house you've got here."

"It's a little drafty," Loretta said, "but it's the warmest place I've found all day." She wondered whether to tell him that Bill was responsible for it.

Jeff nodded and began to eat. "It's been a hard day," he said, "for everybody. The cattle were cantankerous and the horses were mean." He looked at her. "Sorry you came?"

"No."

He cut a big bite of steak. "You used to ask what we did on the trail in bad weather. Now you know. We do the best we can till the weather changes." He chewed for a minute, silent. "It'll be easier," he went on, "when we get the herd trail-broke. And the weather should improve. But it's still going to be a long, hard trip."

"Are you sorry I came, Jeff?"

He ate in silence, thinking, before he answered. "Three wagons will slow us up, especially in rough country and when we hit high water. But I didn't intend to hurry the cattle, so maybe it evens out. No, Loretta, I'm not sorry you came. But you may be, before we get there."

"No, Jeff. This is where I belong, with you. But I do wish there was something I could do to help. I feel so useless!"

"Take it easy while you can." He went back to the cookfire for another cup of coffee.

"You're awfully tired, Jeff," she said when he returned to the bench. "Can't you come to bed now and get some rest?"

He shook his head and he glanced at Lissie, asleep in Loretta's arms. Jane, who had trailed him back from the cookfire, stood at his shoulder, almost asleep on her feet. He said to Loretta, "You go ahead. A night like this, I've got to have double guard on the cattle. They'd spook and run pretty easy. I've got to check them again, and there are a few other things to do. You go ahead. I'll be another hour, at least."

He finished his food, mopped his plate with a chunk of bread. Then he picked up Jane and put her in the wagon. He helped Loretta up, with Lissie, and he said, "Good night," and walked away in the rain and the darkness. Loretta heard him talking to the cook, then heard the splash of his horse's hoofs as he rode off toward the cattle.

She lay awake for an hour, waiting. Jeff didn't come. She slept, and she didn't know how late it was when he finally came to the wagon, was in bed with her. She wakened, feeling the cold in him, and she smelled the tiredness, actually smelled it. She snuggled close, to give him of her own warmth, and she kissed him and he put an arm around her. He said, "I'm glad you came, Loretta," his voice hoarse with weariness. He hugged her once, then his whole body relaxed and he was asleep. Loretta listened, and the pelt of rain on the tilt overhead had stopped. Then she, too, slept, content.

The next thing she knew it was thin dawn filled with noise. The cook was beating the dishpan with the big spoon, rousing the men. Jeff was up and into his pants and shirt and boots and out of the wagon before the banging stopped. A new day had begun, with groans and shouts from the riders, nickering of horses, braying of mules, bawling of cattle. A day, happily, with a clear sky, a warming sun.

For days on end the pattern was the same. They were roused by the cook's din before sunup. There was the seeming confusion of men and horses, then the hurried breakfast, the departure of everyone but the cook to get the herd off the bed ground and under way.

Then the wagon drivers returned, wrestled the mules into harness, hitched them. The wagons jolted over the hills, caught up with the cattle, passed them, went on to the nooning ground Jeff had ridden ahead and selected. The cook built his fire, got out his gear, prepared the noon meal. And Loretta and the children had an hour or more to get down from the wagon, walk, sit in the sun, do as they pleased. Then the herd came up and the men came in twos or threes and ate, standing up and always in a hurry. They ate and went back to the cattle which had been grazing slowly ahead.

Afternoon was in the same pattern as morning. The cook cleaned his gear, packed it, and the wagons rolled once more, caught up with the herd, passed it, went on to the night ground that either Jeff or Bill Sanders had chosen. Camp was made, the evening meal cooked, and when the cattle arrived they were grazed for a time, then bedded down in a loose herd. Supper eaten, the night herders took their posts and the other men talked, played cards, played mouth-organs and sang. And bedded down in their blankets. The men slept in the open unless it was raining; if the weather was bad they found what shelter they could, under the wagons or merely under tarpaulins.

The cattle, as Jeff had warned, had first call on everyone. After the first week, when they were being trail-broken, they seemed to know the routine. But stragglers had to be watched, stampedes guarded against, truculence curbed. They had to be watered. They had to be grazed. And the horse herd and the mules had to be hobbled or herded at night. There was little spare time for anyone, though there were eight men in the crew besides Jeff, three of them wagon drivers who also took their turns on night herd. They seldom traveled more than six or seven miles a day, except on the one dry march between streams, but that came later. As Jeff said, they didn't really travel; they just grazed, and cattle are slow grazers.

Loretta knew in general the route they took, but she couldn't have guided anyone over it. They went up Denton Creek and across to Red River Station. They followed the Red River all the way to the Panhandle, then went north across the Indian Nation to the Arkansas. Somewhere in there they had the long, dry drive, more than two days without water. Then they followed the Arkansas west for a time before they turned north again, north and west. The route didn't matter. Jeff took care of that.

99

When they first moved to Denver, people sometimes asked Loretta when they came to the Bijou. She told them it was in '66, and they said, "Oh, it couldn't have been then, could it? Nobody came over the trail that early." Loretta said, "We did."

The questioners were still incredulous. They turned to Jeff. Jeff said, "Yes, it was in '66. We could have been the first ones, but I doubt it. Oliver Loving brought a herd up from the Panhandle in '59, all the way to Pueblo, and he wintered them on the Arkansas. Loving told me that John Dawson brought a herd all the way to Denver here that same year, '59. And just after the war, in '65 I think, Loving and Charley Goodnight brought a big trail herd up from Fort Belknap through Fort Sumner and went all the way to Wyoming. We weren't the first ones."

"But they didn't bring their families, did they?"

"No, I guess not." Jeff shrugged. "Maybe somebody else did, though. All I know for sure is that we came through in '66."

There was no trouble to speak of until they reached the Canadian River, and Loretta had begun to think it was going to be only a long, wearying trip, day after uneventful day. Then they came to the Canadian and it was in flood, a dark, swirling, muddy current half a mile wide. Jeff looked upstream and down, twenty miles each way, for a crossing. The most promising place was ten miles upstream, so they moved cattle and wagons and settled down to wait for the water to slack off.

Jeff said later that that was the most fortunate move of the whole trip. There was a good campsite and there was plenty of grass for the cattle. And, as it turned out, it was well adapted to defense.

They were there five days. Jeff had the men cut and trim cottonwood logs for the raft they would need for the crossing. Then they dragged those logs and piled them in a kind of pen a hundred yards from the wagons. Jeff didn't tell Loretta why. Nor did he tell her why he kept double guards on the cattle, day and night, and posted a lookout on the high hill just behind the camp. He did tell her never to get out of sight of the wagons and never to go down into the timber along the river.

The weather was mild and clear. Loretta still remembered the particular mildness of that one night and the way the stars glittered. She had put the children to bed but she couldn't sleep. She went to the front of the wagon and sat looking out at the stars, listening to the night, and waiting for Jeff. It must have been ten o'clock when she saw him riding in from the herd. He had just reached the cook wagon when the lookout from up on the hill rode in, hurrying, and called to him. They talked, but all Loretta could hear was something about a signal fire. Then the lookout rode away and Jeff came to the wagon. He called, "Loretta!"

She said, "Yes?"

He said, "You'll have to move to the log pen. I want you and the children to sleep there tonight." His voice was tense.

She knew Jeff well enough not to ask why. She got the children up and Jeff roused Bill Sanders and Sam Royce, and they helped take the children and the blankets to the log pen. Jane was awake, and she kept asking, "Why, Papa? Why do we have to sleep here?"

Finally Jeff lost his patience. "Because I told you to!" he snapped. He got them settled and he saw that Sam Royce had two rifles and told him to stay there with them and keep his eyes open. Then Jeff and Bill rode back to the wagons and roused the hands who were sleeping. The men went back to the cattle.

Lissie and Tommy were soon asleep, but Jane was wide awake. She kept asking Loretta what was the matter, why they had to sleep here. Loretta tried to shush her, finally told her this was their chance to count all the stars. She and Jane started counting, and at last Jane fell asleep in spite of herself. But Loretta lay awake for what seemed hours, watching Sam Royce standing in the far corner of the log pen, listening to coyotes howling and the occasional bawl of a steer on the hilltop. But at last she, too, slept.

The attack came just as dawn began to lighten the sky. Loretta was jolted from sleep by a volley of gunfire, a drumming of hoofs and a chorus of yells. She sprang up, looked over the log barrier and saw forty or fifty mounted Indians racing through the camp, shooting at the wagons. They thundered through the camp and went up the hill toward the cattle, and in a moment there was a still heavier volley of gunfire from the hilltop. Gunfire and screams of pain and anger from the Indians.

Then the light of dawn seemed to come all at once, lighting the hilltop in a pink glow. Loretta could see the cattle there, in a tight herd, the men riding around them, holding the herd and shooting at the marauders. Having failed to stampede the herd in their first rush, the Indians split into small groups and tried to break into the milling cattle.

After that it was all confusion, gunfire and yelling and bawling cattle and the screaming of wounded horses.

Then Sam was at Loretta's side, handing her a rifle, saying, "Don't shoot till I start shooting."

Three Indians left the attacking party on the hill and headed for the wagons again. One got down from his horse, gathered a bunch of dry grass, lit it to fire the wagons. Sam Royce shot him as he crouched. Loretta heard the thud of the bullet, saw the Indian jerk and spurt blood and fall over. Sam fired again and one of the Indians on horseback was jolted, almost fell, grabbed the horse's mane and galloped away. The other horseman fired one wild shot and fled. Until they had gone, Loretta forgot the rifle in her hands.

It was all fantastic, unreal, a nightmare. Then Jane was tugging at her skirt, crying, "Mother, Mother, Mother!" Tommy, on his pallet, was shouting with hysterical laughter. Lissie had buried her head in the blankets.

Jeff heard Sam's shots. He and a hand named Purvis came down the hill at a gallop. Jeff saw the dead Indian beside the cook wagon, swung his horse toward the log pen and shouted, "Anybody hurt? You all right?" Sam shouted, "Everything's all right here," and Jeff and Purvis went back to the cattle on the hilltop.

The attack probably didn't last twenty minutes, if that. The Comanches were after the cattle, and when they couldn't break into the herd in the first few minutes they began to fall back. Jeff's men were armed with the new repeating rifles as well as revolvers, and the Indians couldn't face such firepower. They began to pick up their walking wounded and withdraw. By full sunup they were gone.

The men moved the cattle down closer to the wagons. The cook started breakfast and Jeff tallied up the damage. One man, a rider named Randolph, was dead, shot in the first rush. Another rider, Clint Cooper, had a bullet through his arm. Aside from those two, there wasn't another man hurt. And except for three cows killed by the Indians' shooting, they hadn't lost any of the herd.

"Just plain lucky," Jeff said, and he turned to Loretta and said, "If Randy hadn't seen that signal fire, and if we hadn't got you moved out of the wagon—" He shrugged. Loretta's wagon had ten splintery bullet holes through it, put there in that first charge by the Indians.

They ate breakfast, Jeff cauterized Clint Cooper's arm and bandaged it and put it in a sling, and they gave Curt Randolph as decent a burial as they could, there beside the river. Jeff read the burial service and they put the rider's hat, his spurs and his quirt in the grave with him. And as they walked back to the wagons Jeff said, "We'll make the crossing today, right now, before the Indians get up their nerve for any more fighting."

After the attack, the river crossing seemed uneventful. The men hauled the logs down to the water, lashed them into a raft, rolled a wagon on and towed the raft across the stream with their lariats. The mules were swum across, hitched to the wagons as the raft brought them in, and hauled them onto high ground. All three wagons were safe on the new campsite by midafternoon. Before dark they had swum the cattle across. They camped on the hilltop that night, with guards wakeful despite the long, hard day. But the Indians did not come back. The next day they resumed the journey northward.

Loretta paused to rethread her needle. It all seemed so long ago, so far away. Yet it was only five years ago, six years next summer. Only five years since they arrived on the Bijou with that little bunch of cattle. It was October and the cottonwoods still had quite a few leaves, stiff, rusty leaves that chattered in every breeze. And the magpies screamed at them and flaunted their long tails among the trees. The cattle spread out on one hillside in buffalo grass eight inches tall, the best natural feed in the world, Jeff said. Just a handful of cattle, but a beginning. And Loretta and the children lived in the wagon for three weeks, while the men built the house.

Strange, she thought, how common danger brings people together. Before the Indian attack there on the Canadian they were just a trail outfit cumbered by a woman and three small children who had to be tolerated because they were the boss's family. Only Bill Sanders, of all the men, was really friendly. But after the attack they were like a close-knit family. The hands no longer stood apart from her, doing the necessary chores for her with no more than quiet courtesy. Now they did the unexpected things, the undemanded things. Sam Royce found a patch of wild flags along a creek and picked a great armful and brought them to her wagon for Loretta, just because he thought she'd like them. Finch Purvis caught a baby jackrabbit and tucked it in his shirt and gave it to Jane when he came in for supper. The cook taught her to make son-of-a-gun stew; oh, she knew the men called it son-of-a-bitch stew, but that name was never spoken in her hearing. And Sam insisted, despite her denial, that it was Loretta who shot the Indian who was trying to set fire to the wagons. She had to be a heroine.

Maybe that was one reason every man in the crew stayed when they reached the Bijou and Jeff asked for volunteers who would stay on for an extra month and help raise a house and build corrals. The season was late and Jeff wanted to get Loretta and the children under a roof before the snow came. Every man in the crew volunteered, even the cook, who said, "I'll swing an axe between meals."

Loretta said, "Maybe I can do the cooking. I should be able to help somehow."

So she took over the cooking, to free another man.

She knew the meals were terrible the first few days, but the men made no complaint. She had never cooked for so many hungry men, and if she had enough bread she ran out of stew, or if she had enough stew she ran out of coffee. But the cook took odd moments to tell her how much of this or that to make, when to start each pot or Dutch oven heating, and how to come out even and on time. And in less than a week she was feeding the men just as well as the camp cook ever had. Better, the men said, heaping praise on her. And they cut and peeled logs, notched them, raised walls, raftered and roofed them. They hauled stones, built a fireplace and chimney. They built corrals, and a shed to shelter the horses. And one Sunday, when they should have had the day off, they built a table and benches and put up bunks, specially for Loretta.

Jeff said it was a marvel, the way that house went up. "They built it for you, Loretta," he said. "They would have put up a cabin for me, a shelter, just a line camp. But they built a real house for you. I hope you appreciate it."

"I certainly do," she said. "Oh, Jeff, pay them extra!"

Jeff slowly shook his head. "I figured it close when I asked them to stay on an extra month," he said. "If Bill should want his pay and go back, we'll just about come out even. I'll have ten dollars left, maybe fifteen. No more."

Loretta had managed to save most of the money Jeff sent to her from Baxter Springs. It was all the cash they had. Jeff had hoarded it to pay off the men at the end of the trip. But when the building was finished and the men started packing, Bill Sanders told Jeff he was staying on. "Just as I said when we were here before. I want to be foreman here, Jeff."

Jeff said, "There's no crew to be foreman of, Bill."

Bill said, "There will be. Till then, just let the pay pile up. I've got no place to spend money."

So they came out all right, and Jeff paid each man a ten-dollar bonus, as Loretta had asked him to. Jeff hesitated at the last minute, but Loretta said, "Just like Bill, we haven't any place to spend money. We've got a house, and we won't go hungry."

Jeff paid them off and the first week in November they said good-bye and headed for home. And Bill began building a lean-to addition on the house. "My bedroom," Bill called it, and Loretta silently thanked him. They would have made out, with blankets strung up for a partition; but it wouldn't have been right. They were making a new start, and she and Jeff deserved a little privacy. Bill knew it, bless him.

Oh, she thought now, the trip and the first winter on the Bijou —those were times to remember! The war was over, and the old hurts were healed. And we were—we were a family, for the first time. We were starting over.

Why, she wondered, is starting so important? Starting anything, a trip, a marriage, a family, or starting over, as we were. Is it because you have dreams? Maybe. Dreams lift your heart, make you rich with a richness that you seem to lose as you go along. It is so much easier to have dreams when you are starting fresh, at anything. You start, with all the dreams, and you go along, and some of the dreams come true, but you don't actually know it, and then the time comes when you wonder what happened to the dreams. Why does a dream die when you make it come true? What happened to our dreams, Jeff's dreams, and mine?

Jeff dreamed of the ranch. So did I, because it was so important to him. To us. Cattle on the hills, more cattle than you could count. Grass, and water, and cattle. So we built the ranch, and we had the cattle. The dream became the ranch, and somehow the ranch became a prison. I don't know how. It wasn't a prison for Jeff, and it wasn't really a prison for me. Yet Jeff saw it as a prison for both of us. We had to get away from it, move to Denver, and this became the dream. This big, beautiful house. And then this house became a prison. Why? It's the same house that was a dream, and now it's a prison. Jeff has to get away. Maybe you never can live in a dream. As soon as you move in, the dream becomes something else. Why?

Loretta finished the hem and sighed and straightened her shoulders. She rubbed her eyes and shook her head to clear it. It wasn't often that she got to thinking this way. It was the girls who started it, the stories she had told them. And, probably, the fact that Jeff might be coming home this evening.

Oh, she thought, I don't want to be morbid! It's not my nature, and it never was. Jeff and I never had but one real quarrel. And, she told herself firmly, I'm not going to think about that now.

She looked at the hem. The stitches weren't as small or as even as she liked to have them, but she wasn't going to do it over. She would have to let this same dress down again in another month or two. She would go down to the kitchen and put the flatirons to heat and press it, and that would have to do.

She remembered what her mother used to say about a complaining woman or a woman who always had the blues and sick headaches. If she was a young woman, her mother said, "She's just trying to get out of doing something she's duty bound to do." If she was in her forties, her mother said, "It's her change coming on, and if she don't watch out she'll go crazy." And if the woman was beyond fifty, her mother said, "She never could get along with anyone, including herself, and she gets worse as she gets older."

I'm thirty-four years old, Loretta thought, and I certainly haven't any sign of the change. So I must be trying to get out of something I'm duty bound to do. I wonder what it is?

She smiled, and she thought: Why, I'm not blue at all! I'm almost happy! Jeff probably will be home for Thanksgiving. Oh, I hope he is!

And she went to her bedroom and combed her hair and powdered her nose before she took the dress downstairs to press the hem.

7

It was early dusk when Jeff reached home. He swung down out of the saddle, opened the stable door and led the ponies inside. Before he had closed the door behind them Bill Sanders was limping down the alleyway, lantern in hand throwing long shadows in the darkening stable.

"Well, hello!" Bill shouted, and he hurried to open the stall doors. His voice was welcome itself.

Jeff turned the ponies into the stalls and Bill hung the lantern on a peg and began loosening the latigo. "Figured," he said, "that you'd be back tonight or tomorrow." He swung the saddle from the pony's back, tossed it onto a low partition. "When she crusted over and that new snow came," he said, removing the saddle blanket, "I figured it'd take you till just about last night to get all of them up out of the timber. How are they doing?"

"Doing all right," Jeff said. "We accounted for all but about five hundred head."

"Good, good," Bill said. "They're probably up at South Camp. Look there?"

"I told the boys to look there today. How are things here?"

"Fine, Jeff. Just fine. You go along in. Loretta's expecting you. She said something this morning about a Thanksgiving goose tomorrow."

Thanksgiving tomorrow? Jeff had forgotten about Thanksgiving. "We'll talk later," he said, moving toward the door.

"Sure, sure. Go on in. I'll tend to these two." Bill picked up the saddle and blanket, started toward the saddle room.

Jeff went up the brick walk to the back door of the house. He was stiff from hours in the saddle. He should have stopped an hour ago and loosened up, but he was in a hurry to get home. Ten days ago he couldn't get away fast enough, and now he was like a runaway kid, couldn't wait to get back.

Jenny heard him come in the door and she hurried to the front hall and shouted up the stairs, "Mister's here!" while Jeff stamped the snow from his boots. He stood there for a few moments, feeling the warmth of the house and sensing the odors, so different from those of the ranch house. The steamy cooking odors, the faint smell of soap, of furniture, of rugs, of clean human beings. A faint feminine smell, lightly perfumed, scrubbed. Sensing it, Jeff took off his ranch boots before he went to the front hall and up the stairs.

Loretta was waiting for him at the head of the stairs. She looked fresh and clean and lovely. He kissed her and she laughed and rubbed his cheeks, and for the first time he remembered that he hadn't shaved since he left for the ranch.

"Oh, Jeff! I'm so glad you're here! Was it bad getting out there? You've been working awfully hard, haven't you? Are the cattle all right?"

"Yes," Jeff said, smiling. "Yes, to all your questions. I had to leave the wagon at the ranch. Came back in the saddle."

"You are tired out. And hungry as a bear. I'll tell Jenny to hurry supper."

"No need. I've waited this long. By the time I've shaved and cleaned up it'll be regular supper time, I guess. How are you? How are the girls?"

"We're all fine." They went down the hallway, toward Jeff's bedroom. For a few moments Jeff felt a complete stranger here, had the sense of walking down the corridor of a hotel somewhere. Then the feeling passed. He was home.

They went into his bedroom and Loretta closed the door. "Jane," she whispered, "had her birthday. A cake and everything."

Jeff blessed her for reminding him. "Plenty of presents, I hope. What did I give her?"

"You," Loretta said, still whispering, "gave her a darling little gold locket on a chain. She loved it."

Jeff was stripping off his shirt. "How's Tommy?" he asked.

"Tommy's all right." Loretta seemed to hestitate, then said, "I thought he was coming down with a cold, but he got over it. . . . Now! You'll want hot water. I'll get it."

She left, and Jeff stripped out of his ranch clothes and was in a robe when she returned with a big pitcher of steaming water. "Supper," she said, "will be ready in half an hour. Will that be time enough?"

"Plenty."

He washed and began shaving, and for some reason that feeling of being in a hotel returned. The Planter's Hotel, in St. Louis. How many times had he arrived there after a trail drive, looking just about this way, whiskered and wind-burned and trail-dirty? Go to his room, clean up, shave, get into clean clothes, and go downstairs and eat kitchen meals again, napkin meals, just as though he had never been on the trail. Change, within an hour, from one way of life to another. The Planter's, of course, didn't smell like this. The Planter's was a men's hotel. But it wasn't a ranch house. A man's hotel. But even so, a lot of memories of Amy were involved with the Planter's.

He put that thought away. This was home, his own house. This was Loretta. Even here, in his own bedroom, Loretta's soap-and-lavender smell was as strong as his own sweat-and-horse smell.

As he put on a clean shirt he thought: I had to get away, and I'm glad to be back. I'm like an old saddle horse. I have to get out and run, graze on the flats, but I come back to the barn for grain and a curry comb and shelter from the storm.

He finished dressing, glanced at his watch and went downstairs.

Loretta and the girls were waiting for him in the dining room. Jenny was putting the food on the table, a table covered with white linen and set with china and silver and crystal. And the furniture was polished walnut and mahogany.

Lissie cried, "Papa!" and ran to him. He leaned down for her hug and kiss, and Lissie exclaimed, "Oh, Papa, we're *so* glad you are home!" She clung to him.

"I'm glad to be home, Lissie," he said, and he led her to her chair.

Jane stood back of her chair, watching him with cool eyes. "Hello, Jane," he said, and he went to her and lifted her chin and kissed her. She gave him the dutiful kiss, and he glanced at the locket on the chain around her neck. It was a pretty little thing, in perfect taste. Jane saw his look and said, "Thank you, Papa, for the lovely gift." She glanced for an instant at Loretta, and Jeff knew that Loretta had given Jane her orders. Jane had followed them, to the letter.

"You are welcome, Jane," he said. "Your mother tells me you had a very nice birthday. I'm sorry I couldn't be here."

He went to Loretta at the end of the table, held her chair for her. Then he went to the head of the table, the girls sat down, and Jenny came from the kitchen and set the roast of beef in front of him. Instinctively he reached for the carving knife, then saw Jane glance at him and bow her head. And Jeff remembered to say the blessing. Then he began to carve and serve the plates.

As he ate, Jeff had the feeling that he was two persons, one sitting here eating, the other sitting aside and watching, listening. Watching a middle-aged businessman, a prosperous ranchman, here at dinner with his family after a wearying trip. Hearing his wife ask about the trip, the expected questions; hearing him answer, the expected answers. Watching his young daughters eat, mannerly as could be and speaking only when spoken to.

It was all remote, impersonal as a scene in a stage play. Why?

He remembered his own youth, when he was the age of Jane. His father came home from a trail drive, home to the place in Lamar County, and there was feasting and celebration. And so much talk that young Jeff could hardly get a question in edgewise. His sisters, both older than Jeff, were full of talk about who had been courting them, where they had gone, what they had worn, what each boy had said. Jeff's mother, telling about the Indian beggar the dog chased, the skunk that got in the chicken house. And Jeff bursting with questions about the trail, the cattle, the far places his father had been. Later, Jeff and his father were at odds, Jeff resenting the farm work thrust upon him. But at the time he was remembering now, when he was twelve, Jane's age, he was full of eagerness and questions. And his father was laughing, talking, recounting tales twice heard, telling of people met, places seen. Answering some questions with a word, ignoring others, using still others as reminders of amazing stories. Homecoming. Talk. Laughter.

Warm memories. Why were they so warm, so different from here and now?

Because, Jeff thought, we weren't all bound up in ourselves. With strange, obscure hurts, as Jane is. With things we don't talk about, as Loretta is. As I am.

Then he thought: We were all there, when I was a boy. The whole family. There wasn't a missing child upstairs, helpless, hopeless, unable to understand even the simplest words of a nurse taking care of him. And we weren't afraid of opening old wounds or causing new ones.

Loretta was talking about tomorrow, Thanksgiving. She and Jenny had made mincemeat from a recipe Mrs. Lawrence had given her. Mrs. Lawrence was from Massachusetts, where Thanksgiving was even more important than Christmas. And they were going to have mincemeat pie tomorrow. Did Jeff ever taste mincemeat pie?

"Yes, I had it a time or two, in St. Louis."

"Did you like it?"

"It needs plenty of good brandy in it, I understand."

Loretta laughed and even Jane smiled. "We put so much brandy in ours," Loretta said, "that Jenny began to get tipsy, just from smelling it."

"Then it should be good." Jeff cut another slice of roast. He and Lissie were the only ones who wanted more. Jane put her knife and fork on her plate and sat waiting, hands in her lap.

"You may be excused, dear," Loretta said to her. "I am sure your father will excuse you if you are finished. But there is spice cake for dessert."

"Thank you, Mother," Jane said. "May I be excused, Father?"

"Don't you want some cake?" Jeff asked.

"No, thank you. But if you say so, I'll stay at the table." She said it so politely that Jeff wanted to shake her.

"All right," he said, "run along. You too, Lissie. You are both excused."

"I don't want to be excused," Lissie said. "I haven't finished my meat, and I want some cake."

But Jane left them, went upstairs.

They finished dinner, and Jeff wondered why the cake was

111

so tasteless. It wasn't the cake. It was Jeff, himself. He was so annoyed with Jane that he couldn't taste, and that was senseless. Why should he be so annoyed by a twelve-year-old child?

Later, when the girls had been sent to bed and Jeff's anger with Jane had eased away, Jeff and Loretta were in the sitting room and Loretta said, "It must have been beautiful at the ranch." She looked at Jeff, then smiled. "I know," she said, "you didn't have time to think whether it was beautiful or not, but I remember the way the creek looks jet-black after a snowstorm, and the way the drifts curl over the water. The way the big pines north of the house hold the snow, so they look like great Christmas trees."

Jeff nodded. "They still do. The creek was black, and the drifts curled. Yes, it was beautiful. When I had time to look."

Loretta said, "And the house, it's just a cow camp now, isn't it? It would have to be. Jeff, I love that house!"

He sat silent, staring away. Then he looked at her. "Do you still feel as young as you look, Loretta?"

The question surprised her. "I—I don't know, Jeff. Sometimes I feel—" She broke off. "I was thinking about our first winter there. It was a happy time, Jeff, a very happy time. I felt very young, then. Maybe that's what you saw just now, my remembering."

"You look as young, or at least as pretty, as you did when I married you."

She shook her head. "I was an old maid then, Jeff. An old maid and getting desperate." Then she laughed. "I shouldn't tell you a thing like that! No woman should say a thing like that!"

"Why not?"

"It's one of those secrets a woman keeps to herself. No matter how much she wanted a man, she's supposed to pretend she wasn't waiting for him. But Jeff, I never could lie to you, not even pretty, harmless lies. I thought you never were going to know I even existed."

He kept looking at her. Finally he asked, "Don't you sometimes feel that you're married to an old, old man? When I come home looking the way I did today?"

"Of course not!" she exclaimed. "Do you know what I was thinking when you came home today? I was thinking how much younger you look than you did ten years ago, how much more vital. You're tired now, and you were annoyed at the table, and

112

you're a little more chunky than you were ten years ago. But right now you look distinguished."

"Distinguished? That sounds old."

"I didn't mean it to. You've been working hard, and you've been worrying, and it shows, of course. But you'll gain back everything with a good night's sleep. I don't think any woman does, after she's passed twenty-five. Jeff, when you came in all whiskery and cold and tired, you still looked as strong and vital as you used to when you came home from a trail trip before the war. Then at supper you were annoyed at Jane—"

"You saw that?"

"Of course! I know you, Jeff."

"What's the matter with that girl, anyway? Sometimes I think she hates me."

"It isn't that she specially dislikes you. She's the same way with me, sometimes. She's at a difficult age, and it can be very painful."

"When is she going to begin to straighten out?"

"I don't know. Mother used to say I was an impossible child till I was almost seventeen. Then the boys began to court me and that made me feel important, I suppose. But even then I must have been frightfully difficult to live with. She said I was, anyway. I was helping Mother with the dressmaking, though, so she put up with me. And kept hoping I would get married and be taken off her hands."

"Maybe," Jeff said with a wry smile, "you'd better start dress-making for Jane's sake and put her to work."

Loretta smiled. "I don't think it's that simple, Jeff."

"Probably not." Jeff sighed. "But I probably won't have many run-ins with Jane this winter. I won't be here."

"What?"

"I'll have to be at the ranch most of the time. At least until Bill is able to go back and take charge. Sam Royce just can't get it through his head that a steer won't pull through a tough winter penned in a yard in the timber with nothing to eat." Then he forced a smile. "But that's nothing for you to worry about. That's mine to handle." He yawned.

"And you'll handle it. Don't you know, Jeff, that I don't worry about the cattle? You're the only thing I worry about."

"Me? Why worry about me?"

She avoided the question. "I did my worrying about the cattle that first winter out there. It was so important to get a start. If you'd lost the cattle that winter, everything you dreamed about would have been lost. I don't worry about that any more."

Jeff thought of Pete Wallace, the dreams Pete had, the way Pete had talked that evening at East Camp. Yes, the ranch had been Jeff's dream, and he had followed it. If he'd lost all his cattle that first winter there wouldn't have been much left of that dream. He'd staked everything on it. Everything. But he didn't know, until now, that Loretta had worried.

He smothered another yawn and said, "Well, don't start worrying about the cattle now. Nor about me, either."

Loretta laughed at him. "You can hardly keep your eyes open. Why don't you go to bed?"

"Pretty soon. Loretta, remember that orphan boy I picked up here in Denver? That tow-headed farm boy from back East who wanted to be a ranch hand. Pete Wallace. I took him out to the ranch."

"That boy whose father was killed out in the mines?"

"That's the one. Well, Pete's making a good hand. What I started to say, though, was that coming in from East Camp the other night his horse played out. The snow was knee-deep and crusted. His pony's legs were so badly cut up that it couldn't go another mile, so Pete had to walk in. Five or six miles, and that crust ice chewing up Pete's legs at almost every step. He got in, and when I asked him if he ever thought he wouldn't make it he said no, he knew he could make it because he still had things to do."

Loretta winced. "He must have been very heroic."

Jeff shook his head. "He wasn't heroic at all. He just had courage, and he had things he wanted to do. You said the ranch was my dream, and I guess it was. Pete's got dreams, too. He wants to be a ranchman. But the point is that dreams aren't worth anything unless you've got the courage and the purpose to carry them through. You have to want something enough to carry through. It isn't enough to dream about it."

"I guess that's what I meant, in a way. I was thinking about the boy's trip in, though, not the reason he made it. Aren't there times, Jeff, when the trip is at least as important as where you are going?"

"No," Jeff said firmly. "You never make a trip without a purpose. Why should you go, if you haven't a reason to go?"

"Maybe," Loretta said, "I was thinking about life. Life is a kind of trip, isn't it? I'm not sure where it leads, but it seems very important to me. Just living. Just the trip itself."

"I don't know where it leads either," Jeff said, and he yawned again.

Loretta laughed at him. "I know one trip you're going to make right now. And I *do* know where it leads! To bed. Come on."

The next morning, while the house was abustle with preparations for Thanksgiving dinner, Jeff went to the stable to talk with Bill Sanders. The weather was unchanged from the day before, mild and sunny, and the remaining banks of snow in the yard were underlaid with slushy puddles. Jeff could amost hear the trickling run of melt down all the hillsides along the Bijou, see the spread of open grass on the hilltops and down the slopes to the shallower draws.

The stable doors were open. Bill had finished cleaning the stalls and was spreading fresh bedding. He didn't see Jeff approach and he stopped often to rest his bad leg, leaning on the pitchfork. It had been a bad break, both bones, and when it happened Bill had dragged himself up the creek bank and lain for several hours, drenched and in excruciating pain, before his horse went back to the ranch and Sam Royce came out and found him. Sam put temporary splints on, went back and got a light wagon, made a bed of blankets and brought Bill to Denver. The doctor reduced the fracture, put the leg in a cast, and said Bill couldn't get back in the saddle again for two months, at the least. That was only five weeks ago. Bill should still be on crutches, but he was mule-stubborn about such things.

Jeff found a fork and helped spread the bedding. Then they went back to Bill's room and sat and drank coffee and talked. Bill wanted every detail about the ranch.

Finally Bill said, "You never know, when it starts snowing, when it's going to stop. All you can do is keep fighting it, because you know it can't snow forever."

Jeff said, "Why, in God's name, can't Sam get that through his head?"

Bill didn't answer the question. He said, "I've got to get back out there, Jeff. I'm going out next week." He drained his coffee, got to his feet to pour a fresh cup from the pot on the stove.

Jeff watched him, saw the way he winced when he put his weight on the injured leg, then tried to hide the limp. Even from the back, Jeff could see the jaw muslces bulge as Bill felt and resisted the pain. Bill stood beside the stove a long moment, his weight on his good leg, then came carefully back to his chair and sank into it.

Jeff said, "You're going to stay right here till the first of the year."

"Judas H. Priest and God Almighty!" Bill snorted. "I'm no cripple, and you know it! Besides, all I'd have to do is *be* there. See that things get done, and done right." He ended pleading.

"All right," Jeff said with a thin smile. "We'll go down and see the doctor tomorrow. If he says you can go—"

He didn't have to say another word. Bill sighed. He knew what the doctor would say. The doctor wouldn't budge an inch. He would ask if Bill was still using his crutches, and no matter what Bill said Jeff would tell him the truth, and the Doc would give Bill hell. The crutches were standing there in the corner of the room, hated and unused.

Bill said, "You're going to let that doctor tell you how to run the ranch?"

Jeff said, "You know damn well who's running the ranch. When I get too old to run it, I'll quit and let the bankers take over, or whoever wants to. But I'm not that old yet."

"No, I guess not," Bill said, rubbing his grizzling head. He smiled. "Haven't heard you complaining about your rupture, anyway."

"Rupture?" Jeff asked. "I haven't got any rupture."

Bill laughed, and Jeff bristled.

"I was thinking about Abe Kritchell," Bill said. "You never knew Abe, I guess. He had a ranch over on the Brazos and I worked for him the year I was fifteen."

"No, I never knew him."

"Abe was just about the horniest man I ever knew," Bill said. "He had a son named Zack who was only a couple of years older than I was, and Zack took to calling his father the Old Man. Abe wasn't more than thirty-five, thirty-six, and he didn't like it one bit. Finally Abe said to Zack, 'Son, when you've forked as many horses and as many women as I have, then maybe you can call me an old man. Till then, by God, you call me Pappy.' Then he said, 'A man ain't old till he hangs up his spurs and starts worrying about his rupture before he gets in bed.' "

Jeff smiled. "Probably right, at that. I'll try to remember Abe Kritchell." He went to the stove and poured himself a fresh cup of coffee, and he stood staring out the window for several minutes before he came back and sat down. Then he said, "I haven't hung up my spurs yet, and I don't think I will for a while yet, but sometimes I do wonder what it's all about."

"What's what about?"

"Well, you start out, and you come to a fork in the trail, and you pick one fork and follow it. What would have happened if you'd picked the other fork? Your whole life would have changed. But would it have made any difference, in the end?"

"Of course it would," Bill said. "At least the preachers say so, those that I've heard."

"I'm not sure they know. They took the fork that led toward preaching, and preaching's a good deal like anything else, in a way. You follow the rules of the business you're in. I knew a preacher once that gave up preaching and tried farming, and he found out he had to farm just like anybody else. He couldn't wait for God to do his planting or his picking. He had to plant and pick, just like anybody else. And he got the same price they did for his corn when he sold it."

"He should have stuck to preaching," Bill said. "Then he wouldn't have had to plant corn, or pick it either."

"If I'd stayed with it and become a lawyer," Jeff said, "I wouldn't be going out in a storm to see that my cattle had grass. I'd be arguing cases, like the other lawyers, from the same statute books. Maybe I'd be a congressman, by now, if I'd stayed on that fork in the trail. But even if I was a congressman I'd follow the rules and try to pass laws that would get me re-elected. Why? So I could go on being a congressman. Just the same as I worked the cattle out of the timber and up onto the grass, so I can go on being a cattleman. So what's it all about?"

Bill frowned. Jeff was talking about things that never had bothered Bill, never raised questions in him. But he tried to follow Jeff into this strange territory of speculation. "I don't know what's chewing at you, Jeff. But I do know this. First trip we made up here, you were looking for grass and water for a lot of cattle. Well, you found it, here on the Bijou. Now you've got the ranch and the cattle, and you wonder what it's all about."

"I wonder," Jeff said, "what would have happened if I'd taken another fork. That's all."

"Well," Bill said, "if we'd taken another trail on the way up here, that first time, maybe we'd have been ambushed, like Oliver Loving and Bill Wilson were on the Pecos in '67, when the Comanches jumped them. Remember? But we didn't take that fork, as you say, and Loving's dead and you're alive, and so am I. And neither one of us had to walk barefoot over a hundred miles of cactus flats to stay alive, either. I don't know what you're fussing about. Looks to me like you took the right fork every time."

"Maybe you're right." Jeff got to his feet. He set down his coffee cup and turned to Bill with a smile. "At least, I haven't hung up my spurs yet, and I'm not worrying about a rupture. I shouldn't be surprised if the women have got that goose cooked by now. Change your shirt and come on in and eat with the white folks."

But Bill, when he did come in, insisted on eating in the kitchen, as usual, and no argument could make him change his mind. So Jeff and Loretta and the girls sat down in the dining room, just the four of them, to Thanksgiving dinner.

Jeff remembered to ask the blessing before he carved the goose, and as he served the plates he thought that Bill probably was right. Jeff had made his choice at a number of forks along the way, and he had come out here. What more could a man want? Seven years ago he was a cavalryman, almost too sick to sit in the saddle, a member of a doomed army, within a few months of discharge. A man who would go home to a bankrupt business and try to pick up the pieces, make something of life. Today he was a ranchman with one of the best ranch layouts in the territory, successful by any measure you chose. Sitting here at Thanksgiving dinner in a luxurious house, one of the best in Denver, with a damned pretty woman for his wife and two pretty daughters. What more could a man want?

The talk flowed around him, family talk, and Jeff said the proper things about the roast goose and the stuffing and the rest of the food. And the strangeness was gone, the strangeness of last night. Jeff Ross was husband and father, not a stranger who had walked into a hotel somewhere and sat down to eat with people he scarcely knew.

Then he thought: It always happens this way. I come back from the ranch and for a few hours, overnight, I feel like a stranger. Then I slip back into place. I am the head of the family again, Papa, and Mister, and Jeff.

Sitting there now, this Thanksgiving Day, he sensed this and accepted it, even while he was wondering how it happened. He wondered if his father felt the same way when he came back from a long trail drive. Probably, though he never showed it. A man covers up such feelings, never talks about them. Just the same, Jeff at least lived two lives and never quite brought the two of them together, never completely. He wondered if Loretta did too, if she didn't sometimes look at him and wonder what her life would be like if she had taken another fork, if she had married someone else.

They ate and talked, and Jeff asked if he had ever told about the geese he shot on one trail drive. Loretta said no, he'd never told them about shooting geese.

"It was somewhere up in the edge of Kansas," Jeff said. "On a little creek not more than ten feet wide. There were these two big geese, strange-looking birds for wild ones, but geese. And so I shot them and hung them on my saddle to give to the cook to dress out when we caught up with the wagon.

"Well, we rounded the next bend, and there was a cabin that hadn't been there the year before. Just a log cabin with a mud-and-stick chimney. And as we approached it a woman came out and stood looking at us, her hands wrapped in her apron. I watched her and she yelled at me, 'You shot my geese!'

"There wasn't any use denying that I'd shot the geese. There they were, right in plain sight. So I rode over to her and she gave me what-for. She'd been saving those geese to make new pillows."

Loretta smiled. "What did you do?"

"I offered her a beef for them. But she didn't want beef. She wanted feathers. She said we had to pick them for her. I held up the herd for two hours while we took turns, the hands and me, picking those geese and chasing feathers. I never knew there were so many feathers on a goose. We always skinned ducks and geese, but she wouldn't hear to that. We had to pick them for her."

"So she got her pillows," Loretta said.

"And we got the geese. I was set on having goose to eat, so I paid her a dollar apiece for them. She was as tickled as a kid with a kitten, and I couldn't figure why. Not till that evening, when the cook went to work on them. They must have been forty years old."

"Tough?"

"Tough as rawhide. Cook said he could have split one, put cinches on and used it for a saddle." Jeff cut himself another small slice of the goose in front of him, ate it, and said, "That's why my mouth didn't water when you said we were having roast goose today."

They all laughed, and a few minutes later Jenny brought in the mincemeat pie. Loretta said she was afraid the crust wasn't short enough, but she served it and Jeff announced that it was as good as any he'd ever tasted, anywhere. And he thought that it was good to be here, good to be here at the head of his own family table with Loretta and the girls, this Thanksgiving Day. There was only one thing missing. A son, a boy ten years old who should have been there at the table with them, eating and laughing and asking questions about far places and distant cities. A son who would grow up to be a whole man, a man to take up where Jeff left off.

They ate, and they went upstairs to the sitting room and the girls started a game of parchesi. Jeff went to the window and stood for some time, looking out at the steadily melting snow and not seeing it at all. Finally he turned abruptly and left the room. Loretta watched him, wondering what had happened. Then she sensed his purpose and she got to her feet to follow him and ask him not to go, tell him that Tommy would be sleeping now, that Bessie didn't like to have him wakened. Then she thought: Tommy is his child too.

She sat down again, and a moment later she heard the door to the third floor open and close.

Jeff went up the stairs and quietly opened the door to Tommy's room. The afternoon sun lay in a broad beam across the floor, almost dazzling after the darkness of the hallway. Then he saw Bessie Magruder, in her rocker, her knitting in her hands. She was always knitting, every time he saw her. He wondered what she did with those things she knitted, or if she raveled them out each night to have something to do the next day.

She turned, saw him, and got to her feet. Bessie, he thought, was a strangely unattractive woman, with no appeal in her for a man. Yet there was a wistfulness in her face, especially in her light blue eyes.

She put a finger to her mouth, cautioning him. He went in and Bessie whispered, "He's just got to sleep, Mister Ross. Maybe the missus told you he had a cold, but he's most over it now. But he needs his rest."

Jeff nodded. He tiptoed to the crib, looked down at the sleeping child. And he wondered why he had come up here. There was nothing he could do, nothing he could say. Here was a life, a twisted bit of life, his own child, his and Loretta's, which had no meaning and never would have. Jeff's begetting and Loretta's pain, and for what?

Oh, he had gone over it time and again. There was no answer. The doctors all said it happens now and then, some quirk of nature, some whim, perhaps, of God. Why should God be whimsical?

He turned away. Unbidden, the memory of Amy flashed at him. Amy, in the lobby of the Planter's Hotel in St. Louis, the last time he saw her. Just before the war. Amy saying, "We have things to remember." Saying, "I have a son. A son two years old."

He glanced again at the crib and wondered why a whimsical God had chosen this child to maim.

Then he felt Bessie Magruder watching him, had a vague feeling that she divined his thoughts. He glanced at her. "You say he's over the cold?"

"Most over it," she said.

"Good. I've been away, and—"

"Yes, I knew."

There seemed no more to say. He moved toward the doorway. Then he asked, "Did you have some of the roast goose?"

She nodded. "'Twas very good, thank you." Then she frowned. "But the pasty, it was a bit of a surprise. It tasted of hard liquor."

"Oh, the mincemeat pie." He saw by her look that she disapproved of hard liquor, even when its alcohol was all cooked out in mincemeat pie. He refrained from mentioning the brandy or saying that he thought the pie was very tasty. Loretta had said that Bessie was very good with Tommy, and she certainly was the neatest, cleanest nursemaid they had ever had. No need to offend her.

He said, "You seem to be doing very well with the boy, Bessie. I hope you know we all appreciate it."

"Thank you," Bessie said.

And Jeff turned and went back downstairs.

He hesitated at the second floor, then went on down to the first floor, got his hat and coat and went outdoors. To walk. To stop thinking, stop remembering, stop wondering about the forks in the trail that led here, to this place, to what he now was and what he now had.

He walked for an hour and came back and went to his bedroom and lay down and slept till dark, the weariness of the days at the ranch still upon him. When he got up, everything was back in place. He was a ranchman, a prosperous businessman, here in Denver, with his family around him on Thanksgiving Day.

They sat down to supper, and even Jane was in one of her sunnier moods. There was, Jeff decided, a good deal to be thankful for. A good deal more than he ever dreamed he would have when he first came up here into this country.

Later in the evening, when Jeff and Loretta were alone, Jeff spoke of Tommy. It was the first time in months that they had more than casually mentioned Tommy's name. Jeff spoke of his afternoon visit to the third floor and said, "Bessie seems to be working out all right, does she?"

"Very well indeed."

"And that cold he had, it's better? He was asleep when I went up."

"He has stopped coughing and he doesn't seem to have any fever. Yes, I think he's about over it. . . . Oh, Jeff, he's such a helpless little person!"

"I know. You had the doctor in, I hope."

"Of course. I sent for Dr. Crane, and he came and left some medicine and said we should use mustard plasters. To keep the cold from going into pneumonia."

"What else did he say? Anything?"

Jeff had talked to Crane back in August about Tommy. Crane had said, "There's not a thing anyone can do for the boy, Mr. Ross. He may live another ten years, or he may die in a convulsion next week. Nobody knows. But I doubt that he'll ever be any better than he is right now, no matter how long he lives." Jeff had gone to Crane's office after Crane had been to the house on a routine call and had examined Tommy and said the usual reassuring, hopeful things to Loretta. Crane was a kindly man, but in the office he had talked straight to Jeff. Jeff had asked him not to tell Loretta what he had just told Jeff, not even to tell her that Jeff had been to see him. And Crane, a tall, lean man with silvery hair and a cropped gray beard, had snapped, "Mr. Ross, what kind of a goddamned inconsiderate fool do you take me for?" And Jeff had said, "Thank you," and walked out.

Now Jeff asked Loretta, "What else did he say?"

"Practically nothing else. Just that Bessie seemed to be a very able nursemaid and that I was fortunate to have her. And he said for me to call him any time I needed him. But the plasters and the medicine he left broke up the cold, so I didn't send for him again."

"He's a good man," Jeff said. "Send for him any time."

Loretta said, "Jeff, we've never talked about this, and I hardly know how to say it now. But I know, I've always known, that you needed a son who—" She stopped, unable to go on.

"Tommy is my son," Jeff said firmly.

"Yes. But you need a son—well, a son who would grow up to be a man like you."

Jeff stared across the room. He didn't answer.

"Oh, Jeff, I hoped and hoped, and I prayed and I prayed!"

"Keep on hoping and praying." Jeff stared at his hands. "But if he's never any different—" He shrugged.

"Oh, Jeff! If I could only have another child!"

"I know." He glanced at her. "I bullied it out of old Doc Carter, there in Dallas. Before I took that trail herd to Baxter Springs."

"You went to see him then?"

"Yes."

The tears came, tears of relief, of secrets long kept and now revealed, as well as of heart-hurt over Tommy. She wiped her eyes with a handkerchief and said, "I'm glad you know. I'm glad you have known all the time, though I never could have told you."

He took her in his arms, then, and he felt her tears warm on his shirt. He stroked her hair and he said, "It's all right, Loretta, it's all right. This is the way it is, and there's no need for tears. Save the tears for grief." He kissed her, and he said, "Let's have no more talk. We've said what needs saying."

He blew out the lights in the sitting room and they went to her bedroom. It was a day of thanks.

8

A few days later Jeff met John Iliff on the street in downtown Denver. Iliff, an Ohioan who had come to Denver from Kansas in 1859, now lived in Cheyenne but had come down to Denver on business. He and Jeff were friends and fellow cattlemen, but they hadn't seen each other since the previous spring. Iliff suggested they step into the Hotel Tremont lobby and compare notes.

As they sat down, Iliff asked, "How many cattle have you got out there on the Bijou this year, Jeff?" He still spoke with a slight Ohio twang.

Jeff said, "About ten thousand." Then he amended, "If my men can turn up five hundred head or so that I couldn't account for last week."

"You were out there in that storm? It was a mean one." Iliff was a big man and he wore a clipped, rusty beard. He was only a few years older than Jeff, but he had ranches scattered almost two hundred miles along the South Platte as well as in Wyoming, and he owned shipping pens and a slaughterhouse in Cheyenne.

"My foreman's laid up with a broken leg," Jeff said. "I'm short-handed."

"Too bad. Any of my stock drifting your way?"

"Not that I know of. The only drifters we've seen were Bar H stuff, and just a few of those."

"Hilliard cattle." Iliff shook his head. "Unless Mrs. Hilliard gets things in hand those cattle will be scattered all the way to the Arkansas by spring." He glanced at Jeff, sharply. "I understand you know Mrs. Hilliard."

"I knew her some years ago." Jeff wondered where Iliff had picked that up. "She's a niece of John Laughlin, a commission man I used to deal with in St. Louis."

"She mentioned your name, said she knew you. A personable woman, and capable, I suppose. But she's got a problem on her hands with that ranch Matt started. You knew Matt?"

"I never met him."

"Matt was a shrewd trader, but no stockman. He seemed to think a ranch would run itself, like a farm. And the man he put in charge there was so incompetent I had to fire him. Do you know Tim Roberts?"

"I met him just once. I understand Matt Hilliard is dead now."

"Died last spring. Matt was getting along in years. She's much younger, as you know. Quite pretty. After Matt died she came to me and wanted me to buy the ranch. I told her I had no need for the place, but I did offer to take the cattle off her hands. Matt didn't have much of an investment there, and I advised her to give up the place. But she didn't care for my advice. Said she would run it herself rather than do that. She got quite angry when I told her the crew she had there was a bunch of riff-raff."

Jeff could see Amy bristling. Amy would have a high opinion of her own business judgment, and she would take it as a personal affront when Iliff, or anyone, criticized the men working for her.

"So she's running it herself?" Jeff knew she was, but he wanted more of Iliff's opinion of her.

"After a fashion. She sold her beef last summer, but not to me. Then she brought in a fresh herd. Sent Tim Roberts to New Mexico for them, I believe. And if I know Roberts, she paid first-class prices for third-class cattle. What I've seen of them were a scrubby-looking lot. She's a pretty stubborn woman."

"She always liked to have her own way."

"What she doesn't realize—what nobody but a cattleman realizes—is that it takes more than grass and water to make a going ranch. But you and I have discussed that before. We agree right down the line. . . . Are you going to let me have some of your beef to ship next year?"

"That depends, John."

"On what?"

"On my beef, and your price."

Iliff smiled and got to his feet. "We'll talk price when I see your beef." And as they went to the door he said, "If my cattle start drifting your way, I'll thank you for holding them if you can. My men will do the same for you, though your stuff won't drift north unless they get mixed up with the buffalo."

"I'll do that." They were on the street. "Tell me, John, what kind of a winter are we going to have?"

"A bad one. Every winter's bad, Jeff, one way or another." Then he smiled. "But if we didn't have rough winters, everybody in Texas would move in on us. As it is, only the bold ones, the real ranchers like Jeff Ross, come and stay. . . . Good to see you. Come see me, in Cheyenne. And convey my regards to Mrs. Ross."

When Jeff told Bill Sanders what he had heard from John Iliff, Bill said, "I shouldn't be surprised if this winter cleans out the Hilliard ranch."

"Why do you say that?" Jeff asked.

"I saw the herd they brought in last summer. Never saw such a bunch of scrubs. We gave better culls than that to the Indians."

"Oh, I thought you meant the weather was going to clean them out."

"It will."

The weather had been mild since Thanksgiving, and Jeff had begun to hope, until last night, that it might continue good until the end of the year. "Then you don't like the look of it?" he said.

"I don't like the smell of it."

Jeff laughed. "Stop smelling. When you start smelling weather, you always smell trouble."

"You saw that moon last night, didn't you?"

"Yes, I saw that circle around it. It could mean rain."

"You're talking like Sam Royce, Jeff!"

"I know it." Jeff shook his head. "I just keep hoping it won't come, Bill, for another month. All I want is one more month for them on all the grass they can eat. Then they can take it."

Bill pointed to the sky. "See that high haze? Thin, but haze, for sure."

"I guess we'd better put new shoes on those two ponies I brought in from the ranch," Jeff said.

The storm didn't come that day, but the overcast thickened

by noon of the next day and the wind shifted to the east. The temperature began to fall and there was no sunset, just a creeping shadow of night. By full dark the wind had shifted to the northeast. Jeff went out to the stable about nine o'clock, and felt the first few spits of snow in his face. He went to Bill's room, was surprised to find Bill sitting beside the stove, smoking his pipe and drinking coffee. Bill usually went to bed on the dot of nine.

Bill looked up, startled, as Jeff came in. Jeff had the feeling that something was up. "Any of the horses sick?" he asked.

"Well—" Bill hesitated. "Well, I was just out and looked at Lady. And the ponies. I was just going to turn in."

"With your boots on, I suppose." Bill was fully dressed.

Bill grinned sheepishly. "I was out looking at the weather, Jeff. Damn it, she's coming on to snow again. I told you I smelled it coming."

"So you decided to head for the ranch."

"No! No, Jeff, I was just—well just wishing I *could* go."

"Take off your boots," Jeff ordered.

"What for?"

"Take them off."

Bill slowly worked the boots from his feet. Jeff picked them up, turned toward the door.

"Hey!" Bill cried. "Where you going with those?"

"Back to the house. I'll bring them out to you in the morning, when I'm ready to go. You won't need them till then." Jeff smiled. "I just want to be sure you're around to saddle a horse for me, not freezing to death in a snowdrift somewhere between here and the ranch, with a crocked leg. . . . Good night, Bill."

And he closed the door behind him. He could hear Bill cursing until he left the stable, but he knew Bill had only the one pair of boots here in Denver, and he knew that even Bill would not ride away without his boots.

He took them into the house, put them under his desk in his office, closed the door and went upstairs and to bed. He would be up early, make a pot of coffee, take Bill's boots out to him, come back and eat a snack of breakfast, and be on his way to the ranch. For another bout with a storm, and with Sam Royce.

He went to sleep almost at once, but he wakened about an hour later, went to the window and looked out. It was still snowing, harder now, and the wind still held in the northeast. He went back to bed, wishing it was daylight.

He slept again, and again he wakened. This time he knew it was a noise that had wakened him. He lay listening. All he could hear was the tick of a clock. Then he heard a door open somewhere. Downstairs, he thought. He got out of bed, went to the window. There was about three inches of snow on the window ledge. He stood there listening, and now he heard the cautious sound of a door being closed. At the back of the house. He wasn't sure, but he thought he saw a figure moving in the snowy darkness, going from the house to the stable. Then he heard the faint squeak of a hinge on the stable door, opening and closing.

Jeff quietly closed the window, pulled on his pants and tucked in his nightshirt. He picked up his boots and hurried downstairs. The clock in the hallway was striking midnight.

He lit a match, saw that the door to his office was open. He went in, looked under his desk. Bill's boots were gone, just as he had expected. He put on a heavy coat, took hat and gloves and went out the back door. Fresh footprints led to the stable.

He hurried through the stable, hoping he was in time. But Bill apparently had the ponies ready before he came to the house to get his boots. Both ponies were gone, and Bill's saddle was missing. Jeff went back to Bill's room, found a lantern and lit it, picked up a bridle and hurried to Lady's stall. Lady, Loretta's horse, was the only decent riding horse left. He thrust the bit in her mouth, slipped the headstall over her ears and led her to the doorway, not even waiting to get a saddle. He mounted bareback and rode down the alley. The ponies' tracks were there ahead of him, less than ten minutes old.

Jeff caught up with Bill at the edge of town. Bill was riding at an easy trot, just settling down for the long trip, when he heard Lady loping behind him. He pulled over close to a clump of cottonwoods and stopped, hoping Jeff might not see him, knowing that was impossible. He simply waited, and Jeff rode up, drew Lady to a stop and said, "To the rear, Sergeant Sanders. Back to bivouac." There was both amusement and exasperation in his voice.

Bill didn't say a word. He reined his pony around and they rode back to the house side by side, up the alleyway to the stable.

Bill got down and opened the door and they led the horses in and to their stalls. Bill loosened the cinch on his saddle, swung it off the pony. Jeff reached to take it, return it to the saddle room. "I'll bring mine," he said.

Bill turned to him and snapped, "I'm no cripple, goddamn it!" His eyes were afire with anger and frustration.

"Sergeant," Jeff said, in his most officious cavalry officer voice, "the penalty for cursing a superior office is forty-eight hours confined to quarters."

They were the first words spoken between them since Jeff had caught up with Bill at the edge of town.

Bill said, "Yes." Then added, "Sir." He hesitated just a moment, then said, "I suggest, sir, that you take off that nightshirt and change to the uniform of the day before you start."

"Very well," Jeff growled, and he turned and went through the stable and back to the house. He held in his laughter till he was in the kitchen.

He started to build up the fire and make coffee, then changed his mind. If he knew Bill, there would be fresh coffee on Bill's stove by the time he had changed clothes and said good-bye to Loretta. So he went to his room, put on his ranch clothes and went across the hallway to Loretta's room.

He wakened her and she sat up with a start and exclaimed, "Jeff! What's the matter?"

"Nothing. I'm heading for the ranch."

She looked at him, bewildered. "What time is it?"

"A little after midnight. I couldn't sleep so I decided I'd better get going."

She yawned and rubbed her eyes, then started to get out of bed. "I'll go down and make coffee."

"Don't bother. Coffee's making." He leaned over the bed and kissed her. "Don't expect me back till you see me coming. No telling what this storm is going to do."

She clung to him, rubbed her cheek against his. "Oh, I wish you didn't have to go. But you do, don't you?"

"Yes, Loretta."

"I had a bad dream, Jeff. I dreamed you were still away, in the war. And you were hurt, somewhere."

He stood up again, holding her hands. "Go back to sleep, and

130

dream a pleasant dream." He patted her cheek and blew out the lamp he had brought from his room. "Good-bye," he said again, and he closed her door and went down the stairs and back to the stable.

As he had expected, Bill had the coffee made. He was sitting on his bunk, waiting, the two tin cups set out on the table. Bill was in his sock feet, his boots under the table. It was his gesture of capitulation. He got up from the bunk, poured the coffee and Jeff took his and stood there, trying to sip it. Bill took his cup and returned to sit on the bunk and wait for it to cool.

"This could be it, Jeff," Bill said. "This could be a bad one, one of those that start slow and keep coming."

"It could be."

"I just hope there's enough wind with it."

"To keep the ridges bare."

"Ride hell out of Sam, Jeff. He ain't afraid of work, if you just tell him what to do."

"I'll keep him going."

Jeff looked at Bill over the rim of his coffee cup, at Bill's long jaw and beaked nose and sun-faded blue eyes. They'd seen a lot of miles together. He saw Bill's crooked left arm and thought of that day on Pea Ridge, and of that other day at Corinth. He remembered Bill saying, at Baxter Springs, "I'll go along, Jeff. Where are you going?" And at the Bijou, the day Jeff knew it was the place he had been looking for; and Jeff asked Bill to be his partner, and Bill said all he wanted was to be Jeff's foreman. Bill was his right hand. He almost told Bill to pull on his boots and saddle the other pony and come along.

Then he saw Bill reach for the boots, and Jeff knew what he had to do. He drained the cup and set it on the table and said, "I'll close things up. You go on to bed. Get some sleep."

Bill looked at him, reproach in his eyes and with it a measure of relief. Jeff knew that those three or four miles in the saddle had set Bill's leg to throbbing, maybe twinged the slowly knitting bones with a warning.

Bill said, "You can push those ponies right along, Jeff. They're in good shape. I've been graining them hard."

"Go on to bed," Jeff said, and he knew his voice was gruff. He picked up the lighted lantern and went out into the stable and led the ponies from their stalls. He opened the alley door, led the ponies outside, blew out the lantern and hung it on its peg at the doorway. Then he closed the doors, mounted the flea-bitten roan that Bill had saddled for him and was on his way.

It wasn't a bad night to be traveling, not half as bad as that night three weeks ago when Jeff was making his way to the ranch with the blacks and the light wagon. It was cold but not bitter, and the snow was coming in soft, wet flakes instead of icy pellets driven by a lashing wind.

Jeff settled into the saddle and let the ponies take up the slow, easy foxtrot that ate up the miles without shaking a rider's guts loose. The led-horse, the spare, held back for a mile or so, then resigned itself to the journey and trotted alongside. The snow wasn't yet deep enough to be bothersome.

Jeff thought of Bill, thought what a bungler he would be as a burglar. Bill just wasn't cut out to do anything underhanded. Then he thought of the look Bill gave him when Jeff ordered him back to the stable and put on the hell-for-leather cavalry officer act. He had half expected Bill to laugh at him. Jeff had almost laughed at himself. But Bill was too chagrined to laugh.

Strange, Jeff thought, jogging along in the snowy darkness, that he should have been playing soldier with Bill just when Loretta was dreaming about him in the war. It all seemed so far away and long ago. It was long ago, and it was far away; and yet Loretta still dreamed about it, and Bill carried it with him every day of his life, in that crooked arm. And something of it was in Jeff, though he had thought he purged himself of it long ago.

When he joined up with Van Dorn he told himself it was for The Cause, because he was a Texan and a Southerner. Which was true, but certainly not the whole truth. He went off to the war to get away. It was one of the few times in his life that he consciously ran away from anything. But there he was, in a marriage of his own making that didn't seem to have any meaning, on a road that seemed to lead nowhere. It was his own fault. He had made the choices. But there he was, in his own trap, and the war seemed to be a way out. An honorable way. So he went, not caring very much whether he ever came back.

But out of that going, that attempt to get away, he came to everything that mattered now. In the war he met Bill Sanders, who meant more to him than any other man alive. And he came back to Loretta and eventually made his peace with life, life with her. And, strangely, he came to know, to respect, and to dislike Earl Van Dorn, who was one of the two or three outstanding men he ever met.

Jeff drew the ponies to a walk and looked around for landmarks. He should be coming to Schuyler Station before long. He could see only about two rods in any direction, seemed to be in a little circular world of shifting white that hadn't changed one iota since he left Denver. But he knew that the ponies weren't on a treadmill, and his instinct told him that he was still following the wagon track with the railroad just there to his right. To be sure, however, he reined his pony around, rode five rods or so south, and came to the tracks, each rail with a shallow drift on its lee side. Satisfied, he returned to the wagon road and turned east again, the wind on his left cheek. He would follow the road to the Kiowa Crossing, then angle northeast to the ranch, take the short cut. If everything went right he would be at the Kiowa by daylight.

He rode on, watching for bare patches on the hilltops, for proof that the snow was blowing and that the ridges might be clear. But the wind wasn't blowing hard enough to move the heavy, wet snow. It seemed to pack right into the grass, stay where it fell. He wished the temperature would drop or the wind would rise, or both. It would make harder going for him, but it would be better for his cattle. A ranchman thinks of his stock before he thinks of himself.

He smiled, remembering the Dutchman and his rules for officers. Jeff could see the emphatic thrust of Van Dorn's goatee as he said, "Forage for your horses before you forage for your men. Hay won't win battles, but lack of hay will lose them."

Thinking of it now, Jeff knew that it was one of his own rules as a ranchman. Grass can't create a herd of cattle, but lack of grass can leave you with nothing but rotting carcasses. Keep your cattle foraged and you'll never starve.

Van Dorn, he thought, would have made a cattleman. He had the drive and the basic understanding of a problem. Instead, he was a soldier, son of a Mississippi lawyer, and a West Pointer. The name was Holland Dutch, but the Dutch blood was well diluted by the time it got to him. On his mother's side he was related to Andrew Jackson's wife. That accounted for the other nickname, the one Van Dorn detested—"Old Slippery Elm." Nobody called him that to his face, but he knew about it, and undoubtedly he knew the reason for it. He was inordinately proud of the tenuous Jackson connection and often spoke with admiration of "Old Hickory." He hoped to go as far as Jackson did.

For a time, Jeff knew Van Dorn rather well. He was on Van Dorn's staff for a couple of months and Van Dorn liked to call him in on some pretext and spend an hour talking. Lecturing, really. He had been in Mexico and the Seminole hostilities, and he had arrow wounds from the action against the Comanches at Washita Station. He was an able cavalry leader and he aspired to large command in the Confederacy. Command was his passion, his obsession.

One day he called Jeff in and, without preamble, said, "Ross, a man has to follow his star, and that star is his conscience. Nobody knows as much about any man as he knows about himself. The tragedy comes when he refuses to face his own knowledge."

"You mean, sir, that every man should know his own weakness?" Jeff asked. He had no idea what Van Dorn was coming to, whether he was going to give Jeff a dressing down or what.

"Precisely," Van Dorn said. "I also mean that he should know —*must* know—his own strength."

And Jeff knew it was just another lecture, probably on command. He settled back.

"And," Van Dorn went on, "if he aspires to distinguished command, he must be able to communicate that knowledge. To his men, of course. But also to his superiors in command." He hesitated, glanced at Jeff, then said, "Old Hickory had that ability to a superlative degree. Every outstanding leader has it."

Jeff had always been one to speak his mind. He wondered, even then, if that wasn't why Van Dorn kept him on his staff. Jeff said, "I wonder, sir, if successful command doesn't also depend on the forces you have." He remembered that because of Van Dorn's answer.

"No commander," Van Dorn said, "is any better than the reserves at his disposal. He must be prepared to exploit a favorable situation." Then he smiled. "I believe the women have a rule that applies. 'Never wear your most devastating gown unless you know the man you want will be at the ball. *But have the gown!*" He chuckled. "I have observed that the clever woman always manages to produce the enticing gown. She has her reserves."

Jeff had never thought of Major Van Dorn as a ladies' man, but you never can tell. He was married to a charming woman to whom he occasionally referred as "my lady, Caroline."

Jeff remembered no other details of that morning's talk. It probably lasted for an hour or so, and no doubt Van Dorn brought out an assortment of rules and aphorisms. He had an odd mixture of textbookishness and frontier common sense. And now and then he came out with something like that rule of foraging for your stock before you foraged for yourself.

Jeff learned a good deal from Van Dorn, and it could be that Van Dorn learned a few things from Jeff's practical, trail-spiced observations. The only other talk he remembered in any detail was their last one. He saw Van Dorn a few times after that, but only briefly and in the presence of orderlies, for Van Dorn became a general officer. This talk was in the summer of '61. Van Dorn sent for him. Jeff walked into his office and sensed that something important had happened. He saw it in Van Dorn's face, in the set of his chin and goatee.

"Lieutenant Ross," Van Dorn said, "I have a question to ask."

"Yes, sir."

"If you were presented with the opportunity to advance into a position of higher command—" Van Dorn hesitated, then said, "I am speaking in confidence."

"I understand, sir."

"Would you accept?"

"If it were in the cavalry, sir, I would consider it."

Van Dorn frowned. "I spoke of *higher* command."

Jeff waited a moment, then said, "I prefer to remain in the cavalry, sir."

Van Dorn cleared his throat and shuffled the papers on his desk. "You are a forthright man, Ross. I appreciate that, but—" He cleared his throat again. "You have a capacity for command."

"I am not a professional soldier," Jeff said, "and I don't intend to become one. I have been a drover, and I intend to become a cattleman."

135

"I need men like you." It was the nearest to a plea that Jeff ever heard from him.

"I am at your service, sir," Jeff said, "as long as I remain in the cavalry."

Van Dorn sighed. "Very well." He picked up a paper from his desk. "I sent for you to present this."

Jeff took the paper, glanced at it. It was a commission as captain of cavalry, C.S.A. It was made out to Thomas Jefferson Ross. Jeff said, "Why, thank you sir. This is a surprise!" It was, a complete surprise.

"Merited," Van Dorn said stiffly. Then he held out his hand. "I wished to present it to you in person." He gave Jeff a thin smile. "Good hunting, Captain." And he turned back to his desk.

Two days later word came, officially, that Major Van Dorn was now Brigadier General Van Dorn. It was months before Jeff saw him again, even at a distance. In September Van Dorn became a major general, and in January he became commander of the whole Trans-Mississippi District. And Jeff knew that he had, that day in Van Dorn's office, turned down the opportunity to go up with Van Dorn into the area of top command.

He had often wondered what would have happened had he agreed to go along with Earl Van Dorn. But there he was at a fork in the trail, and he made his choice. There had been moments of regret, but they were long past. He knew now that he had chosen right. His destiny lay the way he had come.

Strange, he thought now, that Van Dorn came to his mind the first time he met John Iliff. There was little physical resemblance between the two men. Both wore beards and both were big, disciplined men. But there was a rasping quality about Van Dorn, a military waspishness, that made many men dislike him. John Iliff made friends, and kept them. But both men had the drive, the ambition, the sense of purpose that mark a leader. Both could see the big picture beyond the details. And both knew what they wanted, never lost sight of it.

Jeff first met Iliff in the summer of '67. Iliff had set up a cow camp on Crow Creek not far from the Union Pacific construction camp at Cheyenne and was selling beef to the railroad construction crews. Jeff had about two hundred head of grass-fat cattle from the herd he'd brought to the Bijou the year before. There weren't enough to trail to a distant market, but he wanted to turn them into cash and go down to Charley Goodnight's place on the Arkansas and buy Texas cows. So he took a spare horse and a bedroll and rode north to see Iliff at his Crow Creek camp.

Iliff was reserved but friendly. "You say you've got a place down on the Bijou?" he asked.

"That's right. I came in there last year."

"Where from?"

"Texas. I brought my wife and my family."

Iliff looked surprised. "Oh? You plan on staying, then?"

"As long as I live. As long as there's grass and water."

Iliff smiled. "I thought you might be a drover who got caught up here and had to winter over." Iliff's camp was just a couple of unpeeled log cabins and a layout of sheds and corrals. Iliff didn't waste money or labor on buildings. He provided adequate shelter, plenty of food, and expected his men to tend cattle. Cattle fattened and multiplied; buildings didn't.

"How many fat cattle have you got?" Iliff asked.

Jeff told him. "Not enough for a long drive to a big market, but next year I'll have more."

Iliff nodded. "That's good grass you've got." He had been sizing up Jeff, apparently approved. "I guess I can take them off your hands," he said.

Jeff shook his head. "I don't want anyone to take them off my hands. I want to sell them, at a fair price. More than I would get in Denver."

"I'd have to see them."

"Mr. Iliff," Jeff said, "I've heard that you are a fair man, a man whose word can be depended on. I give you my word that these are good cattle, not culls. They are grass-fat and good beef, all young stuff. No cows and no old rannies. I'm keeping my cows, and I didn't bring in any rannies."

Iliff considered and finally named a price. It was too low, but it was a bargaining point. They dealt back and forth and finally reached agreement. "If," Iliff said, "they are as you represent them. When can you deliver them?"

"Three weeks from today." Jeff wanted time to gather them and time to graze them all the way, not travel the flesh off of them.

They shook hands on the agreement. Iliff asked, "Where are

you going for your new herd? Back to Texas?"

"Next year," Jeff said. "I haven't time or men, this year. I'll have to buy from Goodnight this year. But the time will come when I will grow my own steers. I think I can grow bigger steers up here than they're growing in Texas."

Iliff smiled. "Right! How do you plan to do it?"

"By picking the best cows I can find and breeding them to the best bulls. Probably not Texas bulls, but—"

"Mr. Ross, I'd like to show you something." Iliff was holding down his sense of excitement, but he was obviously pleased. He led the way to a far corral. In it were a dozen steers as big as Jeff's two-year-olds and somewhat heavier. Their horns were shorter than those of Texas cattle, their legs were shorter, their shoulders and rumps broader. Jeff liked their looks.

"How old would you say they are?" Iliff asked.

"Two-year-olds."

Iliff smiled. "They're long yearlings. I picked the heaviest Texas cows I had and bred them to a Shorthorn bull. This is the first cross. When I breed the heifers to the Shorthorn, the get will be even better."

Iliff had already done what Jeff hoped to do. They thought along the same line. Jeff knew that even Texas calves grew bigger on this northern grass. If he had better calves to begin with—well, Iliff was showing him, right now, the results.

Jeff said, "You're one jump ahead of me, Mr. Iliff."

"You'll catch up," Iliff said. "Anyone who wants to stay in business up here will have to come to it. There's a market for Texas beef right now, but things are changing. It won't be long before we ship cattle directly to the eastern market by rail. You can't really fatten a Longhorn, make prime beef out of him. What will be needed is heavy beef, and we can grow it even from Texas cows, if we breed to good bulls. Get some Shorthorn blood into your calves."

"Where," Jeff asked, "can I get Shorthorn bulls at a price I can afford?"

"I'll look around. Maybe I can put you on the track of one or two when you bring those cattle in."

That was John Iliff, and that was the beginning of Jeff's friendship with him. Iliff saw change coming, anticipated it. He was what

Jeff called a big man, a man with a sense of command.

Jeff and Bill took the fat steers to Crow Creek and Iliff found them as Jeff had represented them. When the deal was closed he said, "I have two bulls for you. Do you want them?"

"I'd have to see them," Jeff said, and Iliff smiled, remembering his own words.

They went to the farthest corral. There were two bulls, one red and white, the other roan. They were blocky, heavily built animals, and they had the mark of the yoke on them. Jeff looked at them, frowning.

When Jeff made no comment, Iliff said, "Well?"

Jeff said, "That's a pair of work cattle."

Iliff nodded. "Yes. They came from Iowa under yoke. An immigrant came through with them last week, and I swapped him a pair of good work steers for them. They're grade bulls, and they're about seven years old. But they've got a lot of calves in them. They're better than anything you've got, aren't they?"

Jeff asked, "What's your price?"

"What are they worth to you?"

"I just sold my beef to you at your price," Jeff said. "Are you offering these work bulls to me at my price?"

Iliff's beard twitched; then he burst into laughter. "Name your price and we'll see." Then he added, "I guarantee nothing about them except that they are sound. They are bulls, and they are Shorthorns, but certainly not pure bred. They are thin and trail-worn now. Maybe they won't get a calf for you. Do you want to gamble?"

Jeff named a price. They finally agreed on a hundred and twenty-five dollars, the going price for a pair of sound work oxen in Denver.

So Jeff bought his first Shorthorn bulls, thanks to John Iliff. The blood of the roan bull still showed in his herd. He was a good bull, active and with a predominant strain in all the calves he sired. His yoke-mate, the red and white one, never sired a dozen calves. As Bill said, he wasn't worth his keep. But Jeff kept him on. And two years later he brought in six really good Shorthorn bulls from Ohio. By then he was handling five or six thousand Texas steers a year besides his own calves. He was on his way.

And by then John Iliff had cow camps scattered along the

South Platte all the way to Julesburg. John Iliff was a rich man, the biggest cattleman in the whole region.

Jeff put the memories aside. The pony he was riding was beginning to tire in the deepening snow. Jeff drew up and got out of the saddle to relieve himself and stretch his legs. The cold wasn't biting too deep; it wouldn't have cut into him as deep, anyway, because a man in a saddle is exercising all the time.

There were about six inches of wet, heavy snow, the kind that Jeff particularly disliked. Not only did it stay where it fell, but if the weather turned cold it would ice over with a cruel crust.

He loosened the cinch, put the saddle on the spare pony, which danced and humped its back. He bridled it, put the lead rope on the pony he had been riding, and mounted again. The brief exercise had loosened his muscles, warmed him comfortably.

He rode on, and half an hour later saw the first hint of dawn, a faint lightening in the sky ahead. Then he began to see landmarks, knew he was approaching the Kiowa crossing.

He crossed the Kiowa, took his bearings from the ridge beyond the creek, and headed northeast, directly toward the ranch. The wind was in his face now, and the ponies didn't like it. Jeff had to hold them into it for almost a mile before they got it into their heads that they were going home. Then they set their own course and pace, shuffling into a heavy-footed trot on the down slopes. They, too, now were eager to get under shelter and have something to eat.

Jeff thought again of Earl Van Dorn and John Iliff, two strong men who followed their stars, as Van Dorn had put it. "A man has to follow his star, and that star is his conscience." Jeff could accept the first part, but he wasn't so sure that a man's conscience was really his star. Anyway, they followed their stars, the soldier and the cattleman, as Jeff had tried to follow his own destiny. Van Dorn was dead now, the war fought and lost. John Iliff was the most successful cattleman in the whole region.

What now of your star?

Jeff didn't know, couldn't figure it out. But he did know that he had made the right choice when Van Dorn had suggested that Jeff was meant for military command. Jeff had turned it down. He had chosen the right fork. Maybe all the other forks along the way had been of minor importance. Or does a man ever know?

His pony pricked its ears and looked to the right. Jeff turned and thought he could make out a group of moving shadows. Cattle, maybe? He reined the horse and rode toward the shadows, and even before he could make out the details he knew it was not a herd of cattle. Cattle drift ahead of a storm, and these animals were doggedly heading into it. Buffalo.

Jeff rode toward them until he could make out the herd, make a rough count. There were only fifty or sixty head of them. He watched as they went past, their shaggy heads and heavy shoulders plastered with the snow. Of the whole herd, only one old bull paid him any attention. The bull paused, turned his head and looked for a long moment at the man and the two ponies, then shook his snowy head and plodded on, nose down, beard almost touching the snow.

Jeff waited several minutes, to see if another band was close behind. Apparently not. This must be just a small, isolated band, not part of a big herd. But their presence was disturbing. They should be far south of here, below the Arkansas. They might have drifted north in the previous storm, but when it cleared they should have turned back south again. Apparently these hadn't, and now they were moving still farther north, heading into the storm as buffalo always did. He wondered how many more were out there somewhere, plodding relentlessly northeast.

There was no telling. He finally swung the ponies into the tracks left by the buffalo band and followed them about two miles along the ridge. Then he turned east, pointing toward the ranch again. Another hour, maybe an hour and a half, and he should be there.

9

Only Harvey Bird and Pete Wallace were at the ranch. Sam Royce was riding the camp circuit. "Thought he might be in last night," Harvey said, spooning pancake batter into the frying pan. "Guess he holed up at East Camp."

Jeff sat in front of the fire, steaming coffee cup in his hands. The morning chores were finished when he arrived, and the house was swept and orderly. Both Harvey and Pete were dawn-risers and both had a sense of neatness. Pete was at the table, carefully cutting narrow strips from a grained cowhide, working round and round. Harvey was helping him braid a rawhide *reata*.

"Where'd you learn to make a *reata*?" Jeff asked.

"Down South," Harvey said vaguely. He reached for a tin plate, put the pancakes on it and set it on the end of the table for Jeff. Jeff reached for the molasses jug and began to eat. Harvey set another batch of cakes to fry for him.

"Seen any buffalo?" Jeff asked.

Harvey shook his head.

"I ran onto a little bunch."

"Where?"

"On the ridge this side of Kiowa Crossing."

"How many?"

"Fifty, sixty head."

"Just one bunch?"

"That's all I saw. But if they're this far up, there may be more coming."

Harvey nodded. He took a pot to the big bag of dried beans, scooped in a dozen handfuls, added half a pot of water and set the pot in the coals at the end of the fireplace. He tossed in half a dozen chunks of venison and three dried chile peppers from one of the strings at the end of the mantel. The beans would simmer all day and be ready to eat by evening.

Jeff looked at the strings of red chiles and thought of Loretta. When they came north, Loretta brought along a bag of dried chiles and as she used them in cooking that winter she saved the seeds from the best ones. When spring came, Bill Sanders took a spade and made her a little garden patch on the sheltered south side of the house. She planted chile peppers, weeded, watered and tended them as carefully as though they were flowers. When they ripened she made strings of them and hung the colorful pods beside the fireplace. When they moved to Denver, Bill took over the chile patch. Those strings of red pods hanging there now were from Loretta's original seeds, though Bill had grown them.

Loretta once said, "I think I would grow chiles even if I never used them. Just seeing them hanging there makes me know that summer is coming again, no matter how hard it storms."

Jeff looked at the warm red of the peppers now and thought: Yes, summer will come, all right. But not tomorrow. We're going to get a lot of storms, a lot of snow, before it's summer again.

Harvey had finished his house chores. Pete put away the hide and the *reata* strips and they got into their bad-weather gear. As they started out the door Jeff said, "Saddle a fresh pony for me."

Harvey said, "You've been out all night."

"Only half the night." Jeff reached for his boots.

Ten minutes later the boys were back, leading a fresh pony with Jeff's saddle. He got into his coat and went out and mounted.

They crossed at the ford and headed downstream. The snow was six inches deep and still coming, with no sign of letting up. The wind held in the northeast, light but steady.

They worked downsteam, watching for cattle in the timber. The snow, which had drifted hardly at all, was as deep on the hilltops as down in the timber. The cattle weren't really yarded; they were merely taking shelter and they weren't difficult to move. But once they had been driven to the hilltops they found nothing to eat and as soon as the men had ridden on the cattle returned to the timber. But they had broken trail, tracked up the snow.

By noon Jeff knew it was hopeless. The snow wasn't going to let up. If anything, it was getting worse, and the wind had begun to rise and the temperature to drop. They were still three miles above Cottonwood Camp. Jeff said, "Pete, you go on down to Cottonwood. Have a good look along the way, see how many cattle are in the timber, but don't waste time getting them out. Just have a look, then head for home. I don't like the feel of this. The smell, as Bill would say. Harvey and I will head out toward Kiowa a ways and see if we can find any trace of those buffalo."

Pete left them, was soon lost in the thickening curtain of snow. Jeff and Harvey turned west, onto the hills between the Kiowa and the Bijou. They rode two miles, the horses slogging through the snow, the wind rising. Jeff was about ready to turn back when he thought he saw tracks on the hill just beyond. They pushed on.

Jeff had been right. On the hilltop were the meandering furrows, now half snowed over, of what must have been his band of buffalo. They had been traveling slowly and several times they had backtracked to eat the tall grass that had been uncovered by their passage. Harvey's horse kicked up a fresh buffalo chip, the typical round, compact dropping, quite different from cow dung. And Jeff knew it had been a band of buffalo and that they had been past here about two hours ago. The tracks led northeast.

The wind had begun to have a bite and frozen pellets of snow rattled against Jeff's saddle like sand in a dust storm.

"Let's go home," he said, "while we can get there. By tomorrow those buffalo will be halfway to the Platte. Or bunched up in the breaks north of Cottonwood."

They turned and headed for the ranch, the wind quartering behind them. The temperature was dropping and the wet, heavy snow was beginning to crust. Before they had gone a mile the pellet snow was drifting ahead of them in swirling waves on the hardening crust.

Jeff wished he hadn't sent Pete on to Cottonwood. Or that he hadn't told him to come back to the ranch. Pete might have some bad going, and this wasn't going to be a night to wander in the open.

For an hour or so the drive of the wind and the prospect of food and shelter urged the horses on. Then the crust began to cut their legs, and for the last two miles Jeff and Harvey took turns breaking trail. Their horses were wincing at every step.

It was full dark when they reached the ford. As they crossed the black water and headed for the barn Jeff saw a light at the house. It was unlikely that Pete had beaten them home, so it must be Sam.

At the barn they found Sam's horse. Harvey looked at its legs, saw that they were unscarred. "He got in early this afternoon," Harvey announced. Jeff grained the horses and Harvey got the turpentine and axle grease to dose their legs.

"I wish Pete was here," Jeff said.

"He'll be in."

"It would be a bad night to have to walk in. Or hole up with the cattle in a yard somewhere."

"He'll be in," Harvey repeated.

Harvey was right. They were just leaving the barn when they heard a shout from the ford. Jeff waited and Pete came in, stripped off his saddle and said, "Thanks for breaking trail!"

"You followed us all the way in?"

"All the way." Pete laughed and went to work on his horse with the turpentine and axle grease. Jeff went to the house.

Sam grinned at him from the fireplace, where he was raking fresh coals up over the Dutch oven. "Thought I'd have company for supper. So I made biscuits to go with the beans."

"When did you get in?"

"A while back. No use holing up, with a storm building."

"Did you see any buffalo?"

Sam laughed. "This time of year?"

"They're on the move."

"They can't be! They're all down south."

"Not all of them." Jeff hung up his coat and came to the fire to warm himself.

Pete came in.

"You too?" Sam said.

"Me too." Pete turned to Jeff. "I followed those buffalo tracks up to where you and Harvey cut them, then followed your trail on in."

"Did you see them?" Jeff asked. "The buffalo, I mean."

Pete nodded. "I thought at first it was a bunch of elk. They were just west of Cottonwood, and—"

"I'll bet they *were* elk," Sam said.

"Yeah. Shorthorn elk, with beards." Pete turned to Jeff again. "They were heading northeast, probably toward those breaks."

"You saw them, then?"

"Rode right up to them. But I didn't follow them. It was starting to blow and you'd said to come back here. I figured if I was coming in I'd better come. So I followed their trail back. Till I found where you and Harvey struck the trail and turned around."

"Well, I'll be damned!" Sam turned back to his biscuits. "Buffalo are all supposed to be down south. Down below the Arkansas."

They ate, and even before they had finished the wind was howling in the pines and whistling at the corners of the house. The pellet snow rattled like sand on the door and at the windows. Another hour and the room began to chill uncomfortably despite the roaring fire. The temperature dropped steadily.

It was a bad night, and the next day was no better. The wind blew a gale and the snow continued, drifting badly. They reached the barn and did the chores, but when Jeff tried to get to the creek for a pail of water he had to give up. The earlier snow had a two-inch crust of ice and he couldn't stay on his feet in the open. The wind knocked him down, sent him spinning. Jeff groped his way back to the house and they melted snow for water.

There was nothing to do but wait it out.

The blizzard roared for two nights and two days. The temperature dropped till they could hear the trees popping. Jeff made a guess at somewhere between thirty and forty degrees below zero.

When the wind finally eased off there were ten-foot drifts back of the house. Where the wind had blown full blast the earlier snow was thick-crusted and polished by the storm. It was a white world, not a bare hilltop in sight, not a spear of grass. And, while the crust would bear a man if he could stay on his feet, it wouldn't support a horse. Or a steer.

And Jeff Ross had ten thousand head of cattle somewhere in that dazzling white wilderness. If he was lucky, they were alive and yarded up in the timber along the streams. Even if he was that lucky, though, they were prisoned by the ice and getting more

146

hungry by the hour. By now they would have eaten all the browse, every twig within reach and even what bark they could strip from the aspen and cottonwood trunks.

Jeff appraised the situation. Horse travel was almost impossible, with the heavy crust on the old snow. Even if they could get to the cattle and drive them out of the yards, there was no grass for them to eat. The grass was all locked beneath that glistening glaze, and cattle wouldn't paw to get at it.

Horses would paw for grass. Jeff wondered if the answer lay in driving the horse herd onto the ridges, forcing them to chowse up the snow and paw for food. If he did that, he would starve his horses and lame them, practically put himself and his men afoot. That didn't matter right now. They were already afoot, and would be till this glaze began to rot. But if the weather eased in a few more days they would need horses, sound, well-fed horses, to get the cattle out of the timber. Another week without grass, or even without browse, would weaken the cattle dangerously.

There was no easy answer. Any way he decided meant big risks. But the sensible thing probably would be to get going, on foot, and cut cottonwoods and aspens in all the yards they could reach. Get enough trees down so the cattle could reach bark and fine twigs and get a little something into their bellies. It was a difficult job, almost an impossible job, but it was the sensible thing to do.

He gave his orders. The men bound their booted feet in feed bags to get some measure of grip on the icy surface. They took axes and started out on foot. It was slow, difficult going, but they found about a hundred steers in the first yard, less than half a mile from the house. They felled a dozen cottonwoods and aspens and watched the hungry, bawling cattle rush to reach the browse. Then they went on, to the next yard, and the next.

They worked all day, and they cut browse for perhaps a thousand head of imprisoned cattle. But as they returned to the ranch in the brittle-cold dusk Jeff saw that in every yard where they had felled trees that morning the boles and bigger branches were stark white, every bit of bark stripped off, and all the small branches and twigs were gone, eaten or broken off and tramped into the icy soil. By tomorrow afternoon those cattle would be almost as hungry as they were this morning.

They returned to the ranch, tired out, and Sam said, "Jeff,

it won't work. You can't win this way."

"Why not?" Jeff demanded.

"It will take us ten days, at least, to get browse to all of them, and by that time the first ones will be starving again."

Jeff knew that was true. "Maybe the weather will break."

"If it's going to break, why not wait? When the weather breaks we can get 'em out and open up the grass."

"And let them starve a week meanwhile? No!"

Sam shrugged and went to the fireplace and dished up a plate of beans. They ate and fell into their bunks.

The next day they went at it again. As they passed each yard where they had felled trees the day before the prisoned cattle bawled at them, demanding food. But they went on, to cattle which hadn't had anything to eat since the second day of the storm. And again they felled trees.

They worked till early afternoon, and they were six miles from the ranch house. Jeff was working on a big aspen when he heard an unfamiliar sound. He paused, listening. Harvey Bird was working on another aspen nearby. He too stopped and looked toward the ridge to the west. The sound came again, a low bellow, lower in pitch than the bellow of a steer. Then another bellow. And then Jeff thought he heard a crunching, almost like the sound of ice breaking up in the creek in a late winter thaw.

Harvey glanced at Jeff, questioning, and Jeff said, "Buffalo?"

"Can't be anything else."

"Drifting back south?"

"They shouldn't be drifting north today."

They stuck their axes in a stump and climbed out of the cattle yard. They climbed the slope above the stream until they could see over, onto the ridge. There, less than a quarter of a mile away, were fifty or sixty buffalo looking coal-black against the dazzle of the snow. They were slowly plodding south along the crest of the ridge. Two old bulls were in the lead, breaking trail, going a few steps, then pausing till the pressure of the cows behind forced them on again. There was a light breeze from the west, so they did not smell the men.

The herd was traveling in a loose bunch, not single-file. Now and then a cow paused and thrust her muzzle down into the snow and found a bunch of grass. But they weren't really grazing. They were moving south, urged by some instinct toward open grass where the storm had not iced everything in. They could travel a long way, even through this heavily crusted snow, for their forelegs were heavily coated with long, tough hair. Their shins wouldn't be slashed by the ice. They weren't as vulnerable as cattle.

As Jeff watched them he knew that here was an answer to his problem, here in this band of buffalo that seemed, when he first saw them, to be a threat. A herd of buffalo drifting into a storm can pick up and absorb a whole herd of cattle, carry them in the drift despite the steer's instinct which tells him to go with the storm, not into it. That had been Jeff's fear. Now the buffalo were opening a broad trail along the ridge, breaking up the crust, uncovering a little grass. If he could get his cattle out of the timber and up onto the ridge, into that broad trail, they could make out. The sun would go to work on those buffalo trails. In a few days the cattle would be eating. If he got them up there.

He turned to Harvey Bird. Harvey was thinking the same thing. They went back to the nearest cattle yard, got their axes and began breaking trail toward the hilltop, swinging their axes to break the imprisoning crust.

It took more than an hour to open a narrow trail from the yard to the buffalo tracks. Then they went back, cut clubs and drove the cattle from that yard into the fresh trail. They crowded them up the slope, kept them going, and finally broke them out onto the hilltop. In the open, where the buffalo had passed, the cattle stood sullen and bewildered. Then one hungry steer found a tuft of grass and began to eat. Others did the same. They wouldn't paw the snow to reach the grass, but they nosed into it and began to find it.

They moved on to the next yard, and Jeff sent Harvey to summon Sam and Pete. All the rest of that day they broke trail from the yards in the timber up onto the ridge where the buffalo had passed. By dark they had close to five hundred head broken out.

The next day they went at it again. What had seemed like a hopeless task now offered chances of success, and Jeff's spirits began to rise. He could even laugh when Sam Royce said, "This is no work for a self-respecting cowhand, chopping ice to get a cow-critter out of a fix she shouldn't be in in the first place."

"A cowhand's job," Jeff said, "is to take care of cattle, whether that means chopping browse or chopping ice or just sitting in the ranch house waiting for spring to come."

Sam grinned. "My mammy always used to say I'd be a fool ever to leave home. Well, I left. I came up here. I'm telling you, my mammy was right!"

"Come on," Jeff said, "we're going to get those cattle up on the ridge."

And they did. They chopped ice for two days. Then the first cattle they had broken out were strong again, able to break crust. And the sun had begun to rot the ice. They cut out the strongest steers among the freed cattle and drove them down the slope to the timber, breaking trail to yarded herds of steers that had been imprisoned by the ice for almost a week. The cattle in those yards were weak and bone-thin, some of them too weak to make their way out. Jeff wrote them off, didn't even take time to skin them out when they died there in the yards. He left them for the wolves and the coyotes.

By the fifth day they were able to reach the Kiowa, using steers to break trail. The cattle there were in bad shape, but they got most of them out. But when they finally reached East Camp they found conditions even worse.

Tallying up after two weeks battle with that storm, Jeff found that he had lost close to five hundred head. He was, he supposed, lucky at that. Five hundred head meant only about five per cent loss. If his luck had gone the other way he might have lost fifteen or twenty per cent, even more.

They were coming in from East Camp, the last cattle broken out and the hilltops showing the first traces of grass through the rotting crust. Jeff was dog-tired, though he hadn't realized it till now. Sam, up in the lead, sagged in his saddle. Even Harvey Bird and Pete Wallace, blessed with the vitality and resilience of youth, were slack-shouldered with weariness. They could all do with a few days of rest.

Jeff tried to remember when he had been so tired, and his memory reached all the way back to the war. Back to the crushing battles. Then, as now, the tension of the fighting kept a man going. But when it was all over, the exhaustion hit him. Worse, then, for too often the weariness was also a weariness of the heart and soul, the bitterness of defeat. It was one thing to fight to exhaustion and have the satisfaction of victory. It was something else again to come out of desperate battle with the ashes of defeat in your mouth as you harried your men into some semblance of orderly retreat. As you did your utmost to salvage at least the integrity of your troop, to escape capture, to fall back more or less intact, to hope for another day, a better-starred engagement. And with the weariness of body and soul there was always the final taste of gall, the knowledge that the gaps in your ranks meant not only loss of effective force but men wounded, maimed, dead.

At least, he thought now, I am coming back with my force intact. None maimed or missing, not even a wound. And we won the battle.

He sat slack in his saddle, shoulders low in weariness, and he thought back to the retreat from Elkhorn, his first major battle. That was where he first knew the bitterness of loss and retreat. That was where Bill Sanders got his crooked arm. And saved Jeff's life.

It was an ill-starred battle from the start, and yet it could have gone the other way had Van Dorn had adequate reserves instead of those 2,000 untrained Indians under Albert Pike. At the crisis of the battle, when Price and McCulloch were about to turn the flanks and crush the Union forces, Van Dorn had to throw Pike's Indians in to hold the center. And they withered under artillery fire, turned and took to the woods. The Union forces poured through, and the battle was decided.

The plan was sound. Give Van Dorn credit. There was Price, retreating from Springfield, Curtis hot on his heels, trying to capture him and his Missouri volunteers. Price was retreating into those rugged Ozark hills of northwest Arkansas, and Van Dorn brought up McCulloch and Pike's untried Indians. He chose Pea Ridge for what was to be a trap. McCulloch moved into position and when Price arrived Van Dorn deployed his forces on the other flank. Curtis came charging in, and Van Dorn swung McCulloch in from one flank, Price from the other, to close the circle, with the Indians holding the center. But the Indians didn't hold.

Jeff was leading his men down Pea Ridge, around Price's flank, looking for Union outposts. The timber was thick and full of blow-down. You couldn't see a hundred yards. Then they came to a clearing of about ten acres, certainly no more than that. Some hill farmer probably had spent five years making that clearing, some man who had dreamed all his life of owning a little corn patch and a cow and a few hogs. So he had come here, to this rugged hilltop, and he had chopped and burned a clearing in the woods, his dream come true. It wasn't a very old clearing, for the stumps still stood, scarcely rotted at all, and the corn stubble was there, not over two years old, and the furrows in the rocky soil. Then the devil that dogged the man caught up with him. Maybe he was careless in building his chimney. Maybe, dog-tired at the end of a day, he fell asleep without banking his fire properly. Something. And his cabin burned. The charred logs lay in a jumble, there at the edge of the clearing. And now it was deserted, growing up to weeds and soon to sprouts, weeds brown and sere in early March. A dream that died.

They came to the clearing, and Jeff knew that from the far edge he could see the whole valley and the ridge beyond. He started to lead his men around, but the wind-fall made a tangle that a man could scarcely penetrate on foot, let alone on a horse. He wound around and through the tangle for a few hundred yards, then said, "We'll be an hour, this way. Come on!" And he set spurs to his horse and led his men at a smart trot into the open, to get across directly and in a hurry.

It was miserable footing for the horses, the weeds masking the furrows and the stumps. And Jeff thought he saw men on the far slope, just across the steep valley. Union soldiers. He lifted his horse to a gallop. And the Union guns opened up on them. Half a dozen smoke puffs appeared on the opposite ridge. He heard the crash of cannon fire. And the balls began plowing the field all around them. More puffs, another salvo, and the cannon balls were right among them. The gunners over there had the range.

A horse screamed. Jeff turned and saw a saber spin in the sunlight, knocked from the hand of a trooper who never knew what hit him.

They were halfway across the clearing when the third round came. It was deadly. Six of Jeff's men simply vanished in a geyser of mud and rocks. Then Jeff's own horse stumbled, sagged to its knees and fell heavily, pinning Jeff's right leg. It was a freak hit. One cannon ball had struck a heap of rocks piled round a big stump, shattered the rocks and flung the pieces like shrapnel. One fragment the size of a man's fist had struck Jeff's horse just back of the shoulder and practically gutted it. Six inches further back and it would have taken Jeff's leg off at the knee.

Jeff tried to free himself. Another round of cannon fire began to fall, geysering mud. Then Bill Sanders was on the ground beside him. Bill yelled two other troopers from their saddles and the three of them lifted Jeff's mount just enough for Jeff to squirm his leg from the pinioned boot. Bill grabbed him, somehow hoisted him onto a horse, yelled, "Get the hell out of here!" and whacked the horse across the rump. The horse bolted for the woods. Jeff looked back and saw Bill haul himself up behind another trooper and flail the horse toward the sheltering timber.

Then they were in the woods, out of that hell-pocked open field. Jeff tallied his men. Twelve were missing. While Bill and a young lieutenant got the detail organized, Jeff wrote a message locating the Union battery and sent a cherub-faced young trooper named Tully back to headquarters with it. He never saw Tully again, never knew what happened to him. But remembering Tully now he knew why he had wanted to help Pete Wallace when he found him, orphaned and alone and bewildered, in Denver a year ago. Pete reminded him of Tully, the lad he sent off with that message, alone; the lad who never came back.

That was on the second day of the battle. The first day they had driven the Unionists back half a mile beyond Elkhorn Tavern, put them into position for the pincers to close. The first day was a day of victory. But this was the second day, the eighth of March.

He led his men down the ridge, searching for Union outposts. And he heard Union artillery fire from the center. The center, where Van Dorn had only Albert Pike's Indians, though Jeff didn't know it then. The artillery pounded. Then there was a rising roar of shouting, triumphant shouting. The shouting eased away and the rattle of rifle-fire rose to a roar.

Jeff halted his men, and through the thinning woods he saw a surging rush of Union forces half a mile ahead. But he still thought they were merely rushing into the deadly trap, soon to be closed by the junction of Price's flank with McCulloch's.

He watched and waited, and the Unionists thinned and vanished. Hoping he had found a gap, a way through to reach McCulloch's forces, Jeff gave the order and led his men through those thin woods. Not knowing that the battle was already lost, that the Indians had given way and that in the breakthrough McCulloch had been killed and McIntosh, who succeeded to the command, was killed only minutes later. Not knowing that McCulloch's forces were demoralized. All he knew was that here was a gap and by all the rules of tactics and common sense he should take his men through and make contact with the other flank.

The workings of choice and circumstance are beyond understanding. Had they made it through the gap they would have run squarely into Union forces, mad with victory, who were tearing dead McCulloch's army to pieces. Had Jeff waited another fifteen minutes, a second force of Union infantry would have closed the gap, probably have wiped him out, man and horse. Or had a handful of Union cavalrymen not been lost in the woods under the command of a green young lieutenant frightened into foolhardy bravery by the necessity of unexpected command, Jeff would never have had that encounter, never have been found by the courier.

He led his men into the gap with a rush. And out of the brush to their left came this handful of Union cavalrymen. They weren't a hundred yards apart. Jeff expected them to turn tail and run, the only sensible course, since they were outnumbered three to one. Instead this fool of a young lieutenant charged. In a moment they were in a hand-to-hand melee, saber and pistol and charging horse. And on ground no sensible man would choose for cavalry action, thin woods but thick underbrush.

Jeff's men met the charge and swarmed over the Unionists, rode them down. But they fought to the last. The issue was already settled and not more than a dozen of them were still in hopeless action when the young lieutenant charged Jeff, closed with him at saber-length. Jeff parried and thrust, and was already getting the better of it when the lieutenant's horse tangled itself in the brush, was knocked off balance, and fell heavily. The lieutenant leaped clear, pistol in hand, only to stumble in the brush and fall as he backed away.

Jeff was down from his horse, rushing him. And Bill Sanders, come out of nowhere, leaped between them, flung himself on the lieutenant just as he fired the pistol. It was point-blank range. The shot would have blown a hole clear through Jeff's belly. But Bill took the bullet, through his outflung left arm.

Then they were both on the lieutenant, in a fighting sprawl

like three cats in the underbrush. A few minutes later the lieutenant was a prisoner, disarmed. And Jeff was twisting a tourniquet about Bill's arm, stanching the flow of blood from the shattered elbow. Telling Bill they must get to a surgeon.

He helped Bill onto a horse. His men got the prisoners mounted, were ready to proceed. Only four of Jeff's men had been wounded, and Bill's the only serious wound among them. Jeff was just getting into the saddle when the courier arrived, breathless, his horse lathered. He gasped out the news to Jeff. McCulloch was dead, his army in rout. Pike's Indians were demoralized. "The General," the courier said, "has ordered a retreat."

Jeff tried to sort it out. With McCulloch's force routed, he had no choice but to return to Price's flank. "Is Price intact?" he asked the courier.

"He was still holding the last I knew."

Jeff gave the order. The troop wheeled, started back. And at that moment the vanguard of the second infantry force appeared, double-timing it toward the action at the breakthrough. They saw Jeff's men, fired a scattering of shots. Jeff shouted orders, led his troop back into the heavy woods, back toward Price.

They never really reached Price. The retreat was on, the vanquished retreat. They did catch up, finally, with the battered army, but in the confusion there wasn't a surgeon to be found. Jeff stopped long enough to remove the tourniquet from Bill's arm and bandage it as best he could. Then they went on.

Bill rode with that shattered arm for five days before a surgeon so much as looked at it. By then it had begun to knit, the surgeon said, in the position it would always have, that crook dictated by the only ease Bill could find for it, his hand thrust inside his shirt just above his belt.

"You're lucky it didn't gangrene," the surgeon said. He was a harried man with sleepless eyes, a man who had seen too much suffering, too much death. "I could break it and reset it straight, but there's not much else I could do. If it's handy that way, I'd leave it. It's healing."

So Bill left it that way. And they went on and on. To Vicksburg, to Corinth, to other defeats. There were skirmishes won, and brief satisfactions. But the battles were lost, and it was the defeats that lingered, the lost men, the growing sense of hopelessness. The weariness of soul was worse even than the weariness of bone and body.

And, with the weariness, the growing wonder if life held anything beyond this. There were the few furloughs, the months-apart visits with Loretta. But those visits were strange and strained, brief excursions into a world of unreality. Bedding briefly with the woman who was his wife. Hearing her voice, seeing her face, knowing she represented something he had once valued and wanted, yet knowing that Loretta was a stranger, always had been a stranger. And the worst was knowing that a man must have some belief, his life must have some meaning. Knowing that he had no belief, no meaning.

When he went home to stay, mustered out, almost too sick to sit in the saddle—that seemed the final irony, the ultimate mouthful of ashes. Back to Loretta, the stranger. Back to the daughter who was still more strange. Back to the son who was even a stranger to life, who was born to be a kind of nothingness.

So he had to get away again. Out onto the trail, which once had meaning. If a man must die, let him die where he can at least see the trappings of the dreams he once had.

So he went, and he recaptured the dream. A part of it. The part that had made him what he was now.

He put away those memories, and he looked again at Sam Royce, there in the thickening dusk, Sam sagging in his saddle. And at Harvey Bird, riding slack and weary, and at Pete Wallace, so like that lad named Tully who was killed or captured and never seen again.

They were coming back from a battle. A battle with a blizzard. And Jeff's forces were intact. There was some satisfaction in that. They were coming back with a large measure of victory. That eased some of the weariness.

If he hadn't come back to anything else, he had come back to this, which couldn't be taken away from him. I have this, he thought. A man must have something more than memories.

His horse shuffled through the snow and the dark closed down and the early stars began to shine. Jeff looked across the dimming distance, softly star-shone, and had a sense of man's inconsequence.

A man could be lost and forgotten here, and it wouldn't alter the hills one iota, wouldn't shift the wind by an inch. A man could live here, and die here, and the grass would go right on growing, unchanged. A strong man—a man, as Earl Van Dorn once said, who was endowed with the capacity for command—could use the grass, for a little while, could even be master to a degree of the vastness. He could own a few of these boundless hills, as much as a man ever owns any piece of ground until he possesses it in death. The summers would scorch and burn, the winters would blast and blight, never aware of him. But he could outwit them, for a little while, as Jeff had now outwitted the blizzard, in a measure. A strong man could survive the worst they had to offer, perhaps even keep his cattle. If he was lucky. Perhaps that was a man's importance.

They plodded on, and the darkness thickened and the stars glittered. And at last they dropped down the last slope, the Bijou just ahead. The ranch house, shelter, rest.

They came in sight of the ranch house, and Jeff saw a light. Who could be there? He frowned, wondering, and he urged his jaded horse past the others, into the dooryard.

The door opened and there stood Bill Sanders. Leaning against the doorway, easing that bad leg, his face long and lean and bone-thin with pain and weariness. Bill said, "Jeff!" and Jeff read the whole message in his tone of voice.

He got down from his horse and handed the reins to Sam Royce, and he said, "Saddle up a fresh horse, Sam, and pick me a good spare."

The others went on to the barn and Jeff went inside.

Bill hobbled to the fireplace, reached for the coffeepot. Jeff snapped, "Sit down! Get off that leg." He set out two cups and poured the coffee. "Loretta sent you?" he asked.

"No. I told her I was coming. I knew you'd want to be there."

"Tommy?"

Bill nodded.

"Is he dead?"

"Not when I left. But the Doc didn't think he had much of a chance. . . . You'd better eat something before you start."

Jeff got a plate and spooned out a heap of beans. The weariness was all through him, in every muscle. He forced himself to eat, and he said, "We got the cattle out. Most of them. How's the traveling?"

"Bad. But you can make it."

"Was it pneumonia?"

"Loretta said not. She said they couldn't stop the convulsions."

Jeff finished his coffee, set the beans aside and got to his feet again, bracing himself against the table. He forced the iron back into his body and put on his coat. He said, "I'll be back when I can," and he went out to the barn.

Sam had the horses ready. Jeff mounted and rode down to the ford, crossed and headed for the ridge, Kiowa Crossing, Denver.

10

It was a hard trip, as Bill had said it would be. Jeff didn't reach the house in Denver till after daylight. He put the horses away, went into the house and found Jenny the only one downstairs. Seeing her tear-swollen face, he knew the answer even before he asked, "Am I too late?"

She said yes, and she tried to tell him all about it, between sobs, but he cut her off, asked about Loretta. The Missus, Jenny said, was still upstairs, asleep.

Jeff took a cup of Jenny's abominable coffee and went into his office. He knew what had to be done, and he wanted to get it done and over with, get this whole thing finished. He drank the coffee and went upstairs.

Loretta was awake. She said she hadn't slept, waiting for him. She cried in Jeff's arms, and he tried to comfort her. He said they would hold the funeral in the parlor downstairs and no one would be there but him and Loretta and the two girls. And maybe Jenny. A family should bury its own dead, in privacy.

"Bessie must be there," Loretta said. "She asked, especially. Bessie loved him, Jeff. She was good to him."

Jeff said all right, but grudgingly.

"Besides," Loretta said, "I think I'll keep Bessie on for a while. The girls like her, Jane especially."

"Later," Jeff said, "we'll talk about that later."

"Have you had anything to eat?"

"Not yet."

"Why don't you go down and eat, Jeff? Then we can plan."

So Jeff went down and tried to eat the tasteless porridge and leathery eggs that Jenny served him. Before he had finished, Dr. Crane arrived. He brought with him a chubby little man named Owen, an embalmer. Jeff sent Owen to the second floor sitting room to wait and took Dr. Crane into his office.

He had come early, Dr. Crane said, to see if Jeff had arrived and to see if he could do anything for Mrs. Ross. Then he said, "Mr. Ross, you are worn out. Do you know that?"

"I know that I'm tired and need some sleep," Jeff snapped.

"I'll take care of that. What happened to the boy?"

"Well, you remember that I told you last summer there was no hope for him." Crane spoke with a Connecticut twang that annoyed Jeff now.

"Or," Jeff said, "that he might live for another ten years."

"That's right."

"What killed him? Did he get pneumonia?"

"Pneumonia? Oh, no. He didn't have pneumonia. But the heavy cold he did have probably put a strain on his heart. Late yesterday he had one of those periodic convulsions and—well, his heart began to falter. He had a series of convulsions, in fact, and he just faded away. As near as I can say, he died at twelve minutes after ten. That is the time I put down in my report."

As though it mattered, Jeff thought. As though the exact minute mattered! "So that's what happened?" he asked.

"That is what happened, Mr. Ross. We did all we could, all of us." He hesitated. "It is really for the best. I hope you can see it that way."

And Jeff thought: What do you know about it? Do you think you are God? But he held his tongue. After all, the boy was dead. Maybe it was for the best; but that was for Jeff to decide.

Jeff got to his feet. Crane seemed surprised at being dismissed, and Jeff wondered what more Crane or anyone else could say. He moved toward the doorway. "Thank you," he said. "Send me your bill."

"Mrs. Ross," Crane asked, "how is Mrs. Ross this morning?"

"She is all right. If she should need you later, I'll send word."

"A brave woman. A very courageous woman. Oh, by the way, I

took the liberty of choosing Mr. Owen. Mrs. Ross didn't know when you would arrive, and—"

"She told me about it. Thank you again."

All Jeff wanted was to be rid of them, all of them, get the details over with. He saw Dr. Crane to the door, then went upstairs. He found Mr. Owen talking to Bessie Magruder in the sitting room. Bessie flushed when she saw Jeff and hurried out.

Mr. Owen was a bald little man with an ill-fitting black suit and scuffed boots. All the time they talked Jeff kept glancing at those boots and wondering why the man hadn't blacked them.

"The funeral service will be tomorrow afternoon," Jeff told him, "in the parlor downstairs. You will see to the coffin?"

"Yes, sir," Mr. Owen whispered.

"And will you see to having the grave dug?"

"I will," the embalmer whispered. "It will be expensive, you know? The ground's frozen?" He seemed to be asking questions.

Jeff's nerves were taut, and the man's whispering was too much. "Talk up!" he ordered. "Of course the ground's frozen. What of it?"

"The grave will be expensive." The man still whispered. "It will cost ten dollars more than if it wasn't frozen?"

"Good God!" Jeff exclaimed. "Did you think I'd bury him in a snowdrift to save ten dollars?"

"No, sir. No, sir." Mr. Owen rubbed his hands in agitation. "But I thought I should mention it. The cost, I mean? The extra cost? Some don't like to pay it? It's cheaper when they go in the summer."

"Have a grave dug." Jeff gestured toward the stairway to the third floor. "The boy is up there, the room on the left."

"Thank you. Thank you, sir." Mr. Owen took his bag of instruments and started up the stairway. Jeff went back downstairs.

Loretta came from the kitchen as he reached the downstairs hallway. Her eyes were red and the lack of sleep showed in the lines around her mouth. "Where are the girls?" Jeff asked. "I haven't seen the girls."

"They're in Jane's room. I asked Bessie to look after them today. Jeff, you're so tired! You're worn out. Please get some rest. Come on."

She took his arm, but he shook his head. "This afternoon. Now

I've got to see the preacher. We'll have the service tomorrow afternoon."

"Yes."

He saw the look in her eyes. "Loretta," he said, "I'm sorry. I haven't had time to say that, but I am. You know that, don't you?"

She was on the verge of tears again. "Yes, Jeff. Now go do your errand, and get back. Get Reverend Ordway."

"I will. And you go up and lie down."

He went to the stable, saddled a horse and rode over to the parsonage. Jeff wasn't much of a churchgoer, but he knew the Reverend Mr. Jonathan Ordway by sight. He was the pastor at the church Loretta attended, Loretta and the girls. He was a wiry little man with a shock of gray hair and a deep voice, a man with a strange combination of unction and practicality.

Jeff told him why he had come and said he wanted the service kept short.

"I shall keep it as brief as possible," Mr. Ordway said. "But there is a minimum of essential observance."

"There will be only the family and servants. There's no need for a eulogy. You didn't know the boy."

"I knew *of* him," Mr. Ordway said with a properly sympathetic smile.

"Omit the eulogy."

"Very well, Mr. Ross. I shall keep the service as brief as its purpose permits. Tomorrow, you say?"

"Two o'clock tomorrow afternoon."

"Yes. I do think, though, that Mrs. Ross would like—"

"Mrs. Ross and I are in agreement." Jeff was not going to give him any chance to argue. He turned to go.

"Do convey my condolence to Mrs. Ross," Mr. Ordway said. He looked grave, puzzled and shocked. "I do wish—"

"Thank you," Jeff said, and he turned and left.

He went home, put away the horse and went upstairs. Loretta was in the sitting room. The embalmer had left.

"Are the girls still in Jane's room?" Jeff asked.

"Yes. But please don't try to talk to them now, Jeff. I told them you are here and that you would see them later. This evening, probably."

"I'll get it over with now."

"Please, Jeff, no!"

"Why not?"

"Jane is quite upset. She'll be all right later, but—well, death is hard for a child to understand, Jeff."

He had steeled himself, sensed somehow that Jane would be a problem. He didn't know why. It was almost a relief not to have to talk to her now. Yet he had hoped to get it over with.

"Please," Loretta repeated.

He gave in, too tired to insist. He was dead on his feet, and he knew it.

Loretta went with him to his bedroom, tried to help him undress. But at least, he could take his own clothes off. He got into bed. And Loretta went to her room, came back a few minutes later in her nightdress and got into the big bed with him. Jeff was already asleep. He half roused, and she kissed him and lay close against him, and he slept again.

Jeff, she thought, is the one who needs comfort now. I have known, accepted. He refused to know, to accept. I must be the strong one now.

Then Loretta, too, slept, her arms about the man she loved.

It was evening, dusk, when Jeff awakened. He was alone in the bed, alone in the room, and the shades were drawn. He looked around, bewildered, thinking at first that he was in his bunk at the ranch, that he had dreamed of Tommy's death. Then it all came back to him, the ride in from the ranch, the house, the presence of death, the doctor, the whispering embalmer, the Reverend Mr. Jonathan Ordway. And he saw the familiar furniture in the familiar room, knew where he was.

He got up and washed in the cold water in the bowl, shaved, dressed. And went out into the hallway, to the sitting room.

Nobody was there. The house seemed deserted. Then he heard sobbing, in Jane's room. Sobbing, and the tones of Loretta's voice. It rose in command. Then silence. And the door opened and Loretta came down the hallway, to the sitting room.

"Oh, you are awake!" She came to him and kissed him. Her eyes were still heavy and red-rimmed, but there was an air of decision about her, a strength, that hadn't been there before. "You

163

were so tired, Jeff. But you did rest, didn't you?"

"Very well. Now I shall talk to the girls and I think everything will be taken care of."

"Now, Jeff?"

"Now."

"One thing, Jeff. Jane is still very much upset."

"You are saying I shouldn't see them?"

"No. You should, if you want to. But—please don't say too much now, Jeff. Later you can be of more help. After the funeral . . . I'll bring them in."

She went back to Jane's room, was gone several minutes. Then she came back with them, stood in front of Jeff, holding the girls' hands. Jane's face was swollen, her eyes red. She didn't even look up at her father but stood staring at his feet, her lips tight, her jaw set. Lissie, too, was red-eyed, but as she looked at Jeff her eyes were bewildered and pleading, still almost baby eyes. Lissie clung to Loretta's hand with both her own chubby hands. Jane stood there clasping her hands together in front of her.

"Lissie, Jane," Jeff began, "you know what happened. Your mother told you." He paused, met Lissie's pleading eyes and tried to reassure her with a look. Then he said, "Tommy was sick all his life. He never was well, as you two are."

Lissie was biting her lip, fighting the tears. Jane still stared, tight-lipped, at Jeff's feet.

"We all hoped," Jeff went on, "that Tommy might some day get over his illness. But hope wasn't enough. And when this new sickness came, he hadn't the strength to fight it off. He left us."

Jane at last flashed him one look, a look of anger and almost of hatred; and her mouth opened as though to say something. Then she clamped her lips again and looked down.

"Tomorrow," Jeff said, "we will say our good-byes to him. And we will go on with our own lives. That is the way of life. We don't know why things happen as they do. Some things we can manage, but death is not among those things. Life and death are out of our hands. Some day, when you are older, you will understand these things, as much as any of us ever understand."

There seemed nothing else to say, and he felt that he had said rather poorly what he had already said.

He said, "There were three of you children, and now there are two. And we love you very much. God bless you."

Then he leaned over and kissed them. Lissie held up her arms and hugged him, clung to him for a moment. But Jane didn't even look up, didn't make a motion, as he kissed her on the cheek.

Loretta said, "Jenny will bring your supper to you. Your father and I want to be alone this evening." And the girls went back to Jane's room.

Loretta watched them go, then turned to Jeff. "I don't know what more anyone could have said. Thank you, Jeff."

Jeff looked at her, surprised. He hadn't asked for her approval, hadn't thought she might disapprove.

Then she said, "Supper should be ready."

They went down to the dining room, just the two of them, and Jenny served them. Jenny had done her crying, apparently. She was almost back to normal. Loretta had told her to take the girls' supper upstairs, and she left them. Loretta asked Jeff about what had happened at the ranch. Jeff told her briefly about the blizzard, the problems with the cattle, the providential appearance of the buffalo. It seemed far away and long ago. Yet that was the reality, to Jeff, not this; and Loretta knew it even as Jeff was talking.

She listened, asked the proper questions, and they ate. Jenny brought the dessert. But Jeff had no hunger for it. He pushed it aside, and Loretta said, "I don't want any either. Let's go into the parlor."

The blinds were drawn in the parlor. Jeff lit a lamp, and in the dim light he saw that the small coffin had been placed on a low table at one end of the room. The cover was on the coffin, he was glad to see. The dead deserve their privacy.

He crossed the room and stood beside the coffin, thinking how pathetically small a box it was. Then he thought: Tommy was never more than a baby. A maimed child who never had a chance, really. Never was at home in this world. But my son.

He turned away. Loretta had sat down on a sofa at the other end of the room. As he went over to her she said, "I'm going to sit with him tonight."

"No. I'll sit."

"You're still tired, Jeff."

"I slept all afternoon. You didn't."

"Suppose you take the fore part of the night, then. I'll rest a while. Then I'll come down."

"Get some sleep, Loretta. I'll wake you, if I get tired."

But she didn't go. Jeff sat down beside her.

"Jeff, we did everything we could."

"Everything."

"Dr. Crane told you last summer that there really wasn't any hope, didn't he?"

"I already knew. Crane just confirmed it."

She nodded.

"Did he tell you? He promised that he wouldn't."

"No. But I knew, long ago. Even before we left Dallas and came up here to the ranch. A mother knows." She sat silent for a long moment. "I'm glad you have the ranch, Jeff."

"Why?"

She didn't answer. She got up and crossed the room to the coffin. She stood there, finally put out her hand, seemed almost to caress it. Then she turned and came back to Jeff. She was almost smiling, not a happy smile but a remembering one.

"He had his happy times, Jeff."

"Happy?"

"Yes. We didn't understand, but—" She paused, remembering again. "The night the Indians attacked, on the trail up here. Remember? We were in the log stockade, the children and I. And the shooting began. And he laughed! I was frightened to death, and his laughter gave me courage. Isn't that strange? I've never forgotten."

Jeff shook his head, not understanding.

"Remember the crazy old trapper? Jake— What was his name? Starling? The one who came to the ranch and saw him and told that story about the boy like him among the Indians. I sometimes think Tommy had things to tell us, if we could only understand."

"Things like what?"

"I don't know, Jeff." She smiled, sadly.

Jeff said nothing, and Loretta said, "I loved him, Jeff. I prayed that some day he would be able to love you, admire you. As a son should. It's enough for a mother to love her child, I suppose. But a father needs his son's love and respect. I prayed, Jeff."

"Yes, Loretta."

She waited for him to say more. And at last she said, "Would you rather be alone?"

"Please." He stood up. "And you should get some sleep." He smiled at her, then, and he drew her close to him and patted her shoulder and kissed her on the cheek. "Thank you, Loretta."

He went with her to the door and closed the door behind her and returned to the sofa. A man alone in a room with his son, his dead son in a coffin.

No, he thought. Not with my son. With a box and a cruelly maimed and dwarfed body inside it. My son was the child who was born while I was at war, the child I dreamed about in a dozen bivouacs. The child who learned to walk and talk and grew to boyhood and youth and manhood in my dreams. That was my son. Then I came home on furlough and saw a child that had been named my name, a child of my begetting with Loretta; and yet not my son. I knew it. Mine, and not my son. The son I had, there in those dreams, died when I came home and saw Tommy and knew without asking, knew the truth about him. My son died, never having lived outside my own dreams, and Tommy was there in his stead. All these years. Tomorrow we are going to bury the body of the child in that box, that coffin. But I buried my son long ago.

Loretta had said it was enough for a mother to love her child, but that a father needs his son's love and respect.

Love? Respect? Were they the goals of fatherhood, the purpose of a man's life? No.

What, then, he asked himself, are my purposes? As a man?

And there were no easy answers. Sitting there in the dimness and the silence of that December night, there in that room with the coffin of the child who had been christened Thomas Jefferson Ross, Junior, that child of Jeff Ross and his legally wedded wife, Loretta, Jeff went over and over the question he had asked himself.

He went over the days of his boyhood, when life itself was sufficient, its own reason; when each dawn was a Genesis, each day new discovery. Over the days of his growing up, dreaming of love, yes, respect, yes, wealth and power and greatness. But love taken, respect demanded, wealth and power earned.

He went over the days of trying to read law, the impatience of youth to be out and doing. The sense of time passing swiftly, yet the belief that life endures forever. Over the early trail drives, his first knowledge of a world in its vastness, its unexplored newness. Over the days of his youth, when one must go and do and live, must drink life in great gulps, hoping to taste it all.

He went over the days of his young manhood, confident in his own strength, believing there never would be a horse he could not ride, an Indian he could not out-fight or out-bully, a river he could not cross. Or a woman he could not have.

He came to the days of manhood, the days of angry arrogance. Marriage, to prove that manhood. And the growing bitterness when that proof was not enough, even for himself. The doubts, the thwartings, the confusions of purpose; and the escape, into war. War, which is its own purpose, like a tornado or a blizzard, and you a part of it. The days of war, and the knowledge that somewhere there is another world with its own meaning, the realization that you are an exile from it, a stranger to it.

He went over the days of his return, the days when death was closer than during the war, a business of death itself; when he defied life, that he might not die in a prison of his own making. And went away, daring death to take him. Why? Because life had lost its savor, had no meaning. He went away, daring death. And he lived. And came here, and found meaning in grass and water and a sky that arched like forever. He accepted life, and came here. Why? Because grass grew and water flowed, and a man could possess that grass and water. Possession, for a little time. The right to leave his own mark on this land. To impress a footprint on the margin of a stream, perhaps, that would endure for a few winters. To match his manhood against a blizzard. To make something grow and fatten and multiply where only the wind blew before he came, where only the hawk soared.

Love? Respect? Were those what a man demanded of life? No. No!

He bowed his head and he thought: A man hopes for a son to walk in the footsteps of his father, a son to go farther than his father went. And if a man has no son, then he must walk alone.

Jeff shook his head to clear it. He was bone-tired.

He got to his feet, stood there for a moment. He walked across the shadowed room and stood beside the small coffin on the low table. He looked down at it and he said to himself, "My son died almost ten years ago. Tomorrow I shall bury my son's memory."

He was still standing beside the coffin when the door opened quietly and Loretta came in. She crossed the room and touched his arm and said, "It's late, Jeff. Go on to bed."

The funeral service was no doubt comparatively brief. The Reverend Mr. Ordway said his set prayers and read the prescribed passages from the Bible. He did, as Jeff had told him to, omit a formal eulogy. Instead he preached a sermon on death and salvation. A brief sermon, no doubt, by his own measurements, but to Jeff it was an endless droning on of meaningless words. Death was a fact and salvation was a hope that a preacher must dwell upon. But Jeff decided, as the sermon went on and on, that its purpose was to bring the family to tears, the family and everyone within hearing. Jenny, of course, was sobbing before he reached the sermon. Then Bessie gave way to tears. Loretta wept quietly during most of the sermon, and Lissie began to sniffle, then to cry. Jane refused to give in till the sermon was half over, and she, like her mother, cried silently.

Then, at last, the service was over. Jeff had suggested that only he and Loretta go to the graveyard, that the girls be spared. Loretta had said, "No. We are all going." So they went, all of them, in the liveryman's carriage. The black one with the black fringe, drawn by matched black horses and, since it was a blustery, cold day, the side curtains in place. The liveryman himself brought the rig and intended to drive it; but Jeff told him to wait at the house. Jeff took the reins, drove to the graveyard.

The bitter wind was cruel. Jeff wondered why graveyards were always on hilltops, where the wind got a full sweep. He had once heard it was so that the godly would have a head start when the exodus to heaven began. Maybe so, but it was hard on the mourners on a day like this. Loretta was shivering before the preacher uttered his first word at the grave. But Jeff thanked that wind because it chilled the Reverend Mr. Ordway as much as it did the rest of them. He hurried through his first prayer and Jeff suspected that he was shortening the burial service here and there.

Then it was all over and they were in the carriage again and on their way back to the big brick house on the hill.

They went home and got out of their funeral clothes, and Jeff went downstairs to his office. It was a strange place, cramped, for some reason. He didn't know why unless it was that he didn't belong there.

He sat wearily in the chair at his desk, and he thought how ironic it was that Tommy, his son, was out there on that wind-swept hilltop and he, Jeff Ross, was here in this sheltering house. Tommy, the weak one, the maimed, the child who needed care and shelter all his brief life. And Jeff, the strong one, the one who had always needed to go and do.

He went to the south window, stood there looking out toward the plains. The overcast had thickened. It was going to snow again. Another storm was building up. It might hold off till tomorrow, but he doubted it. The wind was getting around to the northeast, the bad quarter. There in the graveyard it had come straight out of the east.

He was still standing at the window when there was a knock at the door. He said, "Yes?" and Loretta came in.

"Jeff," she said, "can we talk a few minutes?"

"Of course."

She sat down, after closing the door. She waited a moment, then said, "I hardly know where to begin."

"Whatever's on your mind, say it."

"Well, I spoke of keeping Bessie on."

"For the girls."

"Yes."

"You want to keep her?"

"She would be a help. Especially with Jane." She hesitated, then said, "Jane has taken Tommy's death very hard."

"And you think Bessie can help?"

"I think she may be able to. Jane can talk to her."

"Why can't she talk to anybody else?"

"I don't know, Jeff. It's partly her age, of course, but—well, Jeff, to be truthful, she resents you."

"I know it. Why?" He waited for an answer and when Loretta

170

didn't speak at once he turned and walked to the window and stood there for a moment. Then he came back and asked again, "Why?"

"I don't know, Jeff. I can't say."

He knew she was avoiding something, but there was no need to press it just now. He said, "I'd like to talk to Jane."

"I'll bring her down."

"Send her down. I want to talk to her alone."

Loretta hesitated, then got to her feet. "Jeff, please don't be hard with her."

"Send her down," Jeff ordered quietly.

Loretta left and a few minutes later Jane came to the door. Jeff bade her come in. She closed the door behind her and stood staring at Jeff across the room.

She's tall for her age, Jeff thought. And thin. She's got more of me in her than of Loretta.

She stood there, defiantly stiff, waiting, watching him. Her mouth was set in a thin-lipped line and her eyes were both wary and hostile.

"Jane," Jeff said, "come on over here."

She crossed the room and stood in front of him, her look unchanged.

"Your mother tells me that she may keep Bessie on to help with you girls. Do you like Bessie?"

"Yes."

"Why?"

She hesitated, then asked, "Aren't you going to let Bessie stay?"

"Why do you want her to stay?"

"Because she was good to my brother."

"And now your brother is gone."

"Yes!" It was like a challenge thrown at him.

"Why do you say it that way?"

"Because I loved my brother."

"We all loved Tommy. Don't you know that, Jane?"

"No."

He wasn't going to get into an argument with a child, but he had to be firm about this. "Yes we did, Jane."

"*You* didn't." Her words were cold, accusing.

"Tommy was my son, just as you are my daughter."

"You didn't love him. You wanted him to die."

"Jane!" The word snapped.

Jane stiffened, as though from a blow, but she didn't retract. She stood there, still accusing him.

Jeff fought down the anger, the impulse to slap her. Then, not even trusting words, he turned and walked across the room and came back. "Jane," he said, "we are all upset by Tommy's death. But that is no reason for any of us to be cruel. Nobody wanted Tommy to die. Your mother didn't. I didn't. I'm sure Lissie didn't. And you didn't, did you?"

"No."

"Tommy never would have been well, as you are, no matter how long he lived. Did you know that?"

She slowly shook her head. Her eyes said that she didn't believe him.

"That is what the doctors told us. Perhaps your mother or I should have told you, but it seemed cruel. And we didn't want to admit, even to ourselves, that Tommy never would be able to walk and talk."

"Never?"

"That's what the doctors said."

There was the look of tears in her eyes, but she flared at him, "That's not true! He talked to me!"

"He what?"

"He talked to me! I was going to teach him to walk!"

"When did he talk to you, Jane? What did he say?"

"He said he loved me! He was the only one who *did* love me!" Suddenly her face contorted and the tears came. She fought them for a moment, then covered her face with her hands and went to the sofa and flung herself on it and began to sob.

After a moment Jeff went over to her and tried to comfort her. She drew away from him. He knelt on the floor beside the couch and put an arm around her. She turned her face to him and said, "I hate you! I hate everybody!" Then she turned to the cushions again and went on crying. And after a moment she said, "Why did you let him die? He was my brother, and I loved him!"

And at last she cried herself out. She lay there and the sobs subsided. Jeff got out a handkerchief and said, "Here. You'd better dry your face."

She sat up, took the handkerchief and wiped her eyes. She straightened her dress and smoothed her hair.

Jeff sat down beside her, beside this stranger who was his own daughter. At last he said, "Jane, some day you will have a child of your own. You'll grow up, and marry, and have children, and you'll wonder why there is pain and hurt and disappointment in life, as well as love and happiness. We all wonder, Jane."

She didn't comment.

"I don't know why Tommy wasn't whole and well," he said. "And I don't know why he died. Perhaps he is whole and well now, wherever he is. We all loved him, in our own ways. You thought he talked to you. Maybe he did, in his way."

"I wanted to take care of him," Jane said.

"You wanted him to be well and whole."

"Yes."

"And because he wasn't, because we thought he never would be, you thought we didn't love him. Was that it?"

She didn't answer.

He watched her and he saw in her the thing in himself that always had, always would, demand that life shape itself to his own wishes. He wished it wasn't in her; but he knew that it would be there to the end of her days.

He said, "Jane, there's only one thing I want for you. I want you to be able to accept life, the sweet and the bitter, the sad and the happy. Life is all those things. We pick and choose, and sometimes we find happiness. But we have to take life complete. I hope you are strong enough to take it. That, Jane, is the way I love you. Some day you will understand."

She drew a deep sigh, a long, quivering breath, and she gave back his handkerchief. She stood up, about to leave him. She said, "Thank you, Papa." Then she said, "Tommy never spoke to me in real words. But I know he loved me, and I hoped that some day he would say it in words."

Then she turned and left him, quietly left the room.

He sat watching the doorway, wishing he could have said more, done more to prepare her for the years to come, for life. He wondered how much Jane was ridden by jealousy and resentment as well as by that deep, deep need for love and approval.

Then he thought: We all are, aren't we, to some degree? Is

it life that hurts, or is it the way we manage life? Is it the choices offered, or the choices made?

He was sitting there on the couch, his head in his hands, when Loretta came in a little later. She came in and he looked up and she asked, "Was it difficult?"

"Yes." He got to his feet feeling very tired. He went to the south window and looked out into the deepening dusk. The snow hadn't started yet, but he knew it would come.

She said, "You don't have to go right back to the ranch, do you?"

"Not tonight. Tomorrow."

"But Bill's there now."

"Bill's still got a bad leg. Besides, they're my cattle." He turned and came back to her. "You'd better move Bessie downstairs, near the girls. Close off the third floor."

"Tommy's room?"

"We buried Tommy today. Let's not keep on living with him."

"I'll try not to, Jeff."

The room was almost dark.

"It's been a long time, Loretta."

"Ten years."

She heard him sigh.

"Are you hungry?" she asked. "Ready for supper?"

"No, I'm not hungry."

He took her hand. They went out into the hall and climbed the stairs. Jeff paused at the landing and looked at the door to the third floor. Then he went on, Loretta holding his elbow, guiding him, on down the hall to the bedroom.

11

The snow began during the night. When Jeff came down before dawn to grain the horses and prepare for the trip to the ranch there were four inches on the ground and the northeast wind had a bite. It was drifting the snow. Drifts a foot deep fanned out from every tree and bush in the yard and a drift almost knee-deep had piled up on the sheltered side of the stable. It seemed incredible that more snow was piling up, with the bulk of any normal winter still ahead; but here it was, coming down steadily.

He returned to the house. Jenny was not yet up, but Loretta had heard him get up and had come down in robe and slippers to see him off. She had coffee made and ready for him.

He sat down at the kitchen table and Loretta said, "Another storm. Must you go, Jeff?"

"Yes, Loretta, I've got to go. And I don't know how long it will be before I get back."

She sat down across the table from him. "I know. But I had to ask." She reached across the table and took his hand. "I've never said, 'Don't go,' have I?"

"Never."

"And we haven't quarreled, have we? Except once."

"Only once . . . I probably won't be home for Christmas. Let's see, it's a week from tomorrow, isn't it?"

"Yes. But Christmas won't matter, this year."

"I wanted it to, Loretta. I wanted to make it a good Christmas, for all of you."

"There'll be other Christmases. When we feel more—more like celebrating . . . Jeff, remember our first Christmas at the ranch?"

"A foot of snow, and cold as all get out."

"And wonderful! Really it was, Jeff. The pines were like a whole grove of Christmas trees. When the sun came out that morning, after the storm, they were dazzling. The whole world was."

"You knitted a scarf for me." He smiled. "And I gave you a saddle of venison. I wanted to get a turkey, but there wasn't one in the whole valley. I gave you something to eat, for Christmas."

"You gave me the house. Don't you remember? When we got the house finished and moved in you said it would have to be my Christmas present because we were flat broke. We only had—how much? Twenty dollars?"

"Closer to fifteen. And I owed Bill eight months' wages."

"Anyway, you gave me the house. It was the nicest present I ever had."

"I thought it was a joke."

"I didn't. It was—well, very important, to me. And we were all together, that Christmas, all five of us. After all the going and coming, and the war, we were together." She paused, looked down at her coffee cup. "We were starting over, Jeff."

Jeff didn't answer.

"And maybe we are starting over again now. After yesterday. Yesterday was an ending, a chapter closed. Jeff, for a long time we've lived just for Tommy. All of us. We don't need to any longer. Tommy doesn't need us now."

"No."

"I promised myself I wouldn't talk about it. You had it all in place, didn't you, Jeff? I thought I did, but—" She hesitated. "But I'm still listening for him, thinking about him with the back of my mind. I'll probably go on doing that for weeks to come." She straightened up resolutely. "Well, you do have to get going."

"I should. This storm's not going to get any better." He finished his coffee.

"Jeff."

"Yes."

"I'd like to say just one more thing about Tommy."

"Go ahead."

"Tommy needed me. That's why I loved him so much, I guess. A woman needs to be needed. I need you, and I need the girls. But Tommy needed me. Do you understand that?"

"I think I do. And now Jane needs you, Jane especially."

"You knew that?"

"Of course."

"Oh, Jeff, Jane needs you too! . . . Jeff, there are so many needs! The needs of oneself, and the needs of others. I suppose we can't take care of all of them, ever. We have to choose, don't we? Decide which needs are the most important. That's the really hard part, the knowing, and the choosing."

She took a deep breath, then stood up. "I'm sending you away, Jeff. Into the storm." She smiled. "I never tried to keep you from going, did I? I've tried so hard not to. And I am sending you away now. Sending you off, when I don't want you to go . . . Good-bye, Jeff."

He took her into his arms and held her for a long moment. They were closer than they had been in a long time. He kissed her, and she clung to him for a moment, then drew away.

He put on his coat and turned and looked at her before he opened the door. She was beautiful. He had always known that. But now there was something almost gallant in her.

He said, "Good-bye, Loretta," and he went out to the stable. He saddled his pony, put the spare on the lead rope and rode away into the storm.

As he reached the open country he settled down to what he knew would be a long, wearying ride. It probably would be the worst trip yet, for the way it was building up this storm could be a full-scale blizzard before the day was out. But if he didn't get through to the ranch today it might be another week before he could get there.

He put the ponies to a fast trot, forcing them early, knowing the storm would slow them down as the day wore on. But with any kind of luck he should be at the ranch by dark.

Strange, he thought, that Loretta should have said that he gave her the house at the ranch. But, as he told her, he thought of it as a joke. The house out there hadn't seemed important to him. Shelter, a place to live.

The Denver house was the important one, and he had given that one to her. It was in her name, legally.

He smiled to himself, remembering how he had come to buy that house. He had thought of moving Loretta and the children to Denver, but never to the point of actually looking for a house. He had promised Loretta that she was going to have pretty dresses and jewelry and a fine house, that first summer after they moved to the Bijou. That was one of the reasons for the quarrel she spoke about this morning. But he was so busy with the cattle he just never got to it.

Then, two years ago this coming spring, he was in Denver for supplies, putting up as usual at the Tremont House. And he met Amos Steck. Steck had served as mayor of Denver a few years before, but Jeff had never met him.

Someone, Jeff forgot who, introduced them and Steck said, "So you are Jeff Ross. John Iliff has talked about you." Steck and Iliff had been partners in a banking venture ten years earlier. "How many cattle have you got out there on the Bijou?"

"About seventy-five hundred head," Jeff said.

"How did you make out this past winter?"

"Not too bad. I had about two per cent loss."

Steck's eyebrows lifted. "That's as good as Iliff did." Then he asked, "When are you going to move to Denver and live like a gentleman? And don't tell me you can't afford it!"

Jeff smiled. "I've never seen the house I want," he said, thinking to dismiss it.

Steck turned to other matters, but a few minutes later he said, "I know the house you should have."

"Where is it?"

"Out on the hill. It's the Jack Bayard place."

Jeff shook his head. Jack Bayard was a speculator, a plunger. Jeff had heard about him. He had heard about the house, too. Bayard had built it two years before, when he was on a wave of success. It was said to be something of a mansion, big and expensive. He said to Steck, "I'm afraid that's not my kind of place."

"Have you ever seen it?"

"No."

"You should take a look at it. It's just the place for a man like you, and it can be bought right." And Steck told Jeff why. After he built the house, Bayard had a streak of bad luck. He lost heavily in several speculations. Last fall he plunged on a venture at Chinaman's Gulch, an early, worked-out gold camp, hoping to recoup his losses. To finance the plunge he mortgaged the house for every cent he could get. Now the Chinaman's Gulch venture was teetering on the brink of a crash and the house mortgage would be due in another two weeks. Bayard had approached Steck for a loan to pay mortgage interest. "Bayard," Steck told Jeff, "is in a squeeze. You can get that house for the face of the mortgage."

"If it's such a good deal, why don't you take it over?" Jeff asked.

"Hell!" Steck exclaimed. "I'm land-poor now! Let me take you out and have a look at it."

But Jeff was wary. "I suppose every banker in Denver knows about this," he said.

Steck smiled. "Nobody knows about it except me. I've loaned money to Bayard before. That's why he came to me. If he went to a bank, his whole Chinaman's Gulch thing would crash tomorrow. He is playing a touchy game, and he just might bring it off. But if word gets out that he's in this kind of jam the wolves will get him overnight." He smiled. "These bankers are so damned smart, I'd like to see Bayard pull this one out of the fire."

The reference to the bankers made Jeff say, "Let's go have a look." If Steck was right, this might be Jeff's chance to repay an old score and get a big, fine house at the same time.

They went out and looked at the house, and Jeff liked it. He asked Steck if he could get a ten-day option for him, and Steck said he thought he could. That evening Steck sent word that he had the option.

The next morning Jeff changed into his ranch clothes, clothes that were just on the decent side of respectability. Then he went to the bank he had visited on that first trip to Denver, the one where he had cooled his heels and finally been told, practically in so many words, that he was unwelcome as a customer.

He went to the bank and sent his name in to George Kelcy, the president. This time there was no waiting, no shunting off to an underling. He was ushered at once to Mr. Kelcy's office and Mr. Kelcy got up from his desk and came to the door to greet him. He took Jeff to the chair beside his desk, offered him a Cuban cigar and said, "I'm glad to meet you, Mr. Ross. I've heard a good many things about you."

The reception itself was almost enough to satisfy Jeff. He savored it, and he let Mr. Kelcy do the talking. Mr. Kelcy asked about the range, the winter, Jeff's herds, Jeff's health. At last he asked, "What's on your mind, Mr. Ross? What can I do for you?"

Jeff said, "I'm thinking about buying a house and moving my family to Denver."

"Splendid. I think we can help you find just the house you want."

"I've already found the house."

"Oh?"

"I thought you might want to finance it."

"Undoubtedly we would, Mr. Ross. Do you want to tell me more about it?"

"It's the Jack Bayard house."

Mr. Kelcy's eyes opened. "I—uh, I suppose we could get it for you. At a price."

"I already have an option on it."

"An option? I didn't know it was for sale. At what price?"

"What do you consider that house worth?" Jeff countered.

Mr. Kelcy hesitated. "Let's see. I believe Bayard mortgaged it last year. For twenty-two thousand five, as I remember. What did you say he was asking?"

Jeff still didn't answer. "Would you be willing to give me a mortgage on it for that amount, twenty-two thousand five?"

Mr. Kelcy drummed on his desk for a moment. Finally he said, "I would consider it favorably, Mr. Ross. Very favorably."

"At ten per cent?"

"Ten per cent!"

"Perhaps," Jeff said, "I should have gone to my bank in St. Louis, but I thought that since I'll be living in Denver I might move my business here, my accounts. As I said, I'll be selling several thousand head of beef cattle in a few months, and—" He let the sentence hang, a half promise.

"Mr. Ross," Mr. Kelcy said, "we can't meet St. Louis rates out here. But I'll make an exception for you. I'll meet you halfway. Twelve and a half per cent?"

Jeff hesitated long enough to give it the air of reluctance and concession. Then he said, "Please put that on paper."

Mr. Kelcy took a sheet of foolscap and wrote it out, a loan of $22,500 to Thomas J. Ross, to be secured by a first mortgage on that Denver property known as the Jack Bayard house and plot, the interest to be twelve and a half percentum per annum. And he signed it.

Jeff said, "I'll be obliged if you will draw up the papers and have the money available to my order this evening. I hope to close the purchase tomorrow."

Mr. Kelcy smiled. "I shall do that, Mr. Ross."

Jeff got to his feet.

Mr. Kelcy took his hand. "It is a pleasure to do business with you, sir."

"This," Jeff said, "is a particular pleasure to me." He folded the agreement and put it in his pocket.

"You still haven't told me," Mr. Kelcy said, "what you are paying for that house."

Jeff smiled. "As long as you get your interest, Mr. Kelcy, and as long as you consider your loan adequately secured, I believe we have no other obligations. Am I right?"

"Quite right." Mr. Kelcy sighed, and he went to the door with Jeff.

Jeff held in his triumphant grin until he was out of the bank. The old score was paid off. In a way, Mr. Kelcy had bought the Jack Bayard house, the big brick house on the hill, and given it to him, trapped in his own smartness. He had loaned Jeff exactly the amount of the face of the mortgage, and Jeff closed the deal for the house the next day. He paid $22,500 for it, and every cent was the bank's money.

He owned it clear now. He paid half the mortgage that first fall and the rest a year later, and he put it in Loretta's name at that time. But the original deal, the bank loan for the full price of the house, still stood as a triumph in his memory.

Looking back now, though, he knew that he had promised the house to Loretta the first summer on the Bijou. In a way, he had.

And, in one way, it was that promise that led to the quarrel, that quarrel she had referred to this morning.

He hadn't often thought of that quarrel, though he'd never forgotten it. In some ways, it still rankled.

The cattle had come through that first winter in pretty good shape. Then spring came with a rush, a rush of warmth and a rush of water. The Bijou boiled down the valley and every draw and slew was brimming with melt. Jeff and Bill were busy for days hauling cattle out of the boggy places and saving early calves from the swarming coyotes. They worked eighteen hours a day.

But by late May the pressure began to let up. By June his young steers were fattening on the new grass, and soon they were almost ready for market. Jeff went to see John Iliff and made the deal for them. They would have put on more weight if he had held them till fall, but he needed the cash. He wanted to go down to Goodnight's place on the Arkansas and buy two thousand yearlings, and he wanted to go early and get his pick of the herds. Goodnight would take his note, but he could get a ten per cent discount for cash, and that ten per cent was important.

So he went to Iliff and made the deal and came home, and Loretta seemed moody. Jeff thought it would pass. He was too busy to pay much attention. He and Bill gathered the fat steers and took them to Iliff up on Crow Creek and got sixty-five hundred dollars for them, more money than he had seen in years. He bought those two bulls, and brought them home, feeling triumphant. But Loretta was still upset, so he changed his plans. He sent Bill down to Goodnight's alone to buy the yearlings and to hire a crew to bring them back.

He saw Bill off for the Arkansas, thinking that now he was really on his way. In just a few more years he would have his own cattle on all these Bijou hills. He saw Bill off and came back in the house and said something like that to Loretta. He thought she would be as pleased as he was.

Loretta was washing dishes. She didn't say a word. She finished the last dish and looked at Jeff, a look he couldn't fathom, and she carried the dishpan outdoors to empty the water in it. Jeff followed her to the doorway. As she turned to come back in he said, "Didn't you hear what I said?"

"I heard," she said. She stepped past him, into the house, and hung up the dishpan, and she dried her hands and flung the towel on the table. She turned to him and said, "So that's what you want, is it?" Her voice was tense.

"Of course that's what I want," he said. "That's what I came up here for, to cover these hills with cattle."

"Why?" she demanded.

It was a strange question, to start with. On top of that, she wasn't given to questioning him. Something was wrong, but he didn't know what. Maybe, he thought, she was having one of her bad times, a monthly. But she had never acted this way before.

He said, "Why? Because I'm a cattleman. You know that, Loretta."

She just stood and looked at him, her eyes blazing.

He said, "There are only two things that are important to me. The cattle. And you and the children."

She still didn't answer. She just stared at him, tight-lipped.

"I know it's been hard on you up here," he went on. "But I wanted you to stay in Dallas till I got things going. You wanted to come, so I brought you. All I've got here is just a sort of a cow camp. But in a few more years, when things work out, I'm going to see that you have a big, fine house, and pretty dresses, and jewelry, and all the things—"

"Jeff!" Her voice was a whiplash.

He waited, silent, thinking she would come out with what was really bothering her.

Instead, she snapped, "You fool! Talking about big, fine houses and pretty dresses and jewelry!"

"Well, what do you want, then?"

"I want you to stop treating me like your kept woman!"

"Loretta!"

"It's been this way for six years, Jeff Ross! For six years you have treated me this way! Oh, yes, I made a home for you and I bore your children. I *wanted* to be your wife, tried to be. But would you let me? No! And now you talk about paying me, with things!"

"I didn't say a word about paying you. Good Lord, Loretta!"

"You didn't have to say it! You didn't even have to think it! You have acted it. Of course I wanted to come up here with you. What else should a wife do? I'm the woman you married,

Jeff! Married! I *am* your wife! Oh, you've gone through the motions of marriage, but you never did marry me where it matters, down inside. Never!"

He was stunned by the outburst. There wasn't a thing he could say, and if there had been he couldn't break in, for she was like a stream in flood. The words rushed at him.

"What do I want? What does any wife want? I want my man! Not what is left over, from someone else. You know what I mean, of course you do! Jeff Ross, you have a wife, a family. Tommy is your son, as well as mine. Is that what you are holding against me? Do you want to get away from your own son, as well as from your own wife?"

"No!" he finally shouted.

"You're running away from something, always running away!"

"I had to go up to Crow Creek and sell those steers! What did you expect me to do with them?"

"That's not what I mean, and you know it!"

"Well, what *do* you mean?"

"You're running away even when you stay home!"

"That," he said, "doesn't make sense."

"It's true!"

"It's ridiculous!"

"You've been running away ever since—ever since the day we were married, and—" Tears came to her eyes. "You even ran away when you went to war."

"You told me to go! You said you wanted me to go!"

"Because I knew you wanted to!"

He shook his head. There was no way to answer such a charge.

"And when the war was over you ran away. From your own wife and your own son!"

"Loretta, I took a trail herd north to make some money! What did you expect me to do? Stay home and starve, let you starve? I don't know whether you ever knew it or not, but my own father told me to stay home and plant potatoes, live like a pauper in a potato patch! Did you know that?"

"No." Now she was crying. And suddenly she said, "Oh, Jeff, I so wanted a son for you! And when he was born I named him for you, proudly, when you were far away and I didn't know if you would ever come back. It hurt, it nearly killed me, when I knew that he wasn't right. When I knew that you knew it too. When did you know, Jeff?"

"It doesn't matter when. Don't you know that, Loretta? It doesn't matter at all."

Then she was in his arms, sobbing. And at last she said, "I'm sorry, Jeff. I didn't mean to make a scene. But— Oh, Jeff, don't you know what I want?"

"What?"

"For you to be mine. And to be happy, proud. I want my man to be proud of—of everything! It isn't that I don't want you to go away. It's that I don't want you to *run* away, ever!"

"I wasn't running away when I went up to Crow Creek."

"I know. But it was the old loneliness again. I just couldn't stand it, Jeff. And you wanted to go down to Goodnight's, and that was too much."

"I didn't go."

"I thought you wanted to go. Jeff, we've been together here for almost a year now, going on a year. More than a year, counting the trip up here. Longer than we've ever been together ever. And—" She stood back from him a moment, gripping his arms almost fiercely. "Jeff, I *do* want you to have the cattle, more cattle than you can count. I want you to have the best and biggest ranch in the whole of Colorado. If that's what you want. But not so you can buy things for me. I don't need a big house, or pretty dresses—"

"You'll have them yet."

"I don't need them! And Jeff, never, never make me think you are buying things for me just to pay me. I—I couldn't stand that! I have my pride too, Jeff. I'm not your kept woman."

And the storm was over, the only real quarrel they ever had.

Yes, he thought now, she had her pride. That was one thing he always respected in her. He was proud of her pride. And that was one reason that he eventually got the big house for her, and the pretty dresses and the jewelry. She wore the dresses proudly, and the jewelry. For him.

And he didn't think he had ever run away after that. Not from her, or from Tommy. From the choices he had made, perhaps. Or from himself, though how can you run away from yourself? You take yourself right along. He found that out, long ago. That was the problem: what to do about yourself. You got to the point where you disliked yourself so much that you had to get away, see if there wasn't some place where you could hide from yourself. And there never seemed to be such a place.

Or, looked at another way, you tried to go some place where the self didn't matter, the self you couldn't live with any longer. Out with the wind and the weather and the grass and the cattle, where a man wasn't what he thought or wished or remembered, but only what he could do. Maybe that was it. He knew one thing. If you think about the past long enough you lose contact with the now and the future. And, right now, if he didn't watch the present there wasn't going to be much of a future.

The storm was getting worse. He had pushed hard to Schuyler Station, then changed horses. He kept pushing most of the way to Box Elder, then changed again. And now he was between Box Elder and Kiowa, and the snow was close to a foot deep. In some places the drifts were so deep they came almost to the horses' bellies.

The wind was driving the snow like sleet. It cut at Jeff's cheeks and the horses couldn't face it. He could keep them headed east, but they crabbed their way, going almost sideways as they tried to face away from the wind. Finally, somewhere between Box Elder and Kiowa, Jeff could no longer take it either. He got off and walked, with his saddle horse on the windward side to give him a little protection.

It was thirteen miles from Kiowa to the Bijou, and it was another ten miles down the Bijou to the ranch. Those last ten miles would be almost directly into the storm. Jeff wondered how either he or the horses could take it. The day was slipping away, and with dusk the storm would increase in severity if there was any change, certainly not let up.

Jeff got back into the saddle, tried to increase the pace. But it was no use. The ponies were tiring and the snow was a constantly deepening problem. From time to time, in the lower draws, they wallowed through drifts so deep he could feel his stirrups dragging.

He rode for a mile and had to get off again. The bitterness of that wind was too much for him. His whole left leg was numb from the cold, and he was sure his left cheek was frostbitten.

He got off, rubbed his cheek with the coarse, granular snow until he got the circulation going again. Then he struggled on foot, between the two horses. He was stumbling in the snow now. To keep his footing he clung to the coiled lariat tied to the pommel of his saddle, and he had to stop and rest more and more often. Rest and flail his arms, and lean against one of the ponies to absorb some of its animal warmth.

He went on, walk and rest, walk and rest, a hundred yards at a time. His only objective now was to reach the Bijou. One thing at a time.

He thought back to the only trail blizzard he had ever faced. Other drovers weren't as lucky as he'd been. Renzo Howard ran into an April blizzard up in Indian territory and lost three men and all but two hundred of a herd of almost fifteen hundred cattle. Renzo tried to keep the cattle headed into the storm, thinking it would let up, and it didn't. The cattle finally turned and stampeded right through his men and scattered from hell to breakfast. They knocked down one team of the mules hauling his cook wagon and overturned the wagon. The cook was trampled and died before they could get a fire going. Two riders tried to stay with the cattle, rode off a cutbank in the blinding snow and froze to death. They found the bodies a week later, when the storm was all over.

Jeff's blizzard was not that bad, but it was bad enough. It was his first trip as a trail boss, and he wanted to get an early start. They left the second week in April. The storm struck them the first day of May, when birds should have been singing and the grass should have been green.

He had twelve hundred head of cattle, a big herd for those days. They had camped in a lowland, beside a stream, with a high clay bank at their backs, to the north. Jeff checked on the night herders at midnight, and everything seemed all right, though a heavy cloud bank covered the whole northern sky and a biting wind had risen. He gave orders for the herders to keep the cattle well bunched, and he went back to his blankets.

The cold roused him before daylight. He got the cook up and ordered early breakfast, wanting to get the cattle moving as soon as possible. They had them off the bed ground by dawn and headed them north. Before the cook wagon caught up the snow had started, flinty pellets on a knife-edged wind. The cattle didn't like it, and it was all the men could do to keep the point headed into it. Jeff didn't like it either, but he thought that it couldn't last.

By noon it was snowing and blowing so hard you couldn't see twenty feet ahead. They didn't stop for a noon meal, but kept on going, hoping to reach the next stream and the shelter of the trees there. But they never made it. The cattle simply wouldn't face the storm. They finally had to let them go, let them drift. They drifted till dusk, and all the riders could do was drift with them, try to hold them together. And as dark closed in on them they came to a stream. The cattle surged down a steep slope to the water and headed downstream.

There was nothing to do but stay with them. They drifted downstream another hour, then slowed up and began to bawl. Jeff rode to the front of the herd and couldn't believe his eyes. Even under the mask of the blizzard, he recognized the place. They had come back to the place they had left that morning, had taken shelter under that high clay bank.

The cattle moved into the timber and stayed there, and Jeff went back and brought up the cook wagon and made camp in the same spot where they had camped the night before.

They stayed there three days, while the storm blew itself out. Then the sun appeared, a warm wind came up from the south, the creek began to flood, and they lined the cattle out to the north again. He had lost only twenty head, and he hadn't lost a man. Just plain lucky. He could just as well have been caught the way Renzo Howard was and lost the whole herd.

And he could be caught now, he thought, stumbling through the snow and clinging to the rope tied to his saddle.

He should be getting to the Bijou. One thing, he couldn't miss the Bijou. But how was he going to make those last ten miles, downstream and into the teeth of the storm? The horses simply couldn't face it. Maybe he would have to hole up. There was a stand of pines about a mile downstream. If he could get there he would have some protection, and maybe he could gather enough dead wood to make a fire.

Then he thought of South Camp. South Camp was south of the railroad. The camp had a cabin, and firewood, and food. And a shelter for the horses. All he had to do was turn south and go *up* the Bijou instead of down, drift with the storm instead of trying to fight his way directly into it.

The thought of South Camp sustained him for the last couple of miles, seemed to give him new strength. It was still walk and rest, walk and rest, but now he thought of the Bijou as a release from the punishment of the storm instead of as a final doubling of it.

And at last he stumbled down the slope and came to the ice in the stream. He had made it. He turned to look for the railroad bridge. It had to be there, not fifty yards away. But he couldn't see ten yards. He urged the horses toward where the bridge should be, and he came to the pilings. He looked up, for the beams and ties that were no more than ten feet above him, and there was nothing but snow. Wind-driven snow, like a shifting white ceiling. Then there was a momentary rift and he got one glimpse of the bridge. Then it was gone, hidden.

The horses, their tails to the wind at last, seemed to have new strength. Jeff had to struggle to keep up with them. He clung to the rope and was dragged when he floundered in a drift. Once the pony on his left, the one with the saddle, stumbled off a cutbank into six feet of snow and almost dragged Jeff after it. Luckily, he still clung to the lead rope of the other pony, which reared and helped Jeff drag clear. He hauled himself away from the flailing hoofs of the pony down in the snow and it scrambled out of the hollow. He caught the reins and they worked their way to higher ground. And made their way upstream.

The camp was on the east side of the stream, and Jeff had turned up the west bank. Between the snow in the air and the gathering darkness he couldn't see the far bank. Unless he got over there, he could drift right past the camp without knowing it. There was a good ford just below the camp, but he wasn't sure he would recognize it now. He had to get across somehow.

He got back into the saddle, forced the ponies down to the water. He wasn't sure where he was, but the ponies sniffed the ice, tossed their heads and refused to take it. They turned and hunched their way up the bank again. He tried two more places, and both times they refused. He knew he wasn't far below the camp now.

He kept watching for another place to try to get across. And then, without his bidding, his pony turned left, crowded through a patch of willow brush that whipped Jeff's face cruelly, and came to the stream. Without a moment's hesitation it started to cross the stream. The lead horse was right alongside. They crossed and climbed the steep bank. They turned right and in less than a hundred yards they were at South Camp. The horses had found the ford.

Jeff got out of the saddle and stumbled and fell, his knees too weak to support him, his legs too numb. As he lay there he saw the ponies go around the cabin and into the shed. Jeff made his way, on hands and knees, to the cabin door and pushed it open. He got inside and closed the door and was in an unbelievable world of shelter from the blizzard. He crouched there several minutes, catching his breath, the first full breath he had had, it seemed, in hours. Then he flailed his arms, working the circulation back.

He tried to get to his feet, but still couldn't make it. He crept to the fireplace, and thanked God that whichever of his hands had been there last had left a supply of kindling. He got a heap of kindling together. Then, holding to the table, got his feet under him and found the can of matches. His hands were so numb he had to hold the matches in his fist to strike them. He struck five of them before he got the flame to catch on a sliver of kindling. He pushed the flaming sliver under a bit of pitch pine and watched the flame grow. He had fire. He was safe.

It took half an hour to get his hands warm enough to unbutton his coat. Then he took the coffeepot to the door, packed it with snow and set it on the fire. While it melted and the coffee cooked he got more snow and rubbed his hands, his cheeks, his nose and his ears. His left ear and the whole left side of his face were frostbitten. And his left hand had two frosted fingers that would be sore for days. But those were his only wounds from the storm.

He hacked chunks from the frozen salt meat in the food box, set them to cook. Then he went outside, to see that the ponies had grain as well as hay. The hay was stacked at one end of the shed, so they could get at all they wanted with a minimum of effort. He unbridled the horse he had been riding, and took off the saddle and blanket. He wished he could do more to protect them, but the house protected them from the worst of the wind and the snow had already drifted back of the shed, closing it in. He shouldered the saddle and made his way back inside. And wondered if he could have pulled through in the pines, if he had had to make camp in the open. Probably, if he could have got a fire going. But he was glad he hadn't been put to the test. Here in the cabin he could last out any storm.

Jeff ate, and heaped wood on the fire and dozed sitting in front of it. And at last he got into the bunk, almost too tired to pull the blankets up over him. But he slept.

He slept till midnight, when the cold wakened him. He got up, replenished the fire and slept again. Twice during the night he had to get up and put wood on the fire, and even then his breath was a cloud of frosty crystals when he saw a streak of light at the cabin's one window. It was getting daylight. His watch showed that it was almost eight-thirty. The wind still howled, and the snow still filled the air, though it was hard to tell whether the snow came from the sky or the ground.

He built up the fire and ate again, and he waited. Eventually this storm would have to blow itself out. Eventually he would get to the ranch. Meanwhile, it would be suicidal to try. Anyway, there wasn't anything he could do at the ranch. Not one thing.

Here, at least, he had food and shelter.

He remembered the story they told about George Jackson and his dogs.

It was in the winter of '58 and '59, before they had found more than a quill of gold in the whole Denver region. Jackson, a cousin of Kit Carson, got tired of just sitting, so toward the end of December he set out from the little cluster of cabins there on Cherry Creek, back into the mountains. He took his two big dogs and went up Clear Creek, hoping to prospect for gold. It was bitter cold, but by building a fire on a gravel bar George could melt a little gravel and pan it out. He didn't find anything till he came to a little run near the South Fork of Clear Creek, but there he found a gravel bar that showed real promise.

He'd eaten all his supplies so he marked the place and started back to Denver. But a blizzard caught him and he had to hole up and wait it out. Without any food he got hungrier and hungrier. He had those two dogs, but he couldn't bring himself to kill and eat them. But both dogs had long, fat tails, and finally Jackson called the dogs and picked one and led it over to a log and made it sit down. Then he took his axe and chopped off the dog's tail.

The dog ran howling off into the storm. It was gone for an hour or so. When it came back, George was eating a meat stew.

Folks used to say that if George had had to hole up a few more days he would have come back with two bob-tailed dogs. But the storm blew itself out and George got back to Denver safely, with both dogs. The next spring he went back to open up his mine, but it soon petered out, just a little pocket of placer gold. Gregory's Gulch, just up the way a little bit, became the first bonanza.

George always denied that he had eaten his dog's tail. He said old Drum got it frozen off. But when folks asked him how come the other dog's tail didn't get frozen off too, George had no answer.

Strange, Jeff thought, how the gold stories fascinated most people. Not one in a thousand of those who came out here for gold ever found it. And nobody seemed to realize that the grass they passed right over in their hurry to get to the gold was worth more than they had yet taken from those mountains. You didn't have to mine grass. It wasn't in a seam in the rock that pinched out to nothing. It grew fresh every spring, as lush as it was the year before, and it cured into standing hay every fall. All you had to do was put cattle on it, let them eat and grow fat. Then you took the cattle to market, and the grass grew again, year after year, for more cattle to eat and fatten on.

You could buy Texas steers for ten or twelve dollars a head. They weighed 600 or 700 pounds. You brought them north and put them on the grass for a year and they fattened to around a thousand pounds. You took them to market and got anywhere from thirty to forty dollars apiece for them. You tripled your investment by letting those cattle eat grass. Some of Jeff's own steers, those from his Shorthorn bulls and his best Texas cows, were as heavy as 1,100 or 1,200 pounds. They brought as much as forty-five dollars a head. And Iliff did even better than that. He contracted his own beef to the Indian agencies and got seven or eight cents a pound for it, on the hoof.

How many men digging for gold could show such returns? Not many. But there weren't many real cattlemen, either. Maybe that was it. Iliff was a cattleman, and Goodnight was, and Jeff was getting to be one. But there weren't more than a dozen real cattlemen in the whole of Colorado. Not yet. There would be, in time. With all the cattle coming up from Texas. This past season, Jeff had heard, half a million head came up. And some of the late herds didn't find buyers and were thrown on the grass by the drovers. They were out there to the east somewhere now, trying to carry those cattle through. And in a winter like this they would lose a lot of them because there wasn't shelter and there wasn't water. Jeff knew. He had come across that country the summer he found the Bijou. He remembered how he had thought then that a blizzard would blow cattle on those high, shelterless flats all the way to the Gulf. And he hadn't known how bad these blizzards could be.

He knew now. And he was thankful that he wasn't out there somewhere trying to carry a trail herd through without any shelter, without even a good, solid cabin to hole up in. This storm would thin those herds out. But it wouldn't hurt the grass. That grass would be there till Kingdom Come.

He put a mess of beans to cook. He went out to check on the ponies, found them dry and warm enough and eating hay and snow in place of water. They laid back their ears and waited for him to try to saddle them, full of meanness. Yesterday's rough going hadn't hurt them one bit. Some men in Denver, even some livery stable men, laughed at Texas ponies, said they were runty and mean and not worth the hay they ate. They preferred horses like Lady, dainty and handsome, horses with the mark of the eastern thoroughbred. But Jeff wouldn't swap one Texas pony for a dozen Ladies for ranch work. Sure they were mean, and they were ugly, and they ate as much as a draft horse, when they could get it. But they were rawhide-tough. And, he thought, as he went back into the house, they could find their way home. Those two out there had found the ford and made their way here last night, when Jeff didn't know where he was within a mile.

He went back in and fed the fire and waited. And the wind howled and the snow kept coming.

It was almost dusk again, and the wind was just beginning to let up a little, when he heard the bellowing.

He listened, and the sound was unmistakable. And close by. He went to the window and scratched a hole in the heavy frost. The snow was still blowing and the drifts were almost up to the window sill, but when there was an eddy in the blown snow he saw the buffalo. Dozens of them, maybe several hundred. The whole hillside was black with their moving bodies. They seemed to squirm like maggots in a dead cow. The snow blew over them and around them, and it eddied over them like a cloud. The nearest ones weren't fifty yards from the cabin.

He watched, and he saw how their faces and shoulders were plastered white with the driven snow. Then the herd surged closer to the cabin as the leaders passed and the bulk of the herd came along. Several of them came right up to the cabin, and he could see the icicles on their chins, the deep fringe of frozen snow over their eyes. Their stubby black horns looked twice as black thrusting out from the snow-packed hair of their heads.

They wallowed through the drifts, those in front pressed on by those behind. Occasionally an old bull paused and bellowed. That was the sound he had heard before he looked out.

Buffalo, drifting into the storm.

They would keep on going as long as the snow continued, as long as the wind blew and the snow filled the air. Too stubborn and too dumb to go back where there was open grass. Maybe not too dumb, but certainly too stubborn. And too full of the instinct for survival. They could face a storm, with that heavy mat of long hair on head and shoulders, but they couldn't turn and drift with it. If they did, their lightly pelted rumps would be exposed to the full force of it. They had to bull their way into it.

So they plodded into the storm, over the hills and down through the valleys, through the timber and across the streams. And if they encountered a bunch of cattle, they simply absorbed them, drew them into the herd. The herd provided some protection, some shelter from the killing wind, some mass warmth that a steer couldn't resist.

Jeff watched, wondering if this was a really big herd. If it was, they would go right down the valley, gathering his cattle along the way. Drifting them north. If the storm lasted another night and day, they would go all the way to the Platte. Maybe the Platte would stop them. Maybe it wouldn't. Unless they got trapped in the ice or bogged in quicksand they would keep right on going till the storm was over. And even if the leaders bogged in, that wouldn't stop them. Those behind would walk right over them, oblivious.

He watched for maybe half an hour. And the herd passed. It had been a herd of maybe two hundred head, at most three hundred. Just a band, really, not a herd. But five or six times as big as that band he saw two weeks ago.

He watched the last of them pass and turned back to the fire. Even a band this size could take a lot of cattle with them. And if they got as far as the Platte there would be a lot of dead cattle. Weakened by the cold and the storm's beating, the cattle would get caught in the ice of the Platte. The buffalo would bull their way across, at least a part of them, but the cattle wouldn't make it. They would go down in the icy water and they would drown like rats in a barrel.

Well, there wasn't anything he could do about it. Not a thing. They were going down the ridge. If they stayed on the ridge they wouldn't pick up many cattle. There was nothing to do but wait till he could get out of here, make his way to the ranch, see what had happened.

Dark was closing in. He couldn't get out tonight, even if the wind died down. And though it had lessened, it still was very much alive.

12

Jeff dreamed about Tommy that night. Tommy and that crazy old trapper, Jake Starling. Jake rode up to the ranch in a blizzard and he came in and said, "I've come to take the boy." He looked across the room to the crib where Tommy was lying, and Tommy sat up in the crib and said, "I'm ready, Mr. Starling."

Jake said, "Then come on, young'un!" And he walked across the room and picked up Tommy, in his nightshirt, and carried him outside. Jeff and Loretta followed them to the door and watched Jake set Tommy on a horse he had waiting, then get on his own horse. And Tommy wasn't a baby any longer, and he wasn't crippled. He was a boy almost grown, and his legs were straight. He didn't have on the nightshirt, either. It had become a buckskin hunting shirt, like Jake's except that it was clean and new and honey-colored, not smoke-black and greasy like Jake's. A clean, new buckskin shirt, and new buckskin leggings and a breech clout, and a shapeless wool hat.

They got on the horses, and suddenly there was a herd of buffalo, so many buffalo they filled the whole valley. Their bawling and the clicking of their hoofs was even louder than the roar of the storm. They swept past the house in a dark brown flood, and old Jake and Tommy just sat there, waiting.

The buffalo rumbled past, their heads white with snow. And then cattle came, cattle by the hundred, right in with the buffalo. Every one of the cattle carried the Pothook brand. Jeff could see the pinkish white brand on the ribs of every red or roan steer.

They streamed past, cattle and buffalo. And finally Jake began to whoop and holler. Then Tommy started, his senseless words, the kind of talk he always made. Jake turned and looked at him and grinned and said, "You make a lot of sense, young'un!" And he and Tommy heeled their horses and rode right in among the cattle and buffalo flooding past. They went with the herd, right through the grove of pines just north of the house. They vanished, and the buffalo thinned out, and the cattle, and then Jeff and Loretta stood there alone in the open doorway, the storm beating at them. And Loretta turned to him and said, "He's gone, Jeff! He's gone!" And her eyes were beaming and tearing at the same time.

Jeff said, "He's gone," and suddenly the cold got to him. He was freezing, especially his feet. He wanted to get back in the house and close the door, and he couldn't move.

Then he wakened.

It was a long minute before he knew where he was, the dream had been so vivid. One by one, in the thin glow of the dying coals in the fireplace, he made out the fireplace itself, then the table, then the tin food box, then his coat hanging on a peg beside the door. And he looked down the bunk and saw his own feet. In his turning and twisting he had pulled the blankets up around his shoulders and uncovered both his feet.

Shaken by the dream, he sat up. His feet were numb with the cold, but he managed to get to the fireplace and feed fresh wood, get the flame going. He sat there fifteen minutes warming himself before he went back to bed.

He went back to bed, but he didn't go right to sleep. The dream was still with him.

There was no mystery about the dream except the appearance of the old trapper in it. And even that wasn't really mysterious. The night before the funeral Loretta had mentioned Crazy Jake and what he said about Tommy. Jake's story about the crippled child among the Crows had stayed in Jeff's mind, probably, freshened by Loretta's reference. And the appearance of the buffalo, flooding past the cabin here, had put that idea in his mind, the buffalo and his cattle drifting in a blizzard.

Old Jake was dead, so the Cheyennes had said. Undoubtedly true. Jake was an old man when Jeff first saw him, a remnant of the old days of the fur trappers. Tommy was dead, too. Maybe they were together somewhere, in some Hereafter. Who knew?

Tommy deserved a Hereafter. This world couldn't have been a very happy place for him. Yes, Doc Crane was right. It was better this way. But, damn it, Crane wasn't the one to say so! Tommy wasn't Crane's son. Crane wasn't involved. It was Crane's job to take care of the living, not to sit in judgment on the dead.

Jeff listened to the storm, the wind still blowing a gale. It wasn't as bad as yesterday, but it was still a blizzard. He stared at the firelight and thought: How long have I been in a cabin like this, all alone, waiting out a storm? Is a man always alone in some cabin, dreaming, and waking, and waiting? Waiting for what? Wondering which is real, the dream or the waking?

Then he was weary again. The beating of the storm began to lull him. He slept again.

It was daylight when he wakened, and the storm had begun to blow itself out. The wind still howled and there was a good deal of snow in the air, but the sky was lighter. Between the blasts of wind-driven snow Jeff could see patches of blue, and now and then the sun burst through to turn the swirling ground snow into glittering clouds.

Jeff built up the fire and ate his breakfast. He went out and saddled one of the ponies, which didn't like the saddle one bit. Jeff knew he would have to ride off the pony's frosty meanness, but he also knew that a horse couldn't do a first-class job of bucking in a snowdrift.

He was going to try to make it to the ranch, see what was happening there. Maybe they didn't need him, but his cattle were at stake and he couldn't hole up here at South Camp till the spring thaw.

He cut fresh kindling, carried in firewood from the rick at the end of the horse shed, stowed the food and put out the fireplace fire. He put on extra socks and tied the muffler over his ears and got into his saddle coat, and he went out and led the ponies through the drifts to a place where he could mount. The iron-gray, the one he was riding, made the snow fly for a few minutes, but Jeff was set for a fight with him and rode him out. Then he headed for the ranch.

He had hoped that the track made by the band of buffalo would be of some help. But it wasn't. Overnight the track had drifted full of packed snow and made even harder going than it was through the undisturbed drifts. But by working his way from one ridge to another he could keep to the shallower snow, and he worked his way downstream. Before he had gone two miles, however, he had to leave the valley, where the drifts were six feet deep in places, and work his way out onto the broken flatlands where the going was made more punishing by the wind but where the footing was better. One thing, there was no icy crust.

He came to the railroad tracks and stopped long enough to change horses. He rode the meanness out of the bay pony, crossed the tracks and kept on north. The wind had scoured the ridges. By constant zigzagging he could keep to places where the snow was less than a foot deep. And by changing directions constantly he gave his face and arms a chance to alternate the bite of the wind and the comfort of the sun. The sun had now broken through the clouds. It was far to the south, but even its scant warmth was a comfort. And it provided a compass point on which to guide.

Noon came and passed, and the sun began its descent down the narrow arc toward the horizon. The cold began to stiffen Jeff and he dismounted and walked for a mile. But that only slowed him up, because he had to stop for breath every few hundred yards. He changed mounts and rode again, trying to push the ponies.

The sun was almost down on the horizon and it was almost three-thirty. Jeff turned down a ridge to the west, toward the Bijou. He struck the valley only a mile above the ranch. Then he turned north along the crest of the valley's hills. The sun sank in a dazzle of blowing snow, and the long blue shadows began to fill the hollows. And at last he saw the big grove of pines and the ranch house and the log barns and sheds and the corrals. A long streamer of smoke was blown out from the house chimney, smoke only a trace darker than the streamers of snow that still plumed from every hilltop.

Jeff made his way down to the house and into the dooryard, and he shouted and the door opened. Sam Royce stood there against the inner light and stared for a moment and exclaimed, "Good God almighty, look who's here!"

Then, as Jeff dismounted, Harvey Bird and Pete Wallace came to the doorway, shouldering into their coats. They took the ponies and Jeff went inside.

Bill Sanders got up from a bunk and limped over to Jeff.

"Where in the name of the good Lord did you come from?" Bill asked. "Not from Denver." Bill looked haggard. There were pain lines around his eyes and mouth.

"From South Camp," Jeff said, beginning to strip off his outer gear. He came to the fireplace to warm himself, and Bill sank onto a bench, elbows on the table.

"South Camp," Bill said. "I was afraid you'd try to make it here in that blizzard." Then he asked, "Everything all right in Denver?"

"Everything's all over," Jeff said.

"Too late?"

"He died around ten o'clock."

"Sorry, Jeff."

Jeff nodded. Sam handed him a cup of coffee.

"How's Loretta?" Bill asked.

"All right."

"The girls?"

"They're all right."

Pete and Harvey came in from the barn. They glanced at Jeff and knew the answer to the unasked question. Bill had told them the situation in Denver the night that he arrived. Now they hung up their coats and sat down in silence.

Sam said, "Supper's about ready." He banged his pots in the fireplace for a moment, then turned to Jeff. "Jeff, I'm going to say it and get it over with. We're sorry about the boy. I guess that's about all there is to say, because—well, the good Lord must have His reasons." Sam paused, embarrassed.

Jeff said, "Thanks. I'm grateful to all of you." Then he asked, "How are the cattle?"

There was a sense of relief in all of them, even in Bill. Jeff had put the whole matter back on a basis where they could accept it, understand it. A man handled his own grief, his own personal loss, and once you had said your say you had done all you could. You didn't have to keep chewing at his feelings. You respected his privacy, and you hoped that was what he wanted. Most men did. Jeff had closed the gate on his son's death. In effect, he had said,

"It's over and done with. Our business is cattle. Let's get back to business."

Bill said the cattle were doing all right, as far as they could tell. They got their plates and filled them from Sam's cooking pots and began to eat. Bill said nobody could get out in the storm yesterday to have a look at the cattle. "We were out a while this morning," Bill concluded, "but so much snow was blowing we couldn't do anything or even see very much."

"You were out?" Jeff asked.

"A little while." Bill was defensive.

"I told you to sit, damn it!" Then Jeff asked, "How many cattle do you suppose those buffalo picked up?"

"What buffalo?"

"Didn't they come through here? A band of two or three hundred passed South Camp late yesterday."

They all shook their heads. "They didn't come this way," Bill said.

Jeff frowned. For a moment he wondered if they could have been a part of that dream. No, they were real. He saw them before he went to sleep. And he saw their track this morning, a track that even a night of blowing couldn't completely hide. "They passed South Camp, heading this way," he said. "I don't know where they went from there."

Bill shook his head. "That's all we need now, buffalo."

The wind eased off during the night. Next morning all except Bill saddled ponies and worked their way downstream to survey the situation. When they returned to the ranch in midafternoon and compared reports Jeff said he wanted Sam to go out to East Camp the next day, Pete to go down to Cottonwood, Harvey to go over to Comanche.

"If there's any grass open at all, get the cattle out of the yards. I found a little grass open today. Once the cattle get on it, they'll open more. Don't stay more than a week. Then come back here and report in. Meanwhile, I'll break out what I can around here."

It was a difficult assignment, and Jeff knew it. But they had found only about sixteen hundred head of cattle in the timber along the Bijou today. Somewhere out there he had another eighty-four hundred head, or close to it. At cost, those steers represented over a hundred thousand dollars.

So the next day they started for the camps, each man with a string of extra ponies. The horses would have to break trail, and when the men reached the camps they would need spare mounts for the strenuous job of getting the cattle out and onto the ridges.

Bill insisted that he was going to help Jeff work the home valley, until Jeff said, "I'm bossing this job. When I need you, I'll say so."

"You'll need me," Bill said quietly.

"I'll know it when I do."

And Jeff went to the barn, saddled a pony and went to work.

The first two days Jeff got just under eight hundred head of cattle out of the timber and up onto the ridges. He worked from before sunup till after dark, and he came home and ate and fell into his bunk, too tired to talk. Bill asked questions and Jeff answered in monosyllables. Was the snow melting? No. Were the cattle starving for water yet? No. Wolves killing any cattle yet? A few. How many cattle were still in the timber? Don't know.

And, always, the final question. "Need me yet?"

"No."

The third day was even harder than the first two. There had been no melt, but the drifts had settled enough to make the snow almost as compact as sand. Jeff took three spares with him and changed mounts every hour or so, and by midafternoon all four horses were so tired they walked with dragging feet and hanging heads. Jeff kept at it till sundown, and he got another three hundred head of steers out onto the ridges. Then he headed for home. He was as tired as the horses, and he still hadn't freed all the cattle within ten miles of the house. Even as he started home he could hear the steers in another yard just downstream bellowing. Tomorrow, he thought. I can't get them out till tomorrow. A man can do just so much.

He rode home, and as he crossed the ford he saw that the house was dark. Instead of putting his horses away he went to the house and inside to see what was wrong.

Bill wasn't there. His bunk was empty, the fire was out, the house was cold. He looked for Bill's cold-weather gear. It was gone.

He went to the barn, knew before he looked that Bill's saddle would be missing. And five ponies were gone.

Jeff saddled a fresh pony and went to the ford, looking for Bill's tracks. None there. He went back across the yard and found a wind-blown trail that led up the slope to the east. When he followed it to the hilltop he saw that it turned south. Bill had gone to South Camp.

Jeff settled into the saddle and followed the trail. There had been a light wind all day, just enough to sift snow into the tracks but not enough to obscure them. It was a clear night with a crescent moon in the west, and all the stars in the universe were out, making the snowy world full of eerie shadows. The shadows lay in the drifted tracks of Bill's ponies, picking them out as far ahead as Jeff could see.

A mile above the house he came to the first place where Bill had broken a bunch of cattle out of the timber. They had chowsed up the snow on the ridge, had grazed for a while. Now they were down in the timber again. A steer bellowed, hearing Jeff on the ridge, and the echoes bounced off the hills, strangely loud in the cold night stillness. Jeff listened and thought that only the yammering of a coyote was a more lonely sound on a winter night than the bawling of a steer in a yard in the drift-deep timber.

He rode on, past one place after another where Bill had got the cattle out of the timber and up onto the ridge. He counted seven bunches that Bill had found before he came to the railroad tracks.

He crossed the tracks. From there on he found only three more places where Bill had moved cattle out of the timber. Evidently they hadn't drifted far beyond the railroad, not many of them, anyway.

At last he came into sight of the cabin. His pony lifted its ears and whickered, and a pony in the shed at the camp answered. A moment later the cabin door opened and Bill stood there against the dim glow from the firelight. Jeff rode up and Bill said, "I was afraid I'd have company."

"You have," Jeff said, and he went around and put his horse in the shed. He unsaddled and went inside and dropped his saddle in a corner.

"Eaten yet?" Bill asked.

"No."

Bill moved a skillet of fried salt meat onto the hot coals. When the fat began to smoke he spooned thick batter into the grease, made quick-and-easy sore-thumb bread. He poured a cup of coffee and set it on the table in front of Jeff.

"How many did you get out of the timber?" Jeff asked.

"Three hundred and forty-two head."

"Any more there?"

"I just worked this side of the creek. Probably another three hundred head on the other side."

"We'll get them out tomorrow." Jeff put his elbows on the table, let his head sink into his hands.

"Any of the boys back yet?" Bill asked, turning the bread in the sputtering grease.

Jeff shook his head.

"Good sign. They found cattle."

Jeff didn't answer. Bill scooped the meat onto a tin plate, put the fried bread beside it and set the plate in front of Jeff. Jeff straightened up, tried to eat. He downed one of the sore-thumbs and a few pieces of meat, dipped another sore-thumb into the congealing grease and took one bite. He leaned his head on one hand and went to sleep. Jeff was worn out.

Bill waited a few minutes, then got him to his feet, led him to the bunk and helped him in. Jeff never really wakened. Bill pulled off his boots and drew the blankets up over him. Then he spread the two saddle blankets on the floor in front of the fire and spread a ratty old buffalo robe over them. He sat down on it and pulled off his own boots, gritting his teeth as the boot came off his bad leg. Over the woolen drawers and the sock he wore on that leg was another layer of gray wool, part of the leg he had cut from a spare pair of heavy drawers. He peeled that off and rolled down the sock and held the leg toward the fire to warm the ache out of it. There wasn't much pain in the leg if he kept it warm, but the cold set it jumping like a bad tooth. And even that extra thickness of wool didn't keep it warm in this weather. But, he thought with a glance at his stiff, crooked elbow, a man learns to live with pain.

He looked at Jeff, dead to the world in the bunk, and he thought that Jeff had learned to live with pain too. A different kind of pain. Or had he? Had he done what he was doing now, worked so damned hard to forget that he just numbed himself to it? Jeff's pain was the boy, though he had never admitted it. One pain, at least. There was something else that always baffled Bill, something that happened before the boy.

Funny, you work with a man for years, live in the same house and eat out of the same pot, and never know all about him. What was that old saying? "Wear the other fellow's boots for a week if you want to know why he limps."

Something happened to Jeff before the war, before the boy was born. Something Jeff had never mentioned. Nor Loretta either. But Loretta wouldn't. Loretta was a lady, right down to her toes, and she never complained or talked. Not about Jeff. Or the boy.

Bill pulled his sock back up and put the woolen drawer leg over it. The throbbing had eased as much as it would tonight. He put more wood on the fire, he drew the buffalo robe up around him and he lay back to sleep. Whatever it was, he thought, Jeff had to handle it alone. That's the way he would want it. The same as Bill had to handle the leg. Nobody can help much with something inside your bones. Or in your heart.

Bill thought about the girl who had promised to marry him when the war was over. He'd never mentioned her to anyone, not even Jeff. When he got his first furlough he went back to see her, there at the crossroads settlement on the Angeline River, and everything was fine. Then they were in the battle at Elkhorn Tavern and he got the crooked arm, and he wondered if she would want him, that way. He couldn't bring himself to write to her about it, because she'd never learned to write and couldn't read much and someone else would have to read it to her. So he waited another six months, till his next furlough.

He went back again, and strangers were in the cabin where she had lived with her family. They told him that she and her whole family, her father and mother and both her younger sisters, died in a fever that swept the town and took almost half the people. He went to the burying ground and looked for her grave, but he never found it. There were twenty or thirty new graves, but only a few wooden markers, and none had her name on it. So he went back to the war and tried to forget.

He eased his leg into a more comfortable position and closed his eyes. And thought of a girl sitting beside him on the bank of the Angeline, and her saying, "We'll have six boys, Bill. I want six sons just like you." But try as he might, he couldn't bring back her face clearly, or the actual tones of her voice. All he could see was a face that looked like Loretta's, and all he could hear was Loretta's voice.

He thrust the confused memory away, feeling guilty, somehow. It wasn't right even to think about Loretta that way.

Then he thought that if he had a son, even a crippled son like Tommy, he'd try to work hard enough to forget when the boy died. Take away everything else from a man, and there's still work to be done. He'd found that out a long time ago.

Work, and sleep, and be ready to work again tomorrow.

Bill's guess was wrong, but only by ten head. They worked the west side of the creek between South Camp and the home ranch the next day and found two hundred and ninety cattle in the timber. They got them out onto the ridges and they were home by dusk.

Sam Royce was there ahead of them. Sam had come in from East Camp that afternoon. He had an unhappy report. He had spent four days searching the breaks over east and he turned up only sixty head of cattle.

"That band of buffalo," Sam said, "went through there and they must have picked up all the rest."

"How many?" Jeff asked.

"Damned if I know, but I'd guess at several hundred head. I trailed them ten miles and there were a lot of fresh cow chips in with the buffalo chips."

"Which way did they go?"

"North-northeast, right into the storm."

Bill said, "They didn't go too far. That was the last day of the storm, wasn't it?"

"It kept on blowing all that night and the next day and the next night," Jeff said. "They could have gone most of the way to the Platte." He turned back to Sam. "No sign of the buffalo on their way back?"

"Not a sign."

"God damn those buffalo." It wasn't profanity. It was more like a prayer. "They eat your grass, they steal your cattle, they're no damn good to anyone but the Indians."

The next day the three of them worked the yarded cattle out of the timber along the Bijou in the places that Jeff hadn't been able to reach alone. They got another four hundred head out, but they left close to a hundred head in the yards, carcasses cut down and half eaten by the wolves and steers still alive but too weak to move. The losses were beginning to pile up.

The next day they got down to Cottonwood and joined Pete. Pete had been working the timber downstream from Cottonwood Camp. He reported about a thousand head already out, another two or three hundred still yarded. "Getting weak," he said. "I don't know how many can pull through." Then he added, "Quite a lot of Bar H stuff is mixed in."

"How many?" Jeff asked.

"Two, three hundred head. Beats me how those scrubby cattle can pull through at all."

"Any sign of buffalo?" Jeff asked.

Pete shook his head. Both his cheeks were peeling from frost-bite and windburn.

The next day the four of them got out those cattle Pete hadn't been able to get to. Almost half of them were scrawny, long-legged Bar H cattle.

Then they moved on to Comanche Camp.

Harvey Bird was in trouble. Both his feet were frostbitten, one of them so swollen he couldn't wear his boot. Two days before, while trying to drive a bunch of steers out of a yard, a Bar H steer on the prod had hooked his horse with its horn, driven the horse onto the ice and into the creek. The horse was so badly gored that Harvey had to shoot it. Soaked to the skin and three miles from camp, Harvey tried to light a fire. But his matches were wet. His clothes were beginning to freeze, so he caught one of the spare horses and made his way back to camp, alternately riding and walking. Both feet, in the wet boots, got frosted. By the next morning his left foot was so badly swollen he couldn't get his boot on. So he cut strips of blanket, wrapped the foot to protect it somewhat from the cold, and went back to work, getting the cattle out.

"Why, in God's name," Jeff demanded, "didn't you come on back to the ranch?"

"There's a lot of cattle here," Harvey said simply.

"Let's see that foot."

Jeff stripped off the blanket wrapping and removed the sock. The foot was grotesquely swollen, the toes as big as a man's thumb.

207

But the toes were uniformly red and feverish, not mottled. There was a little mottling around the ankle, but the skin hadn't begun to slough. There was no sign of gangrene. With luck, Harvey would come out of this without losing his foot, might even save all his toes. He had rubbed the foot with snow, the night it happened, till he got the circulation going. And the exercise since then may have helped.

Jeff drew the sock back up over the swollen foot and Harvey wound it in the blanket strip. Watching him, Jeff was sure the dark blood in him was Indian blood; only an Indian would have that much stoic courage. Then he looked at Pete Wallace, and he thought of the night Pete's horse played out and Pete walked in. He looked at Bill Sanders. He looked at Sam Royce. And he decided that Sam was the luckiest one of them all. Or the shrewdest; he couldn't say which. Sam never seemed to get himself into a corner.

He turned back to Harvey, saw the pain lines in his lean, young face. "Thanks, Harvey," he said. And he asked, "How many cattle are still yarded up?"

"Four, five hundred."

The next two days the five of them, only three of whom were really able-bodied, worked the shelter along the Comanche and got the live cattle out onto the ridges. Harvey had been right. There were close to five hundred head; but almost a hundred of them were dead or dying. The wolves were having a feast.

Returning to Comanche Camp the second evening, Jeff mentally tallied up. They had accounted for less than sixty-five hundred head of cattle, and of those between eight hundred and a thousand were dead or dying. The totals were appalling. There inevitably had been some drift to the south, even though they had found only a few bunches yarded up between the railroad and South Camp. Maybe another thousand had gone south with this last blizzard. God knew where they might be by now, maybe clear down on the Arkansas. A few hundred head might have been caught in that band of buffalo and gone north. They might be up along the Platte. But even if you added those in and said there were fifteen hundred head still alive up north and down south, the total came out at only eight thousand. That left two thousand unaccounted for. Plus the thousand or so that he knew were dead or doomed right now. Close to three thousand head. At least seventy-five thousand dollars.

Then he figured it another way. If he had seven thousand head, and if he carried them through and sold them as fat cattle next summer, say at thirty dollars a head, he could just about break even. But that was figuring that he could carry all seven thousand through the balance of the winter, come out next spring with seven thousand still on their feet and grazing. And it would be a tight squeeze to come out at all. If he still had seven thousand.

Another thing. He had about two thousand cows in those herds. Cows he had bred to his Shorthorn bulls, for a calf crop in the spring. They weren't beef stock. Suppose he'd already lost five hundred cows. That would leave fifteen hundred cows. Take fifteen hundred away from the possible seven thousand and you cut the number of market cattle to fifty-five hundred. Fifty-five hundred steers, even at thirty dollars a head, wouldn't pay off the notes.

Any way he figured it, he was in trouble. Plenty of trouble. And there was a lot of winter still ahead. He counted back, reaching for what date it was. As near as he could figure it, it was the first of January, New Year's Day. Either the first or the second, he wasn't sure which. In any case, January and February and March were ahead. There might be breaks in the weather now and then, but he couldn't expect the real break-up and new grass till late March or April. And right now April looked ten years ahead.

Well, you play the cards as they fall. There wasn't any way out now except straight ahead, day after day.

They returned to Comanche Camp and they ate in silence. Bill looked up and asked, "How many did we get out today?"

"Two hundred and ten," Harvey Bird said.

Bill nodded, and Jeff knew that Bill was adding up his own totals. A few minutes later Bill looked at Jeff and started to say something, then thought better of it. Jeff knew by the look on his face that Bill had come out at about the same point Jeff had. Trouble. More trouble than either of them wanted to talk about.

They started back to the home ranch the next morning. The sky was overcast, the wind was raw, but nobody mentioned the weather. They rode in almost complete silence.

They were within two miles of the ranch house when Jeff heard a steer bellowing down in the timber. A frightened, frantic bellow. He reined toward the creek, forced his horse through a drift and down a gully to the water's edge. On the far bank, beyond a deep pool completely iced over, half a dozen steers were in a yard, backed against the snow, facing two big timber wolves. The wolves had hamstrung a steer. It was down and bellowing, trying to get to its feet. The wolves were about to close in, get to its throat and finish the kill.

Jeff jerked his rifle from the scabbard and shot one wolf. It jerked, snapped at its ribs, tried to run and fell, dead. Jeff was so mad he fired a quick shot at the other wolf and only broke its leg. It scrambled to the drift at the edge of the yard and Jeff, trying to get a clear sight for another shot, jabbed his pony with a spur. The pony jumped, lost its footing for an instant, and was on the ice. The ice gave way, the horse scrambled, and Jeff was in six feet of water, the horse on top of him.

The horse thrashed madly. A flailing hoof caught Jeff in the ribs, made him gasp, then gag at the icy bite of the water. Instinctively he fought his way to the surface, only to be knocked under again by the struggling horse. His arms and legs felt paralyzed, his lungs bursting.

He was at the surface, grabbing at the ice. The ice crumbled. He was sinking, going under the ice. Then someone had him in his arms, was shouting, "Here! Grab here, Jeff!" And even as he grabbed the edge of the ice he felt something slip past him, clutch desperately at his coat and slide away. Then he saw Pete Wallace, Pete and Sam Royce. They had him by the arms, were hauling him out onto the ice. And he heard Harvey Bird shout, "Bill! Where's Bill?"

The next thing he knew, Jeff was lying in the snow on the bank and Harvey Bird and Pete Wallace were still there on the ice, Pete calling, "Bill! Bill!"

Then Jeff was sitting under a pine tree, in front of a fire, wearing Pete Wallace's pants and Sam Royce's coat. Jeff was shaking and retching, bringing up water that burned his nose and throat. Between spasms he saw Harvey Bird hobbling along the black ice, looking, looking. Downstream a little way, where the creek shallowed into an ice-free rapid, Pete Wallace, in his underdrawers, was watching for Bill Sanders' body. And Jeff felt nauseated by the shock of what he knew must have happened and yet could not believe.

They stayed two hours. Then dark closed in and they had to give up. They rode home in stunned silence, the four of them, leading a fifth pony with an empty saddle.

They rode home, and while the boys put the horses away Sam took Jeff inside and wrapped him in blankets and built a fire and got the whiskey bottle and made a strong toddy for him. Then Sam made coffee and fried meat and bread.

They tried to eat, but nobody was really hungry. Finally Jeff said, "Somebody tell me just what happened."

"Your horse hit the ice," Sam said. "Next thing I knew, there was a hole in the ice big as a wagon bed and you were in it and your horse on top of you. Bill went in after you. I still don't know how he got there so fast. I wasn't even out of the saddle."

"Bill had been riding with me," Pete said. "He put his horse right down the bank and I don't think he even got off. He just dived in, right from the saddle!"

"Time we got there," Sam went on, "Bill had got hold of you. He got you up where Harvey and Pete could grab you. And the next thing I knew, Bill was gone. The current must have took him right under the ice."

"Bill," Jeff said slowly, "couldn't swim a stroke."

And suddenly Pete Wallace slammed his plate on the table and cried, "God damn it to hell!" He ran outdoors, crying.

Jeff watched and slowly shook his head. Pete had never before seen a man die, not that way. Pete had to scream and curse and cry tears. When he was a few years older he would cry inside, keep his mouth shut and cry inside.

A little later Pete came back in, went to his bunk, pulled off his boots, pulled up the blankets and faced the wall. Soon afterward Harvey Bird hobbled to his bunk and got in.

Sam and Jeff sat staring at the fire for another fifteen minutes. Then Sam asked, "Getting warm yet, Jeff?"

Jeff nodded. "All warm, Sam. I'm all right."

Sam glanced at Bill's empty bunk. Jeff followed his eyes, looked at the shelf above the bunk. On the shelf were Bill's shaving mug, his razor and a half-empty bottle of linament for sore muscles, the linament he had used on that aching leg. Nothing else.

Sam said, "We'll miss Bill."

Jeff said softly, "God rest his soul."

Sam bowed his head and whispered, "Amen."

The next morning Jeff wakened with a pain in his ribs. It stabbed at him as he sat up in his bunk, and he couldn't draw a deep breath. He winced and wondered what had happened to him. Then he saw Bill Sanders' empty bunk, and he remembered. And a deeper pain went all over him, a pain that smothered and made him forget the physical pain in his ribs. Bill was gone. Bill was dead.

He lay back in his bunk for a long minute, trying to tell himself it was a dream, a nightmare. Then he knew it was true. He sat up and reached for his pants and his boots. He had a cracked rib or two, maybe a couple of broken ribs, from that kick his horse gave him in the water. But ribs mend. They knit and heal. The deeper pain would be there a long time, for the memories heal slowly.

They rode down the creek that day, all four of them, and they searched the stream, every rapid, every open pool. But they didn't find Bill's body. And Jeff knew they wouldn't find it till the spring thaw, if then.

They rode home again in the dusk. There was a spit of snow in the air.

13

The snow didn't amount to much, an inch or so, but for a week the wind blew, a bitter wind that kept the fine snow drifting. Some of the hilltops cleared, but the air never warmed enough for the sun to take hold. January's cold had settled down, with no break in sight.

There was little they could do for the cattle. They put the horse herd out on the ridges to pick what grass they could and paw for more, open the grass for the cattle. And to save the hay. Every mouthful of grass the horses ate was a mouthful of hay they wouldn't need. Jeff had gone into the winter with ten big stacks of hay, cut from the best hay draws near the ranch. That would have carried his horses through any normal winter with a stack or two to spare. But not this year. More than half those stacks were already gone.

They did the chores, and they nursed their wounds.

Jeff got nothing worse than a slight cold and a cough from his near escape from drowning. The cough was worse than the cold because when he coughed he felt as though his injured ribs were being torn apart. Sam prescribed a cough syrup of whiskey and sugar, but it didn't help. Harvey's remedy was more successful. He sent Pete out to get chokecherry bark and oak and sumac bark. He made an infusion of chokecherry bark for Jeff and laced it with whiskey. Jeff didn't know whether the stuff eased the cough or the cough wore itself out, but he began to feel better.

Harvey stewed up the oak and sumac bark, added epsom salts and soaked his frozen foot in the mixture. Some element in it re-

duced the swelling and toughened the skin. By the end of the week
he could wear a boot again. Not his own, but one of a spare pair
they found under Bill Sanders' bunk. Bill's feet were two sizes
bigger than Harvey's.

They waited a week for the weather to ease, hoping that January
would yet make amends for December, the worst December Jeff
could remember. And at last it did ease. The wind died and they
had two days of calm and clear sun and melt.

Cautious hope began to rise in Jeff as he rode out to look at his
cattle. For some reason, his cows were in better shape than his
steers, seemed to have lost less flesh. Then he looked again. The
cows weren't in better shape at all; they were carrying calves, Jeff's
spring calf crop. They were just as thin as the steers, rib-thin, gaunt,
starved. Actually in worse shape, because they had calves in their
bellies, an extra drain on them.

The farther he rode, the more cattle he saw, the more that pain
in his ribs began to throb. Damn it, the winter couldn't do this
to him! It couldn't put him right back where he started, with a
little bunch of cows and not a cent to his name! And not even
Bill Sanders to stand by, to get his shoulders under the load along
with Jeff.

If he lost his cattle, what would he have left?

He turned back toward the ranch, the cautious hope dead within
him. Feeling more alone than he had felt in years. And he knew
that, despite himself, he had been listening for Bill's voice every-
where he turned. Looking for Bill. Wondering where Bill was.

He turned back, and he saw a cloud bank begin to roll up from
the western horizon. The wind began to lift and he thought: Is
this the way it's going to end, in a blizzard and a snowdrift? Have
I come this far to have it end this way? Would it have been better
to have had it end under the ice, quick, clean? Certainly better
than to become a paupered old man mumbling about the days
when his cattle covered the hills.

He rode home and found Pete at the barn and told him to bring
in the horse herd. Pete went, and Jeff unsaddled and went to the
house. Before he reached the door he felt the first wet flakes on
his face. He went in, and Sam was standing at the window, looking. Sam said, "Here we go again," and Jeff heard the wind begin

to moan in the pines, the gusts begin to whistle at the windows.

By bedtime the wind was howling and the snow was like sand at the panes. By morning another blizzard was on, full force.

It stormed all that day. Toward dusk it seemed to ease, and Jeff thought it might stop. But with full darkness it was as bad as ever, slashing, moaning, rattling the door and windows.

It was the bellow of buffalo that wakened Jeff. He had no idea what time it was, and as he lay and listened he thought at first that it was the dream again. Then he heard Sam get up. Sam had been more alert, more concerned for the cattle and for Jeff, since Bill was gone. Jeff went to the west window, and Sam went to the door. The frost was so thick on the panes that Jeff couldn't see anything outside. Then Sam, at the door, said, "They're on the other side of the creek."

Jeff went to the door and listened. Between blasts of wind he could hear them crashing through the underbrush. "They're on both sides," he said.

Sam closed the door. Jeff struck a match. It was almost four o'clock. Three more hours till daylight.

"Maybe they'll stop in the timber," Sam said.

"Depends on how many there are."

Harvey was sitting up in his bunk and Pete was awake. "Buffalo?" Harvey asked.

"Yes."

Harvey reached for his pants.

"Get your sleep," Jeff told him. "There's nothing we can do now. Come daylight, we'll see."

"Couldn't we turn them, maybe?" Pete asked.

Jeff shook his head. It would be like trying to turn a spring flood in the Bijou. He went to the fireplace, stirred the coals, laid fresh wood on them. "Go back to sleep, all of you."

"What are you going to do?" Sam asked.

"Stay up and wait."

The others returned to their blankets. Jeff sat in front of the fire, waiting, listening. Wondering if that bellow of the bulls out there in the storm was the bellowing of fate. If so, he would face it alone. He'd learned to walk alone. Bill had been there, somewhere within range of his voice, when he needed to know that he wasn't entirely alone. But even Bill was gone now. He could shout at the top of his lungs and Bill wouldn't answer. He was alone now.

Alone.

He shook his head at the irony. He had run from traps, time after time, and now he was trapped in a house he had built. Trapped and alone in a house, while everything he had was being wiped out in a blizzard, stolen by a herd of buffalo.

He sat and listened, waiting, and the bellowing seemed to die away. He wondered if his hearing was playing tricks on him, and at last he went to the door. The only sound was the roar of the storm. There was no more bellowing, no more crashing in the brush.

He went back and sat down. Maybe it was just another small band, a few hundred head, of buffalo. Maybe he was getting so nervous that he saw doom in every threat. Maybe that, too.

He stared at the fire, and he remembered his father, the way he grew old. He remembered his father's words when Jeff told him he was going to move up here to the Bijou. The old man called him a damned fool, reminded him that he was broke, "like the rest of us."

And Jeff said, "That's why I'm moving. I'm going to make a fresh start."

"With what?"

"With a twenty-dollar horse and a wagonload of nerve."

Well, he told himself now, I've got quite a herd of twenty-dollar horses now. And damn little hay left to feed them. They'll soon be down to cottonwood bark, like the cattle. A lot of twenty-dollar horses. And I never sold or gave away that wagonload of nerve. Did I?

No. But maybe it shrank a little, with the years. Or maybe I didn't have a whole wagonload to begin with. Maybe I was just lucky, and the luck has run out.

"A little luck, and a lot of work . . ." Bill's words.

Then he heard biting words that had been flung at him once: "Jeff, some day you'll find a river you can't cross, an Indian you can't bluff, a horse you can't ride!"

He had laughed at Amy when she taunted him that way. He had said, "No!"

And she had said, "You will."

Had he finally found that river, that Indian, that horse?

"No," he said to himself. But his voice lacked the conviction, the authority, it once had. Why?

He drew a deep breath, and his ribs ached. He was tired, tired in every sinew, tired in mind and spirit. He'd come a long way. Maybe this was as far as he was going to go. He hadn't wanted to come alone, but he had to make the choice. And here he was. Right here. And there was no going back now.

The first sign of dawn came through the windows at about a quarter till seven. Sam roused and reached for his pants, and Jeff got stiffly from the bench where he had been drowsing with his head on his arms on the table.

"How about those buffalo?" Sam asked.

"They went on through," Jeff said. "Just a small bunch, I guess."

Sam got the coffee started. Harvey and Pete got up, had coffee and went to the barn to do the morning chores. The blizzard was still in action.

When the boys came back in they reported that the buffalo had gone down the ridge on the far side of the creek.

"Some were on this side," Jeff insisted. "I heard them."

"A few of them came down and crossed at the ford," Harvey said. "Not many."

They ate breakfast, and Jeff said they had a morning's work out at the stack yard. He was going to protect what hay he had left from the buffalo. So they went out and dug spare poles from the drifts and lashed them to the fence around the stacks. By noon they had a solid wall six feet high, braced and strengthened so that only a big herd of buffalo could break it down.

They were eating the noon meal when the next band of buffalo came, following almost the same trail the herd in the night had taken, along the ridge west of the creek. Jeff knew that this might be the big herd, so he told the others to take rifles and plenty of ammunition. They went out to the barn. Jeff told Pete to move the loose horses into the corral north of the barn, on the downstream side. Jeff and Sam went out beside the stack yard to watch the buffalo.

They came flowing down the ridge, a white-fronted stream of

brown life, doggedly flowing into the face of the storm, like a flood of brown water speckled with white foam. They came down the ridge and spilled over, into the timber. There the flow hesitated, like an eddy, then was thrust forward again by the pressure of the stream behind. On through the underbrush it flowed, small trees going down beneath it, big trees merely dividing the flow for a moment.

Then the brown stream began to thin out as the main herd passed. The stragglers lagged, trotting to catch up, then lagging again. The weaklings, those that would not last out the storm. And with the stragglers came the wolves, not more than six or eight, trotting in the trampled snow right in among the stragglers. They seemed almost unaware of the buffalo. And the buffalo were unaware of the wolves. When the wolves hungered they would bring down a straggler, snap and snarl and fight among themselves, gorge, then lope after the herd, catch up once more and trot there like patient dogs until they hungered again.

The buffalo passed, and the wolves, and there was only the wind and the snow and the storm. Pete had come and stood beside Jeff, watching, and Pete said, "It makes you feel—well, practically *crawly,* inside."

Jeff glanced at the boy; he hadn't even realized that Pete was there.

"They never even saw us," Pete said. "They didn't even look."

Jeff knew what Pete meant. They were like something from another world, a nightmare world. Like some primitive force, elemental as the storm itself, unaware of mankind, unknowing, uncaring.

"The horses all moved?" Jeff asked.

"Yes. All of them except those tied in the barn."

They turned back toward the house, and Jeff heard another bunch on the ridge to the east. They were too far away to see as more than a moving mass on the hilltop, some flow of white-flecked brown that writhed and thrust into the storm, some incredible force that seemed to roll upon itself, counter to all the laws of wind.

Jeff was about to go into the house when he heard Harvey shout from the barn. He turned, and he saw them coming, still more buffalo. They came down the valley directly toward the barn and corrals.

Jeff ran back toward the barn. Before he got there he heard the crack of a rifle shot. Then another, another.

He reached the corner of the barn just as the buffalo hesitated at the far corral fence. Then the fence went down with a cracking of poles and the brown herd surged forward again. And there was Harvey Bird shooting buffalo at the stack yard fence, the barrier they had reinforced only a few hours before. Three buffalo were on the ground in front of it, but the surge of brown bodies made it shiver and sway. Jeff began to shoot. Sam was there too, and Sam was shooting. A barrier of dead buffalo built itself at the base of the stack yard fence and the herd divided, flowed around the yard and around the barn. The men stood on an island in the midst of the hairy brown flood. The buffalo were so close that Jeff could hear their wheezing and see the dirty yellow icicles around their muzzles.

Sam was there beside him, feeding fresh cartridges into his rifle. Then Pete was there. Pete said, "Good Lord, don't they ever stop coming?"

Jeff reached into his pocket for cartridges, began reloading his own rifle.

Suddenly Pete lifted his gun and fired into the mass of buffalo plodding past not ten yards away. A cow staggered, went to her knees and fell. For a moment there was an eddy as those following her tried to go around. The pressure from behind forced them on. They walked right over her.

Pete's face twisted in anger. He lifted his gun again. Jeff put a hand on his arm. "It's no use, son."

Pete lowered the rifle and they watched as the fallen cow was trampled into a grisly patch in the snow, her bones cut apart by the inexorable hoofs, her skull finally kicked aside, still steaming.

Jeff began to feel the warmth of the herd, the faint animal heat of all those plodding brown beasts. It was more a smell than an actual sensation of warmth, vaguely like the smell of a trail herd of cattle on a warm afternoon. But more rank, as buffalo meat is more rank to the taste than beef.

It was the first time he had ever sensed that warmth of the

herd. Now he began to understand why cattle, once caught up in a herd of buffalo, would remain there, even in the face of a storm, defying all their own instinct to turn tail and drift the other way. There was a sense of shelter and of warmth, the same kind of warmth a bunch of cattle yarded in the timber must get from each other. He watched, and the smell, the feel, the sense of implacable force and movement was almost hypnotic.

Finally he turned and went into the barn. He was saddling a roan pony when Sam Royce came in.

"Where are you going?" Sam asked.

"Down the valley."

"You're not going to try to head them, Jeff!"

Jeff reached under the pony's belly for a latigo strap.

"You can't stop them, Jeff."

Jeff went for a bridle. The roan laid back its ears, fought the bit, but Jeff forced the bit between its teeth, slid the headstall into place. "Nobody can stop them," he said, buckling the throatlatch.

Sam took his own saddle blanket from the rack, put it on the nearest pony and reached for his saddle.

"No," Jeff said. "I'm going alone." He put his rifle in the saddle scabbard. "Give me some more cartridges."

Sam put his saddle back on the peg. He gave Jeff a handful of cartridges. Jeff dropped them into his coat pocket. "Stay here," he ordered. "Get out to East Camp as soon as you can. And over to Comanche. I may stop at Cottonwood."

"You will?"

"I may."

Jeff led his horse to the barn door. Sam put his saddle blanket away and followed Jeff to the doorway. Jeff seemed unaware of him.

The buffalo were still coming in a solid mass, but now there were a few cattle mixed in with them. Only a few carried the Pothook brand. Most of them had strange brands, from ranches far to the south. Sam had seen those brands only on spring roundup, when he was down on the Arkansas looking for Jeff's winter drifters. These buffalo had come a long way.

Jeff stood watching. Sam said, "By morning this storm may be all over with."

Jeff didn't answer.

The herd began to thin. The buffalo were no longer packed tight, shoulder to shoulder, and there were more cattle, tired cattle. But the cattle, like the buffalo, plodded straight ahead, not even swinging their heads to look at the men or the barn or the house. They eddied and flowed past the buildings, oblivious of everything not directly in their path.

Jeff led his horse outside. He thrust his toe into the stirrup and swung up. Sam shouted, "See you at Cottonwood!"

Jeff didn't answer, didn't even look back. He rode in among the mixed cattle and buffalo and ducked his head against the storm. A gust of wind and a big swirl of snow hid him for a moment, then eased, and Sam saw him as his horse veered left, with the herd, around the house. After that the snow closed in. Jeff was gone.

Pete Wallace stood staring for a moment, then turned to Sam. "What's he doing? Where's he going?"

Harvey Bird was hurrying toward the barn.

Sam shouted, "Harvey!" and Harvey turned, questioning. "The boss," Sam shouted, "is going down to Cottonwood. He said for us to stay here."

Neither Pete nor Harvey understood. Neither did Sam, for that matter. He couldn't explain it even to himself. He didn't try. He went over and stood beside the barn, sheltered a little from the beating of the storm, and he said again, "He wants us to stay here."

They waited, each with his unspoken questions, and the herd thinned. The stragglers appeared, some trotting to catch up, some plodding step by step, no longer able to hurry, stragglers that never would catch up. And with the stragglers came the wolves, trotting over the hard-packed snow beaten to ice by the implacable hoofs, ice where the storm's new snow already was beginning to swirl and eddy.

The last straggler passed and the snow began to form little drifts behind each knot of buffalo dung, dung that steamed for a little while, then began to freeze.

Sam closed the barn door and he and Pete and Harvey ducked their heads and beat their way to the house. The herd had taken almost three hours to pass. As Sam opened the house door the wind brought the moaning bellow of a buffalo cow from downstream. Then the yelp of a wolf, a wolf howl, the sound of wolves snarling, fighting over warm meat. The wolves had hungered and brought down another straggler.

The men went inside and built up the fire.

At first Jeff was aware only of the herd, the mass of plodding buffalo around him. How many there were in the herd he didn't know, maybe three thousand head, maybe even four or five thousand. He was near the end of the herd. Ahead of him, as far as he could see, they flowed. Immediately ahead were quite a few cattle, red and roan, mostly, as contrasted with the brown of the buffalo, and with long white or yellowish horns contrasting with the short black horns of the buffalo. And with straight backs, not humped as the buffalo were. Lacking, too, the warm mat of long hair that covered the buffalo's heads, necks and shoulders.

Then he saw the buffalo, as individuals, close alongside, saw their little dark eyes, not really as small as they looked in the big, shaggy heads but still smaller than a steer's eyes. A buffalo had limited eyesight to begin with, and the beaten snow had packed into the shaggy brows, lowered them, cut the vision still more. As he watched he saw an old bull strike a big cottonwood with his shoulder, stagger, catch his stride and go on, unblinking but half blind.

The cottonwood's bark hung in tatters, the white inner wood showing. Dozens of buffalo had shouldered it, even struck it head-on. Its low branches were gone, broken off, trampled. And Jeff noticed how bare the valley looked. He knew this valley as he knew the back of his hand, but now he had to look twice to see any landmarks. Every shrub, every bush, every small tree, was gone, broken down, trampled into the snow.

Somewhere ahead and to the left he heard the crash of breaking ice. The valley narrowed with a bend in the creek and the herd was squeezed between the bluff and the water. Then Jeff saw a gaping scar of black water where perhaps a dozen buffalo had been crowded onto the ice. The ice had given way and four of them were still there in the water, trying to heave themselves free and being shouldered back by the buffalo walking, as on a tightrope, along the narrow shelf of bank. Jeff looked again. That was the pool where he had almost lost his life. Bill would have buffalo for company now.

Bill Sanders, who was more like a brother to him than any other man Jeff had ever known. Who twice saved Jeff's life. Why?

Like a brother; and yet, what did he know about Bill? You fight a war at a man's side, and you travel for days and weeks, you work for years alongside each other, and do you ever know the man himself? No. You know where and when he was born, how he grew up, what he did before your paths crossed. You know a little of his life. You know some of his hopes, his dreams, his hurts, but never all of them. Bill Sanders was his sergeant, the man who once said, "If you didn't need me, Jeff, I'd resign as sergeant and go back to trooper." Bill was detailed, at his request, to take him home when he was mustered out, sick unto death. Bill came with him, that desolate summer of searching, up here to the Bijou. They found the ranch, the grass, water and shelter, and Bill said, "You're not a partner kind of man, Jeff. But I'd like to be your foreman." Bill was his foreman, his right hand, his voice of authority. And now, now he was alive and Bill was dead. Why?

Bill was a good foreman, the best. And yet, Bill was not a top boss. The difference was hard to put your finger on, but it was there. What was it? A drive, an inner need, a dream, or what? Was it choices offered, decisions taken? Or was it something in your make-up from the start? If that was it, how could you lose it?

I had it once, Jeff thought. I had it, and I lost it, and I found it again.

And now?

He wanted to laugh at the joke he was playing on life, telling life he didn't give a damn what happened now. Or was life playing the joke on him? He was still alive, wasn't he? Well, whichever way it was, here he was, in a blizzard, drifting down the Bijou valley with a herd of buffalo. It didn't make sense. He was here, drifting with buffalo in a blizzard, and he should be dead, there under the ice. And instead, Bill was there. It was a joke, a grisly joke on life, a grim, grisly joke.

He lifted his head to face the blast of the storm, defy it. The slash of the sleety, wind-driven snow made him gasp and the pain in his ribs stabbed at him. He gritted his teeth and said, "I'm here because I've got ten thousand head of cattle on this range!"

Then he knew that didn't make sense. He was here because a

man who couldn't swim had plunged into paralyzingly cold water to save his life. Anyway, he didn't have ten thousand head of cattle. He had five or six thousand, and hides and bones scattered from hell to breakfast.

Don't be a goddamned fool, Jeff Ross.

He loosened the collar of his coat and drew the scarf up over his face. The scarf his daughter gave him, the daughter who told him he wanted his son to die. Damn it, his son died years ago!

The dusk began to close in. The herd was in bigger timber now, more pines. Jeff had to duck continually to avoid limbs and the passage of the herd seemed to shake clouds of suffocating snow from the trees, though how the snow had lodged there in this wind was beyond understanding. That wind, twisted and warped by the trees, came at him from all angles. Damn that wind!

He looked for landmarks, before the dusk deepened into darkness. The pines themselves were a landmark. The herd was passing Cottonwood Camp. The camp was on the other bank. If he was going to stop at Cottonwood—why should I stop at Cottonwood? What's at Cottonwood? Another cabin, another prison.

There was a ford just about here. No, he had passed the ford. By now the head of the herd was at the oxbow in the creek, approaching the breaks.

He rode on.

Dusk deepened. They were out of the pines. The storm beat at him, full force. The herd plodded on. There were only two forces in the world, the storm and the herd. And he was with the herd, defying the storm. Well, he'd come a long way alone. He could go it alone from here on in.

Full dark, and he knew the herd had reached the breaks, knew by the lay of the land, the prod of the cantle at his back when the pony went down, the pressure of the pommel when his pony climbed.

He wondered if the herd would stop in the breaks, find a high cutbank, huddle there, wait it out. Once the herd came almost to a stop and he felt the storm eddying overhead, sensed a cutbank nearby. Then the herd moved on. Twice it happened, and each time the pressure of the herd forced the leaders out of the scant shelter, into the storm again. And once the herd was moving, once the leaders were forced out into the open, it was like flowing water, pressing on and on. There wasn't a cutbank in the whole valley that could shelter this herd, and the unsheltered ones kept pressing forward.

Out in the open again, out of the trees, on a ridge with the full force of the storm beating at him. There was no stopping this force, and he was a part of it. No stopping the herd until they reached the Platte, and maybe not even the Platte could stop it if the storm continued. And the storm was going to continue forever.

He hunched in the saddle, bowed against the storm, and he smelled that herd warmth he had smelled there in the barnyard. Felt it. Heard the wheezing of the herd around him. Was lulled by the rhythmic rocking of his saddle.

He dozed, and he wakened with a start. He should get up and put fresh wood on the fire. His bunk was cold, and he was alone here. His feet were freezing.

Then he was awake, and he knew there was no fire, no bunk, no cabin. Only the saddle, the herd, the night, the storm.

Loretta was saying, "I never tried to keep you from going, did I, Jeff? I knew you had to be going."

He said, "Yes, Loretta, a man has to go and do. The buffalo came down the valley, and it was storming, and the day was getting late. But Bill was dead. There was no one else to go. Understand? A man has to be going and doing."

He straightened in the saddle and the storm caught him full in the face. "Talking to myself," he said. "I'm talking to myself."

He felt choked, had to fight for breath. He put his hand to his face, felt the scarf, frozen stiff with his breath, close around his nose and mouth. He loosened it a little.

Jane's scarf. Jane, who hated him. Who wanted to be loved. Why was love so important? You learned to live without love. A man did. He didn't know about women. Maybe they did too.

Loretta's words: "I need you, Jeff. I love you."

He didn't want to think about Loretta. Nor about Amy. He didn't want to think. You travel alone. The storms come, and the buffalo, and you haven't any choice. The years pile up, and you lose your cattle, and what is there left?

He drowsed again.

On and on, and ever on. Branches whipped his face and he wakened and put up an arm to shield himself. They were out of the timber, on the ridge once more, and he bowed his head into the storm. And slept. And wakened once more, his horse stopped, the herd stopped around him. Then the leaders, trying to shelter themselves up there ahead, were crowded into the open again. The herd moved. Jeff slept again.

Mile after slow mile, on and on, into the storm. The night crept past, slow as the blind, instinctive herd.

Jeff wakened, stiff and cold. His feet were numb. He felt for the stirrups, found that he had them all the time. He stood in the stirrups, and his coat was frozen to the saddle. He broke it loose. His calves screamed. His toes were full of needles. He rattled his feet in the stirrups, shook his legs. He beat his arms against himself. His fingers ached, his muscles were dead. But he got the circulation going again.

His eyes burned and the beat of the storm drove the snow through the slit above the frozen scarf. He peered around him, made out the shapes of cattle around him, many cattle, a scattering of buffalo. He felt that pungent warmth of the herd.

They were on an upland. He could tell that by the way the wind blew, the feel of his horse's footing. He wished he could get at his watch, but his fingers were too stiff to manage buttons. He thrust a hand inside his coat, to warm it. He only chilled his ribs, and the chill made his ribs ache.

He looked to his right, where the horizon should be, looking for some sign of dawn. Not a sign. Dawn would be late.

He waited, and at last dawn began to come. Not dawn in the east, but dawn in the air, somehow touching the wind and the snow itself. The wind didn't ease and the snow didn't slacken, but he could see a little way. And when you can see, the wind loses a fraction of its darktime force, the snow becomes snow again, no longer a many-lashed black whip. He could see a little way. He was still in a world of shifting white and plodding brown bodies, but a discernible world.

He looked ahead and to both sides and back, and as far as he could see there was nothing but those swaying backs, those swinging heads. He was borne along over shifting white surf on a huge raft of brown and roan and red bodies.

Slowly the light strengthened. Daylight came. Daylight, relief from the depth of darkness, but no relief from the storm. Jeff's belly began to cramp. Hunger. He hadn't eaten since noon yesterday. Was it only yesterday? And the need to relieve himself.

He didn't dare stop, didn't dare dismount. Those cattle and buffalo were all but blind. They wouldn't even see him. They would knock him down, walk right over him.

He reined the pony up, eased him back, let the herd flow around him. Buffalo nudged him, unknowing, but slowly the herd flowed past. And Jeff was among the stragglers. Stragglers and wolves. The wolves trotted there among the stragglers, gray shadows with yellowed, slanted eyes. One or two glanced up at him but the others trotted on, unseeing as the herd itself.

At last he drew the pony to a stop. The herd moved on, was lost in the storm. Jeff got down from the saddle. The pony swung around, tail to the wind. Jeff flailed his arms, finally thrust his hands under the saddle blanket to warm his fingers. And when he had relieved himself he was almost too nauseated to get back into the saddle.

He walked a little way, then mounted, knowing he had to catch the herd. At first the pony refused to face the storm. Jeff had to use quirt and spurs to force him into it. He hadn't realized until then how much protection the herd had given him through the night. Both him and his horse. He quirted and spurred, and he saw the last of the stragglers. He passed an old bull that wouldn't make another mile, then two or three stumbling cows. He passed two wolves that looked up at him and licked their lips with wet red tongues.

But before he reached the main body of the herd he heard the crack of underbrush ahead. Then he was going down a long slope. He was in scattered timber, cottonwoods and willows, timber that ran east and west. And even there, among the scattered trees on the hillside, he heard the cracking of ice up there ahead.

He had come to the Platte. The leaders of the herd were being forced onto the river ice and the ice was giving way beneath their massed weight.

The herd just ahead of him began to slow up. It came to a stop, flowed off to both sides, like floodwaters suddenly dammed. Buffalo and cattle alike spread out in the underbrush, still pushing ahead but now spread out, their forward pressure somewhat relaxed.

Jeff followed one bunch to the left. The snow in the timber was drifted four feet deep. His pony wallowed, struggled back to the path the buffalo had made.

Slowly Jeff worked his way through the brush and timber and at last he came to the riverbank. The river was covered with black ice, clean-swept of snow. As he sat there staring at it, the storm eddied for a moment and he saw the far bank. Just beyond the river was a log building. Then the snow closed in again and Jeff couldn't even see across the ice.

Behind him, downstream a little way, he could still hear the crunch and crack of ice, the panicked bellow of buffalo in the water. Most of the herd was still trying to cross down there.

And suddenly Jeff was too tired to care, about anything. He sat there in the saddle, staring at the swirling snow and the wind-swept ice, and what lay beyond was of no consequence, none.

The storm eddied again. This time he saw several buildings, and pole corrals. Somebody's ranch. Smoke, flat streamers of gray smoke, whipped from the chimneys on two of the buildings.

Three buffalo came out of the brush nearby. They didn't even seem to see him as they wallowed through the drifts and down the riverbank. One of them sniffed the ice, lifted its head and took a few steps. The other two followed. Once on the ice, they kept going, all the way across. They reached the far bank, hunched themselves ashore and plodded on, heads lowered into the wind-driven snow.

Jeff watched them out of sight. Then he rode down the bank and onto the ice and across the river.

14

Within two hours after she left Greeley, Amy Hilliard knew that she should have summoned Tim Roberts to Cheyenne or met him in Greeley and had it out with him. But she didn't like secondhand reports, particularly where money matters were involved. So she took the train to Greeley and hired a rig and went to the ranch to see for herself if conditions were as bad as Tim Roberts had said, and, if so, why they were that bad. It was a most uncomfortable trip and would have been all but impossible if John Iliff had not sent two wagons over the trail the day before, with supplies for the Iliff ranch at Fremont's Orchard. The Iliff wagons had broken trail for her, all except the last twelve miles.

She had intended to stay only two nights and a day. The ranch was a miserable place, crude at best and uncomfortable. She had been there before, with Matt and Young Matthew, but only in the summer, when the stay was an adventure. Now it was a trial, and when this new blizzard came up she was both bitter and angry. She had the cabin to herself, thanks to Matt, who had built a separate cabin for his own convenience when he went to the ranch to hunt or to supervise matters there. But to be trapped here was almost intolerable, and even Tim Roberts' promise that he would get her back to Greeley within another week was small comfort.

"I didn't come to spend the winter here," Amy snapped at him. "Nor even any small part of it. I came because you wrote that you had to have another thousand dollars for supplies."

"Yes ma'am."

"And you say you can't get me out of here for another week?"

Tim smiled. "I could, Mrs. Hilliard. But I'd rather get you out alive."

That was yesterday, with the blizzard blowing full force. Amy, too angry to talk more, had sent him away, told him to come back today. "We'll decide then about getting me back to Greeley."

And Tim had smiled again, that maddening smile of his, and said, "I can do a good many things, but I can't stop a blizzard."

Amy had gone over the accounts last night. She didn't like what she found. Tim Roberts was either a thief or a fool, maybe both. And she decided to have it out with him today. And now it was mid-morning, and the blizzard still held. The blizzard, with its roar, and that bawling down in the timber which was either cattle or buffalo or both, she wasn't sure.

There was a knock at the cabin door. She opened the door and Tim Roberts came in. Before she could speak he said, "There's a man here from down south."

"Yes?"

"I thought you might like to talk to him."

"Why?"

"Well, he can tell you something about what we've been up against this winter. All of us out here."

Tim, she thought, was trying to put off her accounting with him. But she asked, "A man from down south, you say? How did he get here? If he could get here, why can't you get me to Greeley?"

"He came with a herd of buffalo, he says."

"What is he? An Indian?" She laughed scornfully.

"He's a cattleman, from up the Bijou. His name is Ross."

"Ross? Jeff Ross?"

"Yes. He's pretty well used up, after drifting in the storm all night, but—"

"Did he ask to see me?"

"No."

Amy considered for a moment, then said, "Bring him over. I'll talk to him." Then she added, "Alone."

Tim left. Amy stood there, dumfounded. Jeff Ross! It was impossible!

She turned and went to the mirror. She wished this meeting were in her house in Cheyenne. Or in St. Louis. Then she looked at herself in the mirror again. The years hadn't been too unkind. And, she thought, he's just as much older as I am. No man wears his years as well as a careful woman.

She touched her hair, straightened the ruching at the neck of her dress. She wet her lips, nervously. And there was a knock at the door.

She turned from the mirror, went to stand at the fireplace and called, "Come in."

Jeff opened the door and stepped inside and closed the door behind him. His face was stubbled with two weeks of beard. His eyes were red-rimmed and the lines of his face were deep with fatigue.

She said, "Jeff!" and she thought: He's old, he's an old man!

He said, "Hello, Amy." It was Jeff's voice, though hoarse with weariness. He stamped the snow from his boots and came toward her. Tired as he was, he walked with the grace and stood with the poise that always had marked Jeff Ross.

"Take off your coat."

He shook his head. His hair was long. There was a good deal of silvering at the temples. He said, "I'm not staying."

"You're staying a little while. What's the matter? Didn't you expect to see me here?"

"I knew, as soon as Tim Roberts said his boss wanted to see me." His eyes never left her. Her hair was as it had always been, not a trace of gray. Her eyes had that trace of green, enhanced by the green ruching on her brown dress. She was a few pounds heavier, but only a few, and there was no pouchiness under her chin. Her voice was as it used to be, low-pitched, warm.

"You can't just say hello and walk out, Jeff! I'm sorry I haven't much hospitality to offer you, but—"

He smiled, the thin-lipped smile of exhaustion. "A roof is hospitality. A roof and a fire." He took off his coat, put it with his hat and scarf on a bench across the room. He came and stood with his back to the fire, facing her.

He was gaunt, she decided. The skin was taut over his cheekbones and his eyes were sunken. He breathed in quick, short breaths. Then he coughed and winced and smothered the cough with an effort.

"Jeff, you're hurt!"

He shook his head, still fighting the cough.

"You are!" She tried to put an arm around him.

He stiffened and backed away. "A cracked rib. I keep forgetting."

"Sit down, please. Have you had anything to eat?"

"Yes. But since the pot's still on, I could do with some more coffee."

She went to the cupboard for a cup and saucer. He sank onto a bench at the table, so tired he had to brace himself with his hands. She poured the coffee and sat down across the table.

"Tim says you came with a herd of buffalo. That, of course, is ridiculous."

"Yes." He lifted the cup in both hands to steady it. "Ridiculous. But true. With a herd of buffalo and cattle. Quite a lot of your cattle, as well as mine." He sipped, then lowered the cup carefully to the saucer. "You might thank me for bringing them back. They've been wintering on my range." His heavy-lidded eyes gleamed faintly with amused rebuke.

"Thank you." She resented the look. "I have been worrying about them." The tone was ironic, but she knew the irony was flat.

"They're not really worth worrying about."

"Why not?"

"They're culls and scrubs. All your cattle seem to be."

She flushed angrily. "I didn't ask you to discuss the quality of my cattle!"

He sipped at the coffee again. "What phase of your business did you want to discuss, then?"

"Jeff!" she exclaimed. "Stop this nonsense!"

He braced his hands on the table and got to his feet. "Very well. Thank you for your hospitality."

"Don't be a fool! Sit down!"

He stood there, looking down at her. "Amy, you always were arrogant, weren't you? Arrogant and willful."

"And you were cruel. Tough and cruel!"

"The tough ones survive." Slowly he lowered himself onto the bench again.

"And here we are," she said, "you and I. After all these years. How long is it, Jeff?"

"I told you once, Amy, that you had made it something to forget. I've forgotten."

She laughed at him. "You have a good memory for your own words, though."

He braced his elbows, cupped his chin in his hands. He didn't answer.

"Jeff, we were fools. Both of us."

He still didn't answer.

"And yet, how could we have known? Life makes its own patterns."

"We make the choices."

"Who chose this meeting? Answer me that, Jeff."

"I didn't."

"I didn't either!"

"You asked to see me, Amy."

"You came here to the ranch. What did you expect me to do? Pretend I wasn't here? I never hid or ran away from anything!"

His smile told her, without a word, that she was lying.

"I didn't!"

"Amy," and his voice was very tired, "did you tell your foreman to send me here just to rake over the past?"

"You're even afraid to talk about it?"

"There's no need to talk about it. It's over, finished, done. We made our choices." Everybody, he thought, tries to hide or run away from something, some time. There's cowardice in all of us.

"You say the past is closed, then?"

"Yes." He closed his eyes, shook his head, weary.

"Don't you wish it was! Don't you wish it was that easy!" She turned and watched the fire for a moment. When she looked at him again he was asleep, his face sunk in his hands.

She moved the cup and saucer, said, "Jeff. Jeff, you're worn out!"

He tried to rouse, lifted his head for a moment, opened his bloodshot eyes. But his eyes were glazed. She took his elbow, helped him to his feet, led him to the long bench beside the fireplace. It was covered with a buffalo robe. She sat him down, eased his head back, lifted his feet onto the bench, then brought a blanket and covered him. He slept.

She returned to her seat at the table.

She sat there a long time, reviewing the years, the pattern of her life. Yes, she had made her choice, with Matt. But a choice within her pattern. She needed generosity, and caring for. She had planned things that way. And Matt had been generous, kind, loving in his own way. Now Matt was gone. And now, out of nowhere, Jeff had appeared again. The pattern? Her pattern?

She looked at him, sleeping there on the bench. The profile of his weather-beaten face was sharp, clear, even emphasized by the relaxation of sleep. That high brow, that strong, generous nose, that long upper lip and that firm jaw. Beneath that bristling of beard, salted with gray, this still was the face of the Jeff she had known, never forgotten. Grown older now, even more firm, more determined. But in sleep his thin, tight-drawn lips were relaxed and full again, as they were when she first knew him.

She looked again, searching, comparing. Then she shook her head, uncertain. Matt had always said the boy favored her. He had her blue eyes, and a long upper lip and a strong, generous nose. Not Matt's features, certainly. The doctor had said, without reservation, that he was an eight-month baby. But doctors can be prudent. She named him for Matt, and he grew up aping Matt's speech and gestures. Matt never questioned.

Young Matthew was going on thirteen now and in school in St. Louis. She had just returned from a long Christmas visit with him when she received the message from Tim Roberts. It seemed important to come here, straighten things out at the ranch, before she went about selling the big house in Cheyenne. Hold on here until she could sell the ranch to John Iliff. Iliff wouldn't pay what she asked, of course; but, being a woman, she would eventually get an offer out of him. Sell the ranch, sell the Cheyenne house, go back to St. Louis and live a civilized life. She was only thirty-five, still looked thirty. A widow whose husband had left her two hundred thousand dollars. She had a life ahead.

She looked at Jeff again, sleeping there beside the fireplace, and she wondered at life's strange patterns. Choice, he had said. Yes, perhaps choice within the pattern. The pattern that had widowed her, brought her here at this moment, brought Jeff Ross here. The blizzard? It had been a bad winter, one storm after another. Why had Jeff chosen this storm to drift north with a herd of buffalo, if there was no pattern?

She waited, and noon came, and Amy was roused from the remembering and the speculation by the creeping chill. She put

234

fresh wood on the fire. And Tim came to the door again, this time with a steaming kettle in hand.

"Thought you might like something hot," Tim said. "Cook got it just about right today. If you like stew."

She knew that Tim was curious as well as awkwardly helpful. She took the kettle and stood aside that he might see in. "Mr. Ross fell asleep while we were talking. You were right. He was tired out."

"Want me to take him back to the bunkhouse?"

"Later, perhaps. Thank you for bringing this. I like stew."

Dismissed, Tim left. Amy returned to the fire, set the stew on the coals and waited, hoping Jeff would waken. But Jeff still slept and she was hungry. She got a bowl and sat down at the table to eat.

She had almost finished when Jeff stirred, lifted his head and looked around the room, bewildered. He sat up, rubbed his eyes and stared at her. "What happened?" he asked.

"You fell asleep. You were worn out."

He sat staring at her, and slowly it all came back, the ride through the storm, the arrival at the bunk house, Amy's summons, Amy.

"You should be hungry by now," she said.

"It smells like stew."

She got another bowl, filled it and set it on the table. He got to his feet, listened, went to a window and looked out. The wind seemed to be easing up, the storm dying. He went to the table and sat down.

As he began to eat she asked, "Jeff, why did you come here?"

"Why?" He looked at her, faintly amused. "I told you that I brought back your cattle."

"Did you really come with a buffalo herd?"

"Yes. I'm raising buffalo now. Cattle are too much of a risk."

"How did you know that I was here?"

"The same way you knew that I was coming. I'm sure you knew. That's why you were here." He was being blatantly ironic.

"Jeff," she said, wanting no more of it, "you said my cattle are all culls and scrubs. Why did you say that?"

"It's the truth."

"What should they have cost last summer?"

He looked up at her. "What are you trying to do, get me to audit your books?"

"I've audited them myself. Tim Roberts has been stealing me blind."

Jeff made no comment, went on eating.

"You're in trouble too, aren't you?" she asked.

"Not that kind of trouble."

"But you've lost cattle."

"Everyone has. It's one of those winters."

"How many have you lost?"

"Ask me that next spring, after I've made the tally."

"How many can you afford to lose, Jeff?"

He paused, fork in hand. "You sound like a banker," he said with a smile. "A banker that I've just asked for a loan. Did I ask you for a loan in my sleep?"

"I," she said, "can afford to lose every one of my culls and scrubs, as you call them."

"I shouldn't be surprised if you do lose them all, the way things are going. Is that why you wanted to see me, Amy, to compare financial standings?"

"What would happen if you lost all your cattle?"

"I'd be broke, for a little while. But the tough survive. You called me tough. I've been broke before."

"How much land do you own, Jeff?"

"Enough."

She watched him for a moment, then asked, "Do you know John Devereux?"

"I know he's Land Commissioner for the Kansas Pacific."

"John Devereux has been a guest in my house. I also know Robert Carr, the president of the Kansas Pacific."

"You do get around, don't you, Amy? As a matter of fact, I'm not interested in railroad grant land."

"The right person could buy grant land cheap."

"Without water, that land isn't cheap at any price."

"You are using a good deal of railroad land right now, aren't you?"

"Only the grass, Amy. Only the grass. And I happen to own the water that controls that grass."

"Just as I own the water here."

He slowly shook his head. "John Iliff owns all of the Platte that really matters. This place of yours hasn't anything but nuisance value, and not much of that."

"It could provide a Platte River outlet for your cattle."

He smiled again. "Amy, I wouldn't pay a dime for this place. I don't need a Platte River outlet."

"I'm not asking you to buy this ranch!"

"What are you suggesting, then? First you suggest that I can buy railroad grant land, which I don't need to buy. Then you talk about a Platte River outlet for my cattle, and I don't need that either. Just what are you trying to do?"

She hesitated for a moment, then said, "You're just a cattleman, aren't you, Jeff?"

"That's right, just a cattleman."

"That's all you ever expect to be?"

"That's hard to answer, Amy. I was just a drover the last time I saw you. Now I'm just a cattleman. I don't know what to expect next, but as far as I can see I'll just be a cattleman for quite a while longer."

"And if you lose everything you've got?"

He took a deep breath. "Amy, I came up here alone, and I made something where there was nothing before I came. Just grass and water, and nothing else. I could lose everything I've got, and still I'd have what I started with because a ranch is more than just grass and water and cattle to use it. A ranch is also a cattleman. One man, who knows what he wants."

"And you know?"

He paused, weighing his words. "I knew when I came here." He paused again, then he said, "There's one thing a man owns that nobody can take away, and it's probably the most important thing of all."

"What's that?"

"Himself."

She exclaimed, "And you call me arrogant!"

He nodded. "Yes, arrogant and willful."

And suddenly she flung at him, "Jeff Ross, I hope you lose every steer you own! Every last steer!"

"I may," he said quietly, and he got to his feet. "But I'll still own myself." He crossed the room and picked up his coat.

"Jeff!"

"Yes?"

"Don't go, Jeff."

"I've got a long ride home."

She came to him, reached for his hand. "Please, Jeff, don't go yet. I wanted to talk, and—"

"Haven't you had your say?"

"Please, Jeff! Don't go with things this way between us."

"I've come a long way, Amy. And one can't go back."

"I've come a long way too, Jeff."

"Yes. There are the years, and there are the choices, and—"

"Is it because you are married, Jeff?"

"It's because we made our choices, Amy."

They returned to the fireplace and he stood staring at the fire. At last she said, "Why did it have to happen this way?"

"Haven't you had what you wanted, Amy? You made your choice."

She slowly shook her head. "It was my pattern."

"Pattern or not, you chose to marry Matt Hilliard. You had a choice."

"And you married her." Then she asked, "Have you been happy?"

It was an unexpected question. He said, "I think so."

"Happy enough?"

He looked at her, puzzled. "Happy enough for what?"

"As happy as you expected to be, wanted to be . . . Oh, I know you haven't! I can see it in your face."

"Amy," he said, "I don't know what you mean by happiness, but I've done most of the things I set out to do. I expect to go on doing them, one way or another."

"Everything you set out to do?" Her laugh had a note of bitterness, almost a jeer. "You've settled for about twenty cents on the dollar, haven't you, Jeff?"

"I've done the important things, no matter how you value them. The things that matter to a man like me, a cattleman."

"There was a time," she said, "when you insisted that I was the only important thing you wanted. Remember, Jeff? And when I couldn't marry you, you settled for a herd of Texas steers! And now you say you've been happy! Happy enough!"

"Amy," he said, measuring his words, "I've found that you pay for what you get. Including happiness, I suppose, even the kind you are talking about. You pay for it, one way or another. Or you do without. Does that answer your question?"

"No!"

"That's the best I can do. You work for what you get, or you buy it, make a deal. You are the buying kind. Have you been able to buy this happiness you talk about?"

"You're being cruel, Jeff. As always."

"Well, have you?"

"Yes! I've had happiness!" But she was on the defensive now.

"I'm glad to hear that. That isn't what you told me you wanted, once. All you wanted then was contentment."

"I wanted everything! All there was of everything!"

"And you got it?"

She wouldn't answer. After a moment she said, "I still want everything."

"And you still think you can buy it. You think everything is for sale, don't you? Like railroad grant land, which can be bought cheap if you know the right people."

"I've paid for everything I've had!" she flung at him. "I don't owe anyone!"

"That must be a good feeling, Amy."

"It is!"

"Then you should be satisfied."

"With what?"

"With what you bought and paid for."

She turned away for a moment, and Jeff started again toward his coat. She stopped him. "Jeff," she said, "I'm all alone now. Except —except for my son. You knew I had a son, didn't you?"

"You told me once."

"He's going on thirteen years old, Jeff."

"My son," Jeff said, "was ten."

"You have a boy?" There was surprise in her eyes.

"I had one. I buried him last month."

"Oh, Jeff! Jeff, I'm sorry!" But there was something close to triumph in her eyes.

He looked at her, suddenly angry. "Save your sympathy! I didn't ask for your sympathy!"

"I am sorry, Jeff. A man needs a son."

"I said save your sympathy," he said coldly.

"And," she said, "a boy needs his father."

"What are you trying to say, Amy?" he demanded.

"What do you think?"

"I think you are lying."

"And if I'm not?"

"Then you lied to Matt Hilliard."

"Matt is dead."

"And you would barter your own son!" Suddenly he caught her by the shoulders, shook her. "You are lying, aren't you? You either lied to him, or you are lying to me!"

"Jeff, stop it!"

"Tell me the truth!"

"I don't know, Jeff! I don't know!"

He let go of her and turned back to the fireplace. Finally he faced her again and said, "You would sell your own soul, wouldn't you? And I wanted to buy it, once. When you still had a soul, and a heart. But not now, Amy, not now. I don't care who fathered your son, he's your son, not mine." And he said, "God have mercy on your bartering soul."

She stood staring at him, stunned, and he saw the face of a woman as old as Eve. She was a stranger, a familiar stranger, somehow the sum of all the searching, bargaining, loveless women he had ever seen, the women who summarize the lonely winter of the heart.

She whispered, "Jeff!" and there was pleading in her voice. And just for an instant there was Amy, the remembered Amy in her eyes, the eyes he had seen in a thousand dreams. Then it was gone.

Jeff said, "Good-bye, Amy," and he went over and put on his coat. She still stood there at the fireplace, her face set, her hands tightly clenching each other, staring not at him but past him, into all the remembered yesterdays.

He picked up his hat, adjusted his scarf.

Then she said, "Good-bye, Jeff," and it was a last good-bye. He opened the door and went out into the dying storm.

Jeff stopped at the bunkhouse. Tim Roberts was playing cards with the other hands. Jeff said, "I'll be on my way."

Roberts looked up, surprised. "At this time of day?"

"I've got a long way to travel."

"You know your own mind."

"Thanks for the food and the rest."

None of the men offered to help gather his cattle or even to go to the barn and help saddle his horse. It didn't matter. A crew reflects its foreman, and Roberts was a slack man. Well, that was none of Jeff's affair.

He went to the barn, saddled his pony. He made his way back across the river and gathered what Pothook cattle he could find in the timber. Most of the buffalo had gone on, across the river and on north. A good many cattle probably had gone with them, but Jeff finally gathered about two hundred head. The others might drift back in the next storm. Some would die out in the hills. Those that lived would be picked up on spring roundup.

He gathered his cattle and found the trail the buffalo had made coming in, and he started south, toward home, the wind at his back. The wind helped. Once his cattle found the buffalo track the wind urged them on, southward. But it was dusk before he had the cattle gathered, lined out and moving.

It was a long way home. But a man couldn't just sit and wait. It would be just as far tomorrow, or next week. And next week might bring another storm. Jeff was warmed and fed and somewhat rested. What more could a man ask, a cattleman?

Jeff rode, the wind at his back, and dusk deepened into night. And Jeff knew that he was riding away from the past as well as from the Bar H ranch there on the South Platte. Riding back to his own self.

Strange, he thought, how far a man can travel in his own past. Following what began as a dream and dwindled to a mirage. But you have to go, till you find out what it really is, dream or mirage. Maybe Amy was right. Maybe there was a pattern. But there was also a choice. That held the ultimate importance, the choice. Without choice, what meaning was there? And if there was no meaning, why life?

He rode on, and the night deepened around him. He thought: It is only a little painful to watch a dream die.

Not a dream; a memory. A remembrance of something past, something ended long ago. No harder to bury than a son who died, for you, long ago. Not so hard, for the son was a part of you, and she was only a part of the remembering. The remembering that you tried to put away and couldn't. Or wouldn't. Until now.

He thought of the boy, her son. The son she had tried to barter for vanished love. A monstrous thing, no matter who fathered the boy. He was Matt Hilliard's son, to the world and to himself, regardless. Whoever his father, the only decency was to let him remain Matt Hilliard's son. "A boy needs a father," she had said. He had a father. A father to remember. Footsteps to walk in, if he chose, though any man must find his own path eventually. No man can delegate to his son the life he should have lived. Each man deserves to be himself. Has the obligation to be himself.

"Take away everything else, and a man still owns himself." The words had startled him, even as he said them, with their own truth. But he had no time, then, to give them more than glancing wonder. His own words, the unmeditated truth, welling up from some recess of self-respect. Arrogance, she had called it. But it was truth. A man owns himself. Or should.

He wondered about himself. How strong was he, how enduring?

Well, he was strong enough to fight a blizzard. A whole winter of blizzards, even a seventh winter. A winter of storms, somehow the summary of all the inner storms. A strong man survives the inner winter as well. He can survive it, endure it, once he knows it for what it is. Once he knows himself.

Who am I? I am the sum of all the choices I have made. Even those choices I was reluctant to admit. That is who I am, the sum of my own choices. And when I told myself that I chose to walk alone, I lied. I made no such choice. I chose to walk with ghosts. Now I have chosen to leave those ghosts behind. I am alone, at last. Alone with all my choices.

He rode through the night, and midnight came, the cold gnawing his marrow. He reached the breaks, the high cutbanks where the buffalo had paused, only to be pressed on. He stopped there and let the cattle find shelter, and he built a fire and warmed himself for an hour and watched the first few stars blink through the thinning clouds. Watched the stars and wondered at the vast darkness between them.

He sat by the fire, alone, and he thought: I chose to come up here with no more cattle than I have in this patch of timber right now. To make a start, a fresh start. To prove my manhood.

And he remembered young Pete Wallace, the dream on his face, there in the cabin at East Camp. Pete saying, "God didn't owe me anything. It was up to me." Youth, knowing that the world was wide, knowing he could do anything, knowing he had the choice.

I was young once, Jeff thought. Have the years made me old and taken away the dreams? The years and the regrets.

Regrets for what? For choices made and denied.

Amy's questions: "Have you been happy? Happy enough?"

And his own words: "You pay for what you get. Including happiness. Or you do without."

I've done without. Why?

He couldn't face the answer. He tightened the cinch and got into the saddle and rode on.

Refusing to answer his own question, he thought of the cattle. With luck, he would come through the winter with a few thousand head. Four or five thousand, maybe, counting the drift. But you don't count the drift until you've found them. There would be a lot of rotten hides and stinking bones in the hidden gullies and the far patches of timber, come spring.

Meanwhile? You save what you can. You break them out of the yards in the timber, between storms. You maim your horse herd chowsing up the snow so the cattle can pick a few mouthfuls of grass. When your horses have no more hay, you cut cottonwoods to give them bark and browse. Storm after storm, and you do your best. With what help you have. Even without your right hand, who died saving your life. You are broke, and you know it, and still you fight on. Why? Because, take everything else away and a man still owns himself. Because grass is grass and water is water, and a cattleman is a cattleman. And you are a cattleman.

I've made this, he told himself. Until I came there was nothing here but grass and water. I have made it a richness of cattle. Why? Because that was my purpose. I had to do, to be. That is what I wanted. That is what I was man enough to do.

And then he knew the other answer. He could face it.

I had the happiness I wanted, the happiness I deserve. No more than that. Why? Because that is all I wanted.

He bowed his head and whispered, "Forgive me, Loretta."

He rode on and on, and there was one last remembrance. Amy,

standing there at the end, that one flash of Amy, the Amy he once knew, in her eyes. Then the defeat, the knowledge that the dream was dead. Then nothing in her eyes, her face. Nothing.

More stars were twinkling now, and the wind of the dying storm had slackened. Jeff was approaching the breaks below Cottonwood Camp. Another two hours and he would be there. He would stop and rest, warm himself, make a pot of coffee, eat. He smiled, remembering his father. When his mother complained, as she did now and then, that he drank too much coffee, the old man would say, "Mother, you've lived with me long enough to know better than that. A real cowman hasn't got blood in his veins. He's got coffee! Stick a knife in him and he bleeds coffee! If he bleeds blood, he's a sick man, about to die. Now put some more grounds in that pot and build up the fire!"

Yes, he would stop at Cottonwood. To rest, to have coffee.

The stars began to fade. The first hint of dawn appeared. And now Jeff could smell the pines, smell them as he had smelled them the first day he saw the Bijou. He and Bill.

He listened to the cattle, their wheezing breath, their clicking hoofs, and he saw the thin cloud of their steamy breath. He felt the weary motion of his horse, the give of the saddle. He hadn't felt these things, really felt them, or heard or seen or smelled them, in a long time.

He straightened in the saddle, stood in the stirrups, and it wasn't a something remembered out of the past, a memory to age a man's years. It was a man knowing his own pride, his own self, his own being, again.

Then the first glint of sunlight appeared. It was another day.

15

It was the third week in February before there was a break of any consequence in the weather. Storm followed storm. The cold never relaxed more than a day or two at a time. Snow lay as much as two feet deep in Denver, and even if Loretta had wanted to she couldn't have expanded her life far beyond the big brick house on the hill. But she didn't want to.

Tommy's death had released the household from the constant care and should have relaxed Loretta's tensions about him. But it had left a void that couldn't be filled overnight. You don't in a day or a week leave off ten years of watching, waiting, listening. Sometimes in the night Loretta wakened, hearing his cry, and was out of bed and at the door to the vacant third floor before she knew it was a dream, a memory that wouldn't erase. One night it was so real that she went all the way up to his room and stood there in the chill while her eyes focused on the splash of moonlight on the empty cradle. And sometimes in the afternoon, in the sitting room hearing the girls at their lessons, she would pause and listen until Lissie exclaimed, "Mother! You aren't listening to me!" Or Jane saw her look and stopped in mid-sentence and listened too.

With the weather so bad, she had withdrawn the girls from their school and undertaken their lessons with them here at home. It wasn't until Jane mentioned it that Loretta realized that their afternoons now were falling into a familiar pattern. Jane said, "Mother, I do believe that's the very same book you taught me to read from! The one you're teaching Lissie out of. Remember?"

And Loretta remembered, that first winter at the ranch, there on the Bijou.

She said, "Yes, dear, it is. I thought you had forgotten."

And Jane described the ranch house as it was that first winter, in astonishing detail. She told of the way the snow drifted in the pines, the way the purple shadows lay across the snow at dusk, the look of white lace, the fringe of ice, on the black watered silk of the creek. She described the look and taste of yellow cress on the creek bank in April, and the crepe feel of prickly poppy blossoms beside the horse corral in July.

Yes, Jane remembered.

And Loretta knew, then, that she had kept the girls at home because she needed them close by. She needed their memories as well as her own. Oh, she thought, Jeff must go and do, for there's a man's world as well as a woman's world. Jeff must go and do, and I must stay and be. That's it, isn't it? That's the difference. The woman must have the memories, the sweet yesterdays; and the man must make the tomorrows. And yet, can any tomorrow be more than the sum of all the yesterdays? Perhaps we make the tomorrows together, somehow, out of the good and the bad, the sweet and the bitter.

And she wished that Jeff were here.

There was no word from Jeff. But she had learned long ago that no news must be accounted good news. If anything had happened, if Jeff were hurt or in trouble, Bill Sanders would have got word to her. Somehow. And she knew what such a winter meant, on the ranch.

She remembered their second winter there, particularly January. December had been open, almost mild, but January came in with a blizzard. The drifts were hardly settled when another storm came on its heels.

Jeff had only the two hands that winter, Bill Sanders and Sam Royce, and they were caught out in the second storm. They had gone down to Cottonwood Camp to look after the cattle there, and for three days Loretta worried. Then Jeff came in, on foot and alone. She had thought he came back to see that she was all right, but Jeff said, "I came back for more horses. Sam's horse got hooked by a steer on the prod and we had to shoot it."

"But there were still two horses, weren't there?" she asked. "Why did you come in on foot?"

"Because they need the horses to break out the cattle. I'm going right back."

"Jeff!" she exclaimed. "You can't! You've got to rest, and eat. You're worn out!"

And Jeff said, "I'll rest next summer. I've got two thousand steers out there, starving. But I will have a cup of coffee."

He went to the barn, put a spare saddle on a pony, and came back for the cup of coffee. He drank it standing up, and went out to the corral and drove a dozen loose ponies down to the ford and went back to Cottonwood.

That was winter at the ranch.

And this was the worst winter she could remember.

Until that break in late February. When she got up that morning she felt the change. The air was almost balmy. By ten o'clock the icicles on the eaves began to fall and she heard the trickle of running water beneath the ice in the street. Her heart began to lift, but she couldn't let it sing. Not yet. She could only hope that the thaw continued. If it lasted a few days, the grip of the ice at the ranch might begin to relax. Maybe Jeff would be able to get home. But she couldn't permit herself to think that more than fleetingly and with a whole string of maybes. Maybe conditions were bad at the ranch, after these weeks of storm. Maybe Jeff wouldn't even try to get to town. Maybe he would wait till the spring break-up. Maybe, maybe, maybe.

But as the afternoon continued mild she kept hoping.

Evening came and she listened, for the first time, for his step at the door instead of for a cry from the third floor.

Evening lengthened. Darkness brought the night chill and the drip at the eaves ended. Jeff didn't come.

She hadn't really expected him to come, she told herself. Not today. Maybe not tomorrow. No, don't count on tomorrow either. Don't count on any day. Wait. He will come.

And she told herself: I have always waited. I learned to wait. Tommy taught me to wait. Waiting is not so hard. But, dear God, is there not an end to waiting, some time?

The next day dawned clear; and now the chinook, that mild

south wind, came gentling in. By noon there were bare patches in the yard. And when Lissie asked, "Mother, when will there be violets again?" Loretta said, "Before too long."

"Next week?" Lissie asked.

And Jane said, "Silly, next week it may snow again!" But she said it without bite or scorn.

Lissie begged, "Mother, it won't! Say it won't!"

"I wish I could, darling. But Jane is right. And violets won't bloom till May."

"Even at the ranch?"

"Even at the ranch . . . Now we must get to the lessons."

But all through the lessons she was listening, waiting. And hoping.

Then it was four o'clock and the sun was down on the jagged horizon of the mountains. Loretta had come downstairs to see that Jenny had started supper, and she heard someone drive up and stop at the stable. Almost afraid to hope, she looked out and saw him coming up the brick path, striding stiff-legged and tired but with something new in his bearing.

Then he was at the back door and she was there to meet him. "Jeff!"

"Loretta!"

He took her in his arms. He kissed her, and the years fell away, the waiting years. He kissed her and he held her for a moment. Then he asked, "Are you all right, Loretta?"

"Oh, Jeff, of course I'm all right! But you! You're thin as a rail! Oh, Jeff, your cheeks are peeling from frostbite! And your—"

"It's been a rough winter, Loretta." He smiled. "I just stopped to say hello. I've got to go on downtown, get a load of supplies."

"You're not going right back! You—"

"Tomorrow."

Then he kissed her again. "I'll be back for supper. How are the girls?"

"The girls are fine. Oh, Jeff, I wish—well, run along. Get through and get back!"

She watched him hurry to the barn. She watched him drive down the alley to the street and turn down the hill. He had come in the light wagon, with the blacks, and the horses were tired. More tired than Jeff. Jeff—Jeff looked almost young again.

She called Jenny and gave new orders for supper. Mister was home! She put water to heat for him. She told the girls that their father was here. She changed into the light blue dress that Jeff thought was so pretty on her.

It was dark before he returned. He came in from the stable and left his ranch boots in the back hallway, and Loretta brought hot water for him to clean up. While he was shaving she stood in the doorway and asked about the ranch.

"How are the cattle? Did you run out of hay? You must have been snowed in for days at a time. Were there many wolves?"

"One at a time," Jeff said. "I've got things to tell you, but not till after supper."

Something in his voice bothered her, some worry, some hurt, something that he was holding back. But she knew he would choose his own time to share it.

He bathed and shaved and put on fresh clothes, and they went downstairs. Loretta called the girls. They came hurrying to the dining room and Lissie ran to him and cried, "Papa!" and hugged him, begged for kisses. He looked at Jane. She watched him, waiting. He tried to read her eyes. He said, "Jane?"

She came to him, gave him the dutiful kiss. Then their eyes met, and suddenly she kissed him again and whispered, "Papa!" and clung to him for a moment. Then she went to her chair.

Jeff held Loretta's chair, then went to his own place. He bowed his head and said, "For home, for family, for those we love and are loved by, we thank thee, Lord. We are thankful for life, Lord, and we pray for those who are no longer with us. Bless this food and watch over us. Amen."

He looked up, and he saw Loretta's frown of puzzlement, the look of questions in her eyes. Then he began serving.

As they ate, Loretta told him that she had taken the girls from school, was doing their lessons with them here at home. He asked why, and Loretta said, "Because of the weather, partly. It saves a little money, too."

"You haven't run short, have you?" he asked.

"No. But do you mind if I save a little money?"

"That," he said, "depends on how you save it."

Loretta smiled. "I'm also saving Bessie's wages."

"Bessie? Did you let Bessie go?" He glanced at Jane and Lissie.

"I thought you girls wanted Bessie to stay on."

Jane smiled and Lissie giggled.

"Bessie," Loretta said, "got married."

Jeff put down his fork. "I don't believe it."

"Two weeks ago."

"Who?"

"Arthur Owen."

"Owen? Arthur Owen?"

"The embalmer."

Jeff was speechless. He remembered the chubby little man who said it would cost an extra ten dollars for Tommy's grave because the ground was frozen. "I hope he blacked his boots for the wedding," he said.

"More likely she blacked them for him," Loretta said. "She needed someone to look after, poor girl."

"Girl?"

"Well, she was just my age. Four months younger, in fact."

"No. Bessie Magruder was seventy-two, going on eighty."

"And I?"

"You," Jeff said, "are still twenty-three."

"And you?"

Jeff stared at his plate for a long moment, then said, "Sometimes I feel as old as the hills." He looked up at her, and she saw the strain of all the winter's storms in his face. Strain, and some hurt, something she couldn't understand. But not age, really. Jeff was ageless. And she thought: It isn't the years that make you old. It's defeat, the admission of defeat. And she saw no defeat in him.

She looked again, and she knew that he was younger now, in the way that mattered, than he was when he came home from the war.

Supper finally over, Jeff said to the girls, "Your mother and I want to talk. We'll see you later."

The girls went upstairs and Jeff and Loretta went into his office.

Loretta sat on the couch and Jeff walked about the room, restless, and went and stood at the south window. He stood there, staring out at the night, and at last he turned and said, "It's been a bad winter, Loretta."

"I know."

"And it's not over with yet."

"The worst is over, isn't it?"

"I hope so." He paused for a long moment, decided there was only one way to say it. "Bill," he said, "is dead."

"Bill? Dead? Oh, no! No!"

Jeff nodded.

"What—what happened?" She began to cry.

"He was drowned, in the creek. Saving my life."

"Oh, Jeff, I can't believe it. Not Bill!" She mastered the sobs, but the tears kept coming. She found a handkerchief, tried to dry her cheeks. "When did it happen?" she asked.

"Back in January, six weeks ago. My horse went through the ice and Bill came in after me. He was swept under the ice by the current. We still haven't found his body."

The sobs came again. She tried to check them and had a fit of coughing. Jeff sat down beside her, put an arm around her. After a few minutes she said, "That's what I saw in your face. I knew something had happened." And she said, "It's like losing one of the family. I still can't quite believe it. Bill was so— so real. He was like—well, like a brother, almost." She had hold of herself again. "You say he saved your life?"

Jeff nodded. He got to his feet, went to the west window. "Bill saved my life at least once in the war. Now it's happened again. It makes you wonder why." He was silent for a moment, then he said, "It's a thin line. On one side, life. The things you have to do, the chance to do them. On the other side—who knows what? The stars, maybe. Maybe only the darkness between the stars."

He was silent again and he slowly shook his head. Then he came back and sat down at his desk. "Loretta," he said, "I went to the war because— Oh, there were a lot of reasons. I didn't care particularly whether I ever came back. But I did come back, defeated."

"I knew, Jeff."

"I came back, sick and defeated. And all I really wanted to do was crawl away somewhere and die alone."

"I knew that, too."

"You did? Well, I found out that I wasn't going to die that way." He looked at her, his eyes intense. "The darkness is awfully

251

dark, Loretta, and the stars are a long way off. And as long as a man's alive he has to do and be. I came up here, and I found there were things I still had to do."

He was out of his chair again, pacing the room. "Back in January, just after Bill died, the buffalo came north in one of the blizzards. A big herd of them. They came right down the valley and through the ranch. Like fate, defying the storm. I went with them, rode all night long."

He paused, and Loretta said, "And you came back."

"I came back. That wasn't the way I was going to go, either." He stopped his pacing and faced her. "I've lost my cattle, Loretta."

"How many?"

"I won't know till we tally up the winter kill. But too many. I know that right now. I'm broke, Loretta."

"And you've lost Bill."

He nodded. "Bill's gone."

"Jeff," she said, "at the supper table you said that sometimes you feel as old as the hills. Is that why?"

"Partly. Sometimes I feel that I've seen all the winters that ever were. For a while I didn't think this winter was ever going to break up."

"It will. It's already begun to."

"Yes. There's going to be green grass again, and running water, the same as always. There'll be green grass and running water, and cattle, after I'm gone. I won't be here forever, but for a little while, while I'm here—" He didn't finish it.

"Jeff," she said, "you're a cattleman. You always will be."

"Yes, I'm a cattleman."

"You didn't think it would matter to me, did you, that you've lost a lot of cattle this winter?"

"I've got to start over, Loretta. That's what I was saying. Start all over. But you don't have to. I'll see to that. This house is in your name, and—"

"Jeff, there's only one house that matters to me. The house at the ranch. *That's* my house!"

"It's just a cow camp now. You don't have to go back there."

"I'm going back," she said quietly.

"It's lonely out there, and—"

"I've known loneliness."

"—and the winters are rough."

"I've known winter, too, Jeff. But spring is lovely."

He was pacing again. "My life is cattle, Loretta."

"Your life was cattle when you married me."

"It'll be cattle just as long as I can get on a horse. Just as long as I own two or three steers."

"When can we go, Jeff?"

"You're sure that's what you want to do?"

"Jeff, I'm your wife. I made my choice, when we were married. That's what being a woman means, making her choice and standing by it."

"Your kind of woman . . . Loretta, I have to go, and do, and be. I'll always be that way."

"I've always known that."

"You can stay. You don't have to go."

She shook her head. "I can't stay here, Jeff. I've stayed here too long. Oh, Jeff, I want to be at the ranch and see spring come!"

"There'll be other springs." He paused at the window for a moment, looked out. "Some day," he said, "I'll be an old man. Old, and saddle-stiff, and full of groans and growls."

She smiled. "No doubt I'll have my complaints too." Then she said, "Jeff, only today Jane was talking about the taste of the yellow crass along the creek in spring, and the feel of prickly poppy blossoms. Lissie wants to pick sand lilies again, and yellow violets."

Jeff came back across the room and glanced at his desk. "I've got a few things to do here," he said. "Why don't you go up and tell the girls? And tell them about Bill. Bill was very fond of them. Make it easy for them, if you can. They may take it pretty hard."

"I'll try to." Loretta got up to go.

He looked at her and asked, "Remember our first buggy ride, Loretta? When we got caught in the rain?"

"Of course I do!"

"And I showed you how to make coffee?"

"Jeff, do you still remember that?"

He smiled. "Every time I taste that stuff that Jenny makes."

She laughed. "I'll start a fresh pot right now."

She left him and he opened his desk and brought the lamp.

He got out the records, the figures on his winter operations and the memoranda on his indebtedness. The records now not of his wealth but of his losses, the magnitude of this winter's failure.

He totaled the figures and saw that his memory had been right within a few hundred dollars. There was only one favorable factor, and even that was an uncertainty. This disastrous winter would cut deep into every herd on the plains. Beef cattle would be scarce next summer. Prices should be high. Every steer he could save would cut his losses a few more dollars. But the fact remained that he was broke and in debt, deeply in debt. And three months ago he was a rich man.

He put the figures and the memoranda back into the pigeonholes. They had nothing to tell him that he didn't already know. He put them away and looked around the room, this strange place where he didn't belong, never had belonged.

For a moment his mind reached back to a trail that led northeast out of Texas, to a young foreman taking his first herd to market. A boss drover, riding over a rolling upland that danced in the sunlight, the golden dust drifting over the plodding cattle. In that dust and in the dancing light over the hills he saw cattle, thousands of cattle wearing Jeff Ross's brand, on a land of grass and flowing water. God didn't owe him anything. God made the hills and set the grass to growing and the sweet water to flowing, and it was up to Jeff Ross from there on.

He got up, now, and went to the south window and looked out. Somewhere off there, to the east beyond a dark horizon he could not see from in here, lay the Bijou hills, blanketed under melting snow, the sweet Bijou water, beginning to flow again. And the Pothook cattle, what there were left of them.

He had known, when he came across the plains, searching, that winter would come, winter and blizzards that would blight and kill. He had known that this land has no knowledge of man, no caring; that a man could live here only by the grace of God and his own strong courage. But he had known, too, that a strong man, a man who knew what he wanted, could live here and make this land his own, for a time.

A time, a little span of time.

He turned from the window, crossed the room and closed the

desk. Cattle were dead, winter-killed, and years were lost, winter-blighted. Neither dead cattle nor lost years could ever be recovered. But a man started over, went on from here. Spring was coming, green-grass spring. And summer, blazing, work-weary summer. And fall, the crisp days when time, like the aspen leaves, whispered of eternity. Then winter again.

But not yet, not yet. This winter was drawing to its end. He had survived this winter, this bitter seventh winter, and he was still a man who owned himself, still on his feet.

Loretta called from upstairs. "Jeff! I forgot the coffee. It should be done. I'll be down in a minute."

He stepped to the hallway, called back, "I'll be up."

Then he went to the kitchen, got a cup from the cupboard, poured half a cup of the steaming black brew. He tasted its hot bite and thought of Bill, of the coffeepot on the little stove in the quarters at the stable. He heard Bill's voice: "A little luck and a lot of work, and a man makes out." And he thought of his own words: "You pay for what you get, one way or another. Or you do without."

He moved the coffeepot to the back of the stove and went back and finished the coffee in the cup and set it aside. Then he started for the stairs. In the hallway he paused, turned and went to the back door, instinctive. A cowman senses weather.

He stepped outside, saw a few flakes drifting down in the reflected light from inside. He looked up and saw the thickening overcast and felt the drifting flakes on his face. It wasn't storming yet, but it was coming. The wind had got around to the northeast. He would be driving through snow again, slush at the very least, tomorrow. But it was February, late February. In a few more weeks the melt would really set in and they would be jerking cattle out of every slew and boggy draw, every cow and steer they could lay a rope on.

He wondered how Sam and the boys were making out. He had told them to go over to Comanche and start skinning carcasses. Hides were worth a dollar apiece right now. A month from now the market would be glutted, when the snow began to melt in earnest and the winter kill showed up. Meanwhile, you salvaged a dollar a hide from the carcasses of steers that cost you twelve-fifty apiece.

You salvaged what you could, because a dozen dead steers would pay for one live steer next summer, when you started building a new herd.

He went inside again and closed the door. Then he went upstairs, to Loretta.